A NEED TO KNOW

ROGER J. SUTTON

Matador
5 Weir Road
Kibworth Beauchamp
Leicester LE8 0LQ, UK
Tel: (+44) 116 279 2299
Fax: (+44) 116 279 2277
Email: books@troubador.co.uk
Web: www.troubador.co.uk/matador

ISBN 978 1848767 607

British Library Cataloguing in Publication Data.
A catalogue record for this book is available from the British Library.

This novel is entirely a work of fiction.
The names, characters and incidents portrayed in it are the work of the author's
imagination. Any resemblance to actual characters, either living or deceased is entirely
coincidental.

Whilst a number of the locations are indeed factual, the author wishes to emphasize that
the representation of apparent security failures at any of these locations is fantasy and
that on the contrary he has the utmost respect for people and procedures of the security
forces of the United Arab Emirates.

Typeset in 11pt Minion by Troubador Publishing Ltd, Leicester, UK

Matador is an imprint of Troubador Publishing Ltd

Printed in Great Britain by the MPG Books Group, Bodmin and King's Lynn

A NEED TO KNOW

For Elisabeth

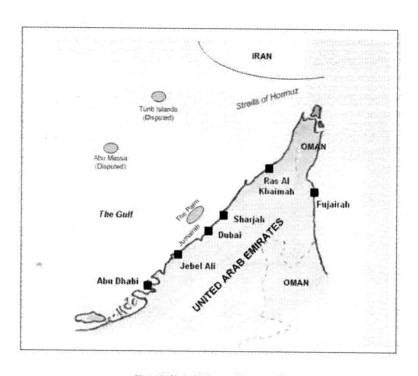

The UAE and the southern Gulf

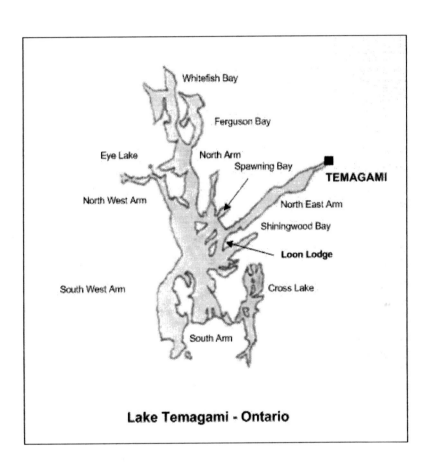

Whitefish Bay

Ferguson Bay

Eye Lake

North Arm

Spawning Bay

TEMAGAMI

North West Arm

North East Arm

Shiningwood Bay

Loon Lodge

South West Arm

Cross Lake

South Arm

Lake Temagami - Ontario

PREFACE

In October, year 2000, the search for a successor to the Data Encryption Standard, *DES* came to an end. The replacement deemed to be the best of the candidates offered was the *AES*, the *Advanced Encryption Standard* submitted by Vincent Rijmen of the Katholieke Universiteit, Leuven in Belgium and Joan Daemen of Proton World International.

Originally produced by IBM and accepted as the standard by the now named NIST (National Institute of Standards Technology) in 1975, *DES* has been used as the default encryption algorithm in the vast majority of communications systems and computer installations. *DES* has been assaulted by what seems to be every analyst in the world, aspiring and otherwise and as early in its life as 1977 the writing was on the wall as to how long the algorithm would survive unblemished. As computing power advanced at a meteoric rate, the time required to carry out a brute force attack to completion, on *DES*, became very manageable and towards the end of the last decade, it fell to a period of about 5 days. Obviously *DES's* time as a secure device had come to an end and it is with much relief amongst the interested fraternities that a new tool has permeated the industry. The application of triple *DES* as a method of extending its useful life improved the situation somewhat by applying the algorithm with two or three 56 bit keys, but Triple *DES* is slow.

Compared to *DES* with its woeful 56 bit key length, the *AES* offers a much higher security against a brute force attack with a 128-bit key and there are options to use longer keys up to 256 bits. The new algorithm is a block cipher and can be implemented in hardware and software in a wide number of environments such as smart cards, gate arrays and PC software. This ability was one of the characteristics, which gave it superiority over its competitors, *MARS, Serpent, RC6™*, and *Twofish*.

The long demise of, and growing suspicions about *DES* stimulated the cryptographic industry to produce numerous alternative algorithms and it will be interesting to see what effect the arrival of the *AES* has upon the rest of the industry. It will take some time though, before it infiltrates the cryptographic niches. No doubt competition for security markets will increase and equally without doubt, will be that every cryptographic seat of learning will turn its attention to uncover any, as yet undetected, flaw in the product. What transpires remains to be seen, but it is all part of the evolution of cryptology and communications security will benefit from the interest and attention. The constant battle between cryptographer and cryptanalyst takes another turn.

A Need To Know is a work of fiction, and although much of it is based on fact, the story line is fantasy. Or is it? In recent years great interest in encryption and the algorithms that are used, has been generated by new technologies, new revelations and new threats. Increased computer power has given the cryptanalysts of this world greater opportunity to break into these algorithms and many universities as well as other institutions have attacked algorithms such as *DES*. The *AES* algorithm now has come under the mathematical microscope and although the plot of this novel is based upon the flaws of secure communications, and does a little more than scratch the surface of related politics. The author wishes to make it clear that he has no evidence that either *DES* or *AES* have been broken, or intentionally flawed in any way. One only has to browse on the Internet to find claims made by numerous parties, that *DES* and various other algorithms have been successfully attacked. Such claims should be treated with caution. Without doubt however, is the fact that security service institutions such as the NSA, GCHQ and the like, utilise great manpower and highly advanced technology in basically, trying to read each others mail. For whatever reason, governments around the world have a need to know and this novel tells a story about some of the motivations and techniques by which they strive to access others' secrets.

Roger Sutton

Three may keep a secret, if two of them are dead.

Benjamin Franklin

CHAPTER 1

Symphony

Some wise man had casually said it of Asian women, and for the life of him Ashley couldn't remember in which bar, or by which sage it had been related. 'Oriental women are like flowers. They blossom with absolute beauty in the sunshine of their home environment. To marry one and drag her off to some distant, cold and dreary land, is just like picking a flower from its life giving ground, to display its elegance all too briefly to a foreign world in some dusty window before it withers and dies. If you are going to marry this lass, take my advice son. Keep her here in her own garden of Eden where she'll be radiant and content for the rest of your lives.'

It held some truth, Ashley had had to admit. From his own experience, he'd seen friends marry *an oriental lass* and whisk her off to South Wales, Newcastle or Glasgow to proudly parade her around like some exhibition piece – a collector's item. And then sure enough, as he'd been warned by this bar room perception, when the European drudgery of day to day life began to wear her down, the flower soon lost the will to live and withered beyond recognition. From the early days, Fitri had complained that as she was to be his wife, it was her duty to follow him wherever his work and ambitions took him. Girls from her kampong, in the same position as she, had married outside the town and moved on with their husbands to the big cities like Jakarta or Solo, and survived, even thrived with the change. Besides it had always been her dream to travel to exciting places like London, Paris and New York. Ashley could see the appeal and had shared her excitement when they flew to England for a vacation and introduction to the family. Despite his reservations,

1

she *had* done well. Certainly there were times when he could see bewilderment and stress in her eyes and the efforts with which she had overcome them or dismissed them as 'tidak apa apa,' no problem! She *had* fitted in with far less discomfort than he had ever imagined, but he felt that time would take its toll. She'd put her arms around him and clung on, her head against his chest to tell him, 'I just want be with you. Any place – no matter. I just want be with you for ever! – You my life.'

Ashley had lowered his head to kiss her hair and seen the tears flow from her opal eyes. He understood that she had been worried that she had failed him, but far from it. Instead he had seen her devotion and determination to make things work. To follow him and serve him and to make him feel like a king. It was an experience that he had never found in a *normal* European relationship. Fitri had cast her spell upon him and without obligation or doubt he felt it his purpose in life to cherish her and protect her from any ill wind. And so it was, after reassuring her that it was no weakness on her behalf he had decided to stay within easy strike of her village, near the university town of Bandung. The hills gave them a balmy European summer-like climate and he was welcomed onto the university's teaching staff. It also offered him enough freedom to communicate with the British Embassy under the guise of British Council's support for Indonesian Higher Education. The faculty also encouraged him to write and present papers and seminars that became increasingly of military bias, to interested parties in the region. For almost two years, this had been the way of life on which they both flourished along with their daughter, Eva, mercifully the image of her mother. Ashley was proud enough to live with one beautiful woman, and the thought of spending what remained of his life with two was almost too much to wish for. Never-the-less, a fear that had been there at the back of his mind ever since they first really came together was eventually realised. The summer time of their life together was destined to end. The recall to UK had been postponed as long as it could have been and though Ashley could find alternative work that would give them the opportunity to move to Jakarta, Fitri persisted that she wanted to see something else in the world. However Ashley remained convinced that it was largely an argument to ease his apprehension, though he had to admit that his wife had matured sufficiently to deal with the problems of moving to London. It wouldn't be forever, they both agreed and Ashley's fear was placated with that. It wouldn't be for ever.

***

He'd only been away for a few days and on his return to Jakarta's International airport Soekarno Hatta, had expected Fitri to be there with Budi, their driver. Nobody of any financial standing drove themselves around Jakarta, and Budi was a trusted member of the family who took up the mantle of the family chauffeur relieving both Ashley and Fitri of the time and stress of inching the car through the congested city. As he fought his way through the crowded arrivals hall, he could see Budi standing in his usual position at the back. Although Fitri's diminutive figure would normally be swamped by those waiting to greet their friends and relatives, what she lacked in stature she made up for with energy and she would be spotted easily, causing such a commotion that anyone would think that they'd been years apart. She'd be excited to hear how his trip had gone and also eager to communicate every bit of kampong news that had passed her way during his absence – as well as Eva's latest advance in vocabulary or play. On this occasion though he hadn't seen her. But he had been surprised to see his old drinking mate, Cameron. At first he had presumed that it was just coincidence that his friend was there to meet some member of his own family. The flight from Singapore was the return leg of what had become a popular weekend shopping trip for the Jakarta privileged, and Ashley had often seen friends on the same aircraft returning to Jakarta after a wallet draining shopping spree along Singapore's Orchard Road. The fact that Cameron was standing with Budi however, hinted that Cameron was here for him. Somewhat puzzled and certainly a little disappointed, Ashley was still delighted to meet both of them.

3

Perhaps a beer was planned along the way home. Budi was polite but stone faced and Cameron's greeting was pleasant but Ashley felt a touch reserved. He was troubled. Budi took the case and Cameron wrestled the carry-on bag from his shoulder and bustled him outside just as the thunder boomed across the airport, and the menacing grey-blue cloud, pregnant with the late afternoon's rain, burst open to deposit its contents upon the crowds of travellers and their escorts. No time to hang around. Budi waved them forward, suggesting that the Jag was parked close at hand, so Ashley followed with Cameron in tow, each bending their back so that their faces would be spared the sting of lashing rain. Sure enough, in seconds they were there. Budi, not bothering to put the case into the boot, had thrown it into the front passenger seat and then scrambled round to jump in behind the wheel. Cameron raced round to climb in behind Budi leaving Ashley to take the rear nearside door. It had only been a distance of fifty metres, or less even, but in that short time the storm had drowned them like rats. Budi started the engine but didn't immediately drive off, but just sat still waiting for the aircon to clear the already misting windscreen. Ashley, for the second time since he'd met the pair, felt a shadow pass over his soul.

Nobody moved. Budi said not a word, but just sat arms resting in his lap, staring through the torrent of water being ineffectually swept aside by the wiper blades swishing across the windscreen. Cameron had taken off his wet jacket and was looking through his window.

'Cameron, what is it?'

Ashley was chilled when Cameron at last turned to face him. Was it just rain careering down his cheeks, or …? He struggled to see the source. Tears? For God's sake not tears! 'Cameron what is it?' He repeated, but with an urgency, a demand that was rapidly turning to alarm. 'My God, Cameron, tell me what's wrong?'

Cameron gathered himself, putting his hand on Ashley's forearm. Budi was motionless. The rain was hammering on the roof and ghostly figures swept by in search of their own transport. Ashley's alarm was turning to anger, but he restrained it with great effort, seeing that Cameron was in no shape to receive it.

'Is it Fitri, Cameron? Is something wrong with Fitri, or Eva?'

The big man couldn't collect his words. His mouth was moving but the air that was passing though could only muster the merest of whispers. 'There was a bomb – we've – lost her Mike.' And then a second time, but with more strength after swallowing to moisten his parched throat. 'Mike – my dearest friend, there was an explosion – a bomb, at The Indonesia Hotel on Jalan Sudirman and Fitri was caught in it. We've lost her!' and followed it with a profound apology, 'I am so sorry,' as if it were all *his* fault.

Ashley was stunned, not blinking, not moving, not breathing, not daring to think. Cameron had lowered his head and covered his eyes with his left hand, weeping silently and wondering why such a toilsome burden had fallen upon his shoulders, yet at the same time knowing that only he was close enough to bring his friend news that would chill them both until their dying days. The rain, the endless rain hammered out its tattoo on the ageing Jaguar. It too seemed to have lost the will to live.

Budi continued to stare blindly out into the storm, not able to drive even if commanded to do so.

Amidst all the terrible drama of that moment Ashley felt a surge of compassion for the two companions who had braved everything to meet him. The bearers of such appalling news must have been in unspeakable agony as they had made their way, to Cengkareng. He felt that he owed them so much and loved them so dearly for their sharing in his grief and being there for him when he needed someone at his side. He took Cameron's hand, held it tight and leant forward towards the driver's seat, reaching over it and wrapping his other arm across Budi's chest hugging him tightly. Budi responded by raising his own arm to firmly grasp his employer's, to let him know that he also was there for him. Ashley never forgot that moment, and in the years to come wondered if he could have ever been strong enough to deal with the immediate aftermath without them. Of dealing with the dawning realisation that he would never again hold his beloved Fitri in his arms. Their support in those moments created an extraordinary bond of companionship.

That she was gone, was all he could deal with at that time. He didn't want details. He didn't want to know how and he didn't want to know why. Plunging now into the dreadful details would just be twisting the knife. He was grievously wounded and knew that any more hurt would drive him over the top. He just wouldn't be able to cope. As it was, he was grateful to be there sitting in the car. If Cameron had blurted the news out in the airport terminal, he would have had neither the strength, nor the will to stand. Even the rain had played its part in delaying the moment until the better occasion, if ever there could be a better occasion for such trauma. Ashley, whether it was strength of character, sheer stubbornness, or just something innate, decided that to get through this he would have to focus on doing the simple things first. All the fallout, all the remorse, the wailing, the countless, interminably sleepless nights, the tormented days and the devastation of their little Eva, would have to come later. He knew that there was no other way to deal with this, than let the passage of time heal the deep scars that were already forming in his heart. The notion of a future petrified him. He knew that he would be haunted by Fitri's death for many, many years, but for the immediate minutes, this had to be put away. He had to recover from this horrendous blow and to do that he had to buy time. If he could manage the next minute, it would become an hour. If he could manage the next hour it would become two – then a day and then days, weeks … and months …

'Change seats Budi! – I'll drive!'

***

He was willing the storm to continue. Whilst its ferocity was maintained, he knew that he *must* concentrate on the driving above all else. The city's storm drains were already full and overflowing, and roads and pedestrian pathways and the like, had all merged into a single flat, fluid plane. The elderly Jaguar was not the best vehicle in the world to handle any depth of water and its low slung suspension made it vulnerable to raised manholes and deep gutters.

The hazards were now hidden under the swelling rivers that in a very short time had replaced Jakarta's thoroughfares. He had to deal with it. Fitri would have expected no less of him.

***

The evening sun settled on the towers and spires of central London as Mike Ashley was escorted by a bright young thing who had *bounced* efficiently through a labyrinth of corridors and checkpoints bringing him eventually to the office of Leonard Clements. As he entered, an authoritative voice boomed from an adjoining room. 'Come on in Mike.' In the semi darkened room, the only light came from the golden beams of the young summer sun, as they cast shadows on the mahogany bookcase. It illuminated the gold and silver ingrained titles of the leather bound volumes, as if they were luminescent of their own accord. The antique Gill & Sons of Aberdeen ticked quietly past six twenty. In front of the bookcase a single desk was dressed with a telephone, brass penholder containing numerous pencils and pens and matching tray, with paper clips and a pipe and smoker's accessories. The lamp with green shade completed the desk set trio. A single red pocket file was centrally placed on the desk. It seemed to the visitor that it had been placed there with the precision of an architect and its geometric alignment with the desk sides lent additional foreboding to that already radiated by its ominous colour. The rich aroma of tobacco and a thin veil of smoke lingering at the window confirming that the host had recently been drawing on his pipe whilst taking in the evening view across Whitehall.

'Take a seat – I'll be with you shortly,' came the firm, solemn greeting from next door. Ashley did as he was bid and at the same time caught the murmur of a telephone conversation through the open door. He eased himself into a leather chair. Little had changed here since his last visit, although the gloss and lustre of the wood furnishings seemed to have improved with time. It enhanced the atmosphere of history and drama even more so than it had when he had first been summoned to this nerve centre of Her Majesty's security services. No, nerve centre it wasn't, for there were no computers, no flashing lights on banks of coloured telephones, nor were there radio links with embassies or agents across the world. Rather a centre of intrigue and strategic thinking. A place where decisions of national consequence were made. He had little doubt that the red file was of such consequence and obviously the reason for Clements' summons. The clock finger touched half past the hour and the last over of the day, a few miles to the northwest in Middlesex, would be drawing the curtain on the first day of the first test match.

The call had come during his vacation, as calls inevitably did. Not that he'd been on some far flung beach this time. Much as he loved the peace and beauty of such places, he always endeavoured to take a few days' leave for a test match, whenever the opportunity presented itself. The weather had been promised to be conducive to the simple enjoyment of his childhood passion. So it was with great reluctance, a simple conditioned response, that he'd received the call at Lord's, the bosom of English cricket. He was taking a cool beer to swill down the pork and apple sauce sandwich in one of the ground's many bars. It was busy with lunch time drinkers who had migrated from the stands, happily chatting about the state of the morning's play. The Aussie drinkers were noticeably less enthusiastic, for their anticipated mid morning English batting collapse had not materialised. It had been a solid start to the morning by the opening pair, promoting a sense of relief even optimism amongst the local supporters. It promised to be an enthralling battle when play resumed after the break and he was looking forward to being there as the afternoon unfolded in the best of a British summer's day.

The mobile in his pocket signalled that it was not to be. Disturbed that his long planned escape from office stress was interrupted, he found a vacant spot to place the remnants of his lunch and took the call. The noisy, light hearted buzz of a new cricket season around him was instantly suppressed to a mere whisper as his eyes focussed on the caller's ID. Butterflies in the pit of his stomach signalled the onset of caution and anxiety. 'Shit,' he had sworn silently as he had accepted the call. A mood of foreboding, a dark shadow, raced in to replace the freshness of that early summer day.

✳✳✳

The sweeping sunbeams crossing the desk caught the file like a headlight catching a fox's stare on a dark country lane. It flashed a red alarm to him that the murmured telephone conversation next door had drawn to a conclusion. The approach of muffled footsteps brought him to his feet – ready to greet Clements' entry.

Commander Leonard Clements extended a welcoming hand and Mike Ashley felt the firmness and confidence in its grip. The man had aged somewhat since they had last met, but the straight back and square shouldered figure still told of a long military past. Although the waist line had spread, he still commanded the air of authority and determination that a senior naval officer assumes over years of combat leadership. 'Good to see you again,' he said as he strode purposely around the desk, motioning his guest to retake his seat and then settled into his own green, leathered chair. Without lifting his eyes, he leant forward over the desk and rested the temples of his bowed head on his finger tips, his elbows straddling the still unopened folder. The brilliance of the white shirt and the vermillion file held within the sun's spotlight, contrasted sharply with the umber of the desk top. The full head of silver grey hair hid the commander's face in deep shadow.

Clements gazed down at the file, seemingly reading its contents through the opaque plastic cover and remained in this pose for some time. Had he been unaware of the old man's demeanour, a newcomer might have been tempted to wake him with a prod from his apparent slumber. But Ashley was no newcomer to this situation and knew that when something heavy rested on the mind of Leonard Clements, it was not wise to disturb his still intellect. The ruddy face, brushed by years of vintage red and age dimmed eyes hid a razor sharp mind and a depth of knowledge that had deflected any thought of retirement amongst his peers. Ashley had the feeling that he was not only assessing the gravity of the file's contents, but also assessing his own attitude and aura from across the desk. Despite his appreciation of Clements' attitude, he had not had a pleasant day and discomfort and frustration were starting to set in as the interlude became even more prolonged than usual. The clock had slowed as if to measure passive thought rather than real time and its beat overwhelmed the din of traffic in the road outside. Still he fought hard to resist the temptation to fiddle. To scratch a fictitious itch. To wipe a dry nose or shift the position of his legs or rump. The tick of the clock grew louder as did his impatience and pulse. Meanwhile Clements was assessing the changes that were even now, after months of rehabilitation, painting a waxy dullness around the fringes of the younger man's face. The trauma of that day of evil in Jakarta obviously still haunted Ashley. Perhaps it always would. But Clements read him well. Though others doubted his readiness for action, Clements was of the firm opinion that what Ashley really needed, more than anything else now, was to climb back in the saddle.

As if sensing the younger man's rising tension, Clements took a slow deep breath, as if it might be his last, exhaled a long sigh, dropped his hands to clutch the edge of the desk. As he leant back into his chair it groaned with reluctance to take up the shifted weight of Britain's spymaster.

'How was it going – the cricket I mean?' The deep throated reflection broke the silence, opening the conversation with controlled informality.

Ashley recognised the effort to ease his own temper and apprehension. Start with the niceties of the day, establish rapport, some common cause or level ground, before getting down to the serious tack. Even though he expected an opening gambit to be the prologue of the interview, Ashley felt much more at ease than in the silence that had preceded it. So much so that the eagerness to get on with whatever he had been so rudely summoned for, gave way to relief that the call to action had at last been sounded. He suspected that he'd been opened up like a can of beans and that Clements' access to his inner thoughts was much facilitated by the seemingly innocuous prelude. Despite a sense of caution at the back of his mind, Mike Ashley was happy to indulge in perhaps the one subject in which he felt that he could match Clements' intellect. Cricket!

Leonard Clements had been a member of the MCC for longer than he cared to remember and whilst he had known personally, many past cricketing giants, it didn't serve his purpose to intimidate the man whose innate talents and pragmatism he once again was in need of. It was in Ashley that he saw the attributes of a classic batsman. Watchful, dogged, back-against-the-wall attitude as one would attempt, single-handedly, to battle against the eleven opposing players and even on many occasions he felt, the umpires too. When he felt that his junior was beginning to speak openly and enthuse freely about the game; Clements moved back into the shadow and bought his hands together in mock prayer. The moment of mirth dissipated rapidly as the time to deal with the matter at hand came about. Ashley could not see the eyes, but felt them fixed upon him.

The quiet voice spoke with a guttural coarseness that came from the years of heavy pipe smoking. 'Mike, as you might guess, it's not an enquiry into cricket that caused me to interrupt your pleasure today,' another extended pause for breath followed. 'But, it seems that we have a problem,' and hastened to add, 'we, being Her Majesty's government – and the problem being potentially one of extreme gravity.'

Mike Ashley nodded, expecting nothing less.

Clements moved forward to the edge of the chair and Ashley, half expecting a whispered *confide* mirrored the action, but it was to the file that Clements' attention was focussed. The intelligence chief opened the folder, now darkened as the sun had passed across the room to dim in a far corner. He withdrew a typed document and placed it precisely on top of the file. It was a single sheet of A4 with print on each side. Realising the sudden onset of late evening and the increasing glow of the streetlights outside, Clements reached across to switch on the desk lamp. Ashley blinked with the sudden influx of light and momentarily looked up at Clements's face, which had never been clearly illuminated since he'd entered the room. The eyebrows carried heavy growths of silver matted hair and it was only when Clements lifted his head slightly, to view the document through bifocals, that Ashley noticed the deep cavernous eye sockets. Tired, yellowed eyes lurked there like those of some sea monster peering from its darkened grotto.

The big hands lifted the paper and once again, Clements paused unduly as if still unsure about revealing more. Eventually he sighed and appeared to come to a decision placing the document flat on the desk. He pushed it in front of Ashley, rotating it around with a finger tip to signal that he should read its contents. Presuming that a smart response was expected, Ashley scanned quickly the first side and then the reverse to get the gist of its story. Then he returned to the original side and more slowly this time, read through it again, pausing on several occasions to digest the information revealed. Clements, waiting patiently and observed silently, his chin supported by his left hand, the elbow resting on the arm of the chair. The intensity with which those eyes were bearing down upon him, related no tone of relaxation even if the body posture did. Rather they imparted a sense of intense scrutiny of Ashley's behaviour and expression as the latter read of the Goodwin's disappearance.

Tea arrived by courtesy of the smiling escort who deposited the tray for Clements to serve. No word was spoken but Clements politely nodded his gratitude as the girl turned on her heel and with the now familiar spring, walked out with an exaggerated flourish. Clements poured but left Ashley to add his own sugar and milk.

Another silence followed and then, only when Clements was sure that the information had been assimilated, he spoke slowly and with exaggerated purpose: 'So you see Mike – one of our relatives has, as the Aussies would say – gone walk about,' and he lifted his bushy eyebrows to let him know, in no uncertain terms that he, Mike Ashley, was being asked the question. Where was Peter Goodwin?

***

12

Ashley's tea had gone cold by the time he had remembered it and he had been severely rebuked by a threatening glance from Clements's secretary, when she returned to replenish the teapot an hour later. Ashley apologised with a shrug that promised that he would not transgress again. To emphasise his regret, he let his eyes and smile linger a little longer than was *really* necessary. Showing that he might have forgotten the tea, but he certainly had not missed the freshness and perfume of her brief interlude.

'Still the same Mike Ashley I see!' Clements let a smile momentarily crease his lips. 'It's quite some time since we had a little job for you Mike, but that is not a bad thing really. Keeps you out of the focus of interest of our competitors.' He paused again. 'Of course there may well be a simple explanation for our friend to take another, unexpected vacation. It's quite a regular pattern of behaviour. But the circumstances are troubling enough for us to be concerned that no harm has come to him, and you – Mike, have all the credentials to follow this up in as subtle a manner as possible. *No* fuss, *no* drama and *no* trumpets!' added Clements in afterthought.

The unusual emphasis raised Ashley's sense of inquiry. The concern inferred was not a common trait of Clements'. He was not one given to needless exaggeration nor cosmetic comment and if he'd missed the more subtle hints of disquiet before, Ashley now knew that something was profoundly amiss in these corridors of Whitehall. For the first time in a long time, intrigue refreshed his troubled mind.

***

Hunger pangs and the last chance to get a beer brought the meeting to a close. After carefully re-assembling the contents of the red folder, Clements cleared the desk of the notes that each had made and pushed them into the shredder. He returned, stepping on the foot switch to turn on the corner lamp stand, as he passed. The sudden increase in illumination brought them both back into synch with the London scene, which by that time had taken on its June night-time robe of a matt black sky decorated with fluorescent jewels announcing whatever delights, or services any visitor could wish for.

Clements had concluded by handing an encrypted CD of the file to Ashley for his *bed time reading*, as he had put it. He would be able to view it on his own laptop computer, once the IT security bods had sent him this month's secret keys. No need for him to carry sensitive paper copies, or a laptop that was always prone to loss or snatches. Over the years, several heads had rolled after security hardware had gone missing although it was pretty certain that any sensitive data stored on them would have been irrecoverable without a hierarchy of passwords and secret key information. For the first time he saw it labelled *Symphony* and wondered, not for the last time, what music it would play and what part he would play in it. Of no doubt was the identity of its conductor, and the last he saw of him that night, as he left the office, was the old fellow standing by the window with a newly lit pipe held to his mouth. Clements was taking his peace as he looked out over Westminster, his eyes drawn there by the authoritative tones of Big Ben striking ten.

For Clements himself, although he had so little information to go on, and no certainty that the picture was as black as he had perhaps painted it that evening, his gut feeling was one of profound unease. Peter Goodwin had gone AWOL before and had always, in the past, drifted back into civilisation when – and not before, he had set himself right with his inner torments. When Goodwin was having one of his black hole things, as they had come to be known, it could be an hour, a week, or longer before he stepped back into the maze of mathematical complexity that for many, described the hidden world of cryptology. This time however, there were too many unanswered factors. Too many coincidences had triggered in the old master a considerable feeling of anxiety. He had selected *Mike Ashley* to delve into it and even though the physical transfer of the Symphony file to the journalist had felt like the passing over of his great weight of concern, he was content that he had the right man for the job. Pragmatic, feet on the ground sort, with a knack of charming his way into many a closed heart or mind. A man with no apparent regard for standing or reputation. 'What you see is what you get!' was his old mentor's introduction when they'd first conjured up a meeting of coincidence.

Now, some ten years later, he sincerely hoped that it would be a quality that would become quickly evident to anyone who cared to check him out. Not one to invite a deeper analysis that might unearth something a little more sinister under that disarming veneer. It gave him reassurance that Mike Ashley's open attitude to life and people had not been unduly tarnished by the devastating loss of his Indonesian treasure. How much he would need that philosophy over the coming months? ... He could only guess.

∗∗∗

Released at last from the stuffy confines of Clements' inner sanctum, Mike Ashley stepped out into the street. The slight chill in the air caught him a by surprise, but its freshness was a revitalising therapy for both body and mind. His pulse quickened as the thoughts about the three or so hours spent in intense debate were, for the moment, dispersed. The cool air surged through his sinuses and the hustle and bustle of pedestrians and traffic alike changed his focus to deal with immediate priorities: Food and drink! He felt like a child released from the classroom prison by the four o' clock bell, alarming the neighbourhood to the charge of a liberated school boy.

The traffic was not so bad at this time of night. Most of the city's work force had flooded the transport system for their homeward journeys some time ago, leaving the streets to the late shoppers, diners and drinkers like himself. A quick mental assessment of train timetables and the distance to Waterloo, plus the train time to Guildford, left him in little doubt. If he was to get a beer or two before closing, it had to be here, in town. He couldn't risk arriving home to a dry city without a couple of pints to help him digest and ponder the evening's debate. Briefcase, with its encrypted CD ROM, firmly clasped to his ribs, he flagged down a cab which then pulled out to rejoin the mainstream flow towards the river. Better to replenish the liquid levels first, whilst considering which steak house, Italian, chinky, or fish parlour would be most conveniently placed for the subsequent dash to catch the train.

As a Northerner, he still found the vibrant city an exciting place to be and nowhere was more impressive than the sight of the Houses of Parliament. The soul centre of Britain and what vestiges remained of its empire. As the taxi took him over Westminster Bridge, he looked back. Elated by physical activity and mental relief, the magnificent building standing proudly illuminated against the dark backdrop of the night sky. At this time he could only dimly see the sombre concrete security barriers that surrounded the perimeter, serving as a reminder that society remained under the continuing threat of terrorism. The thought of a 9/11 style attack against this hallowed icon of the British people horrified him enormously. Little did he know that at that *very* moment, in that *very* house, Prime Minister Blair was looking out across the river with much the same thought in mind.

Once over the bridge, he abruptly remembered the first ambition of the day. Was it really still the same day? He leaned forward and tapped on the glass partition, 'Cricket score!' he fired at the taxi driver. 'Did you get the close of play?'

'265 for 8, gov'ner,' was the reply cast over the driver's shoulder. 'Started well enough – but usual story – collapse in the middle order. Now we're hanging on for the odd run or two in the morning.'

'Crap!' – His elation dissipating rapidly.

The driver must have caught the change of expression in his mirror: 'But it's not so bad, been in much worse positions of late, don't you think?'

'Yep, you're right, I guess,' he thought to himself. But the disappointment after the early promise and the lunch time optimism was depressing him more and more by the minute. 'Shit, how bloody predictable! We never manage to exploit a situation after we've got into a dominant position. It's the same in any bloody sport we play – Never can turn the screw – Always handing a life line to the bloody opposition. And then paying the bloody penalty.' No matter which team, in which sport he supported, his allegiance seemed to be the kiss of death.

Looking out at the shops passing by, he reflected that logic would tell him that his innate tendency to support the underdog would inevitably lead to disappointment. Just for once in his lifetime it would be a glorious, never to be forgotten moment, if *his* team could just win something and give fellow sympathisers just one excuse to celebrate; something to raise them above their mundane day. Give them a cheer and a buzz to brighten their lives. Just once in his lifetime, he begged! My god! How sick he was to hear of the major Premiership clubs feeling sorry for themselves and moaning about the end of the world just because they had not won a trophy last season. They should experience, what he and most others did, when *every* season ended empty handed. When there was nothing to shout about when the accolades were handed out at the end. He wondered if the winners ever got bored with success and thought he'd like to be in a position to experience it sometime.

His latest girlfriend could never understand his passion for sport, just as he couldn't understand hers for the high street windows and shopping malls. He could never get her to appreciate his pain when the results came out and lately he had to confess quietly to himself that he, from time to time, had considered the idea of not supporting anyone. There were times when it was just too damn depressing. Yet on the positive side, it was clear that his sense of perpetual optimism typified the British people, and if ever the nation was unified, it was unified by sport. Not politics, not religion, not some fanatic beating a doomsday drum, but by sport and it was always stirring to see, at major events, everyone waving the same flag, singing the same song and sharing the same hope and emotions.

He must have spoken subconsciously at some time in the short journey, for the taxi delivered him to The Fish Parlour. Or maybe the fellow had some commission agreement for everyone he dropped at the door? In any case the food decision was made, but the pub on the corner promised to satisfy the more immediate requirement of a cool beer. Right now he needed an injection of moral support, especially if he was destined to continue with his saintly mission of supporting the underdogs of this world.

Peter Goodwin could never be described as an underdog, at least not within the confines of his own sheltered world of algorithms, number theories and quantum cryptology. In what he considered to be the more real worlds of social interaction and physical behaviour however, Mike Ashley thought him, with some considerable sympathy, not to be a member of the club. His own hang ups about sport paled into insignificance when he considered Goodwin's regarding everything that could not be numerically defined.

CHAPTER 2

Bayswater

She towered twenty stories above the waterline and at three hundred and thirty metres long, the latest of America's Nimitz class aircraft carriers was as long as the Empire State Building was high. With a crew of over four thousand, depending upon the squadron strength and her mission, and with a flight deck that covered over four acres, she was a colossus in the true sense of the word. Ten thousand spectators made up from crew relatives, dignitaries, and politicians, not to mention the thousands of construction workers, their chests swollen with pride, watched as the floating city set sail on her inaugural mission from her home port of San Diego. Rupert Miller gave the order that the tugs be released and that the carrier's own propulsion units be brought up to drive the ship out into the Pacific. The pulse of the waking giant quickened and every man on board sensed the call of adventure and independence now that she was on her own. It would be a few days before the rest of the fleet gathered around the mother ship, but all the trials, modifications, and red tape had been completed and now she was a fighting ship – The biggest and most sophisticated ship ever to set sail. Admiral Miller was thrilled by the bands, banners and buntings that had presented a tumultuous send off but it was a relief at last to leave all the razzmatazz behind and get on with the job. A quiet satisfaction filled the man as the San Diego city skyline fell behind. Now he was at ease with himself and his command.

***

The house in a Bayswater backstreet held no immediate sign of life as Mike Ashley climbed the steps to the front door. It was a large, red bricked terrace house of the 30's/40's era with what looked to be a conversion of the original four storied house into apartments. Peter Goodwin held the tenancy of this two floor apartment and it was here that Ashley rapped the black knocker against the heavy door. Immediately there came the sound of a dog barking excitedly from the rear of the house. That would be Lucy, he thought. The barking suddenly grew louder as an internal door was opened and he could hear a raised, but softly toned feminine voice admonishing the dog and beseeching it to calm down. Mrs. Morgan obviously did not have much command over the excited animal as it came racing to the door. He could hear the clatter of claws on the parquet floor, as it scampered full pelt down the corridor and then skidded and bumped as it hit the front door. With front legs raised to lift her head above the level of the inset window, she could make out a fragmented figure through the stained glass window, and barked at it with great enthusiasm. Mrs. Morgan came waddling afterwards, chiding the dog as if it were a boisterous child. She took hold of the dog's collar and pulled it back with one hand whilst fiddling with the lock with the other. Once a degree of control was established, making it safe for both dog and visitor, the door was opened to reveal a flustered, dumpy, homely little woman in her late 50s. The spectacled figure had greying hair peeking through a faded dark brown tint, and was collected in a bun at the back. Her black dress and frilly white apron announced her as the maid of the house, a fact that he already knew from Clements's illustration of the previous day. Lucy was far from the threatening beast that had attacked the door. All bluff and gusto as she strained at the collar and continued to bark, but now with less ferocity. Wild sweeping of her tail emphasised that play was the basis of her enthusiasm.

'Oh, don't need to worry about Lucy, sir. She's long past her days of seeing anybody off. 'asn't got a tooth left in her head – and sir would be Mr. Mike, am I right?' Not waiting for an answer, she blurted 'Mr. Leonard from the office called to say that you'd be round. Such a nice man seems to me. Real polite and gentlemanly like. Not to be found often these days, I might say,' she at last paused for breath.

As Mrs. Morgan was obviously expecting him and comfortable with his entry, Ashley took it upon himself to step inside and close the door. The dear lady, still flustered, apologised profusely for forgetting her manners. Lucy was still eager to get to know him more intimately and she skidded across when the maid released her collar. Ashley squatted to greet the collie but was a taken by surprise by the weight of the old animal as she bundled into him almost knocking him over. The source of the musty smell that had greeted him when he first took a step inside was clear. Lucy had a distinct doggie odour that pervaded the entrance hall and his sinuses twitched and filled. He wished for an open window to ventilate the place and dilute the warm, unpleasant stench of dog and stale cigarette smoke. Must have been days since any fresh air was allowed to blow through *this* house, he thought. The dog became calmer and enjoyed his attention as the maid fretted about the clamour and the hairs on Mr Mike's clothes.

She could read his discomfort, but eventually ushered them all into the front room before busying herself to open a small window. The welcoming fuss had left Lucy thirsty, so the dog padded off to the kitchen and could be hard lapping noisily at her water bowl. He protested politely when Mrs Morgan suggested a cup of tea, 'the kettle is already on, I might say, sir,' and she brushed down her apron, leaving the room with no regard to his reluctance.

In truth she needed the time to gather her thoughts and her nervousness persuaded him to hold his peace. She was much more at home in her own world of the kitchen, with just Lucy as company. Elsewhere she was stressed, threatened. In the presence of strangers she was panicky and her only solution was to busy herself with anything to hand. Her escape left him alone in the room and he was happy to have the opportune moment to nose around. A slight draft of cooler air emanated from an open window but it wasn't sufficient to clear his irritated nostrils which threatened to explode into a sneezing bout at any moment. Quickly he moved across to the window and quietly opened it a couple more notches, hoping that she would not notice. The influx of fresh air was welcome relief.

'Milk and sugar?' she called down the hallway.

'Yes and just a half spoon, please,' he replied, as friendly as he could so as to put her at ease.

A kettle boiled and Mrs Morgan continued her agitated monologue with Lucy whilst Ashley cast a glance around the front room. It reminded him of his grandparents' house of many years ago. A typical fifties set up with a three piece suite, a little faded with time, a desk or bureau, characteristic of the era, with the large hinged front door that opened downwards to provide the writing surface. A pair of lamp standards placed strategically in diagonally opposing corners of the room carried the same flowery patterned shades as the heavy curtains and pelmet that dressed the bay window. A television stood on a purpose built table to one side of the tiled fireplace, the grate of which was hidden behind a brass, framed guard that carried a pastel drawing of a Chinese mountain scene and a delicate female figure clutching a cooling fan coyly to her face. Above the fireplace hung a modern print that seemed vaguely familiar but he couldn't quite place the artist. A David Shepherd? he queried, knowing that if he wasn't correct, his guess wasn't far wide of the mark. He wondered if Goodwin had purposely re-created the comfort and security of his childhood home, or had simply walked into it as it was when he took the lease. For Ashley it was too much. Too comfortable, too much furniture, too ornamental and too elaborate a décor. Coupled with the reek of the dog and the lack of air, it felt all too claustrophobic.

Busy noises from the kitchen alerted him that refreshment was on its way. He considered asking her permission to give the place a more thorough going over, but could sense in her a fierce loyalty to Mr. Peter, that she would object. He moved across to the book case. Ashley had always been of the opinion that the contents of a fellow's book case, revealed a lot about the character and it was here that Ashley began to get some insight into the mind of the man he was looking for. There was some fine literature on display. He drew the back of his index finger across Bronte, Dickens, Thomas Hardy, Tolstoy's War and Peace and Anna Karenina and other classics that filled the first shelf. The next shelf had Attenborough's – *Life on Earth, Ascent of Man* – Bronowski, *A Brief History in Time* – Stephen Hawkins, *The Elegant Universe* – Brian Green, *Cosmos* – Sagan, *Origin of the Spe*cies, *The Mystery of The Nasca Lines* – Tony Morrison, *Piltdown man* – Milner Place, *From Lucy to Language* – Donald Johanson, plus a host of other old and new books on anthropology. The next shelf held, *Applied Cryptography* – Schneier, *Security* – Schafer, Sutton's *Secure Communications, Principia Mathematica*, and two whole rows of National Geographic and Nature at floor level. Quite amazing to discover that everything was arranged perfectly in alphabetic order. How tiring he thought, the degree of order in the place contributed to the growing sensation of finicky oppression. He was certain that if he mounted the stairs to the bedrooms, he would find every sock with its partner, every tie hung straight and in order, shirts neatly pressed and hung *to attention* like soldiers on parade. Polished shoes would be arrayed with the same military precision. He found it all so suffocating.

As he moved to the second bookcase, he had the uneasy feeling that he was being watched although he could still hear Mrs. Morgan closing cupboard doors in the back. He turned round and found the big brown eyes of Lucy staring at him. The dog had sensed intrusion into her master's sanctuary and her eyes expressed disgust at his illicit prying. She was an old dog with greying hair and a barrel of a body shape that told a story of pedantic life. She either resigned herself to the situation, or was overcome with the exhaustion and excitement of the visitor's arrival, for she limped in, circled the rug in front of the hearth several times before finding a comfortable spot and spread herself down for a snooze. Ashley noticed that the dog had struggled to walk and saw the incapacity was not helped by the fact that her claws had not been cut for some considerable time. Hence the clatter as she had raced and skidded down the hall upon his arrival.

The bureau caught his attention but he didn't have time to check if it was locked. He guessed not as the small key remained in its place in the top cover, but the two drawers beneath held no key. Perhaps it was a common key? but he couldn't remember if that of his grandparents, had one key or more. It was a long time ago but it was funny, he thought, how things he believed forgotten, came flooding back when a suitable trigger was presented.

Mrs. Morgan bustled into the room with a tray full of tea and biscuits, her short legs working over time. 'If only Mr. Peter were here, he'd be so pleased to have a friend 'round, I might say!' as she placed the tray by an easy chair. Ashley very much doubted it, even if he was a friend of Goodwin's, which he certainly wasn't, and just put the statement down to Mrs. Morgan's compulsion to utter the first thing that came into her head.

She nervously pushed the biscuits towards him and he noticed that her hands were shaking. He wondered if she was just uneasy about his presence, that her employer was missing, or whether this was her natural demeanour. She poured tea and anticipating the inevitable enquiry suppressed the desire to run back to her sanctuary. Instead she perched on a corner of an embroidered footstool close to the door, escape still very much on her mind. She glanced, over her spectacles, across at the open window. He'd been caught out and a flicker of guilt caught him by surprise.

'I am really sorry to impose Mrs. Morgan, but it seems that Peter has taken a vacation somewhere,' he began, sensitive to her anxiety, 'and the office needs to contact him quite urgently. We wondered if you might know where he could be – if he said anything about his trip to Canada?'

She lowered her head, hands fiddling with the frills of her apron. 'He was due back by now – asked me to stay to look after Lucy till he came back.' And added, remembering the question Ashley had initially posed, 'he said he'd a conference in Canada. I think it was, Toronto – yes that's right, Toronto! He showed me a picture, with a big tower. Looked a nice place did Toronto. He's a lucky man, Mr Peter. Getting to see such fine places – never had much time myself for travelling 'round – and my Bert never liked aeroplanes, so we didn't get very far. – Went to Paris for a weekend but couldn't do with the language, I might say.'

'Did he mention any other place in Canada, a place where he might er, just spend a weekend, to relax, say?'

She became aware that her hands were attracting his attention and released the apron, hastily brushed it straight, before looking up and replying 'Oh he was happy to go, I could tell, and he said so too. Pointed at the picture and told me it was from Canada.' She looked up above the fireplace to indicate the picture that he'd seen before. Ashley's eyes followed. He took greater notice this time and promised himself an even closer look before leaving.

'It's a 'Bateman, – Robert Bateman. He's Canadian, you know?' So Mrs. Morgan had caught him by surprise again. He wondered for a moment, if she was indeed an expert in either wildlife or art. 'No!' she read his thoughts aloud and smiled as her confidence grew, 'I only know because I dust it down every week. But Mr. Peter loves it. He's a real nature lover is Mr Peter. Off to watch the birds, does walks in the countryside most weekends, an' he's got lots of books on animals and nature. Spends hours reading. I might say.'

He wondered if she might say more, but she fell quiet as if she had been talking too much. Ashley was conscious that she reticent to show her lack of schooling about these things. She looked down in shy embarrassment that she had opened up so much to a stranger, exposing her simple upbringing and lowly position, especially to such an intelligent gentleman from the office and all. She bent to pat Lucy who had eased over to rest her head on the maid's slippered feet. 'And he adores Lucy, of course,' she added, as if apologising to the dog for neglecting her.

Ashley took his eyes from the dog and they strayed to the bureau again as he thought about the next line of questioning. He considered it unlikely that such a fastidiously tidy chap would leave any loose bits around that might shed light on his departure to places unknown. He would have to manufacture a glance in there, if only to satisfy his curiosity, to put his mind at ease, he might say.   She had startled him again, the silence too long for her comfort. 'Of course you know how he came to name her Lucy, don't you?'

Now he was on the back foot, but Clements would have applauded him, for now she was still volunteering information with little regard for her inhibitions, feeling the need to ease the formal conversation and so give some insight into Mr. Peter's personal life. Initially he'd had difficulty connecting with her, but now she was gaining more confidence, even taking the initiative. 'He named her after one of his books,' she enthused and seeing him puzzled, added proudly '... after one of those skeletons they dug up in Africa!'

'Oh of course!' he recalled with hands spread wide as if to emphasise the obvious, 'Leaky excavations in the Olduvai Gorge, wasn't it?' and looked back at the bookcase to check if he was right. 'No, Johanson it seems. – Did he call, or leave any contact number – Peter, I mean?' seeing that his abrupt leap from the desolation of the Ethiopian desert, back into Bayswater, had confused her. Perhaps if he asked for another tea, he might get chance to get his nose in the bureau.

'Oh!' she started. Lucy lifted her head alerted by the exclamation, 'Yes, for that matter he did.' She checked her apron pocket as if expecting it to be there. 'Now where did I put it?' she tutted in self reprimand, missing the first part of question. She rose to her feet and just as he thought that this might be the moment to ask for another cup of tea, she rolled across to the bureau, twisted the key and lowered the hinged cover.

Ashley was up like a shot and Lucy too, sensing possible action so that he almost stumbled over her in the effort to gain a glimpse inside. He needn't have worried as Mrs. Morgan didn't feel the need to hide anything as he moved beside her. In fact she was happy to have made a contribution and reveal the bureau's contents.

There was even less material there, than he'd first imagined. In fact, as Mother Hubbard might say, *the cupboard was bare*. – Well almost. There was a crossword puzzle, torn from a daily newspaper and a small travel brochure of the type that travel agents slide into the ticket wallet of their client. It was to this, that Mrs Morgan turned her attention, her hands hesitated above it as if it might be hot. 'Ah yes! It must be here,' she said and at last took hold of the booklet, opened it up and turned it upside down. Out fluttered a small piece of yellow posit paper and there, in her juvenile scrawl, was the sought-after number. Not wanting to part with the original, she scribbled it down in the margin of the crossword and feeling very pleased with herself, handed it to him. 'There you are – Mr. Peter never does well with the crosswords anyway. Such a clever man, but I never saw a single line filled in. Strange really, I might say.' Ashley too was surprised to hear this.

They all felt that it was time for him to go and Lucy sensed the excuse to frolic once more, but he wanted to have a closer look at *The Bateman*. Drawing closer, he saw that it was a limited edition, authenticated by the embossed badge, signature and scroll. *Loons of Algonquin* it was entitled. It portrayed a pair of exotic water birds swimming together across a North American lake shrouded in early morning mist. The stilled water had taken on the greenery of the surrounding forest in its mirrored reflections. He could imagine Goodwin's interest in the simplicity of the scene, for in him too, it invoked a mood of tranquillity. Perhaps the only thing in the house that didn't trouble him.

He took his leave of Mrs. Morgan and Lucy and heaved a huge sigh of relief as he stepped out into the fine drizzle. He thought that something had been accomplished without knowing precisely what, and he was satisfied that neither of the household had been unduly alarmed by his morning sojourn. Uncomfortable certainly, but not alarmed. He could call again some day if need be. The gentle rain dampened his hair and clothes, but he didn't mind, finding it exquisitely refreshing after the overpowering stifle of Goodwin's home. He paused on the step, looked about him and took a large breath to fill his lungs with the cool damp air. Not exactly the clean, fragrant stuff that you'd find in a lake side wilderness, but for central London none-the-less, the mist was hugely refreshing. Every part of his body screamed its relief and his sinuses, tightened by the heavy atmosphere inside, shrank as the coolness of the morning flowed through them. At last he could breathe and with that he struck out in the direction of Kensington Palace. He had decided to walk across the park in the hope that the canine odour of Lucy and cigarettes would be diluted in the city's light rain. Striding past the bay window, he heard a noise and glanced over his shoulder to see Mrs. Morgan stretching through the lace curtains to close the window. Lucy, panting by her side, peered over the window sill.

She hesitated; a strained look was momentarily soothed by a nervous smile as she had been caught in the act, her concern exposed to the damp street. A hesitant wave of the hand wished him on his way. Lucy barked a silent goodbye, before they both returned to their own fostered seclusion.

CHAPTER 3

St. Andrew and the Fort St. George

Terminal 4 had been its typically busy self that morning, but the midday departure was not so uncomfortable. So many flights had been at the break of dawn, making the journey to Heathrow a very testing time. He could never be sure about the traffic on the M25. Often referred to as the biggest car park in the country, this motorway carried the heartbeat of the capital and was notorious in the morning rush hour, when nobody rushed anywhere, and again when commuters headed homeward in mid evening. How the hell it ever came to be known as the rush/hour was beyond him. He'd tried many variants but had found none that could deliver him to the airport with any certainty of meeting his check-in time. An outbound departure at ten a.m. meant that he had to leave home at about six-thirty to give him any hope of beating the jam, and even then, on more occasions than he cared to remember, some trivial accident had blocked the arterial road leaving him with a hair-raising dash to the gate. As the situation got worse, he'd adopted the luxury of bedding at the airport's hotels for the night before and whilst this eased the stress of the early morning scrum, it did nothing to ease his expense claims. He'd argued, with some veracity that it was less expensive to pay a hundred and fifty pounds for an overnight hotel, than it was to sit back in the fast lane of that cursed highway and watch your flight wing its way overhead. Not to mention the damage done by explosive blood pressure when grid lock was eating at your critical time. In fact he'd once phoned in to the local radio station, which had some travel experts debating about the threat of Deep

Vein Thrombosis, on long haul flights. He'd vociferously argued that there was greater danger to drivers on the M25, where rigour mortis was becoming the prevalent threat rather than DVT on the way to Singapore. In recent times though, he'd become considerably more phlegmatic and it did, he had to admit, ease his pre-flight stresses and so helping to renew his passion for escaping from flying a desk.

On this particular morning it had been busy but he'd arrived in such time that he'd had a few moments to indulge himself in the business lounge with a light breakfast to supplement his normal start to the day, a bowl of cereals and an orange juice. A couple of croissants and hot fresh coffees, courtesy of British Airways had set him up for the morning and would carry him a fair distance of the way across *The Pond*. Flight BA-93, once free of the pack of mechanical beasts that milled around its soft underbelly, like hyenas at an antelope kill, coasted down the taxiway to await its turn behind the earlier slots. As the airborne conveyor climbed westwards back across the M25 and up over the Surrey countryside, before peeling off on its own path, Ashley could not help but marvel at the sight of two hundred and fifty tons of 747 roaring down the runway and incredibly lifting off into the next dimension. Far from fearing flying, he still felt the schoolboy's thrill on take off and then elation as he settled back into his seat, to relax. It was easy to understand these emotions. After all the traffic stress and the check-in scramble, concern about delays and last minute calls to staff and friends, the moment the big bird broke through the eternal London murk, into the blue, transported him into a new adventure.

The weather on that Monday morning, was that rarest of events, a fine English summer's day and if he could have looked back to the city, he would have seen the England cricketers taking the field for the continuation of the test match. Not so far distant, was the massed supporters of Wimbledon excitedly awaiting the first match on the centre court. The rattle of the drinks trolley brought him back into real time but feeling it a mite too early for a Scotch, elected for a Buck's Fizz to enhance his breakfast elation.

The seat belt sign triggered a buzz of activity as the early coffee drinkers hastened for relief and others reached into the overhead bins to retrieve forgotten books or laptops. Ashley detested working on a flight and intended to avoid it on this occasion too. He delved into the Daily Telegraph, scanning the front page headlines for any worthwhile topic and was less than enthused by the continuing problems facing George Bush and his British cohort in seeking extraction from the self imposed mire of Iraq. The new round of defence cuts that whittled away still further at Britain's armed force's budget alarmed him more so. Something's got to give here, he thought. One day we are really going to catch a pile of shit. It was also the consensus of opinion amongst his military friends as it was of those in *the service*. Not that he had many contacts there. He was only a fringe member of the team, if one could call it that. He'd preferred to remain a peripheral. Apart from some moderate arm twisting by one or two of Clements' peers who wanted contributors under closer control, he remained at arms length. Clements and himself were of the opinion that freelance journalism offered far more opportunity to keep one's finger on the sinister pulses of friends, fiends and foes.

The second page carried a story of yet another volcanic eruption brewing up on Java. Bromo at it again he thought? Or was it Krakatoa – Merapi? A dagger pierced his heart as he remembered those halcyon days in Indonesia with Fitri. The name, he'd found out later, meant *festival*. Festival by name and festival by nature!

✳✳✳

Ashley smiled at the passing towers of cotton cumulus as his thoughts stepped back to the occasion of their first meeting. Jakarta, nine years ago, at the St. Andrew's ball. He'd only been passing through and really gate crashed the event at the last minute with borrowed suit and bow tie. And there she was! Amidst all the kilts and sporrans, DJs, heather and tartans. There, amongst the overweight and over exposed bovine snobbery that represented much of Jakarta's European elite, all important – but only to themselves, stood this

Indonesian jewel, whose beauty was louder than all the ribaldry around.

If Mike Tyson had hit him on the chin, he couldn't have felt more stunned than he was at the sight of her exquisite beauty and reserved demeanour. He always had had a soft spot for Asian women and found them a delight to watch whenever visiting the east. Petite, slim, feminine, graceful in movement, cafe crème skin, demure. The oval faces were a fascination, and especially the eyes – and the long black hair – and, and… And here, not more than a few yards away, face to face, was the embodiment of all those features that he adored. He had been about to toast Cameron, as they had taken the welcome drink of the evening, when he caught sight of her. His knees weakened and an audible groan escaped from somewhere deep inside.

'Don't tell me you've already spotted some tart to screw tonight?' his host had muttered in his ear. 'Nobody sensible brings white trash to society bashes in Jakarta. And certainly nobody takes them home afterwards,' he laughed. 'Unless of course they're already on the leash!' he added. It promised to be an entertaining night and they'd all joined in with mutual merriment. But then his friend had looked again when Ashley had failed to respond to the jibe, and immediately understood. 'Ah well! Not with such local beauty in competition,' he granted.

Such was his fixation that he'd failed to make the slightest response to her first glance. She was not alone, but hanging on the fringe of a mixed group of diners waiting to take their seats once the Chieftain had greeted the assembly.

Please look again, he prayed, but she was lingering on the conversations of her friends. Not apparently making any vocal contribution, other than to smile quietly in polite companionship.

He'd been round the world several times, done this, done that, met him and met her. Advised princes and generals – spoken at seminars and briefly taught journalism in colleges, so he was used to communicating. But at *that* moment, his social experience and confidence left him without any semblance of control. It all drained away through the soles of the fake Clarks bought from the market that morning.

At last the Chieftain entered the room with his heathered beau and the crowd hushed in respect. The MC, fortified by a few early whiskies, announced boldly that all guests were required to stand at their places and the Chieftain was escorted to the top table by a piper wailing out *Flower of Scotland*.

My God, – still she had not looked around and her group were now at their table. If there was really anything at all in telepathy then she could surely sense his agony, ready to do a deal with the devil or anybody else, if only – .

Then it happened! She was looking at him. They were *all* looking at him. He was still rooted to the spot, in the middle of the ballroom whilst the rest of the circus had taken their places for the first course. Embarrassed, he'd blushed, sweated instantly and profusely and with an apologetic bow to no one in particular, made his escape to the vacant seat next to his soul mate Cameron Cameron. As luck would have it, the princess was seated nearby, but with her back to him. A dig in the ribs from Cameron alerted him to the Chieftain's toast and he jumped to join the other men as the old head of clan hailed the beauty of their ladies on that fine occasion. He raised his glass to the vision at table four. Cameron chortled with mirth at his neighbour's explicit infatuation. The others at the table, all guests of his long time pal, had all noticed in amusement that his heart strings had been well and truly plucked,

The dinner formalities had taken an absolute age. Toast to the Chieftain. Toast to Burns. Toast to the Haggis followed by a toast to The Queen. *Ode to the Haggis*, courtesy of a Robbie Burns' effigy who must have been at school with the bard judging by sight of the skeleton that screeched out the recital.

Ashley was dying. Thankfully, and not a moment too soon, some official announced that 'gentlemen may remove their jackets.' Some respite at last. Released from the harness of the borrowed jacket that was at least two sizes too small for him, Ashley persevered through the food having neither appetite for haggis, nor much else on the menu. There was only one thing on his mind – Princess. He'd seen with relief, that she did not have a male escort, but was it just wishful thinking? How foolish and embarrassing it would be, if he presented himself at her table, only to find that she was accompanied or even worse, married. God forbid.

More formalities followed the interminable courses but his anxiety and resolve had not diminished, the forced interlude of the meal, had given him time to formulate a reasonable plan. The alcohol fortified his battered confidence – and then during the serving of coffee, she had taken the most cursory of glimpses in his direction. He couldn't swear if eye contact had actually been made, but he was almost sure that her eyes had lingered quizzically, imagination perhaps? And was there the faintest trace of a smile? Wishful thinking?

The moment he had waited for, suddenly presented itself. A middle aged *grey hair* from her table rose to take his leave. He had been seated with his own lady, a battleship if ever there was one, but he had seen him pass occasional comment to the vision across the table.

Ashley later remembered that he had risen quickly, excused himself and followed the man through the lobby, waiting there whilst his quarry disappeared into the gents. The conversation that followed once *Grey Hair* had re-emerged must have been quite garbled and he couldn't recall any of it. But it had been clear that, yes his attention had been noted by Miss Fitri and her friends. That no, she was not attached and in fact, a new kid on the block, so to speak. A quite shy young woman was Miss Fitri, and although she didn't speak very much English, *Grey Hair* thought that if he was gentle, polite and very patient then it shouldn't be a problem for him to say hello. He'd gone on to say that he was pretty sure that Miss Fitri would be too self conscious to get up and dance, to join in the reels and rollicking of Scottish dancing, and, as the rest of the table was eager to do just that, she would probably be alone at times and might welcome some pleasant conversation. But that would be all! *Grey Hair's* stern tone made it very clear.

Grey Hair returned to his table and spoke briefly to the battleship at his side. She had smiled across the tables at Ashley, obviously not as fearsome as she looked, and leant, as if her sails had suddenly caught the wind, to Fitri's ear. The topic became obvious when the girl turned her head to seek him out, found him and questioned him with raised eyebrows which revealed large brown eyes that sparkled in the ballroom lights. He had offered as warm a smile as he could control and this was mirrored by an inquisitive but non committal flicker from her lips.

Ashley, feeling more confident now that the ice was broken, had done as advised. The White Heather Band had been waiting all evening for this moment and so had Ashley. He felt a last minute panic that some other predator might have the same idea tormented him. So he had to be first!

The pent up energy of the conductor was released in a flurry of baton strokes that commanded the White Heather Band to play their first chords of the night, then he turned to the society, bowed and with an exaggerated up fling of arms, ordered the masses onto the floor.

A quick check that her companions had taken accepted the invite and he was off. In seconds he was there standing by her chair and looking down into her soft brown eyes set in her delightful oval face. The cross room dash was his first mistake and he immediately felt ashamed of his crude approach. In the months that followed she would teach him much about Indonesian culture and gracious manner. At that moment he'd thought that his European impetuosity had ruined his chances. She was so quiet, outwardly undisturbed, and immensely fragile. Yet so much more in control of the situation than he. Not only with her beauty, but with the karma that shielded her from the ignorance and naivety that was him.

'Salamat Pagi,' he introduced himself, holding out his hand. 'Saya Mike,' he followed – and praise the lord! for his second mistake brought laughter to her face and palpable relief to both of them. She hid her mouth behind her hand as if embarrassed and in a touching moment of modesty lowered her head. But the Javanese eyes were still laughing.

'Salamat sore,' good evening, she'd smilingly corrected him.

'Nama saya, Fitri.' Now looking him in the eyes and perhaps

35

seeing more sincerity than had been portrayed by his undignified approach. A typical 'orang putih,' she had later confessed to have thought him, and in doing so immediately forgave him for his western inadequacies.

He was beginning to get hot under the collar again, as the room and music closed in. He was fighting for something original to say, but frightened to further expose his cultural vulnerabilities and in doing so, destroy any chance he had of forging the relationship he so much desired.

But she had seen his body language and eased his dilemma with a motion of her hand inviting him to take the vacant chair at her side. He hoped that The Gay Gordons would continue their stampede across the dance floor in order to give him time to recover before they came to reclaim their table. At least he had not been rejected, yet. The invitation to sit with her was a positive step and the opportunity was there. Dialogue was not easy, for *Grey Hair* was right about her command of English, but with the Indonesian phrases he had learnt during the months of back-pack adventures and volcano exploration, along with her faltering English, they chatted quite nicely. And the long pauses of silence were not silence at all. Little needed to be said and what was said in a mix of pidgin English and pidgin Bahasa, facilitated much humour and ease.

Battleship and *Grey Hair* returned to join the two of them and it was a timely intrusion, perhaps even orchestrated. It gave the hosts a chance to check out the new guy and even offer protection to their charming guest, should she have needed it. She hadn't, and conversation flowed pleasantly between the four of them and with the other couple who, from time to time, took a rest from the inexhaustible White Heather Band. Smiles and laughs told of warmth that pervaded the group as they made him welcome in their company.

They had danced just once – a quiet waltz that sanctioned the band to take a breather, and him to hold her at respectable distance. Once again he sensed her grace, her fragrance and the fragility of her light frame. She seemed so delicate, like a fine piece of porcelain, that he was afraid to crush or drop lest she would shatter into a million fragments. He would never forget her eyes, raw umber, the oriental opal shape and Javanese eyelids that dressed them like silken curtains across the darkest of skies. The shallow bridge of her nose, the small delicate mouth with full pert lips like the petals of a rose, which promised bliss if he ever got to kiss them. When they went their own ways that night, and for weeks, no, months afterwards, Mike Ashley's feet never touched the ground.

After Fitri had left with her party, he had returned to the Cameron scrum of lurid jokes and the good natured banter about not bedding the princess that night. 'Rejected, not passed the test, old whack. Welcome back to the pen!'

'All in its own good time,' he had parried, more than content with the evening's work, and then relaxed with an elated smile that even the next morning's hangover could not erase. He had known full well from her parting smile, that he had not been rejected.

Six months later they were married. The clamour of the traditional Javanese wedding and haunting timpani of the gamelan orchestra still rang in his ears. Just eighteen months after – she was gone. Ashley never recovered.

✳✳✳

A light hand on his shoulder: 'Would sir like a top-up, or are you ready to order your main course?' The BA matronly figure drew his attention from the clouds that still lingered in his Indonesian excursion. Realising that he'd only half drunk the Buck's Fizz, he went for the top-up and – *needed* to have another look at the menu to decide on either the rump steak, poisson au gratin, or vegetarian lasagne verde, – thank you very much.

✳✳✳

The drive up to Cambridge had been a welcome escape from the city and he was happy to find Clements well into a beer at his favourite haunt, The Fort St. George. Backing onto the river Cam, the pub had two tiny rooms besides a main bar and wooden benches on the front courtyard on which a large family of French tourists were enjoying a noisy lunch in the midday sunshine. Clements was in the snug, compressed into a corner by the other three occupants, a local doctor and his two bitches. A bigger pair of Irish wolfhounds he had never seen. From even a short distance they could have been mistaken as small horses. The dogs totally dominated the room, so much so that they had to take it in turns to circle around in order to oversee his entrance. Seeking refuge from the dogs and the shrills and screams from *les enfants terribles* occupying the front terrace, they walked through to the back and found peace on one of the lawn benches.

Clements started to probe about his findings in Bayswater. 'So young Mr. Ashley, I wonder if we could brain-storm a little. What did you come up with?'

Ashley reported on Mrs Morgan and Lucy and said that he'd come to the conclusion that Goodwin *had* suffered one of his famed burn outs, and gone native for a few days. 'He's a nature lover and particularly keen on bird watching, and the wide open spaces of Canada might just have been too good an opportunity for him to miss.' Counter to this theory, had been the fact that the dear Mrs. Morgan and Lucy, for he found it difficult to think of them as separate entities, did exhibit some degree of undue stress. It was difficult to say conclusively whether, despite efforts to remain transparent, his own intrusion into their little world, or Goodwin's disappearance would have been their primary source of uneasiness. It nagged him a little, but in the end he was certain that Mrs Morgan was being supportive in helping him to help Goodwin. She *was* worried.

Clements had paused as the waitress arrived with sandwiches and fresh beer, then paused again before offering his input. 'I hope that it is as simple as that Mike – but there are a few other factors that you should know about, which suggest that this latest Goodwin excursion, as you call it, might not be what it appears, or – made to appear – dare I add?

Ashley was all ears as Clements revealed the original purpose of Goodwin's visit to Toronto. He'd known that there was a cryptology seminar, followed by a small exposition riding piggy back on the seminar to give contributing manufacturers an opportunity to put their latest wares in the world's shop window. A sort of thank-you for their efforts and so providing them an opportunity to exploit the occasion. What he had not known was that Goodwin had been scheduled to present a paper to the seminar. The subject of his paper was an assessment into the integrity of NAMES, the *North American Encryption Standard,* the new ciphering algorithm that had been elected by the industry, read National Security Agency, as the new standard algorithm.

Ashley had read of the competition that had gone on over the last few years between a number of mathematics teams, to produce a successor for the aged, and often considered, insecure algorithm, BASE, the *Basic Algorithm for Standard Encryption.* BASE had been around for years, which to most people with their fingers on the pulse, was not surprising, as its main sponsor was the NSA. And who else would want to be in control of an algorithm that was the encryption security medium for possibly, seventy percent of the world's telecommunications, but the United States' very own NSA? The National Security Agency.

Although he wasn't, by any means, a cryptologist, he had dabbled in it whilst at university, but his mathematical limitations and, it had to be admitted, his lack of interest in large numbers, led it to be a subject to be read about from time to time, rather than let it become the be all and end all of his life, as it had become for Peter Goodwin. However, not knowing precisely how conversant Ashley was with recent developments in the shadowed world of communications secrecy, Clements took it upon himself to briefly run him through some of the numerical intricacies of algorithms and secret keys. He paid greater emphasis on the political and financial consequences of the NSA's interest in having its eyes and ears on every transmitted message, beamed around the world.

'It was sometimes known as the "Never Say Anything" or the "No

Such Agency" after its instigation by President Truman in 1952. To this day, its mandate is signals intelligence gathering. To listen in on, and decode all foreign communications that would be of interest to the security of The United States. Naturally Britain has its own body of interest in GCHQ at Cheltenham,' mused Clements. 'But its budget and scope, pales into insignificance with that of the NSA. They spend billions on listening technology and super fast computers aimed at breaking the coded messages of its foes – and friends!' he added.

Ashley had read, with considerable fascination, books like David Khan's *The Codebreakers*. Books that related the stories of Enigma and its dissection at Bletchley Park, and the largely successful American efforts to read Japanese radio traffic in the Second World War.

'The BASE algorithm is one of many encryption algorithms that, in simple terms, use a mathematical formula along with a secret key to encode messages between two friendly stations. Providing the receiving station has the same key information, it, and *only* it, can successfully decode the transmitted message. Naturally anybody else having the correct key data, and the algorithm, can also read the message. So the goal of the NSA, and other like minded organisations around the world, is either to get a copy of the key, or break the key using one or two techniques that are basically guesswork.'

'But that doesn't answer the question: *why* did the Americans push BASE to the rest of the world?'

'Because BASE is old tack nowadays. It uses only 64 bits in its key. In practice it effectively only uses 56 bits in the encryption and by modern day standards with 1000 bit keys, BASE is ordinary to say the very least. The remaining 8 bits are used in, er, let's say packaging.'

'So if the NSA is promoting what might be classed as a weak algorithm, then it has a good chance of reading my bloody personal mail, free of charge?' quipped Ashley. He had a reasonable working grasp of this stuff. It wasn't a totally new revelation but there was something to be learnt and besides he could see that Clements was in his element and Ashley was reluctant to interject whilst he was in full flow.

'Not only *your* classified material, but half the world's too!' laughed

Clements. 'Just to put things into perspective Mike! In a brute force attack on a key, a modern computer might, let's say for example, make one thousand million checks per second. So with BASE having a key variety of ten times ten to the power of sixteen, that means ten times ten to the power of sixteen possible combinations – it would take something like two and a half years to break the code.'

'So where *is* the weakness then? Two and half years is a bloody long time. And by the time you've broken the key, it will be too late. The information would have become redundant in that time.'

'True,' the old man agreed. 'But then again, the computer might come up with the correct answer on the first try. Who is to say? The brute force attack works by trying all combinations of the key. So it is not safe to expect them to break into your Pirelli Calendar collection only after two years or more. – Besides, with the cash the White House makes available to the NSA, they have many super fast computers on call – the most powerful in the world. Then of course there is the next generation is IBM's *Blue Gene/P*. This beauty can carry out a thousand trillion calculations per second. So if you extrapolate from my first example, and they have a few hundred of thousands of these working in parallel -'

'They would break the code in – twenty four hours!' interjected Ashley, keen to show that he had some numerical skills after all!

'Precisely! – Just think if the White House knew, that within 24 hours, Saddam Hussein was going to attack Kuwait, it would allow them to take certain protective measures, even if they couldn't repel the invasion.'

'So why didn't they?'

'Maybe they did. Or, I should say, I'm certain they did. Reading other people's mail is a double edged sword. It's one thing reading it, but it's another thing reacting on it. If Uncle Sam was there waiting at the Iraqi/Kuwait border with a welcoming party of three or four armoured divisions, along with a few Apaches – even Saddam's cronies would have smelled a rat. Perhaps the most important thing about signals intelligence, is keeping secret the very fact that you can read the other fellow's secrets.'

'So what's special about BASE? How come it's still widely in use, even if everybody suspects that it's been compromised?'

'The fact that it's not so easy to get your hands on high grade encryption tools and algorithms. The Americans, the French and even us British, have strict export regulations governing both the strength of algorithms and whom they can be sold to. Especially the ones you can trust. You can imagine that the Americans wouldn't want to sell their latest 'stealth' technology to likely enemies if they thought that those forces were going to use it against the homeland the minute they'd opened the cardboard box. The same goes for the spying industry. Most people only sell such stuff to the world markets when they are past their sell-buy dates. – Besides – much low grade intelligence can be protected quite adequately by BASE. It just depends on what value you put on the data that you wish to protect. If it's your Pirelli Calendar, then nobody is going to spend millions trying to break the encryption that you might choose to use, just to sneak a look at Miss December, when for twenty dollars they can buy their own Miss December.'

'Oh! if you'd only seen Miss December, sir, you'd be sure to protect her with more than your 56 bits!'

Clements choked slightly on his beer and had to take another draught from the glass to clear his airways. 'Er, yes I am sure …… but the people at NSA have, eventually been forced to look for something to succeed their beloved BASE. On the one side, it must have borne much fruitful intelligence, but on the other side of the coin they've lost a lot of revenue due to the restrictions that they have imposed on people like Motorola and Big Blue wishing to export encryption. They and their US competitors have had to vie against encryption from other countries, like the Swiss, whose manufacturers have been keen to export high grade machines and algorithms, not only at the expense of American trade, but also to the frustration of the NSA. The last thing they would have wanted was people, especially from non NATO countries being motivated into buying encryption that the Americans couldn't break.'

'So there is a stronger algorithm on the market now?'

'Yes, just! – It's NAMES, the algorithm I mentioned previously. It uses 256 bit keys instead of the 56 bits of BASE and therefore is much more secure against assaults such as the brute force attack. In fact if you use the same computing power as before, then it would take longer than ten to the power of twenty four *years* to carry out the same brute force attack!' Seeing him grapple to comprehend such a meaningless number, Clements sought to put it into perspective. 'That is older than the age of our universe! Or – as Peter Goodwin modelled … "If you could build a box that could contain the complete solar system and fill it with sand, then carrying out the brute force attack on NAMES, would be like looking for a single, predefined individual grain of sand in that box!'

The deep silent waters of the River Cam slid by silently under the willows that draped its banks, as they both sat reflecting upon the magnitude of these revelations. For the first time, Ashley began to understand how somebody could become totally engrossed in numbers. Locking themselves away in their own universe, their own dimension, their own time frame. Such conceptions were only for the focussed mind. For the Peter Goodwins of this world, numbers *were* beautiful.

It was a long time before either of them spoke and it was Ashley, who eventually spoke to ask the profound question that drew mock applause from his peer. 'So if it's impossible to break such codes, or keys, well, in practical terms, let's say – the NSA and cryptanalysts from other organisations must be searching for another way in?'

'Ah!' Clements leant across the bench, resting his chin on his interlocked hands and looking Ashley straight in the eye said with great solemnity, '……and there you have it my friend – our little project to find out where Goodwin is and what he knows – welcome to Symphony.'

✳✳✳

The hostess tutted politely, but with intent. He'd not even thought to pull out his table in preparation for the meal tray. She expertly spread the table cloth with one hand whilst holding the starter tray in the other. He wondered why the BA girls could be so precise in lining their things up and the English batsmen so imprecise in lining up theirs. Rather than spoil his meal that lay before him, he closed the newspaper and organised the salad, adding the olive oil/balsamic vinaigrette himself. In anticipation of the fish course to follow, he took a glass of the Chardonnay, 'crisply dry with fresh fruity flavour and bouquet!' as it was advertised. After the second glass, he began to mellow a little as the alcohol reached the parts that mattered, and he relaxed into the meal and service. Now halfway across the North Atlantic he could look out across the deep blue and spot at least four contrails in line abreast. Similar aircraft, all heading for North America and all within the same time frame. It made him wonder how many flights per day were taking similar routes, filling the skies in an aviator's M25. Before he knew it he was mentally tallying the number of passengers a day, a week – a year? Goodwin would know instantly. Thirty eight thousand feet below and a thousand miles behind, rain clouds had replaced the cotton wool cumulus off the coast of Ireland and the heavy rain that was now lashing the Atlantic shipping below, would eventually rescue the five day test match from yet another defeat at the hands of the antipodean marauders from Sydney.

CHAPTER 4

Toronto Bound

St. John's, Newfoundland, gave the first images of the North American continent. As always he had been the last to finish his meal and by the time he'd dispatched the dessert, all the other passengers on the upper deck were snoozing, watching a movie or reading. The Daily Telegraph crossword could wait a little while longer. He slowly stirred the Black Label around so that the ice cubes tinkled lively on the glass – admiring the amber liquid and letting the rich smell alert his nasal passages before taking the first sip. He swilled the delicious liquid around his mouth; he let it slip down the throat to stir warmth into his belly. He'd flown so many times that it had become a conditioned reflex: the after meal digestion assisted by a glass of water to clear the palate, finger on the call button, a brief wait, which gave him time to salivate in anticipation, before the scotch arrived. This was the time when he really relaxed in a flight and on this occasion too, he let the seat recline, put his head back and let the world pass by under his window.

Now the flight was passing over the northern reaches of New Brunswick. Soon it would make a gentle turn in a south westerly direction, down the St Lawrence Seaway and on towards the Great Lakes. He remembered those school day geography lessons thirty years ago when he'd pored over maps of the world, dreaming about visiting such places, without ever thinking that he would get to see them in real life. Yet here he was again living those dreams of a youth whose ambition, like that of many others, was to see the world. What made it sweeter, being a Yorkshire man, was that he was doing it at somebody else's expense. Another slug of the scotch slipped off his tongue.

***

Symphony was revealed in some detail after having downloaded the June keys. They had been encrypted by a one time key. The latter was automatically generated in his computer's tamperproof security module after receiving a random number primer from HQ. The state-of-the-art cipher unit used one key for ciphering the complete hard drive so that even if the computer was lost, nobody should be able to gain access to its contents. In addition to the hard disk encryption, each file, or folder would be encrypted by the individual project keys. The third component was the communication keys. These keys were used to cipher Emails and their attachments, so that wherever he was in the world he could communicate with HQ, with Clements, or any other player in the team, having the same communication key. He guessed that each different link in the network would have a different key to reduce the possibility of anyone being able to read the wrong message, whilst at the same time authenticating the source of that message. In other words one could be sure that if the message was signed by John Smith, then it *was* from John Smith. If it was more convenient to transfer information by CD ROM, flash, or floppy, then the communication keys could be used to encrypt whichever medium was chosen. As an extra precaution, all plain imports from floppy disks or CDROMS had been forbidden by yet another security parameter. This removed any chance of a back-door entry and the possibility of picking up intruding viruses. When it was absolutely necessary to use the internet, all secure parts of the hard disk, or partitions, as they were referred to in the trade, were totally blocked and anyone hacking in would not be able to get at the hard stuff. All of these protective measures were backed up by access controls, such as passwords and as a final guard, the security module was removable. And without it, no contents of the computer's files could be retrieved. So he had few fears about leaving his laptop in a hotel room, or even in his checked-in-baggage in the aircraft hold, as long as the security module was in his pocket.

When engaged on a project, he received the monthly keys for that project and that project alone. He could, of course be working on more than one project at a time and in this case, he would receive a different extra key for that second project. Once a project had been declared *dead and buried*, all relevant keys would expire due to their time-out parameter.

Once every quarter, he would have to bring in the security module for the IT security guys to load in new master keys, i.e. those encrypting the download of project keys and communication keys.

Passwords were a real pain. There was a whole hierarchy of the blasted things and those under his own control had to be replaced every month. It was tedious stuff but he knew that it was essential to use strong passwords in order to prevent some eavesdropper or hacker from breaking in. There were two possibilities for generating passwords in his system. Either he could rely on his own intuition and diligence to produce them, or he could use a facility on the security module to generate one for him, from a random character generator. In the latter case, the passwords were to be considered very strong, but with the disadvantage that they would be difficult to remember as they wouldn't usually mean anything to him. If he produced his own passwords, then they would usually be easier to remember as they would probably relate to some aspect of his life. Here lay the danger and an inherent threat to access controls. Ashley, with some reluctance used the automatic generator, but rejected those that it produced, which he thought he might have difficulty in recalling. There had been occasions when he'd forgotten the current password and then blocked the whole security module by entering the wrong one more than three times. A blocked module meant neither access to his secret files nor his Emails. If he was travelling abroad, then it meant an embarrassing visit to the local British Mission in the hope that the security manager had access to the correct reset/administrator passwords. If not, then there was a frustrating wait for such information to be delivered to the mission by the diplomatic bag. This would also entail a right royal bollocking from the Key Admin and Clements himself, which had to be formally read out to him by the embassy official. Keeping secrets was not easy and he appreciated what a tough task it must be for the heads of network security, managing all those secret keys for all of the payroll spread around the world. A task made especially difficult when it involved rebellious and relatively ill-disciplined users such as himself.

On the other hand, the difficulties he experienced also opened up possibilities of gaining access to other's secrets, especially those who were not so well informed or disciplined. In communications security and intelligence work, it was always an ongoing battle – a search for the weakest chink in hardware and operating protocols, and then its exploitation. He estimated that about ninety percent of communications security failings were due to the human factor, a theory that was supported by the lectures that he'd attended over the years and feedback from within the organisation itself. Back in WWII, the German Enigma was a superb cipher machine. In retrospect it was seen however to carry a few, but critical weaknesses. Yet these were only discovered because of operator ignorance and blunders. In the Pacific War, the Japanese indiscipline and poor methodology also had catastrophic consequences. It was clear to see that fools in this line of work were always found out and paid a heavy price for it.

***

Once IT had sent him the Symphony keys, he'd typed out the eight digit password, entered the CD that Clements had given him and selected the correct key for the files it contained and double clicked the decipher button. The first file was deciphered and after a few seconds automatically stored on the Top Secret partition, in plain text. Ashley double clicked on the file icon labelled Goodwin P. and Microsoft Word broke into activity to display the bio data of the cryptologist.

***

Subject: Peter Goodwin
Birthplace: Portsmouth
Present Abode: London
Status: Single
Physical Attributes: 1.70m, 55kg. Slim build, Blue/grey eyes, Premature
                     greying of hair (light brown), wears spectacles for mild
                     myopia. Suffers slight curvature of the spine, probably
                     caused by extended study and use of computers.
                     Often referred to, by associates as The Grey Mouse.
                     Eidetic imagery retention.
Profession: Lecturer/Researcher in pure mathematics – Cambridge
                     University, UK. Consultant cryptologist for CIPHERCAN Co.
                     Toronto, Canada.

Background: King Edwards Grammar school, Portsmouth, England.
                     Left June 1984 with double As in mathematics and physics.
                     Read Pure Mathematics at Cambridge from 1984 – 1990.
                     with MA in mathematics.
                     1992 – April 1997 worked for Racon PLC, Reading, England,
                     as cryptologist specialising in cryptanalysis. Left in 1997
                     when Racon lost major contract to CIPHERCAN for the
                     supply of digital communications system to UK defence.
                     August 1998 – present time with CIPHERCAN as senior
                     cryptologist.
                     Retains research position at Cambridge and led
                     cryptographic team in producing SQUIRREL as a competitor
                     to replace BASE (Data Encryption Standard).

Psychological profile: Introverted, almost reclusive. Experiences difficulties in
                     communicating with people, despite his lecturing experience.
                     Intense mind-set regarding his mathematical work. Prone
                     to periodic breakdowns which have become more frequent
                     as time passes and on such occasions seeks refuge in
                     nature appreciation, tranquillity, classical music and
                     reading. During drop-out periods, that may last from a few
                     days to a few weeks, prefers to remain incommunicado.

Highly impatient and exhibits some arrogance when questioned about his work by non like minded people. Treats superfluous suggestions or opinions with disdain. Dogmatic, single minded in his work and considered by many to be totally inflexible.

Disappeared for six weeks after the rejecting of SQUIRREL by the NTSI, who were in favour of the German algorithm NAMES as the BASE successor. Became even more introverted after this period and increasingly aggressive to academic colleagues.

Associates:	Mrs. Mildred Morgan, – house maid.
	Claudio Bonetti, – chairman of CIPHERCAN. Cambridge research team.
	Leonard Clements, – MOI.
	Numerous students from Cambridge lectures – some expressing worshipful admiration of their mentor.
	Lucy,- his pet dog.
Interests:	Mathematics, compulsive attitude to crosswords (has, on occasions submitted crossword puzzles for publication in British national press). Ornithology, music, natural history. Enthusiastic royalist. (Thought not to be due to characteristics of monarchical subjects, but rather in preference to, quote – 'Parasitical Politicians').
Motivation:	Of the opinion that everything can be described by numbers as they are melodious and represent purity. Extremely confident in his own mathematical ability.

***

Apart from the record of AWOL excursions, two other salient points attracted Ashley's attention. One was the photographic memory and the other was the Goodwin / Cambridge team effort to produce the successor to the old BASE algorithm, and their apparent failure to do so. He could well imagine the stress that Goodwin would be under after what he must have *surely* considered to be an abject rejection of his work.

Eidetic memory? – Reminded him of a line he'd heard somewhere: 'We all have photographic memories, it's just that some of us don't have any film.' The older he got, the less this seemed like a joke.

Well yes, this would go a long way to explain many of the behavioural observations highlighted by the report, and it was also apparent from his own cursory assessment of Goodwin. He'd witnessed at first hand the intensity of the man on the one occasion that Ashley had met him, lecturing on the surreal subject of quantum cryptology. For what was crystal clear and almost an *orgasmic* event for Goodwin, and, it had to be said, for one or two of his disciples, was totally over the heads of himself and the majority of the audience. Goodwin might have been conversing in a different language for all Ashley knew. During one coffee intermission and snack grab, the boffins were to be seen clustered together in little pockets, enthusiastically debating what had just been presented before them. It somewhat reminded him of the lunch break at Lords, just a few days ago. Was it *really* only days ago? Same excitement, but quite a different subject. After the lecture, the plebs, amongst whom he had then considered himself to be a fully fledged member, succumbed to the idea that they were on a completely different planet altogether. Yet the people around him, and he knew many of them reasonably well, were all highly intelligent people, mostly well respected in their own fields, and certainly capable of dealing with life's everyday problems, which by all accounts Goodwin and many of his fan club were not.

One boffin, with a glass of warm university plonk in hand, expounding on Goodwin's psyche, pronounced that people with eidetic imagery retention often could not cope with a normal life, because they remembered every little thing that was happening around them. In doing so they became so overloaded with trivia that they were often unable to focus on normal everyday things with any degree of clarity. 'Imagine,' he related, 'Goodwin might have a mental image of a wedding shot fully engrained in his memory. Yet the subjective pleasure of the bride and groom would be completely overwhelmed by his retention of what normal people would consider to be irrelevant material, such as the condition of the turf in the picture.' Goodwin's singular objective, it seemed, would be to recount from memory, the blades of grass on which the wedding party posed! Ashley was perfectly content to be a lesser mortal. He considered Goodwin's problem to be further exacerbated when the products of mathematics did not quite conform to what Goodwin expected: ideal results, symmetry of solutions – perfection. Shadows on the lawn were the supreme frustration. When he found his own secret world, his refuge of numbers, let him down, so to speak – the rug was pulled from beneath him. Then Goodwin did not have anywhere to hide from the multitude of tasks, disappointments and decisions that common folk took in their stride. At dinner, he had been known to engage in a passionate debate with himself about whether to start with a carrot or potato, or a...? It was no wonder that the man was largely considered an oddball.

Putting all these characteristics together, along with the supreme intellectual effort in generating the likes of SQUIRREL to become the new BASE algorithm, Ashley began to understand Clements' concern for Britain's most outstanding cryptologist of the modern era. In the face of what must be considered as exceptional competition from esteemed bodies such as MIT in Boston, the ETHZ Institute in Zurich, and the Harvard group, any challenger could perhaps expect that one's own contribution might not become universally accepted as the number one. What had evidently been accepted in good grace by the other losing contenders, Peter Goodwin had not. Dilley, the MIT protagonist, had been quite philosophical in deeming the outcome as a cryptographic evolution and remained more than content with his own contribution despite its international rejection. Goodwin however, had poured scorn on the decision and behaved like a jilted lover. Why then, speculated Ashley, if the NAMES team had produced something that was obviously superior to SQUIRREL and all the other algorithms, and had been accepted by all other parties, why not by Goodwin?

In lay man's terms it was like a pub football team playing – and losing against a star team like Real Madrid. Everyone expects the finest to win the game with the lowly opposition left happy to accept the inevitable and be hugely content in just being involved in the occasion. The best team would win! So why *was* this such a problem for Goodwin? Did we have here, that rare thing – an Englishman who was just a bad loser?

✳✳✳

The popping sensation in his sinuses alerted him to the fact that the 747 had started its descent for Toronto. He looked out of the window to see that they were still flying up The St. Lawrence as it spread into Lake Ontario and left Ottawa behind in its contrail. The subsequent change in engine pitch confirmed that it would be a good time for him to ease the building pressure on his bladder and freshen himself up before the final stampede to the toilet. It always surprised him that most waited until the last minute before they hit upon the idea. On the way back to his seat, he had asked if there was the time for a final scotch before the cabin crew busied themselves with their preparations for landing. Two minutes later, the smiling matron, BA's answer to the delectable *Singapore Girl*, delivered a heavily laden glass, along with a tumbler of water to ease its aftermath and his re-hydration.

Clear skies presented an excellent bird's-eye-view of Toronto, its harbour front and the CN tower rising majestically above the financial district, as the flight did a u turn for its final approach from the south. The circuitous course provided some excitement for those sitting on the other side of the cabin, as the grand spectacle of Niagara Falls passed beneath. Ashley's eyes were on the tower. The dome next to it housed the final two days of COMSEC, the world's biannual conference on Cryptology and its attendant trade exhibition. It was also the last public sighting of Goodwin before had dropped out of sight.

CHAPTER 5

Comsec

Just as Goodwin had done before him, Mike Ashley checked into the Hilton amidst the evening rush of conference delegates. Some had had their fifteen minutes of fame, and were dashing to catch flights home, whilst latecomers like him were arriving to catch the final acts of the conference.

Having completed the check-in formalities Ashley casually asked the room number of his good friend and colleague.

'One moment please. Sir – I am sorry sir, but Mr Goodwin checked out on – July 7th. We were expecting him back after that weekend. He did make a reservation for the 9th. "To arrive in the late evening," it says here. But he hasn't called and he didn't show – yet,' the receptionist smiled apologetically from the computer screen. 'Oh! – there's one more thing, sir. He left some laundry to collect on his return.'

'Any forwarding address, or contact number?'

'Er,' – another scan down the screen. 'No sir, I'm sorry, nothing.'

'Please be kind enough to ask him to call me, if, – when he checks-in again.' He smiled, took his key card and followed by the porter, headed for the lift and the executive floor. With the conference so close by, hotel rooms around The Dome were at a premium, but his club membership had ensured a room for him and an upgrade, to boot.

***

Ashley checked into the conference as it opened the following morning. The simple breakfast, coffees and short walk to The Dome gave him some final moments to get his thoughts together and review his plan of action. The news that Goodwin had intended to return to the Hilton, if not the conference, gave him encouragement as he collected his COMSEC program and site map. He'd been pre-registered by Jane's Defence Weekly and was duly given a blue badge that signified *Press*. Nothing but the truth, he smiled to himself.

His goals for the day were to check out why Goodwin had failed to turn up to deliver his paper to the conference and judge reactions from the conference members. He also had to check out CIPHERCAN, who, on their own territory were here in some force and occupied a prime position in the exhibition hall. Perhaps they could shed some light on Goodwin's behaviour and attitude and of particular interest to Ashley was the subject of his paper. Its title 'Algorithms under Analysis' was both vague and ominous. Certain to bait the inquisitive. He noted that it was scheduled for the first session on the morning of the 11th July. The day after Goodwin had been due back at the hotel.

The first paper on this morning was on the latest advances on Public Key Cryptology and was chaired by a mad professor from the Massachusetts Institute of Technology. A real breeding ground for technical excellence and innovation, thought Ashley. This guy was something of an extrovert, long hair and pointed beard. No sooner had he taken the podium than he started waving his arms around as if he was conducting an orchestra. The tone of Dilley's voice rose and fell as it expounded the great drama that had been taking place within the IT computer bays at MIT. Ashley was grateful not to be sitting too near the front as he could see the occasional shower of spittle from the speaker's lips as his salivary glands worked overtime to cope with the animated jaw and vocal tract. The whole audience had become totally captivated, and none dared fiddle with their mobiles in surreptitious transmission of good morning messages to their loved ones or secretaries. If you didn't know jot about PK encryption before this performance, you certainly did after it.

Ashley always believed that a good teacher had to be an

entertainer, otherwise it would always be an uphill battle, despite knowledge and methodology, to keep the little darlings awake. Such a contrast to the Peter Goodwin lecture he'd attended. Goodwin was so nervous, highly strung and speaking in such low tones that it was exhausting trying to catch his every word. He held his audience in absolute silence lest any pertinent statement be missed. Yet in his own way, he had captivated people of his own mentality with subtle inference and supposition. These were supported by copious scribbles of formulae and statistics that resembled a young child's first experience with a felt tip pen on the nursery wall. Ashley had silently begged someone to push the microphone closer so that he and a host of others did not have to lean forwards to catch the whispered word. It was quite amusing to see the hard-of-hearing bobbing backwards and forwards as if engaged in Islamic prayer. With Goodwin, unless you were on the same wavelength then you wouldn't survive. On the rare occasion that anyone was brave enough to stand up and ask questions, that enquirer had to be very, very close to the mark. Any sign of numerical ignorance or naivety would be treated with disdain, and Goodwin would look through the offender with an icy stare that pinned the poor fellow to the back wall and just pause for effect before continuing his recitation. Ashley would never consider himself as anything but an amateur cryptologist, being more interested in the more practical aspects of communications security. So, much of what Goodwin had to say, when he could hear it, was beyond him. Therefore it came as a big surprise to him that at the end of Goodwin's lecture large numbers of the congregation actually stood to applaud with worshipful enthusiasm. He could only suppose that they and Goodwin had been communicating on a telepathic channel rather than the aural one that the mere mortals had been tuned into.

Prof Dilley, was a completely different kettle of fish. Group participation was the order of the day and the speaker fielded, most capably, the sort of questions that one might expect from a mixed floor of mathematicians, sale personnel, and customers and press alike. It left everyone feeling on a high – that they got something out of it. Ashley was keen to interpose with a question or two about BASE and NAMES, but with the momentum of the subject deviating along a different path, it would have been too much of a sidestep. At one swoop, he risked attracting a lot of unwanted attention to himself. He held his peace and waited for a less salient moment to start his inductive style of enquiry.

Dilley concluded his lecture and left the stage to be immediately surrounded by admirers. The organisers had chosen well, their opening batsman of the day. Ashley too felt enthused and left the theatre to cast his net wider.

Rather than make an immediate bee line for the CIPHERCAN stand, he browsed around a few of the other displays. Sometimes feigning interest and at others genuinely keen to know more about products and their customers. On these occasions he busied himself taking notes for his journal. Apart from the displays, what also was of common interest to some was people watching. Attracting particular attention were the representatives of organisations such as Ministries of Defence and Ministries of Foreign Affairs, officials from all over the world doing the rounds in search of solutions – and themselves watching everyone else doing the same. To further authenticate himself in this company, he engaged in a couple of lengthy interviews with company representatives who were trying to push PC, Internet and GSM security products, as well as the out and out military stuff. Events such as COMSEC always attracted a cosmopolitan crowd and maybe sales were not the primary motivation for being represented. If you were in the market you had to be here. If you were not, then it was noticed and questions would be asked.

Eventually the compelling mix of curiosity and some apprehension drove him in the direction of the CIPHERCAN stand, centred in pride of place within the Canadian pavilion. He was happy to see that there were only a couple of visitors on the stand and one of them departed as he approached. The remaining guest, whose attire gave the distinct impression of him being a student, was tall, slim, long limbed with tousled hair and sporting a heavily acne'd face. He was engaged in a conversation that brought consternation to the face of the blue suited salesman behind the orange CIPHERCAN lapel badge. Ashley mounted the stand and cast his eyes along the hardware presentations and network diagrams that connected Paris with Washington, Sao Paulo, Singapore, London and Dubai. The spotty student was still entertaining the blue suit, which left Ashley free to check on some of the documentation explaining all the company's virtues and why you should buy CIPHERCAN to protect your secrets. He could see that it was equipment that would only interest government bodies, the military and VIPs with deep pockets, even though no prices were actually displayed. The man in the street would have preferred to buy a Mercedes rather than the ciphered GSM telephone Ashley now held in his hand. It all depended on what value you placed on your secrets.

At last, Spotty and the Blue Suit shook hands and went their own way. The Blue Suit came to greet Ashley whilst Spotty hovered around the neighbouring stall. 'Good afternoon sir!' said Blue Suit, thrusting his business card into Ashley's direction. For a second, Ashley, both hands full, thought of taking it in his teeth, before replacing the GSM back on its stand. He took the card, gave it a cursory glance and popped into his breast pocket whilst Blue Suit leant forward to read Ashley's badge and then smiled in recognition of his visitor's role. 'Nice little gadget, this. Guarantees absolute privacy between you and your girlfriend for those intimate late night calls,' as Blue Suit picked up the GSM.

'Just the thing for Charles and Camilla, don't you think? – but they probably couldn't afford it. Am I right?' smiled Ashley.

'Quite right,' laughed the suit and countered with 'but maybe he wished he'd bought one anyway!'

'He'd need two, of course – or maybe more!'

'Absolutely!'

It was tempting for Ashley to reach inside his jacket and pull out his own mobile to compare toys. Like the CIPHERCAN device, it looked, to all intents and purposes to be an 'off-the-shelf' telephone.

But open up the battery compartment and one would find an extra circuit board that certainly would not be present in any high street product. End to end encryption of conversations between himself and Clements was available at his fingertips. 'But I thought the GSM phones were already ciphered?' he tested Blue Suit's knowledge.

'Oh, well, yes that's true.' The man stuttered, caught by surprise by the informed journalist. 'It is certainly a big improvement on the old analog system where you could listen into one or two conversations, whilst making your own. 'However,' regaining his composure, 'In all truth, it's only ciphered over the radio link – the link between the telephone and its nearest base station. The rest of the signal path is over the normal public switched telephone network, and there it's not ciphered. Anyone can tap into the call.'

'So why is your unit more secure?' enjoying the jousting.

Blue Suit was well into his sales verbatim now. 'Because we cipher the signal from end-to-end. All the way. From the moment your voice hits the microphone here to the time it appears at the earphone of the receiver. – No possibility of anyone eavesdropping on your goodnight intimacies,' smiled Blue Suit.

'I suppose you use strong encryption?'

'Well, the normal GSM uses a standard algorithm, produced by the Europeans. But it's not possible to export it to some countries – such as, er – I think China and probably the old eastern block.' The CIPHERCAN man was starting to struggle now and his glib tongue was not so confident as it searched for pauses that allowed more thinking time than he had needed in the introduction.

'But I was talking about your encryption, not standard algorithms. How is your unit more secure?' Ashley slowly turned the screw.

To Blue Suit's relief, rescue arrived in the shape of Blue Suit Two! 'Carlo Bonetti!' the newcomer proudly announced himself, appearing from the little rest room at the rear of the stand. Carlo Bonetti stretched his arm forward and offered a podgy hand to emphasise the greeting. Remnants of some food clung tenaciously to his bottom lip and the tissue in his left hand confirmed that he'd been snatching a quick bite. Once relieved of the handshake, his right hand plunged into the jacket pocket and re-emerged with a silver card holder, from which he retrieved his business card and offered it to Ashley.

'Mike Ashley, Jane's Defence Weekly!' he responded politely, accepting the card with the same, practised cursory glance at its information before depositing with the rest of the collection, in his breast pocket.

Carlo Bonetti, Sales Director, Middle East, – was Mafia all over. *Don Bonetti*, thought Ashley and was certain that he carried a sub machine gun in his jacket and afraid of no one but his mother back in New York City.

Big man, wearing an expensive blue pinstripe that struggled to cope with the one hundred and twenty kilos of Italian pasta. The efforts of the day, indeed the whole week, had taken their toll on his posture and attire. A blue silk tie hung loose and the collar was released from its fight with the folds of fat around the neck that supported a big round head crowned with short black hair held in place with a high gloss gel. The cheek jowls were also bulky and heavy black framed glasses perched on the wide nose magnified his slightly bulging eyes. Everything about Bonetti was big and loud and every movement was an effort that induced sweat to pour from his temples. But what he lacked in physique, he made up for with jollity, confidence and a dynamism that tagged him as an international wheeler dealer. If Bonetti was in town then everyone would know it. Once met, never forgotten.

The Italian, conscious of a minor irritation on his lip had another wipe with the tissue and the crumb was finally dislodged. 'Welcome my friend,' patting Ashley on the shoulder. 'I could not help overhearing your conversation with my colleague here. So the press is interested in serious encryption, it seems? Perhaps I can help. But how about coffee first?' and without waiting for a response, called loudly to some unseen figure behind the stand. 'Marie Anne! – due caffe please! Uno doppio espresso and,' turning to Ashley … ?

'Cappuccino, thanks.'

'… and a cappuccino for my friend.'

Ashley was a touch uneasy about the enthusiastic welcome and overt hospitality, especially as his host must be aware that the press would not normally be arriving with a fist full of dollars with a view to purchasing everything on display. However, if it made his enquiry easier, then he would be happy to go along with the charade.

Bonetti put his arm across his shoulder and guided him to a small wrought iron plastic, pedestal table attended by two similar styled chairs. 'Meester Ashley,' he explained as if reading the journalist's thoughts, 'It's the end of the show and we 'ave 'ad a 'eavy, 'eavy day, 'eavy week, in fact, – and I need coffee, and uno momento to take theese body of mine off my poor bloody feet – so welcome. Besides all our customers 'ave been and gone and ees time to relax a leetle.'

The sound and smell of the coffee espresso machine announced the imminent arrival of drinks and Bonetti turned to Blue Suit and with a subtle clench of the eyes and the faintest of nods, dismissed him to another task. 'My friend ees new with the company and as yet knows a not too much about our products. First time ee come to our exhibition. Good experience for him,' he explained with all the drama and artistic impression of the Italian language.

'I was just asking about your encryption – particularly what type of algorithms you use?' bringing the line of conversation back around to the pertinent question. Bonetti took off his jacket and hung it on the chair behind him, exposing large patches of damp under his armpits. 'For example, in your GSM phones over there?' Ashley indicated with his head to identify the items in question, and wondered if Bonetti was playing for time, when he busied himself undoing the sleeves of his shirt and folding them halfway up his large hairy forearms.

With a perceptible note of caution Bonetti, almost apologetically, announced, 'BASE, *Basic Algorithm for Standard Encryption!* – You see this model here is a beet a long in the tooth now, but we expect to 'ave a new version on the shelf soon.' He went on to explain.

Ashley raised his eyebrows in mock surprise, 'But why not use your own algorithms, BASE is an old solution, by modern standards – I believe?'

'Yes indeed, you're right sir. It came on line in nineteen seventy five. But we 'ave no choice, you see. Canada 'as an export agreement with our big brother across the lake, which forbids us to export strong encryption. So BASE eet ees!' with arms outstretched and palms open to the roof as if seeking the world's forgiveness for this.

Marie Anne arrived with the coffees and an ashtray. She was tall and skinny with short blonde hair, big nose and wore a pink suit that did nothing to enhance her featureless figure. No wonder Bonetti kept her at the back, he thought, as she entered and left without a word passing her lips. Ashley momentarily considered asking for the sugar, but feeling her surly manner, thought the better of it.

Bonetti threw the espresso down his throat in a single act of caffeine infusion and reached back into his jacket pocket to retrieve a packet of Esse cigarettes and a lighter. He slid open the pack and offered one to Ashley, who politely rejected with a shake of his head. 'Now, of course, we 'ave a new algorithm. Eets called NAMES – *North American Encryption Standard* and eets much more secure than BASE. In fact where BASE had fifty six bit keys, NAMES has one thousand bit keys. You see this is much more difficult code to break. Takes many years.' Bonetti added, head back and exhaling smoke through the stands artificial ceiling.

'So you think BASE was weak?' probed Ashley.

Bonetti was well versed about BASE and the latest encryption tools and keen to exhibit his knowledge, especially as most of his customers who had no idea about such matters. The less informed stared blankly at him if ever a conversation progressed to algorithms. He was not keen to talk at length about BASE, for it was a feature that put his company at a distinct disadvantage when competing against competitors from countries who were not so stringent about export regulations of strong encryption. Many, such as the Swiss who produced their own proprietary algorithms, were quick to exploit this niche at the expense of the American and Canadian companies. When his people were asked about this matter, they could see the suspicion instantly aroused when it was revealed that CIPHERCAN employed not only what was now considered weak encryption, and given the resources available to the American NSA, was also considered to be easy meat for their code breakers. This doubt played heavily on CIPHERCAN's prospective customers and had cost them millions of dollars in lost export sales. He had experienced considerable difficulty in selling his products to discerning clients, when at the back of everybody's mind was the fear that the Americans could still read their mail even if it was encrypted by BASE. It was no accident, he had to admit, that perhaps half the world's military and ministries were relying on a code that was already way past its sell-buy date.

Bonetti's salesmanship came to his rescue and he saw the opportunity to impress the journalist with CIPHERCAN's solution. Avoiding a direct answer, he diverted the impetus. 'We, of course strive to give our customers the best security that ees available to us and we are proud to say all our new products are installed with NAMES.

'Have you noticed any increase in sales since you adopted NAMES, any positive change of attitude?'

'Ha! Absolutely, you gotta believe it!' bellowed Bonetti, throwing himself back in his chair.

'Would you mind if I reported on this success for CIPHERCAN, in Jane's?'

'By all means. – Now we really competitive. First we are no longer inhibited by BASE and secondly we are, and always have been, undercutting our competitors. They are sheeting themselves, I can tell you,' Bonetti enthused. 'Marie Anne! … there's a Chianti in the cupboard. Get it open and bring three glasses. Pronto, bellissima mia!'

This was going well, thought Ashley as he turned to pick up his shoulder bag and collect his writing pad and pen. Bonetti took the opportunity to light up another cigarette even though there were already three half smoked sticks stubbed out in the ash tray. Around the rest of the hall, one or two stands were being vacated by sales teams eager to make a quick exodus now that clients and customers were drifting away. Ashley was a little surprised to catch a glimpse of *Spotty*, still in the vicinity, dipping into the pastry dish of a coffee stall just down the hall.

Marie Anne arrived with the tray of clinking glasses and the bottle of Chianti Classico. No doubt Bonetti had been saving it for just this occasion, the big wind-up after ten days of selling CIPHERCAN. Even Marie Anne looked less stressed than before. Attending to a sales stand for a week or more must be exhausting, thought Ashley. The relief around the hall was now palpable. It seemed like everyone had been waiting for some tired executive to pack up and in doing so, signal the moment for all to either celebrate, or get the hell out!

Bonetti was celebrating, and proudly announced, as he sniffed the cork with satisfaction and poured out the red wine, that it came from his 'ome town of San Gimignano. 'Right in the middle of Chianti country,' he advised and waved Ciao to a departing exhibitor from the neighbouring booth. 'See you in Vienna, next time!'

'Salut!' As Blue Suit was welcomed back to the fold, now that the sensitive stuff had been dealt with. Or so Bonetti thought! 'Yes we 'ave made big advances these last few months and even just this week, have we not?' he turned to Blue Suit, who nodded vigorously in eager consent.

'Cheers,' responded Ashley, clinking glasses whilst looking Bonetti in the eyes, observing the continental protocol.

Bonetti sipped from his glass, picked up his latest cigarette from the ash tray, took a long drag and after holding it for a few seconds, put his head back and despatched another cloud into the metal rafters above. Once again, he stubbed out the remains even though almost half was left. Ashley wondered if it was an act of compensation or guilt that he never finished a slender twig. Perhaps he felt in control by not having to persist until the last drag?

Bonetti leaned forward, 'Six months ago we made our first big sale to the Middle East. We've been trying to break into the market there for many years. People are falling over themselves, trying to protect their interests, ever since the militant fundamentalists got themselves into the action. Lot of money there and lot of people worried about looking after it.'

'Was this a military, commercial or diplomatic contract?'

'First one was for UAE military.' Bonetti took his glass, swilled its contents and thought of San Gimignano as he sniffed the red's bouquet. 'Email security and fax machines,' he added.

'Faxes? Now that's a little surprising in this modern day and age, isn't it?

'Not at all. There's still a lot of life in the old fax machine. It's not so expensive, quite efficient and most of all, easy to use. And that's important when you are short of staff experienced in use of computers and internet services.'

Bonetti intimated that Ashley should make way for a top up and he duly obliged whilst Blue Suit hung out his empty glass hopefully, only to miss out when the Italian returned the bottle to the table after refilling his own glass. 'And, this week we signed another contract with Sheikh Hamed – Dubai royal family, to supply the very same faxes. Wants to use them in setting up some communications security for this year's DUBAIREX.'

'DUBAIREX?' queried Ashley.

'Aviation exhibition, November next – Dubai – Persian Gulf, 'getting to be a preetty beeg show nowadays. All the beeg players will be there, Boeing, Airbus, Lockheed, BAE, you name it.'

'Yes quite!' responded Ashley, forgetting, for the moment, the major aviation marketing event of the year. 'And all this stuff installed with NAMES?'

Bonetti took another sip of the Chianti, relishing it more now that it had been breathing a while. 'Sure thing!' he said at last with great satisfaction. 'This crowd in UAE, particularly the Dubai people have invested millions, oh billions! in developing the place. Twenty years ago it was desert. Now they've got one of the best airlines and a sky line that outshines any in the world, with the possible exceptions of Hong Kong or Singapore. They have put in beeg bucks and it's all at risk if some Islamic radical decides that it's not in Allah's taste.'

'So you've made a killing, so to speak?'

'We beat off the opposition and we're optimistic that it's the first step in the door. I personally, am going to act as consultant. To make sure that it works as it should. And then we're playing with the big boys.'

'What about internal sales? Within North America I mean?

'We've always had a home market to underpin the export effort. It's OK. Nothing big but ok!'

'Do you use NAMES in this market too, or do you employ a propriety algorithm? – I mean does every customer get the same encryption algorithm?'

'Depends on the organisation. If it's an international then we have to use NAMES, otherwise we can utilise our own material,' answered Bonetti easily.

'So you have your own cryptographic laboratories?'

'Yes, of course, right here in Toronto – and a leading consultant from Cambridge to oversee it,' boasted Bonetti, but noticeably hesitated a little with the appendix as if he regretted adding it. He took the wine glass once more and lifted it to the light, admiring his birthright and feeling its soothing influence after many stressful days. Once again, he swilled the fine wine around his glass.

'Ah yes,' said Ashley, as casually as he could manage. 'That would be that Peter Goodwin – I expect?'

Bonetti stared through the wine at some distant point, and just for a milli second or so, tensed, letting the wine still, fighting some knee jerk response. A dark cloud momentarily whisked across his face, yet Carlo Bonetti handled the moment expertly. He'd been caught quite unawares and yet hardly flinched. But Ashley had seen enough and whilst Bonetti exercised remarkable control, Blue Suit had not. He'd been sitting casually on a display table at the side, swinging his legs to and fro. The instant Goodwin's name had been mentioned, the legs had stopped abruptly and Blue Suit's eyes had lifted sharply to seek Bonetti's.

'I was hoping to catch his lecture, the other day.' Ashley offered to ease the moment, looking down at his pad and scratching some detail into his report.

Bonetti recovered, by taking a slow sip and countered, 'and so were we!'

***

Ashley joined the rest of the lingerers, vacating the Dome as COMSEC drew to a close. Outside the hall, the early evening sun was still strong and warm. Instead of making his way directly back to the hotel, he turned left down Spadina Avenue and strolled down towards the Harbour front, and Lake Ontario. On summer days and evenings like this, workers from the financial district mixed with tourists to enjoy the relaxed atmosphere with few drinks or dinner at one of the numerous harbour side restaurants that were open to the elements and offered a pleasant view. It was a busy time and it seemed to him that half the city was there to hang out. He shed his jacket and carried it over his shoulder, happy to enjoy the clean air after the oppressive heat in exhibition hall. The fresh air filled his lungs as he walked at an easy pace taking in the events of the day and reworking through his interview at the CIPHERCAN stand. Goodwin's missed lecture had drawn some comments that ranged from: 'Who cares' – 'a pity' – 'would have been interesting' – to some expressions of sympathy and even concern. No one knew the precise subject on which he had decided to talk as Goodwin had failed to turn up on the 10th at the speaker registration and provide the customary prologue to his lecture. It was noticeable that the criticism came mostly from within the small circle of fellow cryptologists and the former from the American contingent, who didn't hold much truck with Goodwin's whimpish attitude. He wasn't the entertainer; he didn't make a splash and therefore was not worth listening to. Ashley wondered if the same people would dismiss Stephen Hawking on the same grounds. Ashley himself was not sure in which camp he belonged. Certainly not one to deride him, but not one to fall at his feet either. Like some, he thought that if people like Goodwin could handle everyday life, it stood them in good stead for coping with other traumas.

In his own life, his interest and participation in sport had helped along the way when storm clouds gathered elsewhere. Healthy in body, healthy in mind was a strong doctrine to adopt. Even a few hours' escape into football, golf or any other game, provided relief and a diversion from a dark path that could easily become a downward spiral. Who was he to speak? He still hadn't fully come to terms with the loss of his dear Fitri, but he could deal with it now – couldn't he? Ashley wondered how the cryptologist would handle the loss of someone so close. Time for a beer. Drown the thoughts.

He was rescued from deeper reflection by one of the touts, menu in hand, out to kidnap customers to their particular eating hole and allowed himself to be cajoled into a steak bar just off Rees. Not to be rushed, Ashley insisted that he needed a couple of beers and a spot of people watching before deciding upon what was to be rare or medium. No chance of a newspaper at this time of day, certainly not an English one, so he dug into his breast pocket to retrieve the collection of business cards that he'd collected over the day and disposed immediately of those that held no interest. He was about to return the others back to his pocket when a crumpled slip of paper fell from between them. Expecting it to be a credit card slip, he bent to retrieve it and was surprised on opening it to find the crossword puzzle that he'd picked up from the bureau back in Bayswater.

The first pint of beer arrived, suitably chilled and inviting. He smoothed out the creased paper and took a long hard draught of Moosehead, and was just about to tackle one down, when a bony, long fingered hand appeared on the back of the opposing chair. Ashley looked up and was preparing to wave it away to some table in demand, when he recognised the spotty student who'd been hanging around the CIPHERCAN stand.

'Sorry to trouble you, but may I join you for a few minutes?'

'Be my guest,' said a startled Ashley, rising to his feet. 'Can I get you a beer?' – happy at least to have someone to chat to. But the guy held up his hand in refusal.

Looking decidedly anxious, Steve, as he introduced himself, spoke quickly and to the point. 'I was a student of Peter Goodwin's; – at Cambridge – a few years back!'

The words stung Ashley. He stopped, caught the crossword paper that was about to be carried off by a sudden breeze, neatly folded it and tucked it back into his jacket pocket. He assessed the strained look on the face and the eagerness with which the man apparently needed to get something off his chest. Now it was Ashley's turn to raise the hand, getting the young man to breathe, and chose the moment to catch the waitress's eye. 'Another beer for my friend, dear,' with a warm smile which sent a message of *all's well* to anyone who might be observing. 'Let's take this slowly, Steve. – What are you doing in Toronto?'

'For the conference, but I'm here on an exchange program between Kings College and Toronto University, and I wanted to see Peter again, he comes from time to time ...'

'Hey! steady on. One step at a time, take it easy, there's no rush. Now, you said that you were studying under him?'

'Yes, I was working with him for three years.'

'Any research?'

'No, not at that time, but now yes. Yes, just this year. But not under Peter.'

'Do you know what SQUIRREL is? – Have you worked on SQUIRREL at all?' inquired Ashley.

They paused for Steve's beer arrival, before he answered, 'Yes I know about it, er, – rather I know of it, but wasn't really involved with it. A bit before my time, you know.'

Ashley took a drink and looked across the water to the City Centre airport, where a Cessna was making its final approach before landing. He'd never met this young fellow and was reluctant to confide in him without knowing much more. It was possible that he was connected, even employed by CIPHERCAN, after all he had seen him engaging in some serious conversations with their staff. He could be just out to check on what he, Ashley was up to. Bonetti had merely told him that he understood that Goodwin had not been well and therefore could not deliver his paper. But he had never actually said if Goodwin had spoken to him about this, or gave any details. Ashley would have expected Goodwin to have turned up on the CIPHERCAN stand, to help promote the company and field any enquiries about ciphering. He was sure that when it got to the serious stuff, both Bonetti and Blue Suit would be out of their depth and expect Goodwin to give them support on this matter. It would be important to clients that the top man was present for show, even if not for technical discussions about algorithms. He was sure that Goodwin would hate it, as it was clear to all that he was not an entertainer and a dedicated introvert might be an embarrassment for CIPHERCAN, if he'd been there. Goodwin on the stand could even be the makings of a customer relations disaster. Perhaps if the truth were known, Bonetti might not want him there, for just that very reason. The director had expressed his anger that Goodwin had not been around after that weekend and put on a very impressive show of disgust with a raised voice delivering a number of unpleasant expletives. If he was being less than truthful, then Bonetti was expertly able to channel his fears and aggression into a convincing act of professional disparagement, but the high blood pressure he could not hide.

Ashley had been diligent in not overplaying his hand and was convinced that neither the CIPHERCAN team, nor anyone else, could suspect that his enquiries were anything other than those of a technical journalist. The question bugging him now was: was the chap facing him across his beer, seeking Ashley's real motivation on behalf of CIPHERCAN, or some other party? Could it be that he really had genuine fears about the well-being of his old cryptology professor?

'Peter often discussed the whole issue of BASE with me, its shortcomings and the competition for its successor, not in lectures but informally when a few of us got together.'

'Did he break the BASE code?'

'I don't know, – but he certainly knew how to go about it and if we'd had the computing power of some of the American universities, then, yes, statistically we could have done it.' They both took a drink and the student added a spontaneous observation, '- personally, in all truth, we would have been quite disappointed if he hadn't broken BASE. He wouldn't have been able to resist the challenge. Algorithms, astronomy, crosswords, you name it, any intellectual challenge and Peter was in to it.'

This was a pretty informed insight into Goodwin's work and Ashley was gradually coming round to the idea that this guy Steve was the genuine article although he hadn't said anything about why he had made the effort to make contact with him. 'Steve, this is all very good, but why come to me about this? Anybody who knew Goodwin well, who was familiar with his work would be aware of, of ...'

'I met him the day before he disappeared!' interjected the student.

'So why is that interesting to me?'

Steve was showing signs of frustration. 'Because I thought you might be able to help!'

'Help? Who needs my help? It seems to me that he just lost his bottle. From what I hear, it's not the first time he's taken off when things have got tough.'

'Shit!' he was getting angry now and took a long swig at his beer, trying to keep his cool. Ashley thought that he was about to get up and leave, but Steve thought the better of it and resigned himself to one more try. 'Peter was absolutely sure that *his* SQUIRREL was perfect. That there was *no* competition! That it was a big mistake, and he meant *really* big, for NIST to select NAMES instead of SQUIRREL to replace BASE.'

His raised voice and the heavy slapping of the table emphasised his irritation, and in doing so attracted the attention of diners at the neighbouring tables. It was all getting out of hand thought Ashley. They both had another drink to take the heat out of the situation. Not saying a word so as to let the temperature settle. Steve looked beyond him, his mouth pulled to one side, stitched tightly in a horizontal frown, as if he was frightened that anything else untoward should escape his lips. He sat back, his long legs under the table and arms folded across a heaving chest. If this guy was in Bonetti's employ, then CIPHERCAN would be nominated for another Oscar next year.

'So why *did* he miss the presentation? This was his chance to inform the world, in front of exactly the right people. The right time and the right place! And he missed the show.' Ashley let a little of his own anger slip into the question.

'That's just what I've bloody well been trying to get through to you. He would *never* have missed it. Shit! – Not for the world! –

Shit! – F**** you!' – And with that he was gone. Standing abruptly, he finished his beer in one, and was gone, striding briskly off in the direction of the ferry.

Ashley was not sure if the fellow had caught the trace of his smile before he stomped off. He would have slept easier if he had. But the whispered 'thank you' that Ashley breathed after him was long lost in his wake.

***

'I think well-done should be the order of the day, my dear, but I'll try medium-rare – and another beer please.'

***

Back at the hotel, Ashley got another break, albeit a small one. The same girl who had checked him in was on reception and caught his eye as he passed by. 'Sir! Excuse me sir, but there's a message for you.' He checked his step and turned to the desk.

She passed him a message slip that would have been on its way to his room had he not passed by at that moment. 'It's for Mr. Goodwin, but you did ask, and he's still not back yet. It's from Hertz.'

He took it with a smile and grateful thanks and read it there and then. It was just a message that the car rented by Goodwin was now overdue in its return. 'Would you please contact this office or the nearest Hertz desk, to inform them of his intentions? Your immediate response would be much appreciated … Blah, blah.' What was important to Ashley was that it gave the details of the car and that wherever he was, Goodwin still had it. At the very least he was still in Canada!

***

Once in the privacy of his room, he prepared and transmitted an Email report of the day's events for Clements. It was his first since their meeting in Cambridge and whilst he didn't have anything conclusive, he did think it prudent to keep his boss informed of the progress or lack of it that had been made. The fact that there was little positive data to feed back to London meant that other avenues of inquiry had to be explored. In this case two heads were better than one. And Ashley, although he was certain of Clements's response, needed the go-ahead to widen the search. Subsequently, Clements confirmed this emphatically with a simple sentence – 'We have a need to know!'

He ciphered the message with Clements's key of the day and then closed the ciphered file so that there was no plain copy on his computer. Finally he blocked that particular disc partition before logging onto the internet and sending the mail immediately. His second report was far from being secret. This one would be published and available for any interested party to see, including Carlo Bonetti himself, or Carlo Billionetti, as Ashley now liked to think of the Italian wheeler-dealer.

Should anyone be checking up on his own authenticity, they only had to pick up a copy of the world's favourite defence journal that weekly reported on the important events in the world's security news. Bonetti and CIPHERCAN would be pleased about the free advertising and it might stand Ashley in good stead whenever they might meet in the future.

CHAPTER 6

North by Temagami

The crossword sprang to mind as he needed some relaxation before he felt tired enough to hit the pillow. So, not for the first time, he smoothed it out and scanned down the clues to check if there were any that triggered immediate answers. It occurred to him that Goodwin must have sat down once, in a similar manner, to address this very crossword. But if that were the case, then it couldn't have been a lengthy attack because no solutions were filled in. Perhaps that day's puzzle from the Telegraph had been particularly demanding and stretched even the cortical neurons of the Cambridge cryptologist. So, there's not much hope for me, thought Ashley.

The first seven horizontal clues didn't illicit any instant reaction, but sixteen across looked interesting.

Gunner has job, it turns out, in South Africa – (twelve letters)

The second part of the clue *it turns out*, usually indicated that there was an anagram somewhere and he didn't think it would be *in South Africa*. This seemed more likely to be the main part of the clue. So the letters from which to construct the answer must come from …
… of course! – Immediately he saw *Job* and then linked it with South Africa, he thought of Jo'burg! A quick check to see what letters were left from, *Gunner has* … If they could indeed make up the rest? and sure enough, there it was – *Johannesburg*! Feeling pretty proud of himself, that it came so easy, he was encouraged to continue.

Well! it wasn't so difficult after all. But how come Goodwin hadn't found it?

Having Johannesburg, he decided to build on it and so tried fifteen down which crossed the first answer at the second letter *o*.

I'm set up in an easily managed residence – (eight letters).

No anagram here that he could discern, but *I'm set up* certainly means that reading from the top, there should be *mi*, in there Already he had the *o* from *Jo'burg*, so that left five letters to find from the rest of the clue, which was easily manage residence. He took a biro and scribbled these letters down jumbled in random pattern, in the margin and then tried all possible combinations along with the *o, m* and *i*. It wasn't long before he'd got *domicile* – quite easy but none the less impressed with himself. He was amused, but then in the same instant realised with a shake of the head, that Goodwin could not have had trouble with this. He was after all, a world renowned cryptographer and cryptanalyst, so he must have been able to tackle a puzzle of this mild difficulty with some ease.

Looking further down the clues, Ashley found seventeen down, it too crossed over *Johannesburg*.

Dull Picture that lost some tea, all stirred, lake in Canada. – eight letters.

He looked across to see that it took an e from Johannesburg but! It was the last part, *lake in Canada* that really woke him up. The printing then caught his eye again but for a different reason. He'd missed it the first time. There – underneath the text, was that a pen mark? He sat up and moved the paper to the bedside table and viewed it under the lamp. Carefully smoothing out the multitude of folds and creases. Yes, he was right. There was the faintest of pencil marks, but faint as it might be, it was definitely there, partly underlining the clue. Goodwin must have made it. He couldn't imagine Mrs. Morgan, either interfering with Goodwin's puzzle or having any idea of what the clue might mean, or its solution. Either *lake in Canada* was the main clue or *Dull Picture*. *That lost some tea,* he reasoned, meant that one of the contributing words had the letter T removed. Off hand, he didn't know of any Canadian lakes other than Superior, Huron, Erie and Ontario itself. It was a long time since he had studied The Great Lakes in geography all those years back at King Edward's Grammar. Superior had eight letters, but the *e* didn't correspond with that in Johannesburg.

Ashley's mood deepened, sensing that there were several pertinent questions to be answered here. It was becoming something more than a simple crossword puzzle.

One.   Here he was actually here in Canada and the clue was about Canada.

Two.   Goodwin had had some reason to show this clue more interest than any of the others.

Three. Those other clues tackled by Ashley, himself, had not been particularly difficult. Therefore why hadn't Goodwin made even a single entry?

Four. If the clue was after a lake, he didn't know any that fitted the bill.

Five. The body of the clue could be Picture and the Canadian part of it, just coincidence?

OK, he thought, we'll have to tackle it from another angle, and searched the room for any maps of Canada. The only thing he could find was a crude one in the telephone directory, giving codes for different regions and not a lot else. He glanced at his watch – already eleven thirty, so the hotel's lobby shop would be closed. Frustrated by not being able to take the puzzle any further at that time, and after having an exhausting day, he quit for the night. He would leave seventeen down until he was refreshed and his head clearer than it was now.

✳✳✳

He woke with a start, not knowing at first what had disturbed his slumber so abruptly. Half expecting the telephone or the alarm to have alerted him to the fact that it was morning, he waited for a second bell – But it didn't come and the darkness in the room told him that dawn was some hours away. A smile spread across his face as he recognised the reason for his waking. Goodwin had not filled in any of the clues of the crossword, he didn't need to! He could, with his eidetic memory, remember every one that he could answer without writing them down! Ashley was just left to wonder if that included seventeen down and what it meant, if anything at all?

It could wait till later. Sleep was still number one down.

***

OK this was it, action day! Ashley had to get on the road and somehow pick up a trail to chase down Goodwin. The question first thing that morning was, where to start?

After the interlude with Steve, Ashley was convinced that Goodwin had intended to take a weekend off, out of town and out of the hustle of the conference circus to garner the energy and confidence to deliver his paper. He thought it unlikely that Goodwin had flown anywhere as this would involve hassle, expense and time. Besides he already had wheels and it didn't take long to get out of the big city and escape into his beloved wilderness. Ontario had plenty of that to offer. From the hotel desk, he knew that Goodwin had checked out on the Thursday morning and was due back on the following Sunday night. If Ashley read the scenario correctly, he considered that Goodwin would not have wanted to drive for any more than a day, in either direction. Otherwise, it really didn't make much sense in going at all. So one day out, three nights there, wherever? And then one day back. Based on nice open, dual carriageway roads, with not a lot of traffic and no particular need to play Michael Schumacher, Ashley reckoned on three to five hours of easy driving to be reasonable. That gave a range of a maximum of three hundred miles out and three hundred miles back. Maybe a little more, but it was a starting point. Ashley laughed to himself – it was a pity that it wasn't London, then he'd only have to look as far as the M25.

On the face of it, drawing a compass line circumscribing Toronto with a three hundred mile radius suggested a mammoth task, but for anything other than a day trip, the city was almost surrounded on three sides by water, thereby introducing some limitations. Ok, give a little bit of leeway to the south west, then north seemed the best bet. After all, Goodwin could drive north to the Arctic Circle whereas going south would soon take him to the good old US of A. Ashley thought that out of the question. Except that the roaring Niagara Falls was down that way. But it was only a day's trip. It was still a possibility, but then the weekend crowds of sightseers and their traffic, would be enough to point him, let alone Goodwin, in the opposite direction. So north, he was confident, was the best bet.

On the map that he'd bought in the lobby before breakfast, he drew a sector with the western line stretching from Toronto to touch as a tangent, the shores of Lake Superior and extending in a north westerly direction. The eastern boundary he drew from the city and up towards Ottawa. There was the small sector to the south west and Ashley thought that he couldn't exclude it entirely, but on thinking about it for some time, it didn't invoke the same idea of a big escape as did the vast forests and wilderness to the north. And that was what Goodwin would be searching for. Peace and solitude were more certain in that direction. Otherwise he had misread many of the signs along the way.

Recollecting his visit to Bayswater, Ashley had considered at the time, both what Mrs Morgan had said about Goodwin's hobby of ornithology and his affection, dare he say fascination, in Bateman's Loons of the Algonquin – and right there in the middle of his sectored markings of Ontario, was the Algonquin national park. He checked the mileage and came up with about two hundred and thirty miles. Certainly in range, and equally certain to be a very attractive proposition to Goodwin. Putting himself in his quarry's position, with his habits, hobbies and frame of mind, it just had to be the favourite destination.

Still searching for alternatives, he looked to the west, along the eastern shores of Superior, but didn't find the string of industrial towns along the great highway at all attractive and Goodwin would have to drive through that, to get beyond Sault St Marie. No, not likely. As much as he explored other possibilities, not wanting to be anything other than objective, he could not find any alternative that would have the pulling power of one of the great national parks of Canada.

The next hour he spent on the Internet, searching for accommodation and found a dozen lodges that looked promising. Three were fully booked and had been for some time, and none had a Goodwin in house, before or now. Two others were so outrageously expensive that he was sure that they were well beyond Goodwin's pocket, but enquired about them anyway. He got on the telephone to the others and found that they were also fully booked for the weekend as they had been for the last month. 'It's usually the case at this time of year,' advised one receptionist. So it seemed like one had to make a reservation weeks in advance, or get lucky with a cancellation, or the odd day or so between weekends. The very last number on the list however, produced silver, not gold, but silver – it was something! A Mr. Goodwin *had* made a reservation for the Thursday night, but wanted the Friday and Saturday also – at Caribou Cottages, but they couldn't oblige. He'd called back later, to cancel his initial reservation for the Thursday.

Goodwin must have managed to find an alternative for the whole weekend rather than a day here and a day there. Ashley couldn't see too many other options that he could chase up, other than, perhaps, camp sites or a bed and breakfast on the outskirts of the park. It was becoming an impossible task. On the one hand, he was on the right path, Goodwin had been looking to The Algonquin for refuge, on the other, he could now be anywhere. Back to square one! – and lunch.

***

He took a right out of The Hilton, walked on Queen Street and then on to Richmond, to the very Hertz car rental office that Goodwin had used just over a week ago. God! It seemed much longer than that since he'd been asked to pay Clements a visit. He took a Pathfinder four wheel drive. In view of the terrain he might have to travel over, it could prove useful. Once all the paper work was done, he drove back to the hotel, to load up his belongings, left a message at the desk, should Goodwin eventually find his way back alone, and then took University Avenue, Yonge Street and out of town on the highway, heading west. After a few miles he met the junction with highway eleven, heading north. The decision was made.

Highway eleven stretches from Toronto, all the way up to Hudson Bay. He remembered from the time when he had been working on a school geography project on the region. Little did he know then, how close he would get to it one day. As he put distance between himself and the big city, his mood became mixed. One minute happy to be on the road and doing something physical, yet the next, apprehensive about what lay ahead of him. Why it was that way, he couldn't exactly say. Perhaps it was the fundamental conviction of Steve that Goodwin would never miss the opportunity to present his paper. That it was imperative to speak at the conference, but then not turning up on the big day, was starting to ferment worries in his own mind. If he had not been so impressed with what the young student had had to say, and more importantly, the passion with which he had said it, Ashley doubted if he would have got as far as he had. In retrospect, perhaps if he had confided in Steve a little more, he could have possibly gleaned a broader insight into what was troubling his mentor. Maybe there was more to be had? On the other side of the coin, he could still not be absolutely sure on whose payroll Steve was. To reveal his very own masters would have left him open to the same threat that Goodwin might be under. In that circumstance there would have been no going back, no wiping the slate clean and probably no chance to help Goodwin, whether he needed it or wanted it.

North Bay was in reality a major crossroads. West to Calgary, The Rockies and Vancouver. East to The Algonquin, Ottawa,

Montreal and further along, The St Lawrence to Nova Scotia. South, back to Toronto and north to Hudson. Had he not been able to solve seventeen down, he could have turned up here and tossed a coin to decide which way to go. His first idea of Algonquin, was still an option, and if he couldn't uncover something in Algonquin, then he promised himself to have a final scout round the park on his way back to Toronto. As it was Ashley had to stop for gas and took the opportunity to grab a quick meal. A wayside Thai restaurant, just short of North Bay enticed him in. Which way to turn? Toss a coin and trust to lady luck or seek inspiration. Waiting for his meal, Ashley spread his map across the table. Then eating with one hand and plotting with the other he scoured the country of a million lakes. Mentally crossing those off that triggered no interest and circling those that might, just might hold a clue to Goodwin's location. Clue! Clue! The crossword bugged him. He *had* what might be construed as a clue, the clue? How to match that with a lake? So many of them! Lakes named after every animal that had ever walked the earth and some that he doubted had ever put foot on terra firma. Some with English names, some French and even some Indian tribal names that mystified him even more. Take for example this. His finger rested on Temagami? Ashley could not guess what it might mean and dismissed it as he had many others. – *Dull picture that lost some tea?*

'Shit!' he exclaimed to the other diners around. The owner/waitress gave him a glare of consternation, fearing that he was commenting on her cuisine and moved to approach him from behind her till. Ashley suddenly realised his predicament and lifted both hands to wave apologies. It wasn't the food. In fact he'd been so engrossed in his survey that he hadn't even noticed the hot Thai spices. No – it was the *Dull picture.* – Matt! – That was a dull! And image was a picture! He searched quickly back over the latest scan, where was it? What was it? – And then he nearly fell off his chair as it rocked back against the wall, alarming his host once again. 'There it was! All the bloody time!' Ashley tapped with such a heavy finger that the map was torn across the fold. Hastily he pushed the parting back together, and, could hardly withhold his excitement. He was there. Goodwin had to be there! Ashley could not believe that it was just a coincidence. He just had to be there.

Delighted and duly satiated and with chillies fomenting trouble deep in his guts, he took off, leaving the perplexed restaurateur standing hands on hips at the window as he left on what he knew to be the final stretch of the day. Time was running and he was getting close. It was an hour later after passing such thought provoking places, as Jumping Caribou Lake, Rabbit lake, Red Squirrel Road and Papa Johns, that he drove into *Dull Picture that lost some tea, all stirred*, eight letters, no less. 'You bastard!' he swore to himself but with no particular target in mind.

The place invoked thoughts of an Alice in Wonderland trip through the looking glass. Well wonderland its was, and exactly what Goodwin would have plumped for. If this really pointed to his second choice after Algonquin, Ashley, though that Goodwin would have been very much relieved. Solving the clue was a long shot by any means but it had to be the reason for Goodwin's faint pencil mark. The crossword from Bayswater had come before the lake, but perhaps the coincidence had just stirred Goodwin into investigating it, after failing to find a bed in Algonquin.

Temagami – or *Matt image, having lost a t* and being *all mixed up*, again. Amazing! He'd found the lake purely by chance, he had to admit, whilst amusing himself with the other fantasy names. It was early evening by the time he drove into the small town resting on the eastern shore of its lake of the same name. Not a big place by any means. Not so many hotels or lodges here and it soon became obvious that it was just a food and fuelling centre for the region, rather than a resort in itself. Outfitters for boots, waterproofs, hiking gear, fish lines and bait, maps, guide books and provisions -anything that a nature lover could wish for.

A thought had crossed his mind on the way up, to base himself here and hire a canoe with some fishing tackle, so that he could explore the lake and some of the shoreline cabins whilst appearing to be just another angler in search of a man-eating trout or bass. It didn't take long for him to ascertain that Goodwin had not checked into any of the town lodges, but there were any number of cabins around the lakes without phones or even road access. Any one of these would be ideal for a few days' escape. With this in mind, Ashley turned left off the main road to drive along the quay-side in search of the Temagami Canoe Rental office. It was a fortuitous decision for when he mentioned this idea of travel mode to the rental proprietor, she was aghast. 'Paddling around Lake Windermere in the English Lake District might have been feasible, but this is Canada my dear. To canoe around our lake? For your advice this is a *real* lake I might inform you, and not some pond that you can get round in a day. Forget it! – It's a non starter!' laughed the girl derisorily. Ashley was beginning to feel stupid for even thinking about it, even before she took out a map to show him the extent of Lake Temagami. He excused himself for being 'a bit out of his tree.'

'Well you's can say that again, my friend' said the girl, delighted that she'd shot him down and bellowed his ignorance to every ear in the store.

Ashley blushed and wished the wooden floor would open for him to plunge into the water lapping beneath. He'd been to many places and experienced many adventures, but his failure to grasp the magnitude of Canada's seemingly boundless expanse, left him feeling quite inadequate.

She rejoiced in his embarrassment, 'Mo' as she called herself, took pity on him and just to show that it was all fun, pulled down the map of the area and spread it along the counter. 'There, my dear, is a lake!' she announced with pride. Hands on the counter and her massive chest extended to emphasise the point. – 'I have it on very good authority that if you'd care to walk around the perimeter shore, then you'd have walked three thousand miles! If you's paddle round it then we'll expect you's back next spring after the ice has gone, and boy you's'll have hell bigger shoulders than you's got now.' The store phone rang and 'Mo' excused herself, taking her leave of him.

Lake Temagami looked vaguely like an octopus with eight outstretched arms. The town was perched at the end of the eastern arm. That alone he now estimated to be twelve miles long. He could see immediately that his idea of covering a bit of the lake each day and at the end returning to the town for the night was as she'd said, a non starter. It would mean a twenty five mile round trip every day, just to get to the hub of the lake, without any chance to explore further a field. Mo returned, looking to tease him more. Suddenly he was aware of a different discomfort. The Thai chillies that had been on a back ground brew, were cultivating something a little more dramatic. 'If I were you, you's could take a houseboat from my neighbour, just back along the quay, there. Then you's could cruise around to your heart's content and in some comfort too. Mark me though, with just a fifteen horse power mercury on the back, it will only just be faster than you's canoe.'

'No good,' he said, wondering who the other you was. 'I've only got the weekend before I need to get back.' It wasn't necessarily true, but it expressed his need of urgency and to some extent explained the frustration that was creeping in. The chillies were also creeping in, doing their worst with his gastric juices and it wouldn't be long before he needed to search for a refuge of his own.

'I'd suggest that you's drive down the access road, you's could find a place there to stay. Then you's would be centrally located and could move around from there to find some good fishing. Most places have a boat to rent. In fact, my sister's got a real good place. Right on the spot and her husband has boats and fishing gear. I can call her if you's likes – it's real homely, if they've got a room for you's?'

Ashley looked again at the map and when he found the Loon Lodge, he could see that it was a sensible option. He conceded and immediately took up the offer as the only sensible solution. 'Yes, that's fine by me.'

Three minutes later, Mo had organised his accommodation. The Loon Lodge it was to be. Now that he'd got a room sorted out, it was time to sort the chillies out and Mo directed him to the *little room*, round the back. Once he got his guts back together, he could concentrate on the route to the lodge. Mo adjusted her bandana knot at the back. She looked more like a Harley Davidson enthusiast than the proprietor of a canoe hire business. She had a jolly disposition and enjoyed the role but he wouldn't like to be on the wrong side of her. Just being in her good books left him a mite nervous.

Ashley, now feeling that he could just about cope with her and therefore the rest of the world with ease, set off back down the quay side to get on to the highway again. As he turned the Pathfinder round to get out of the cul-de-sac, it took him through the car lot and in doing so caught sight of a red car tucked away in corner. He'd been on the look out for Goodwin's red Chevrolet rental all along and had spotted several reds on the way up here. Only one had actually turned out to be a Chevy, but that had a different registration plate to that given by the Hertz. As he slowly rounded the other cars in the lot, he spotted the Hertz backed license sticker, on the inside of the windscreen. His heart missed a beat and felt his guts tighten with excitement as he drew closer. Driving slowly past the front of the car he checked the number and bingo! – Yes it was Goodwin's. A car horn behind alerted him to the fact that he was not alone so he pulled forward onto the side of the road.

Ashley switched off the Pathfinder's ignition and paused to draw breath. Since he'd left England, he'd been plotting and hoping for this minute and now it had arrived, his anxiety grew, wondering what else he might find. He took another deep breath, checked his mirrors and swung out of the four wheeler looking about him to see who else might be hanging around. As far as he could make out, everyone was seriously into their own business and showing not the slightest concern for his. He walked back to the car lot and round to the Chevy. It had collected some dust, so it had not been driven around for a few days. He casually tried the doors and the trunk, finding all to be locked, took a quick look inside the cab, which was clear of anything apart from a cigarette packet lodged in the drink holder. Not wanting to draw attention to himself, he quickly looked around at the bodywork and tyres and seeing no excessive ground splashes or mud caking on either, sauntered back to his own vehicle. So

Goodwin was here, or had been here. Ashley corrected himself – Goodwin's *car* was here. Of course that didn't mean to say that Goodwin had been with it, when it arrived.

Looking around for ideas, Ashley saw that the car lot was opposite the 'Red Buoy Houseboat Centre,' and as he watched, a couple came out, crossed the road, got into their car and drove off. It seemed sensible that if Goodwin had parked the car where it was, then he might have been interested in hiring a houseboat. If he had been struggling to find accommodation, then it might have been the perfect option. Alternatively, if the car had been stolen and then dropped, for example, then one wouldn't expect there to be any connection with the Red Buoy centre. There was only one way to find out and loathe though he was to be seen asking too many questions, the time had come to clear the way for the next phase of his search.

A bell rang as he entered the houseboat centre and a heavily whiskered face popped up above the counter to greet him.

'Sorry to trouble you, but I was hoping to join a friend here for the weekend but I couldn't be sure which houseboat company he'd rented from.'

'What's the name?

'Goodwin, Mr. Peter Goodwin!'

'Yessir,' without needing to check any ledger, 'well you've come to the right place. Mr. Goodwin took one of our boats last week, and he's still got it!

'Isn't that a worry for you?' asked Ashley 'his being late coming back, I mean?'

'Well he left the usual deposit, his car's out there, and he called to extend for the whole week. So it's not a problem.'

Goodwin extending the rental, for a whole week? That hit him hard and low. Could it be true? Could he have really lost his bottle and opted out of the conference altogether?

'Anyway we often have people hanging on for a few extra days, if we can manage it. It's still a bit early in the season and so not such a big problem just now. And you were expecting him to be still here.'

'True,' Ashley had to admit, fearing that his credibility was on the line now. 'I planned to arrive earlier but came up on the off chance that Peter was still here.'

'Well I am sure that he's still around, but don't ask me where. There's many a place to get lost, if he wanted to.'

'Thanks, I'll have a look round and maybe get lucky. Cheers.' Ashley beat a retreat having established what he had been looking for, but maybe at a price. He was pretty sure that the fellow held some suspicions and hoped that this would not cause him any complications in the future. He found it very hard to believe that Goodwin had completely dropped out. Was he really in such a desperate state that he'd written off his lecture, perhaps his whole career?

Having at last some satisfaction that he was now on the scent, he drove back down eleven and turned onto the Temagami Access Road. Road it wasn't, not in the black-top sense of the word. It was a stony track, deeply furrowed, undulating and twisting through the forest. The stone chippings rattled underneath the Pathfinder and threw up voluminous clouds of grey dust behind. God help anyone following. After eleven miles, just as he began to think that he'd missed a turn, the track gave out into a hard standing along the side of an inlet. It accommodated a car parking space and three jetties for boat loading. A telephone kiosk stood at the rear and, as pre-instructed, Ashley got out to call the Lodge, so that they could come and get him with the launch.

With no obviously vacant slot in the car park, he tucked the Pathfinder into a gap between two boat trailers parked on the access road and grabbed his bags to walk back to the jetty. Fifteen minutes or so later, he could hear the whine of an outboard as it approached from behind the headland of the inlet and it wasn't long before the speedboat pulled clear of the trees and wheeled round in a graceful arc towards the jetty. The driver killed the outboard some thirty metres from the land and let the boat coast slowly in. Ashley moved down the jetty to meet it and caught the mooring line when the driver tossed it in his direction. The boat's driver jumped onto the jetty boards and beaming a generous smile, introduced himself as John, John Moskwa. Ashley shook his firm hand and returned the greeting. Moskwa picked up the bags and tucked them securely under the seat and after making sure that his guest was comfortable, pushed out the speedboat from the jetty with an oar. Once clear, the driver opened the throttle just enough to get steerage, swung the boat around and then wound it up so that water hissed underneath the hull. There was a slight swell and once they had cleared the headland, Ashley felt the evening breeze beginning to chill the skin. Moskwa turned and shouted that the weather was turning and to expect rain later tonight and all through the next morning. Ashley nodded his regret and started to take in all the information that he could see around him, noting bearings on inlets, beaches, cabins, buoys and headlands. He would need these telltales whenever he had to find his way back to the lodge. He was also looking for houseboats but couldn't see any. Moskwa shouted that this stretch of the lake was the main thoroughfare and most people used it to transit from one leg of the lake to another. Not a popular spot to moor up for a peaceful night. Temagami's answer to the M25.

Twilight was well established by the time that Loon Lodge came into view and the rest of the lake's residents were settling down for their evening meals as John pulled up to the landing stage. As he stepped ashore, a trio of elderly guests were sitting at one of the outside tables, drinking in the last light of the day. John Moskwa busied himself with Ashley's bags as the lady of the house, on hearing the outboard, came out to greet them.

Jenny fussed around him as if he were a long lost brother. 'We rarely get any English here,' she said, even before he had really opened his mouth. He gathered that word had come through sister Mo, that the English were coming. Seemed like quite an occasion when the three fellow guests stood as one, to say hello. 'Get yourself over here pal and join us for a drink. Jenny! – the man looks in need, and whilst you're at it, we'll all have one more each.' Ashley was thankful for their warmth and promised to be back immediately he'd dumped his gear, changed and rinsed his face. He was beginning to feel weary after a long day and the Thai chillies, although quelled for the moment, had left him noticeably frail. For the moment he forgot all about Goodwin and settled down, content in the knowledge that he'd arrived to a welcoming place, where he felt comfortable in having a roof over his head.

Five minutes later he was back. As promised, an extra seat had been drawn up for him and a cool beer glass was already condensing in anticipation. 'Cheers, gentlemen, so kind of you.' And took a long slow drag.

'Nonsense,' chirped the eldest, 'we're all pissed off with each other's company, so it's interesting to have some new blood around. Pretty exciting don't you think Todd?' turning to his neighbour.

'Sure thing, 'ope he's got some real good story tellin'.'

Ashley laughed spontaneously. If they only knew, he thought. 'Only fish tales.' He cracked.

The old fellows chortled and Todd turned to John to noisily enquire: 'Where *are* all the bloody fish this year, John? We come every year, same time, same place and every year we get fish just a jumpin' into the boat, surrenderin' to us. Not this year though. Hardly seen a bloody thing. I blames global warmin', I do.'

'Ah just listen to this crap. 'bout time yer put away these 'Scientific American' magazines and got back into the Playboy. Much better for yer at your age,' rebuked Dick, the eldest. 'The only intelligence he's got is between his legs.'

'An rumour tells me there's not much there either,' yelled Jenny from the kitchen

They all turned to Todd, sixty if a day, and laughed generously at his own expense.

'Believe me it's great to be here in Temagami.' He pronounced the name as it was written. To which they all roared with laughter.

'Son, it's pronounced Tem-og-ammi,' beamed Dick. But Ashley was by now oblivious to further humiliation.

A gust of wind blew across the darkening lake and with it carried a damp chill. Ashley pulled on the sweater that he'd brought down with him and was grateful for its warmth. He was happy to enjoy the good natured banter and it helped relieve the stress of the day. The cordial atmosphere eased the growing feeling of foreboding that had crept in silently, like a thief, to replace his natural optimism. The coming storm also played its part. The trees behind the lodge were becoming more agitated by the minute and passing boats were now throwing up spray as they hurried on their way to the safety of their own moorings. For a moment, Ashley glanced out across the choppy lake. He could see lights on the opposite shore, blinking behind waving branches and wondered where Goodwin might be amongst this wilderness. Wood smoke from the log fire was twisted and distorted like a writhing snake as it was caught by the strengthening breeze; its aromatic tang pleasurably reinforced the adventure of being out of doors.

Since arriving at the lodge, the pace of life had seen a distinct and rapid change from the hustle and bustle of Toronto and the conference circus. The unhurried saunter into which he was suddenly immersed would be just what Goodwin searched for. He could well understand how Goodwin, on numerous occasions had found it necessary to extract himself from the treadmills of politics and technology. Even the advance fringes of the heavy storm that were already breaking upon Temagami, did nothing to detract from the beauty and tranquillity of the place. Its effect on its residents was undeniably addictive.

'We're brothers, if you didn't guess,' said Dick, dragging him back into group. 'Todd, Dick and Harvey!' he laughed. They all joined in and it was obvious that the brothers, judging by the easy merriment and the rollicking that erupted at the slightest provocation, had been drinking for some time. Each of them around sixty years young and as playful as kids enjoying their annual school outing and damned sure they were going to enjoy it to the limit. Fish, or no Fish.

Ashley asked about the fishing and wished he hadn't, for it opened up an unending vociferous dialogue that went on for ages, long after they'd given up on the day and retired to the restaurant.

'What yer lookin' for, young fellah?' asked Dick

For a moment he wondered if the old fishers had somehow rumbled his real motive for being here. 'Trout!' If they had, then he'd divert their scrutiny and turned it back into safer territory. He went on to explain his passion for fly fishing and expected them to express something similar. But no, he was mistaken.

'My god!' They yelled, each turning to seek agreement. 'Fly fishing? Shit that's too damned difficult for us. Why bother, we just hit 'em on the 'ed with anything that comes in 'andy. Can't be fussed with flies!' The roar of laughter erupted once more.

But Ashley persisted; he was on confident ground now and offered his own stories into the melting pot, relating of his times casting flies into the upper reaches of the Spey, Tay and other Scottish rivers.

'So what yer use for bait then?'

'Just flies, no bait allowed on most rivers. Dunkelds and crane flies are pretty useful, or nymphs when the temperature's up. This was a foreign language to the brothers and seeing their contempt for the fine art of fly casting, he asked: 'So what do you guys use?'

'Leeches! – bloody great leeches,' boasted Todd, to the world, and went on to indicate with his hands, that his leeches were of the man-eating genre.

'Over here, we don't use 'em as bait. We just tie 'em on the end of a line, throw 'em overboard and let 'em have their way with any poor sod that comes along. Really good when they've not been fed for a few days. They just sink them damned ugly jaws into anything that swims by and there you have it. Haul it all aboard and then just the tiniest sprinkle o' salt and they let off the fish, real quick time.' Dick informed him with apparent sincerity.

Ashley was just about to believe it all, hook line and leech, but out of the corner of his eye, he caught Harvey, the quiet one, cover his mouth with his hand and turn his head away, so as not to give the game away. The rhythmic bounce in his shoulders however, revealed the truth and they all collapsed in such riotous laughter that Jenny came to see what was cooking outside. They could all smell what was cooking inside.

'Now you folks out here, you making too much noise for the

neighbours, we've had lots of complaints since you lot arrived!' She was determined to join the fun.

The four of them nearly collapsed in a heap and were quite helpless for several minutes. Ashley was sure that at least one heart would give out. The nearest cabin that he could see was at least three miles away.

'Now hear this, if you lot don't get yourselves in here quick time, there'll be no dinner and I'll send Rocky to sort you all out.'

The three brothers, eyebrows raised to the threatening heavens above, whooped in mock fear and promptly swept up the dregs from their glasses and headed into the bar and lounge. Just in time, thought Ashley as he was caught by the first heavy rain drops. Once again he looked out over the water, thinking about Goodwin, but the grey curtain of rain racing towards him, hurried him inside.

✳✳✳

It would have been most pleasurable to continue the jousting into the night but Ashley had thought it wiser to put a little distance between himself and the brothers-in-arms. So he used this opportunity to go his own way. They were at the Loon Lodge for quite a different purpose and whereas he had to keep a clear head in order to meet his objective of making a rendezvous with Goodwin, they could do as they please.

Throughout the night, the wind had whipped the rain into lashing torrents that had battered against his bedroom window. The violence of the dancing tree branches had provided the background music for nature's symphony. Yet despite the tempest, the fatigue of the long day followed by the monstrous steak meal, augmented by more drinks than he cared to count, induced a sound sleep through most of the night. When the rain, still beating against the cabin finally disturbed him, it was well past dawn and had it not been such dreadful weather outside he would have felt regret that he was not already under way. As it was, nobody had ventured out onto the lake and as a boat was the only way to get around, travel of any sort had ground to a halt.

In the lounge, John, who was a quiet man and one of few words, advised: 'In weather like this, we just settle back to let nature play itself out. In a place like this we have to be flexible. Wilderness runs on a different timetable to the big cities. Underlines the fact that it has the power, makes all the decisions and those that struggle against it are chancin' their arm. Nature doesn't suffer fools gladly. Up here, a fool can get into a whole load o' trouble. Even in our so called civilised places, natural forces rule the roost and it's just that in the city, people are too sheltered from its effect. It's only when it really gets really wild that folks notice it. And then it's noticed big time! Here we're much closer to it. It breathes round us and we have to take notice and respect it, otherwise it's a recipe for disaster. There's little that we can't do today that can be put off 'til tomorrow – or the day after. When the snow comes, Mike, and the lake ices over, we can be a week without goin' any place or seein' anybody. It's our thinking time.' – John concluded his unprompted oration and got up from his chair. He took his waterproofs from the hook on the door, climbed into them and stepped outside into the continuing rainstorm. 'Just checking the boats Jen,' he shouted over his shoulder. He wasn't a man to stay indoors for long.

Ashley had listened quietly and he conceded that much of the world needed some thinking time, none more so than himself. He also acknowledged that as he was getting ever closer to Goodwin, it was not only in the physical sense but also in the philosophical. His initial indifference to Goodwin's well-being was being superseded by a sympathy. An anxiety.

Jenny had called 'Full American?' when he had first ventured in and it took him a few seconds to realise that she was referring to breakfast. Having established what constituted 'Full American,' he plumped for 'halfway,' not being able to face the likes of pancakes and their trimmings. Even halfway was more than the usual health conscious plate that he prepared for himself at home. The smell of crispy bacon and splatter of fried eggs was more, much more than he could resist. Besides, he justified, if he ever got out onto the lake, he would need ample sustenance to keep him going for what might be a long search. In the end he was happy that he'd reneged on the full American, because, judging by the heaped plate put in front of him a full American would have taken till lunchtime to dispose of.

Well there was no rush, with the storm showing no signs of abating, there was little else to do, but hang around and wait for it to ease. Just like playing cricket back in Sheffield. In the early weeks of many a summer when it seemingly only rained on Saturdays, he and his young team mates spent many frustrating afternoons, sitting eating sandwiches, in the hope that the sun would eventually win through. After breakfast he wandered around the lounge, which was decorated with photographs, some aged to sepia, faded by the passing of time. Of thick armed fishermen proudly holding aloft the record catches of the season. Even ice fishing! Jenny confirmed that it was the best season to be here, but Ashley was highly sceptical. His experiences of spending a British summer standing in a river up to his midriff in the cold peaty torrents shed by the sodden Scottish highlands were just about tolerable. Sitting in a cabin standing on a metre of ice and fishing through a hole cut through it, for hours on end, was not his idea of spending a rewarding weekend. 'Best time of year to catch big fish,' she said.

'Not surprising,' retorted Ashley 'any fish with intellect would leap at the chance to be caught. Just to escape the damned cold.'

But the photos on the wall held proof that some hardy people thought that it was the butch thing to do. 'Thick in t' arm, thick in t' head,' his dad used to say. He and his father had rarely seen eye-to-eye. But if he'd witnessed these guys posing in their furs, with breath frosting their beards, then he was sure that they would have reached an easy consensus on this occasion.

The brothers three had not emerged by eleven and Jenny said that it was unlikely that they'd be back in the land of the living till mid afternoon. 'When the sun was up, they'd be up with it. No matter if that was five in the morning or five in the afternoon. On days like this ......' she shrugged, as if it explained everything.

Ashley was starting to chomp at the bit. After all his dashing around from continent to continent, city to city, here he was in the final chapter of his mission yet unable even to get to the boat that he'd rented from John. He sat by the lounge fire, reading an old National Geographic that was investigating the NASCAR lines in Peru and the towering ruins of Macha Pichu. So many spectacular places to visit yet. The sound of voices outside drew his attention. He went to investigate, but it was only a canoe paddled by two drowned rats, who had called for some provisions from the Moskwa store and insisted bravely that they were having the time of their lives. Ashley thought that they might be pretty short ones, as the canoe was heavy with water and it passengers shaking with cold. He couldn't bring himself to believe it when they set off again into the unceasing rain, especially when there was a warm fire and hot food just there for the taking. There but for the grace of God, go I, he thought.

It was about four when the rain began to ease, and Ashley feeling desperate to get something out of the day, persuaded a reluctant John to lend him some waterproofs. 'It's not done yet,' he was warned, but eventually he got into the gear and set off across to the opposite island shore, where at Becca's Haven, he was told that he could get his hands on some live bait. Literally! By the time he'd tied up at the jetty, the rain had fallen away to a drizzle and one or two other boats had ventured out to pass him by on the crossing. The swell was still very choppy and they all fought to stay in a straight line in the cross wind or suffer the consequences of taking it broadside on.

***

The excursion was a success in that Ashley gained some satisfaction from actually doing something and it was useful to get some experience in boat handling. As for the fishing gear, what the old guys had spoken about the night before was reinforced at Becca's. The best advice coming from the man in-the-know was indeed that of using leeches. So he duly bought a dozen of the writhing black monsters along with a rod, line and hooks. He also sought the information about the best sites and what fish were in play at that moment. 'It's not been a good year so far and there are very few trout around. The best bet is for Bass and Walleye and they're more often found in the South Arm than anywhere else.'

His schoolboy experiences, although obviously dated, were coming in useful in building his credibility as a mere tourist out to fish. It was comforting that here at least, he was accepted at face value. It made conversation and relations building a more relaxed affair and therefore facilitated his information gathering.

Having collected the materials, a license and data to enable him to set about finding Goodwin, Ashley loaded everything aboard the aluminium twelve footer. Two young boys were taking advantage of the break in the weather, engrossed in catching some of the frogs that swarmed around the pier. But even as he lowered himself into the back of the boat, more rain was beginning to fall. By the time he had cleared the creek, the rain had resumed its full strength and whilst it didn't pose problems in the lee of the island, he could see that the most recent squall was whipping up the waves in the main channel. His lack of recent experience in handling a boat caused him some concern but from what he could see ahead, he thought that he could manage the resurgent storm. As is often the case, he later reflected, what one deduces from afar, to be a non threatening situation, becomes a totally different kettle of fish when viewing it from the inside. As he drew clear of the island's shelter, the squall appeared to worsen significantly. He realised rather belatedly, that he had something of a battle on his hands. Wisely he had donned a life jacket on leaving Becca's place and he was grateful for this foresight. Nonetheless, if it did come to the event of a sinking or an overturning, the prospects of recovery or rescue were not good. A quick glance around told him that he was out on his own and he cursed his reluctance to accept John's forewarning. Another case of ignoring the ground rules of the wild. He'd had similar experiences whilst climbing volcanoes in Indonesia and on some occasions there, had considered himself a little fortunate to survive some difficult situations. As now, he had recognised, albeit rather belatedly, that he was in a bit of a spot. Naivety of a city dweller let loose into the big outdoors was often the root cause of calamity. Panic was its catalyst. A touch naïve he might be, but prone to panic, he wasn't. His tough childhood environment amongst the steel mills of South Yorkshire had instilled a healthy dose of resourcefulness and tenacity. Those qualities were to serve him well now.

The Loon Lodge was in sight but it was no easy matter to reach it. He had now progressed into mid channel where the wind was at its strongest. The temptation was to swing the bow around in the direction of home and gun the engine in a race to safety. Ashley knew to be patient and not let the situation get away from him. He was, after all, still in the boat, which had shipped some water, but not enough to present an immediate threat. All he had to do was keep it that way. He throttled back until he had just enough power to make way and keep the head just to port of the wind. This angle of attack would take him in the direction upstream of the lodge. The wind fought to drive the bow round and push him square – the worst possible situation for him to be in. Ashley continually juggled with the outboard to keep in line the distant hill that had become his reference point.

Rain lashed down and if he had had time to notice, he would have felt the river of water pouring down his back, chilling his spine. The force of the rain was now hurting his face and head. It was turning to hail. As the bow rose and plunged into the troughs, serious spray was flung up in the air and then whipped back across the boat and straight into his face. Ashley had to grimace, reducing his eyes to mere slits in order to peer through the waterfall that was his face. He was only a mile from the shore but it might as well have been ten. Alarmingly the water level in the boat was rising fast, making it heavier to steer for the hill that he could now barely see. His hands were also taking a pummelling and the chill was slowing the blood flowing through them. One was steadying his position whilst the other gripped the outboard tiller. He longed to release both of them from their task, just to breathe some life into them. To get the blood flow moving again. Just a few seconds of relief. Just a few seconds of lost control and concentration would have spilled him into the tormented sea. Temagami was a very different beast to that which he crossed the day before.

Despite the tempest's efforts to carry him away, Ashley was clinging on. The single-mindedness was slowly winning the day. The next time he saw the lodge, it looked to be no nearer, but in fact he was making some progress, edging slowly closer and giving him encouragement when he needed it most. He was definitely getting closer now, but it was absolutely essential that he kept his nerve, right until he felt solid ground under his feet. His feet were now as cold as his hands and he glanced down to check why. He was alarmed to see the water level had risen above his ankles and every lurch of the boat was exaggerated by the pendulum effect of the water's weight. Important to keep it going, not to let it all slip now. Safety was just a few yards away, so close but not yet certain. Keep it going.

Now only ten yards separated him from the jetty, but he could see that this was going to be the most difficult stretch. One second he was above the jetty and the next a couple of feet below it. He took a long look across his left shoulder and just for a second, thought that he had caught sight of Mrs. Morgan and Lucy at the window, as he had last seen them in Bayswater. A second look gave him Jenny and perhaps it was Dick, or Todd peering alongside. John was outside, standing feet apart, bracing himself against the wind. He was waving frantically, trying to signal something, but Ashley couldn't work out what it was. His shouts were swept away by the howling wind. John persisted in his animations, swinging his arms together backwards and forwards.

He was slipping back, down wind. He was going to miss the jetty and faced the possibility of being swept back into the main stream. That's what John was telling him. Get into the windward side of the jetty. He was trying to line him up, get him to twist the throttle more.   More power to take further upstream and then dive into the jetty as he was being swept past. Ashley did just that and for the first time in a long time, heard the engine noise above the wind. The boat moved forward, at an angle to the jetty and it made progress in spurts as the waves first battered the little boat and then dropped away. Waiting, waiting for it. Too soon and he'd be swung round to face the wrong direction. Just a yard now. Wait, wait, watch the swell. Wai...t. Now! Ashley gunned it one last time and swung the bow round. As the he did so the boat rose and then shot forward, carried on a wave crest, to crash against the staging directly below where John had been standing moments earlier. Ashley nearly lost it and almost pitched forward into the flooded hull, but steadied himself, grasping the seats and ripping a couple of finger nails from their roots in the process.

John had dashed round along the jetty and Ashley grabbed for the line that was under his feet. He had to fish for it, such was the volume of the water within the hull. Seconds passed as he groped for the rope, he was being swept back. Got it! He tossed it over to the left and John caught it first time, hauled it in, hand over hand and secured it to the mooring loop embedded into the jetty structure. A second line from the stern – and the boat was secure. Ashley fumbled for the outboard switch, but his hands were so cold, it was only after several attempts that he was able to kill the motor. John reached down, grabbed Ashley firmly around the wrist and hauling him, finally to safety. Still in the teeth of the dying storm, the pair hugged momentarily and without a word stepped carefully to the door, into the light and home.

CHAPTER 7

The Search

Within an hour of his escape from the storm, the wind had dropped and the rain weakened to a mere drizzle and then to nothing at all. It was as if, having failed to claim him by the sting in its tail, it had surrendered its own will to live. As the evening set in, the skies had finally cleared apart from a few tattered remnants of dark cloud driven by the last of the high winds. The deepening monestial blue sky promised fairer things on the morning.

Inside the cabin, everybody had gathered to shelter in the first place and then watch his drama unfold. The brothers were there, still recovering from their excesses of the previous evening and even the two canoeists had turned back, heading for safety once they saw the squall building up in the northwest. Jenny had the coffee on the stove, its rich aroma pervading the lounge. She was busy issuing orders to all and sundry, getting the place in order for the evening meals. John had emerged from his waterproofs and after placing a couple of hefty logs on the fire, sat in the chair by the hearth. Ashley had joined them once he had been to his room, stripped off his sodden clothes and stood under the shower. For an absolute age he stood motionless. Just letting the hot water bring new life to his chilled body. Encouraging the muscles to stop shaking and the blood to flow once more though his stiffened limbs. As if signalling his recovery, blood began to ooze from his torn fingernails and the whole left hand began to throb with a pain that he had not recognised since the wound was first inflicted. Having recovered physically, he dressed and made his way to the cabin lounge to be greeted noisily by the brothers who had engaged in hair-of-the-dog recovery as a starter for the evening. Ashley took the Moosehead beer he had been given by Jenny, sat opposite John and both raised their glasses. Not a word passed between them and none was needed. As their eyes met in the silent toast, a thousand thoughts were exchanged. The shared danger had brought them closer together. It was a fleeting bond that would diminish in time, but not be forgotten.

***

Ashley rose early, but he was not the first to the coffee pot for as he was making his way across the gangway between his cabin and the lounge, the brothers hailed him from the jetty. Dick was about to cast off whilst Harvey tended the outboard and Todd checked the cool box, undoubtedly to make double sure that there was enough drink to survive the day. Seeing him, Dick turned to wave, 'have a good one, fellah!' and with that the gurgling outboard sprang into life as Harvey steered them out into the channel and Ashley paused to watch them for a while, as their boat cut through the ripples of the light breeze.

'I've bailed the boat out and it's ready to go. Your rod's gone, but the other gear is till there – including the leeches. They look pretty dormant, but some fresh water will bring 'em back to life.' It was John, attending to the practicalities of life that city folk so often take for granted.

Whilst scoffing his breakfast, a houseboat had moored up alongside the Lodge to stock up on feed from the Moskwa store. Ashley, of course, was keen to see its tenants. But it wasn't Goodwin. It was a young couple with a child of a few months whose crying demanded immediate attention. Feeding time he presumed. It was only the briefest of stops and they were soon on their way and Ashley was most interested to see them depart. The young man fired up the fifteen-horse power Johnson and went on their way. Judging by the high revs of the outboard, the young man was giving it full throttle but the floating caravan was barely making a bow wave as it sluggishly pulled away. The driver seemed resigned to a slow cruise as he headed back up the northeast arm to Temagami town. If the wind had been against it, then God knows how long it would have taken them.

Less than an hour later, he was on his way. He had expected to have to return to Becca's to buy a replacement rod, but John had rustled through his store to find a spare one of his own. Thankfully he would not have to waste more time and money in re-equipping. Ashley had taken the opportunity to have a cursory look around part of the island for any moored houseboat during that first eventful trip. There were none that he could see, though that was not to say that Goodwin couldn't be elsewhere on Temagami Island.

In a lake the size of Temagami, and with such complex topography, it had been a difficult decision on where to start his search. If what the houseboat owner had said about Goodwin's call to extend his stay was true then he could be some distance away, anywhere within say, two days of cruising. If not, and Goodwin had only really planned to spend the weekend there, then he had to be – south of, say – Sand Point. He had mentally drawn a horizontal line across from that point. It roughly divided the main lake in two, which reduced the options considerably. When he considered the map of the main lake, Gull Lake, in the far west, was only accessible by portage and the same argument ruled out Wasaksina in the east. Cross Lake in the south east, was only accessed by portage too and so did not need to be covered.

Slowly, he eliminated as many of the remote arms, inlets and bays as he reasonably could. Still not entirely convinced that Goodwin had voluntarily extended the houseboat rental, Ashley was left with the Bear Island region, Shiningwood Bay, Cross Bay and the whole of the South Arm as his prime targets. The Northeast Arm, he dare not ignore but thought it too busy with traffic for Goodwin! He smiled at the irony. There he was, used to the crush on the M25 and now here he was, considering a twelve mile stretch of a remote lake in northern Canada as being congested with traffic. How quickly human perceptions change, he thought.

***

It was still only seven in the morning when he pulled away from the jetty and as he waved to Jenny, he could feel the morning chill through the heavy sweater. The storm had cooled Temagami considerably but he expected the sun to start warming it after the next hour or so, as there were few clouds to burn off first. Already a number of boats were out criss-crossing the lake's hub. One or two he could see flying by, others were lost in the heavy morning mist. Some were catching up on affairs postponed by the storm, but most were, probably like himself, professing to get a full day's fishing, making up for the one just lost.

He steered south-southwest, following the channel marked by green and red buoys. To start off, he kept close to the middle of the channel so that he could scan both the mainland shore as well as that of the island, with his binoculars. Each shore was dotted with cabins and moored boats but he didn't catch an early sight of a houseboat. Red Buoy had said that they had six boats out, when he first arrived. After thirty six hours, most of it lost time, he had been able to cross just one off his list. As the channel opened out into clear water and with both shores falling away into the distance, Ashley hung closer to the island shore. He made good speed but knew that he'd have to slow and maybe stop from time to time to go through the fishing routine. Hopefully he could lose himself and avoid interested eyes, if there were any around.

His second success of the day almost caught him by surprise. Just as he was rounding the southern tip of the island, not fifty yards from the shore, a houseboat pulled round the rocky headland, right across his line. Ashley throttled back, not because there was any real danger of a collision, but more to give him chance to check on the occupants. There were at least four on board that he could see. Three at a window tucking into breakfast and a man looking after the propulsion unit at the stern. Two down, four to go.

From that point, Ashley cut across the open water, directly east, into Shiningwood Bay. The bay was long, but narrow, stretching to around half a mile at its widest point and about four miles in length. He'd chosen to tackle this bay early in his tour as it was within the range that he'd estimated and he thought that he could quickly work through it. As he turned into the bay, he was greeted by his first flat water of the day and was able to push the thirty horse power engine to its maximum. He started scanning the northern shore first but then found it largely sheltered from any breeze or sunshine, by the hilly forest behind. This had left a blanket of mist. A legacy of the preceding day's storm, it was hiding all of the coves and inlets from his view. He had to throttle back as visibility around him dropped to a few yards. Progress had suddenly become painful. He was just considering switching to the southern shore that was exposed to the sun and what little breeze there was leaving it clear of the fog, when in the distance, he heard the deep throated throb of a high powered speedboat. It was approaching from the west. Nothing unusual about that, there were a few residents out and about now, so he would expect to meet the occasional boat. He slowed the Mercury to a crawl and as he did so, the howl of the speedboat engine eased to a deeper throb as it too slowed, but then it was wound up once again as its pilot took it away further down the bay. He presumed it too had entered the fog and then turned out of it. Ashley checked with his compass and turned south aiming to hit the other shore and not use up valuable time struggling along the north shore. He soon broke clear and increased speed to chase down the southern side. There was no sign of the speedboat anywhere.

As he approached the end of the bay, he smelt wood fire as it hung low over the water and he slowed to investigate. It was a campfire. A group of bedraggled school aged canoeists were in the process of breaking camp. Ashley wondered how much sleep they'd had during the previous night.

Checking his watch, Ashley found that he'd been out for nearly two hours and the sun had climbed above most of the high ground. The pockets of early morning mist had almost entirely dispersed now and he lost no time chasing back down Shiningwood. Back into open water. No houseboat in that bay, he was sure.

The next bay was to the south and adjoining Shiningwood. Its entrance was narrow and split by a small, rocky island. The southerly entrance looked to be very shallow, so he took the other and soon found himself inside Cross Bay. It was quite different in shape to the last one, being broader but not so long and having a number of smaller bays branching from it, at the eastern end.

The early morning coffees had percolated through to Ashley's system, so after a quick sweep around with the binoculars, he looked for a convenient spot for him to lay up and ease his discomfort. It didn't take long to find somewhere to beach and he aimed for it, cutting the engine early and lifting the prop out of the water as he approached, to avoid any damage to the blades from the rocky beach. Trying to keep his feet dry, he waited for an opportune moment to jump ashore, taking the line with him. An overhanging branch proved a suitable hitching point before stepping into the trees. The coolness of the shade was a reminder of the rain and added to the wonderful freshness of the air. The smell of damp pine needles infused the forest and ants scurried around in the undergrowth carrying tree debris as construction material for the nest. As he brushed branches out of his way, he was showered with rain drops that had not yet evaporated. He stood quietly for a few minutes, cooled by the water and marvelling at the peace around him, only the distant buzz of another boat broke the silence. The noise increased as it sped into the same bay. Judging by the tone of its engine, it was a similar craft to the one he'd heard before. As it grew nearer, Ashley became convinced that it was the very same one although he could not see it from where he was standing. In any case it shouldn't be of much concern to him, it wouldn't be so extraordinary for it to be dashing backwards and forwards, as indeed he was.

On the off-chance that somebody was looking for him, he sat for a moment on a fallen log, out of direct sight of the lake and just caught a fleeting glimpse of the speedboat. As it disappeared down the bay, it left him once again in the forest silence. A tossed pebble disturbed the fleet of oarsmen as the insects skimmed the lake's surface, and when focussed beyond them, he could see the reflection of the blue sky, dotted with scattered cumulus. It was a very nice spot to be in, but it would be even better under different circumstances, when he could just laze and pass the time of day. The magnitude of his task hung over him and its enormity was becoming more apparent by the hour. With every site that he'd visited, ten others would materialize. There were a multitude of remote berthing slots that could hide a landing stage and boat. Perhaps he could come back some day, to enjoy the therapy of the environment that was wrapping itself around him even as he sat there.

OK, time to get to it. He rose from the log and realised that his jeans had become soaked around his rump, by the damp log. Cursing his absent-mindedness, Ashley moved towards the boat. But at once stepped back into the trees. From the left he could hear the speedboat coming back towards the bay entrance. Concern about the speedboat was beginning to nag him. His own boat was hidden quite effectively, so he held back and waited for the other to pass. It was too far away to see who was at the helm but it had the ubiquitous white hull and a blue top with a large black Mercury outboard hitched to the back.

After letting it past, Ashley thought that it was time that he at least put a show on, just in case he *was* under observation and also to give him chance to observe other lake users. Once the way was clear, he pulled out of the shore, checked which way he was going to float and then moved back towards the bay entrance so that he could switch off and fish for a reasonable length of time without needing to start up every five minutes.

Fitting out the rod, reel and line was not a problem but when it came to dip his hand into the jar containing the leeches, things started to get very complicated. Nothing would be more convincing than to return to the lodge with a sizeable fish or two for Jenny to prepare for dinner, but for that, he needed the support of the slippery beasts in his jar. With the fingers of his left hand still giving him some pain, Ashley used his right hand in trying to control the disgusting, slimy, black beasts. In his childhood, he'd spent many happy hours splashing round numerous ponds in search of newts and leeches. This was different: there are leeches and there are leeches: these were monsters and quite capable of drinking an armful of blood, given the chance. Still in their original water, they had slumbered as the oxygen content had become depleted. But when he stuck his hand in the jar, their lethargy was immediately dispelled. Lunch is served!

Struggle as he may, he could not take a firm hold of any one of them without it slipping away. After numerous attempts, he decided to take the hook, a trident, carrying three vicious prongs, to the bait, to impale an unlucky body. Any audience would have been greatly amused by his pains and he was most happy that he could struggle in private and that John and the brothers were a million miles away. Having painfully hooked his own fingers on more than one occasion, he found the leeches quite uncooperative and distinctly unable to impale themselves on any of the hooks he was offering. Eventually, when one of the beasts had fastened its obscene jaws, to a finger, he took the trident in his injured hand and pressed it through the squirming worm as it fed on his own blood. In the excitement he had spilt much of the water, so topped it up with a fresh fill from the lake. This invigorated the remaining leeches to a new level of activity and Ashley was glad that he'd hooked one whilst it was less lively.

Give me fly tying any time he thought, as he cast Moby Dick into the still waters of Cross Bay, to do its worst with any unlucky bass that had the misfortune to swim by. The general drift of the boat was easterly and he was content to let it float down the longest stretch of the bay so that he could fish whilst at the same time searching the banks, with his glasses, for any interesting feature.

Once again the tranquillity of the place seemed to impose itself upon him and for the first time since he arrived, he saw loons. Some distance away at first, but as he drifted slowly in the slight breeze, he recognized the superb plumage, as a pair of them dived and played together, oblivious of his presence. Ashley could see at once the attraction of watching these beautiful birds. An attraction that had offered Goodwin respite from the pressures of Toronto. Whether it was strong enough to keep him from speaking at the conference, Ashley couldn't say. It might well be. The place certainly grew on him and for someone as vulnerable as Goodwin, who was to say that it wasn't totally captivating? Maybe he'd decided that too much was too much and *had* called the boat centre to extend his stay. Then simply stepped off the treadmill. As if to act in response to his thoughts, the loons started to call to each other. Ashley had read about it, but the printed stories could never do justice to the haunting quaver that now carried across the water. He was compelled to sit and listen. The priorities of his mission took a back stage role for the time being as nature cast its magic spell.

First one, then the other took off, as he started to get too close for their comfort. He followed their flight through the binoculars as they flew past him, going west. The birds dipped below the tree line and it became difficult to pick them out against the dark background but still he followed, expecting them to skim into a new stretch of water. They were low now and moving fast. Suddenly, as he panned after them, something beyond – in the trees flashed by. The momentum of his travel took him onwards a little, but he stopped, lowered the glasses and peered into the distance. He couldn't resolve anything with the naked eye, but something had caught it for a split second. So he lifted the glasses one more time and slowly tracked back from where he'd last seen the loons – He nearly missed it again, but there, almost completely hidden in the trees of the far shore, looked to be his third houseboat, moored to a landing stage.

Ashley had only been fishing for about half an hour, but he was eager to check out this new boat. He started up the outboard and turned the boat around. With the rod held in his left hand, steering the boat with the right, he pointed the bow east and aimed to do a slow speed arc, trailing the line and Moby along behind. In this way it would be obvious to anyone that the houseboat was not the target of his interest and that he was just another fisherman trawling his bait behind as he moved to a fresh site.

It was now approaching midday and the sun was high in the sky as he slowly approached boathouse three and once he'd got into a good position to observe it, he stopped the engine, lay the rod down along the length of the boat with Moby still doing his bit under the surface. It was time for lunch and for the first time Ashley felt the warmth of summer. Although he was not yet feeling any pangs of hunger, sitting there, eating lunch was a good excuse for hanging around a while. He had not seen any occupants of the houseboat moving around and did not wish to make too bold an approach in case he disturbed anyone. If nothing happened whilst he finished Jenny's packed lunch, then he would have to think again. To explore a little closer might need an excuse, especially if the sitting tenant was not sitting.

A tug on the line announced that Moby had struck lucky and Ashley dropped his food back into the cool box and he moved quickly to take up the rod. The line was taut and he could feel the fish moving round and under the boat so it was not merely some sunken log that had snagged his hook. On home water, he would have played the fish for a few minutes in order to tire it before bringing it in to the boat. On this occasion however, he was too eager to land it and the line soon went slack as he reeled in far too quickly. He'd let the occasion get to him and cursed his impatience. When he eventually got the line in, the hook was empty. Moby had met his match. As he didn't fancy another wrestle with the leeches, especially as he was half way through lunch, Ashley left the line trailing overboard without any bait for the time being whilst he went back to his sandwiches.

There was still no sign of any holidaymaker around and the time had come to make a move. He was fighting more impatience now. Half the day gone and he'd only covered a fraction of what he'd set out to do. There comes a time when one has to force the issue a little and Ashley decided to invoke a response, involuntary or otherwise. Another call of nature was the best excuse that he could think of and faced with either landing the boat some distance away and then trying to sneak up behind for the chance to steal a look inside, or berthing up against the other side of the landing stage. He chose the latter and made a meal of it. He over revved the engine to announce his approach and made a hefty bump against the small landing stage to underline his arrival.

Still no movement from inside. There was no doubt that anybody inside would have heard him, Ashley thought. Unless that is, they were either comatose or engaged in some very serious sex. Other than banging on the door to ask for a cup of milk, he couldn't think of any other subtlety to draw attention to him. So he clumped up the boardwalk as if he were wearing his father's old, hobnail boots and sauntered into the trees doing his best to whistle. He pulled off to the right and continued about fifty metres along the shore before turning into the forest. Once again the silence was deafening and the familiar scent of pine needles filled his nostrils and was instantly soothing on his sinuses. Even now, his senses were succumbing to nature's physiotherapy and he really had to pinch himself in order to refocus on the job in hand.

Stepping through the forest, he found that the grass was getting thinner. The afternoon's warmth penetrated the forest canopy eliciting from the numerous small ponds that remained, thin wraiths of steam that contributed to the eerie mist cloaking the ground. His intention had been to swing around the back of the moored houseboat to recce the approaches to the landing stage, but as the terrain showed signs of rising, he extended the penetration, thinking that the hill crest might offer a better vantage point. As he was approaching the top of the slope, the ground became drier and the grass was replaced by a lush carpet of pine needles, which flexed silently beneath his feet. Where were they? On the way back, Ashley would have to check out the houseboat more closely. He was starting to feel anxious for Goodwin again and there was a spontaneous urge to call out. It would have served little purpose and unnecessarily exposed his presence to all and sundry. And for what reason should he call? As it was, he kept his peace and mounted the knoll. His patience was immediately rewarded.

The other side of the hillock descended sharply down to the water of the next bay. In fact where he had landed was one side of a narrow spit of land. Now he could see the other side and there at the water's edge were what he presumed to be the occupiers of the boathouse behind. A young girl was gaily splashing through shallow water with a small branch in hand, whilst mother and father were sitting on a travel rug, back-to-back enjoying the occasion and their daughter's noisy play. Evidence of a picnic completed the scene and Ashley felt seriously ashamed to be encroaching on their privacy. He turned quietly and made his way back to his dinghy, taking care not raise any alarm. He passed close by the houseboat and a glance through the window revealed an untidy scene with children's toys scattered around. Once on board his own vessel, he used the paddle to ease himself away from the jetty and did not start the outboard until he was back in the middle of open water. Once there, another leech was fixed in place and whether it was from experience, or Ashley's sheer determination, this baiting did not follow the original comic scene, thankfully. Once all was set, Ashley got under way, slowly trawling the fishing line behind. Three down and three to play.

And so it went on. After Cross Bay came the main South Arm. Six miles long and two miles wide with at least three major smaller bays projecting from the far end of the central stretch, plus a host of islands to be investigated. It meant that he couldn't afford to spend much time fishing. So he reeled in Son of Moby and started to cruise down the eastern side of the arm. This was straight forward until he got down to the end of the arm. He was about to turn to the west, to cover the southern shore, but what he expected to be the end of the arm looked to hide a small lagoon. He slowed the boat to a crawl and hunted for a map that he'd misplaced during the loss of Moby. When he eventually found it and opened it up on the seat beside him, he was horrified to find that he'd discovered a new lake, Cross Lake. My God! he thought, and once again the reality of the magnitude of the task was laid out bluntly before him. From the map, Ashley estimated it to be some nine or ten miles in length with a maximum width of about two miles. But that only told half the story. The total coast line must be at least twenty five miles and that didn't take into account its own archipelago of islands, and some of those were sizeable pieces of geography. This was becoming impossible. If Goodwin had really wanted to disappear, then he'd chosen the right place to do it. Ashley could cruise around till the ice formed in November and still not have covered the whole lake.

Once again he had not taken heed of the local advice, just jumped in with both feet and with the mislaid confidence of ability and was now suffering the consequences. His confidence had been born on good experiences around various parts of the world, but he'd never come across anything of this enormity. He was in Canada, he kept trying to tell himself that, and on each occasion when he did so, he understood it. But then after a short time, his European conditioning kicked in and once again narrowed his focus. He was setting himself goals that were physically impossible to achieve within an acceptable time frame. The only way to cover everywhere would be by helicopter, or a well equipped, full-scale search team. Neither were practical options.

He felt utterly useless and for a moment became deeply depressed. He was not used to failure, having on the contrary a well earned reputation for getting the job done no matter what difficulties needed to be overcome. Mr Fixit, as he was known by people in-the-know, now had come to realise the truth. His amateurish efforts were not going to achieve anything. It was all just too much and he considered giving up there and then. Back to the Loon Lodge, and out of here, quick time. It was a temptation.

What was it John had said about the pace of life here, and the storm wasted hours? Thinking time! John had described it as, 'it's our thinking time!' Ashley killed the engine altogether. How had he missed this new, huge bloody lake, when making his plans for the day?

Time for a beer. He reached into the cool box and extracted a cold can of Moosehead, but cast out his fishing line before opening it and then settled down to study the map once again, with the rod wedged between his thighs.

Yes, he could see it now. The way the map was folded, if he looked at one side, he saw the South Arm of Temagami. If he turned the map over, he saw what appeared to be a separate lake, Cross Lake. If he fully opened up the map and looked carefully, then he could see that the two lakes were joined by a channel that narrowed at two points. But originally he hadn't looked carefully enough. For where the paper was actually folded, the print was damaged and it was exactly at one of the narrows. He had discarded this lake from his search pattern because he thought that it was separate from the main body of water. Shit, he'd really underestimated the day's effort, by a long way. Ashley took a big mouthful of cool beer and swallowed it slowly so that it chilled his throat. It surprised him to realise how thirsty he was. The afternoon's heat had caught him by surprise, as had other matters that day.

After a few more mouthfuls of beer, he began to reflect on the situation, and in particular on the map that still lay outstretched at his side. Two points slowly emerged that went some way to disperse his anger and frustration. One was that the entry into Cross Lake was at least twenty two miles from Temagami town! A houseboat chugging away on its tiny engine would take, he thought – a day or more. And then another day to get back! If Goodwin was only here for the weekend, then this was too far! This second point led him to quickly retrieve the fishing line and promptly drain the last dregs from the beer can, before getting the outboard fired up again. He steered down the channel into the entrance to Cross Lake. It was not long before he came up to the first narrows, which he negotiated comfortably. After another mile or so, he came to the second narrows and he again passed through reasonably easily, though it was a bit tight. Not a lot of room to spare!

Ashley smiled to himself. He was not quite the fool that he had thought just a few moments back. Although he could get through the second narrows, Goodwin couldn't be on Cross Lake. There was no room for Goodwin, nor anyone else to get a boathouse through! Content, and greatly relieved, he did an about-turn and headed back into the South Arm.

With renewed enthusiasm he set about combing the area and was determined to clear this part of Temagami by the end of the day. Ashley followed the coastline methodically and investigated any inlet that looked as though it might provide a niche for a houseboat to seclude itself. He weaved in and out of the numerous islands and even though the afternoon was all too rapidly turning to evening, took time to fish, both to justify to the residents of Loon Lodge, his reason for being here and to satisfy his angler's pride. Throughout the remainder of the day, there was no view of either Goodwin or any of the missing houseboats, though he did have two interesting incidents to record. On one of the occasions he paused to cast a line overboard, he had been drifting off one of the central islands in this part of the lake. As was normally the case, bar the occasional boat that passed him by at some distance, there was a silence that almost hurt the ears. With hardly a ripple of water to splash against his hull, and the occasional insect, or distant birdcall, the silence was deafening. Every movement he made seemed to generate such extraordinary noise that he felt must have been heard for miles across the water. As if to reinforce this feeling, he started to catch the sound of voices and as he drifted towards the island, the sound of human conversation grew louder. Somebody over the other side of the island was having an animated discussion that was punctuated by short silences and bursts of laughter. It was only when he had decided to try another spot for his observations, dare he call it spying, that he rounded the island spit to find the source of the discussion that had drifted far across the lake. From a considerable distance, he had been able distinguish parts of the conversation. Now much to his amusement, he found it was none other than the three brothers sitting in their boat, rods aloft, busily fishing and equally engrossed in some political debate that held them enthralled until he passed across their line of sight.

'It's Mikey boy!' they cried and waved furiously as his wash gently rocked their boat. Todd stood, rocking it even more, to perform a dramatic mime that invited him over for a beer.

'Not until the sun is below the yard arm!' he shouted happily. He silently reproached himself as he regretted the shout and felt guilty about breaking the stillness. He'd enjoyed the solitude of the day, but he also was quietly looking forward to an evening's entertainment back at the lodge. In deference to the guilt feeling of disturbing the world, he returned his own mime that informed them that he was on his way home and would join them later to discuss the catch of the day. More laughter, a cheer and a unanimous display of thumbs up registered their agreement.

It was a little after that, whilst trawling his line behind and heading slowly back in the general direction of the hub, that he'd cast an eye back to check the line stretched out behind. He had caught the briefest of glimpses of a fast powerboat, jetting across his stern. As he watched, it turned on to a parallel course to his own. It was too far away to be certain, but as it turned, presenting its cockpit to him, he got the impression that it was blue. The very same craft that he'd seen on several occasions before? By the time he had got his binoculars to his eyes, it had disappeared behind another island. He had expected to catch it again as it emerged from the other side, but it didn't. He could hear it race away, but it must have changed direction again, when out of sight. Was this too much of a coincidence? If indeed it was the same boat? He couldn't seriously think that anyone had sufficient motive to be spying on him. As far as he was aware, he had played the fisher role reasonably well and nobody apart from the lodge residents were aware of his existence here. Apart from, that is, Jenny's sister back in town. That there was a strange Englishman on the lake might have become a topic of gossip amongst the natives. But just who was around to engage in gossip? There were probably many boats of similar characteristics and colour on Temagami. He put the question to one side and concentrated on plotting the correct course home. He was happy to be equipped with the map and compass, for there were many channels open to him and to the unfamiliar eye, they all looked the same in the fading light.

The car! – Goodwin didn't renew the car rental, possibly the boat, but not the car! Why hadn't he thought of that before? Goodwin, if indeed it was he who extended the houseboat lease, would surely not have overlooked Hertz, nor indeed the Hilton reservation. He must have had telephone access to call the boat proprietor in Temagami, so why not Hertz or the Hilton? Mobile phones had not yet encroached on the region and were not served by base stations in the locality. The failure of his own mobile to find any provider since his arrival north of North Bay was evidence of that, and it had been confirmed gratefully at Loon Lodge. Ashley thought it inconceivable that somebody as thorough and precise as Goodwin would go to the trouble of making one phone call without making the others. It couldn't be a case of not knowing the relevant contact numbers, as he was almost sure, no, certain! that both would be available on the documentation that Goodwin must have with him. As soon as he got back to the lodge, he would make the necessary calls to check that Goodwin had not made contact since he, himself had set out north from Toronto.

He released the steering of the boat letting it progress of its own accord in the general direction of home, to draw in the fishing line. The focus of his mind had shifted once again as he sought to explore all possible avenues of the enquiry and the need to keep up the fishing façade had taken a step back in the order of priorities.

The trip back had taken him a further thirty minutes. He'd not pushed the outboard, preferring to make comfortable progress whilst keeping an eye open for any telltales that could easily be missed in the fading light. It was also a time for thought. He'd set out on this mission with a feeling of indifference, but as time and events had passed, he found that concern had replaced indifference and now a growing apprehension was casting its shadow.

Ashley felt a sense of urgency which propelled him to greater efforts, that Goodwin needed him, and needed him now. Logically, Ashley knew that there was no point in chasing around in the gathering gloom. Little could be achieved and mistakes would be made. If he himself failed to turn up at the lodge this evening, in a respectable time, then its residents would become concerned about his own security. That would raise a few eyebrows, if not activity, and he remembered Clements' mandate to make no waves. An ironic smile spread across his face as he thought how prophetic that metaphor had been. Here he was doing exactly that. He throttled back as if it were *these* very waves spreading widely across the placid Temagami Lake, to which his peer in Whitehall had been referring to. He needn't have worried for in the context of things to come, they were mere ripples.

Paradoxically, Goodwin had intended to create a tidal wave that would have created a maelstrom in the world of eavesdropping and deception, had he turned up to deliver his paper. Little did Goodwin know that he would succeed, if not in quite the way he had intended. Ashley was back at the lodge before the brothers and could see no sign of them as he stood, after making his own boat secure for the night. Anyway, judging by the amount of alcohol that he guessed had been consumed throughout the day that he would hear them before he saw them. The sun had long since set but the northern twilight lingered long here, as if the day were suspended in time, reluctant to give way to the relentless encroach of darkness that would keep its secrets for another night.

John's boat was tied up on the other side of the jetty and he paused to wonder if it had been used. There was neither smell of fuel, nor the sickly odour of hot oil that inevitably gathers on any combustion engine. Neither were there any of the sounds that would tell of a cooling engine as it contracted with falling temperature. Just the gentle lapping of water trapped between the hull and the jetty. Nevertheless, he stooped briefly to put his hand on the outboard casing. It carried only the warmth of the day's sun. Probably not used all day, and besides it had an orange top.

A beer, he thought, was necessary for both body and mind. So he stepped through the lodge's fly-screen door, the screeching spring announcing his arrival to anyone inside. But there was only Jenny, back in the kitchen preparing the evening feast for tired hungry men, whose noisy exuberance was expected along soon. Reading his mind, she produced a beer from the cooler and a smile that preceded courtesies of the day.

But Ashley was not in the mood to engage in conversation. He could not, on this occasion, reflect her warmth and rather than force himself to communicate in a false manner, waved aside the glass and excused himself to enjoy the last light of the day outside. She took his reserved manner to mean that he had not caught any fish and he was happy to let her feel that way.

Stepping out through the screeching fly door, Ashley made for one of the benches. He'd dropped his bag there on the way in and although he couldn't see it clearly, somebody was there rustling through it. Alarmed, he tensed and the hairs on the back of his neck bristled. The tinkle of cans and glass could not be mistaken, but the perpetrator remained unidentified. Ashley shouted 'Hey you!' For an instant there was silence; and then a furious flight as a small shady figure sped off down the board walk and tore round the back of the lodge. He relaxed as he realised what the black and white bands meant. There came a call from back inside: 'Mikey! Now you take care 'o Rocky, you hear? I let him out 'his cage for a run. Just holla at him if he gets *too* friendly.' Ashley laughed and not having seen too many racoons in Guilford, he stole round the corner in pursuit of Rocky. Hoping to catch a glimpse of the would-be-thief, he walked round the back of the lodge, but Rocky had gone. No sign of the lodge pet, but there *was* the distinct smell of fuel. He remembered that they sold fuel for the outboards here and in the shadows he could make out a tank and various hoses that snaked across another jetty and the inlet that served it. Thinking it a useful opportunity to spy out the location, for his own refuelling that he would need in the morning, Ashley trod carefully along the rocky path. To the left now was the open water of the lake, and between, the berth and fuel tanks. His way in was clear. The water line of the inlet carried his eyes to the right as he turned to retire and enjoy his beer. He froze.

There it was – partly hidden in the trees.

✳✳✳

He felt that John must have seen him, for not long after Ashley had settled at the bench, he came to join him. Neither knew how to start the conversation. Although Ashley had, on the face of it, no real reason to be concerned, the culmination of a frustrating, lengthy day, which had produced nothing positive other than eliminating a small region from his search, and now the discovery of the mysterious, blue power boat, right in the back yard, generated unease, if not stress. His stomach muscles tightened

Both men sat side by side, taking in the peace of the mirrored lake. Not a ripple disturbed the boats that lay motionless against the quay. The only sound was the hum of a few insects hovering close by. Others were oarsmen, like tiny phantoms skating busily across the lake surface. In the middle distance, Ashley could see a family of loons swimming slowly in the last light, dipping silently into the water for any tasty bit that came within range. The monochrome radiance of the rising moon was replacing the departing afterglow of the sun, such that the lake seemed to get lighter against the black backdrop of the far shore. The tranquillity served them both well. John was not quite his usual, placid self. Something was eating at him, and Ashley had a million questions to ask but no way to ask them. Nature was slowly bridging the chasm that existed between them as each of them sought a way to break the ice. The mood was softening helped by their affinity for the beauty around them. Undoubtedly the cool, slightly aromatic Moosehead was contributing to the moment. Ashley could feel the anxiety ebb away and wondered if the Temagami enchantment could similarly cast its magic spell on the warring factions of the world, if they were to congregate here.

Fantasy, he knew.

'More drink you guys.' entered Jenny. It was a statement, not a question and she breezed across to the bench with two more chilled cans of Canadian beer. 'My we are slow drinkers tonight, aren't we?' Both men raised their cans and toasted each other with the replenishment. The door was open.

'What yous lookin' for Mike? – couldn't see much chance o yous catching any bass or trout, the way you was cruising about down the south arm today?'

Ashley was tempted to reveal something of his purpose for being there, but his professional caution warned against it. Yet John's probing surprised him. Was it suspicion, concern, or just plain curiosity that caused him to abandon his natural reserve? John was an observer, not a commentator, and words did not normally come easily to him. One could sense that he was happy to leave each unto his own. Only responding when provoked into doing so. Yet, this was the second time that he'd initiated conversation with this unknown visitor from England.

To insist on his motive being of pure interest in fishing, or tourism, was not going to pacify the host. Even if he lied or evaded the question, John wasn't going to accept it. Perhaps at face value, but that was all. He was a studious man, a proven observer whose curiosity was not going to be satisfied with some simple fob off. It might be more thought provoking and therefore infinitely more dangerous to persist with the charade of innocence than to give a few crumbs of the truth. And furthermore, thought Ashley, to try and make a big secret of it, would just induce greater suspicion and probable conversation to follow. Even so, John didn't need to know anything about Goodwin, or his background. Except perhaps, that he was merely a friend. Ashley also quietly suspected that he didn't want to know more. So perhaps it was concern that troubled his host, as had been apparent during the storm.

The calling of the loons brought him back from deep within his own thoughts. 'Well John, I am looking for a friend.' A heavy weight lifted from his shoulders.

'And he's got a houseboat?'

So John *had* been putting two and two together and there *wasn't* a chance of fooling him! 'Yes, I think so.' 'We were due to meet up in Toronto and then have a few days in The Algonquin.' And to deflect the inevitable follow up. 'But I turned up late and he went ahead. Algonquin was too fully booked, so he left a message that he was here. And here I am to join him.'

Whether he accepted that or not, he wasn't sure, but John had momentarily turned to look him in the eye, a slight nod of some understanding or was it an appreciation of being taken into Ashley's confidence? And then looked back at the loons, crooning and cavorting in the moonlight.

Some time passed whilst the situation was digested. They both enjoyed the moments as the birds called their partners with their distinctive wails.

'There's a houseboat in Spawning Lake – been there a couple of days, or more maybe?'

***

The brothers had been very late getting back and by that time, Ashley had eaten and retired to bed. He had been slightly disturbed as his fellow guests disembarked and whilst they were noisy in unloading and securing their boat, there was none of the humorous play making that had been there on previous nights. Either their antics or intakes, or both, had been excessive throughout the day, or they too had felt the stillness that pervaded the lodge.

***

John couldn't come with him as he had further deliveries to make to various residences on the lakeside. Ashley had been entering the lounge just as the blue powerboat had taken off. Jenny explained that John always used the blue boat to make deliveries from the store, as it was bigger and more powerful than the orange one that was usually tied up at the front. So, he understood, John had been going about his normal business the day before and the times that their paths had intersected had been by pure chance. He suspected that it wasn't quite the whole truth, but could not discern any sinister reason to believe otherwise.

Jenny had met him round by the fuelling stage and he'd taken on enough fuel to last the day, as well as a cool box full of drinks and food to see him through until late evening. For appearances only, he'd loaded the fishing gear and although the few leaches that he had left were either dead or dormant, the survivors stirred vigorously when he recycled their water, as if eager to start the new day. He set off across the straight, remembering the tempest of what seemed weeks ago and then steered to pass to the east of Temagami Island. It didn't take long to clear it and then enter an expanse of water that was marked off with buoys for floatplane landings and take offs. With only a slight breeze to ruffle the surface water, it wouldn't be a problem to fly in on this morning. Following the map and the directions pointed out by John the night before, he headed for the narrows of Spawning Lake. He was eager to investigate the houseboat that John had spoken of. Nevertheless he kept an eye on the shoreline just in case the hirer had moved out of the bay. What was certain was that no houseboats had returned to their moorings since he had first made enquiries four days ago. He had checked that out before going to bed. Neither had any calls been made to The Hilton. A cursory call to Hertz revealed the same situation. It all pointed to Goodwin being here, on Temagami.

After an hour of steady cruising with the outboard only on two-thirds throttle, the entrance to Spawning Bay came into view. By that time, it was developing into a pleasant summer's day and the fresh morning air had been replaced by a balmy breeze that tangled his hair, sweeping any cobwebs way behind. On any other day, on any other mission, Ashley would have been delighted in just being here. Over the past few days, his familiarity with the locale had bred a growing confidence on finding his way around and operating the boat was now second nature. Despite the pressure to chase down Goodwin, he had to admit that at that moment he felt buoyant and even a little optimistic that things would develop favourably – and soon.

The entrance into the bay was certainly narrow. A sandy headland with shallows and a beach on one side and he had to weave left and right to get through the rocky outcrop. Perhaps a little tricky for a houseboat, but not really a serious problem if its captain took it slowly. Spawning Bay was split in two stretches of water by a central isthmus running down almost its entire length. Ashley steered across the entrances of both stretches for a cursory glance but could not see any vessel in either one of them. There was little alternative but to go through the methodical routine and he elected to take the northern of the two bays first.

What seemed a straightforward search at first became somewhat more difficult because much of the coastline had become overrun with weeds and he had to be vigilant in order to avoid them wrapping around the prop. Nevertheless there was nothing to see on his left as he headed in an easterly direction. The blue sky reflected in the lake and the shoreline trees gave a mirror image that shimmered lazily. An unreal chocolate box painting. The last of the morning dew still left traces of fresh pine on the air and he filled his lungs with slow deep breaths so that its cool, soothing qualities could be felt in his eternally troubled nasal passages.

Ashley cruised slowly down to the end of the lake and turned from another fruitless morning leg, to return up the central isthmus and back to the mouth of the bay. The U turn had been a little careless as is often the case when one relaxes too much and takes things for granted. The outboard faltered, but surged again as he gunned the throttle grip, but then died slowly away as the propeller became strangled from below.

'Shit?' He cursed mildly on looking over the back end to discover that he'd steered into a proverbial Sargasso Sea of weeds lying just under the surface. The Mercury had become so highly entangled that when he tried to swing it on its hinge, out of the water, there was a danger that it would have pulled the stern under the surface. But using his right hand to pull the outboard up and back, his left hand tore at the entrails of the fouling weeds, so that he eventually managed to secure the engine on the latch. Individual thongs were quite weak but the mass of vegetation that had accumulated in such a short time came as a surprise to him and it took some hacking away. Even then there were finer filaments more tightly wrapped around the shaft and he needed a knife to cut them free. The water around the boat had become clouded with silt from the roots that he had had to tear from the lake bottom and stench of rotting material bubbled up to the surface. Perhaps ten minutes had passed since the outboard had stalled, before Ashley had stood over the stern and released the engine latch so that he could lower the prop back into the water. It was when he sat back, dried off his arms, and raised the blue fisherman's hat to let the warm air underneath it escape that he heard it. With the outboard running and the commotion and focus on fighting the weedy tentacles, it had been impossible to detect it. But now that it was peaceful aboard and his ears were well tuned in, the alien sound of distant music could be heard from the trees of the central isthmus.

It wasn't terribly unusual to hear sounds of human life on the lake, especially with so many youth camps around with their inevitable portable players causing their own brand of pollution – but it was still worth investigating. The spit of land between the two bays was perhaps a kilometre wide at the top end of the lake and although he took the oar to paddle along the coastline, the density of the reeds gave him no access to the land at that point. Ashley estimated that the music was coming from the near shore of the southern lake and if that were the case, somebody was holding a noisy concert that was being broadcast to everyone in the area. That sort of behaviour and lack of consideration for other folk angered him and he would certainly make his feelings known when he got round to the southern Spawning Bay. Resisting the temptation to start the outboard up, he continued to paddle back up towards the mouth of the bay whilst at the same time trying to bring his binoculars to bear on the source of the offending music. By now he could make out the tune, and strains of Dire Straits' *Local Hero* became clearer as he moved further east towards the hub. Not such a melody one expected from wayward youth, thought Ashley. But even if the choice of music was agreeable, then its volume certainly wasn't. It caused him to pause for thought. Here he was, simply a visitor to the place and yet he was eager to police it as if he owned it. Caution and an awareness of his own fleeting presence undermined his authority, and moderated his disgust.

It took him the best part of an hour to reach the bay entrance and swing into the southern part of it and by that time he had resorted to the Mercury's power rather than that of his own muscles. As he once again headed east, he let the outboard chug along at a walking pace whilst he panned the glasses back and forth across the width of the lake and eventually, about two thirds of the way down, he caught the first sight of the houseboat that John had mentioned on the previous evening. As he progressed, it became clear that the houseboat was moored to the southern shore of the central spit of land. He couldn't make out any human figures moving around it but there were signs that whoever was living there had recently thrown bread out to feed the birds as there was an avian spiral carrying rooks and gulls as they descended to feed. Ashley kept well to the middle of the bay, wanting to make a subtle reconnaissance from a distance rather than charge straight in with all guns blazing.

He closed to within a half mile of the houseboat before turning off the Mercury with the aim of going through his fishing routine. The engine died but the boat's momentum carried it on for a few yards before it slid to a halt in the quiet water. Ashley was immediately disturbed. Dire Straits were still playing to the whole lake and his irritation grew once again. He took the decision not to get the fishing rod out. The music broadcast gave him an excuse to approach directly. A few birds were still wheeling around, screeching their competition in the search for remnants of food that had been scattered along the landing stage. As he closed in on the scene, Dire Straits changed tune and once again the evocative tones of *Local Hero* started up to mix with the shrieks of the fighting birds. Still no movement from any would-be resident, so he called out to announce his arrival but it was immediately lost in the cacophony of sound.

Now he was so close that the birds were sweeping around him, expressing their rage that his arrival was disturbing their feeding frenzy. He nosed the boat up to the landing stage and tied up to the hitch post on the opposite side to the houseboat, then stood to climb onto the wooden boards. Local Hero was reaching its climax as he jumped onto the stage and the birds that had lingered in a final act of defiance took off in noisy flurry of frantic feathers. It was a disturbing scene. His pulse had quickened to a heavy beat so that he could feel the blood throb through his temples. His senses were at peak alert as he stepped along the wooden boards. He could see that their meal was done anyway. Not a morsel of food was left for them to fight over.

Now that the gulls had dispersed, Ashley turned his attention to the houseboat. The music had stopped – so someone had seen or heard his arrival. 'Anybody home?' he shouted, not able to think of a more original announcement at the time.

There was no answer. After the birds and the music, the whole lake seemed peculiarly quiet, even by its own standards. He moved to the side of the houseboat and peering through the window, rapped on its glass to accompany his call, 'hello!' There was no sign of the host and no response to his call. Ashley stood upright and looked around him. It was quite possible that the hirer had gone ashore. It was a beautiful day and he for one would have been out on a trek or a swim from the beach. It would be such a waste just to stick around the boat. He walked down the boardwalk to step ashore. To the left was a dense reed bed that stretched for some distance. To the right was a pebbled beach and snaking through the long grass was a trail leading over a fallen pine log, into the forest beyond. He walked along the trial and climbed onto the log, turning to survey the land before stepping over the other side. Looking down, over the log, footprints in the soft soil, gave evidence that somebody had indeed been down this path. Closer inspection revealed that the footprints were not fresh. Rainwater had severely eroded the sides of the imprints and left some recent, fine residue on the floor of the imprint made by a boot heel. At one time it had been a heavy mark as somebody, seemingly male judging by the boot size had, just like himself, jumped down from the log. But it had not been a print of that day. A beat of wings caused him to look up. He was surprised to see that the birds were still there, soaring around in their watchful spiral. Silent – but for the soft crack of feathers twisting the air in their acrobatics to avoid each other. Ashley walked slowly up the trail as it entered the forest, taking care not to tread on the path itself so that he could follow the footprints without disturbing them. Fifty yards into the forest the ground started to rise and the soft soil gave way to more rocky material that was covered with the inevitable pine needles. It was impossible to trace the footprints any further but it was clear to Ashley that nobody had walked the trail since the storm.

He headed back the way he had come and called out again into the forest. No answer came back. His only listeners were the birds above, still involved in their ariel dance. After re-crossing the log, he approached the point where the landing stage met the shore. He had just turned to take the beach when there was a bellow of noise that caused his heart to stop and his body to jump round. Dire Straits had struck up again!

Alarmed by the sudden onset of noise, Ashley trotted back to the stage and walked along it to the back of the houseboat. He shouted once again, knowing that he would get no answer. Just a polite gesture to anyone who did happen to be inside. He stepped down onto the floor of the houseboat and moved to the door. It was open. Not by much but it seemed to welcome him. He pushed it further open and bent to look inside. 'Hello?'

Dire Straits were deafening at this range and the whole lake breathed a sigh of relief when he moved to the audio deck to stop the recycling tape. He didn't have to search the place to know instantly that he had found Goodwin's hiding place. There on the table was the telltale evidence. Crossword puzzles! Two of them. No entry made, but Ashley now knew that there would never be one. Peter Goodwin was here, but he wasn't in the houseboat. The place was almost undisturbed and Ashley was momentarily taken back to Bayswater. Everything in its place. No evidence of visitors. A thorough search also revealed little. Ashley was keen to look for any written material, particularly anything referring to the Toronto conference. Hotel and airline reservations were there and so were conference brochures and even a timetable that announced what had been his intended lecture. But Goodwin's briefcase did not reveal any secrets. Ashley was frustrated, 'Doesn't this guy ever write anything down?' he asked himself. Goodwin the perfect spy, he thought. Everything confined to that eidetic memory. If any information was going to be forthcoming for Symphony, then it would have to come from the horse's mouth. Not from documentation. Knowing Goodwin, as he did now, he fully expected any computer files that may be found on the BASE algorithm, would be few and far between and securely encrypted by a key only known to the man himself.

Ashley had just about given up his search of the houseboat and was contemplating his next strategy to find Goodwin, when he heard a distant hum of a high-speed marine engine. He looked out of the immediate window only to disturb a gull that had chosen that very instant to land on the stage. Moving across to the other side of the houseboat, he heard the engine growing louder. He looked back towards the bay entrance through the other cabin window saw the bow wave of a blue speedboat making its way towards him.

John had obviously seen Ashley's boat tied up alongside the houseboat and came straight in. Ashley returned to the rear, exited through the door, and was just stepping onto the jetty as the blue powerboat came alongside. As he moved forward to catch the mooring line, there was another sudden panic of feathers and raucous shrieks from under the jetty boards. The pair of gulls that had been feeding on something in the shade, fled from the side. Recovering from the sudden fright and grateful for his friend's support, Ashley made himself busy in securing the new arrival. But John was not returning his cheerful greeting. He was intent on something else. Still in the boat, he had got down on his knees to peer under the landing stage. Whatever was hidden there caused him to lean right over the side so that he could get a better view of where the fleeing birds had come from.

'Looks like a plastic bag,' John muttered, 'can you see it from above?

Ashley aligned himself with where his companion was looking and peered through the gaps in the stage planking. 'Yes. There's a bag there. Mostly submerged. I can't reach it from here.'

John turned back into the hull of the blue boat and retrieved a boat hook, which he used to fish in the murky water. He snagged the bag, lost it as the material gave way, and then snagged it again. It was difficult to reach and Ashley could see the strain John's stretching body was enduring in the effort to release the object.

'Got it!' he cried and drew the boathook out towards him.

Ashley bent over the wooden stage, poked his head underneath, and reached out with his arm to catch hold of the flotsam. It didn't feel like plastic but Ashley had it now. He pulled – released his grip and reached under to get a second hold as the bag floated towards him. His head was almost at water level by the time they had managed to manoeuvre the thing clear.

It floated now. Ashley's head was flung back in horror as Goodwin's white face and empty eye sockets bobbed past within a whisker of his own eyes. Ashley reeled and rolled away from the partly decomposing corpse. He could do nothing as unabated retching wracked his body.

John had frozen. 'My god!' he cried. He fell back into the seat of his boat, looking back down the bay towards the Temagami hub.

Several minutes passed before either man could recover enough composure to brave another look in the direction of the floating body, buoyed up by the gasses of internal decay. Goodwin had drifted out of reach of both boat and jetty. It was the gulls that triggered a response from the stunned men. As the corpse drifted further away, they were gathering once again, to attack what remained of the cryptologist's half-eaten face.

Sheer disgust gave them the strength to drive the birds away and whilst Ashley jumped into the waist deep water in pursuit of Goodwin, John released the blue boat and paddled across to join him, waving an oar above his head to batter any bird that dared come close.

Without looking into the mash that had once been the face of a mild, shy, yet passionate scholar, whose intellect matched any in the world, Ashley took a lifeless arm and waded back to the beach towing the Cambridge man's remains behind. John's uninhibited anger was focussed on the marauding birds. Yet it wasn't the gulls that had killed him, it was some ruthless bastard who'd wrapped a wire garrotte around his neck and twisted, and twisted until it had bitten almost completely through the whole neck, throttling the last flickers of Peter Goodwin's life, bringing it to a grotesque end.

It was a tearful Ashley who pulled him ashore with a tenderness, an affection that had started from the time of interview with Mrs. Morgan and Lucy and steadily grown through an admiration, to a concern for his well being and now, finally, sheer distress. There were a lot of questions to be asked by Symphony, but Peter Goodwin would not be answering any. His secrets were now truly secret – erased by the water of this Temagami Lake as it soaked through the neurones and fissures of what had been his cerebral cortex.

CHAPTER 8

Lighthouse

Bonetti had taken up the offer with delight. It wasn't often that the chance to fly in the personal jet of a Sheikh came by and when the call came for him to board, he was excited by the prospect of royal comfort and service. In fact he was happy to just to get out of Charles De Gaulle International Airport. What a nightmare the place was and even in the cloistered VIP lounge, the chaos and bustle outside made their presence apparent on the faces of the wealthy and influential as they prepared to depart for destinations far and wide. Bonetti had arrived early and had made the usual heavy inroads into the lounge's stock of red wine by the time the hostess came to collect him. The service limousine took just a few minutes to deposit him at the foot of the steps of the Lear Jet. As he climbed aboard, he was relieved of his baggage by the ground staff handler, who loaded it into the small freight bay at the rear of the aircraft. The aircraft was smaller then he expected and he immediately felt claustrophobic as he walked down the short cabin to the only seat that could accommodate his bulk comfortably. At just over six feet tall and close on two hundred pounds in weight, you couldn't get many Carlo Bonettis into a Lear 400. But before he could think of a plausible excuse to unplug himself out of the drain pipe fuselage and transfer to the Emirates Airbus that he'd seen parked by the main terminal, the cabin boy had pulled down the hatch and the pilot was winding up the engines. The fortunate fact was that he was the only passenger in the 5 seat cabin, accompanied only by the single Pakistani cabin crew, who had strapped himself to the bulkhead fold-down seat. Not even the chance to get frisky with the hostess, Bonetti thought in disgust as he peered up at the Boeing and Airbus leviathans that dwarfed the Lear. Unlike the juggernauts which rumbled down the runway for a kilometre or more before clawing themselves into the air, the Lear sprinted off like a sports car and within the length of a football field was pointing steeply at the clouds above. Bonetti had been busy divesting himself of everything tight around his body and had just got one shoe off when the Lear went through rotation and leapt into the sky. If he hadn't been strapped into his seat, he was sure that he would have done a somersault, *a major arse over tits event*, as he would later describe to his drinking mates in The Lucky Palace. At the time the Canadian Italian was in danger of bursting the bulging blood vessels that stood out of his neck and by the time the Lear had levelled off at its cruising height, there was more of Bonetti on the floor than settled into the luxurious leather upholstery of the rear bench seat. All one point seven metres of it!

On seeing Bonetti's plight, Hakim`s his first task was to rescue his ward and recover the jacket, tie, belt and shoes that had been dispersed to every corner. Once the CIPHERCAN executive had regained something of his composure, he brushed away the fussing boy and swore racially in a red faced, eye popping bluster. Speaking immaculate Oxford English, the unflustered Hakim enquired, 'Would Sir like a glass of cool mineral water to relax with?'

Bonetti was about to bite viciously, but still suffering the effects of the VIP Chianti, thought better of it. 'Si, Yes!' And added … 'Grazie!' as an afterthought. The idea of being treated as a VIP was slowly encouraging him to live the gracious part. Just wait till he got his hands on that bastard pilot though.

***

The electric drummer beat his drum as he did every night and had done so for the last eight years – ceaselessly and tirelessly as predictably as the sun rose every morning, yet forever silent. Samir wondered how many times he had raised his arms, neon drumsticks in hand and then dropped them down to strike the yellow drum?

Eight years, nearly three thousand days, thirty five thousand hours of night time duty, say, two million minutes and with one beat every three seconds; – Insha'allaah, maybe forty million times! Ironic, he thought, that if he had forty million dollar notes, like a king in his counting house, counting out his money, it would take him eight years to count it. A smile spread his lips wide as he prided himself with his English sense of humour.

Forty million dollars he didn't have, but there were people in this city that did, and some had much, much more. To him, as he looked out of his workshop window at the effigies and icons of the rich, he saw that western trended plutocracy was desecrating this Arab land, Allah's land. Even as he watched, the glass clad towers that shone and flashed like lighthouse beacons signalled more to join them. The forest of construction cranes swung to and fro continuously, in what seemed an endless race to scar every single square metre of the landscape with dollar making tarmac and concrete. Each building was dressed in every colour of glass or plastic that he could imagine. A children's fairground? No! a playground for the affluent, who paraded around in Mercedes, Ferraris and grand American chariots, like kings and princes with their gold decked women. All of them parasites and prostitutes in his eyes and in those of Allah.

True, there were many mosques around, some still in their original plain attire of dusty adobe style construction. Their minarets were dwarfed by the giant megaliths of immorality, but other more modern structures, were glorified by the very same ubiquitous lights and glass of their satanic neighbours. The red ball of the setting sun hovered over the scene contributing dramatically to the melting pot of colour.

He could just hear the Maghreb. The first call to prayer of the evening. Now days the prayer calls had to battle to be heard above the clamour of the city and of those who heard, many responded only by hereditary conditioning whilst others were seeking business favours from their influential connections even as they knelt in communal supplication. And a few, he thought, like himself, god fearing honest Muslims who were sincerely devoted to the cause. The cause that had been inbred in him, during his childhood and youth spent amongst the ruins of the Palestinian transits that had camped near the Roman ruins of Jerash, to the north of his capital, Amman.

Many evenings spent conversing with his friends had revealed others who expressed similar disgust of the ever growing tide of capitalist encroachment drawn by the black gold that underpinned all the malignant pillars that he could see around him now. Yet, though he loved them and took them in his arms and his heart, none was ever prepared to take steps towards preserving their religious identity and beliefs, in the face of the evil onslaught that threatened the Dubai and world. He alone, it seemed, could remember the preaching of men like his father who as the village Imam long ago had held him captive with enchanting stories from the Holy Book. He, Samir, was troubled heavily by the path that modern Islam was now taking. It contrasted distressingly with what he had held as being the truth, and he at least, had become increasingly determined to contribute to the return of the old order. He was a pacifist at heart and could never condone the atrocities that were taking place in the world's regions of distress, especially when it concerned the innocents, the children. Nor could he side with those who took innocent hostages and paraded them on the television before butchering them in God's name. They were barbaric, disgusting and brought nothing but the world's condemnation upon Islam. But on the other hand, sacrifices had to be made. If it meant that of his own life, then so be it. It was God's will, not his own. The time was near, Al-hamdu-lillah

Once more his eyes shifted to the animated drummer who would continue to drum until the photo cell that he himself had installed. Once it detected sufficient of the next morning's daylight it would extinguish the red and yellow lights, signalling the end of another drummer's night shift. For now, its pulsating illumination was brightly reflected in the newly opened Creek Hotel. Yet another edifice created to help cope with the masses of tourists and business executives that were bleeding the region of its ancestral heritage and culture. One day soon Insha'allaah, he would ensure that the insane rush to turn Dubai into an Arab Disneyland would come to an end. With a dark cloud veiling his mood, Samir left the window and returned to his test bench and the new CIPHERCAN fax machines waiting for his attention. But first he spread out his prayer mat, faced to the west and prayed to Allah for forgiveness and guidance.

They were the last in the line of seventy units supplied by CIPHERCAN to Lighthouse LLC as part of their contract with the navy of the United Arab Emirates. As usual Bonetti, the regional manager had hidden a handful of extra machines in the contract. Samir knew from past experience that they were there for the lining of Bonetti's own pocket in one way or another. In this case Samir had managed to secret two away into his workshop on the pretence of requiring them for either demonstrations or troubleshooting the navy's network. Hopefully they would be forgotten and left to reside under his control, here on the fifteenth floor of the Lighthouse Company building. The company's managing director, Sheikh Hamed had called him up to the seventeenth floor, where the executive office was located, just a few days ago, to announce that Lighthouse and CIPHERCAN had just signed a new contract to supply another twenty units for the Sheikh's other business interest, the Dubai International Air Show. It was more commonly known by its acronym of DUBEXAIR.

Samir correctly suspected that in the light of the terrorist activity in the world today, it would not be extraordinary for such a progressive emirate to draw the attentions of Al Qaeda and the like. In fact he thought that the most surprising thing was that it had not already been targeted. But then perhaps it had, but in a clandestine manner that was not apparent to the outside world. Sheikh Hamed and his brother had often been heard debating about the need to preserve security for several Dubai strategic operations. Not nearly so well blessed with bottomless oil wells like its close neighbour Abu Dhabi, Dubai's insatiable thirst for prestige, particularly recognition amongst the Arab nations was largely founded on a myriad of ventures that ranged from tourism, promotion of sporting events, a free trade port, countless shopping malls, real estate investment and as a centre for international exhibitions. In the latter case alone, the DUBEXAIR now rivalled both the Paris and Farnborough air shows, in international interest, influence and sales. It was the stage where local aviation giants, such as the Emirates and the new fledgling Etihad, used the back cloth to announce multimillion dollars worth of investment in new aircraft. It was therefore apparent to anyone who spent a little time to study the scenario that unlike the major contributor and influential member to OPEC as Abu Dhabi was, Dubai's emergence as a major influence on the region was built like a pack of cards, based on finance. It was a structure built on confidence. Confidence in the stability of the location, the foresight and imagination of the Royal family along with the integrity of its banking and commerce. One bad incident, even the suspicion of a threat would pull the rug from under many an investment and one could imagine the playground emirates' population, bloated with foreigners, quickly returning to the Bedouin lifestyle from whence it had emerged some twenty or thirty years ago.

Such threats were Bonetti's bread and butter. As with most defence suppliers, he was always eager to help out organisations or governments in stress or under threat, even though he occasionally was the one sowing the seeds of anxiety. Anything that contributed to satiating his own avaricious desire to enter the realm of the world's millionaires was not acceptable

Samir was going to help Bonetti on his way!

The fax machines in front of him represented the first step. They were part of the final delivery of a contract signed two years ago and were not the latest machines on the market. Neither were they carrying the new NAMES algorithms but being supplied by CIPHERCAN, they relied on the old BASE security. The UAE navy had bought hundreds of these machines and they were spread far and wide throughout the Emirates and beyond in overseas missions. Samir knew almost every aspect of the network and on more occasions than he cared to count, had carried out the installations himself. Years of his presence in secure locations, ports, offices and headquarters had made him a familiar figure in the region and he knew all the people that counted and their habits and means of access to the communications posts. He always made a fuss of the normal Arab protocols and greeted all with enthusiasm as if they were brothers of the flesh rather than merely brothers of race and religion. His cheery wave and beaming smile from the window of the dusty Toyota and the compulsory exchange of Alsalam Alaikoum – Alaikoum Alsalam, granted him easy access to almost every military camp in the region. It was in sharp contrast to Bonetti, who often walked the same corridors and visited the same offices as Samir, and who gained his access with the air of a raging bull. He would bulldoze his way past guards and secretaries in search of the senior echelon of decision makers and particularly the men with the cheque books. If Carlo Bonetti was in town, then everyone knew about it. He was a very successful salesman but it wasn't the swagger and arrogance that was his marketing influence, it was his connections with royalty and the alleged willingness to cross a few palms with silver that bought in his contracts. Many senior military figures shared the same interest in money and what it could buy and so they accepted him despite his lack of respect for anything, or anybody less fortunate than himself. It was his conviction that everything, even integrity, could be bought, maybe at a price, but it could always be bought. Uppermost, it was his lack of respect for the religion for which Samir loathed him. And he was not alone in this hatred. Official subordinates, the ones who were usually left holding the can when things went wrong, got nothing from Bonetti. He was just interested in making the sale and offered almost nothing in support when things were not going to plan. It was a niche that Samir was happy to exploit and it offered a golden opportunity for him to be the ears and eyes of the *Brothers of Islam*. For many, Bonetti brought stress and headaches and it was Samir the engineer, Samir the security manager, Samir the tea drinker, the listener, the fixer who was the one who brought relief of their problems. When generals banged their desks and bawled out their technical crews, it was Samir whom they crawled to. Samir would rescue their careers and their pride. And he never let them down. Always available, never turning the mobile off and the first to arrive at the navy gate when the fleet was about to sail and communications were down. Many a stripe, many a shoulder pip, many a promotion had been rescued by Samir's sweat. It was on this wave of gratitude that Samir rode, and he rode it well. On not just a few occasions did he find himself amazed at how easily he was accepted into the most secure of locations, even asked for advice on what should have been top secret tasks. Of course as time had passed by, technicians, officers and signals security personnel had come and gone. But Samir's reputation merely skipped from one new head to another. He knew their birthdays, their children's birthdays, their wife's and even their mistresses' birthdays. If they didn't have a mistress, then Samir knew where to find them one. Samir knew them better than they knew themselves and there lay their vulnerability, though they never were aware of it.

So it had been with the integration of the fax network. The shortage of trained, reliable people had left him with the task of implementing the security program, of advising when and what secret keys to change, setting each machine's parameters as *he* thought fit. The military often could not be bothered to study the manuals had they ever bothered to unpack them from the shipping packages that collected the desert dust in rarely opened cupboards. Why bother? Samir was here!

About algorithms, he knew little, though he had read seminar reports gleaned from Bonetti's desk and cast his eye through the many web pages that provided far too much pertinent material for public digestion. In any case he didn't have the ability to exploit either the software or hardware implementation. Neither did he have the resources nor the mathematic prowess of a university research establishment to align a sophisticated attack. But that didn't matter, because the real weakness lay not with the ciphering algorithm, but with everything else around it. No good buying a Rolls Royce, if you didn't know how to put the key in the ignition. It was the human element that he had explored, coupled with the flexibility that sometimes lay hidden in the depths of a machine's operating menu. He was searching for an Achilles' heel that would let him into the navy's secrets and give an insight into the day-to-day operations planning of the Jebel Ali Naval HQ.

***

Ali's Hill, as it translates, was just twenty kilometres west of Dubai city centre. Originally a small fishing port and then the UAE's first tanker port and oil terminal, Jebel Ali had grown into what was arguably the most strategically important deep water port in the Persian Gulf, with the possible exception of Bahrain far to the north. Around it had grown a flourishing free trade area with some heavy industry and the main source of electrical power in the region. In fact its easterly growth, back towards the Dubai metropolis had met the expanding face of tourism. A cluster of five star hotels clutching the beaches of the southern gulf were spreading in the opposite direction towards the port. Such was the dynamic growth of each that they now lived together cheek by jowl. Naval port, oil terminal, power station and free trade park all perched on the emirate's northern Jumeira coast line. Samir could remember, just a few years past, driving out there with his family. The *Defence Roundabout* then marked the city's periphery and was the trigger for his children's excitement at the thought of a day at the beach. They would leave the city behind and drive across the empty sand flats that carried no construction other than the road to Abu Dhabi, one hundred and thirty kilometres away across the shimmering desert. Then they'd turn off the road and follow a track through the sand dunes to spill out the children, sunshades and picnic bags on to the deserted, pristine sand of Jumeira beach. The smile of his cherished family pleasures dispersed as he considered that he would now have to drive half way to Abu Dhabi in order to find a plot of coast that was not overrun by the Sheratons, the Hiltons and Les Meridiens to name but a few of the west's top branded hotels, each charging the earth for the right of visitors to walk their beaches. Beaches on which he'd dug castles and splashed happily on many weekend days until the children had dropped with exhaustion and he'd had to carry them, one by one, to the back of the car, before heading back to the distant lights of what was the tallest building for maybe a thousand kilometres in any direction – The Trade Centre building. Now what had once appeared as a huge monolith growing out of the desert, dwarfing all around it, was in fact dwarfed itself by the very towers that Samir had come to despise as the decadent trappings of the west.

Jebel Ali and Bahrain, each was a priceless jewel for the coalition forces during both Gulf wars. Samir smirked at the term – coalition. A big dog with many tails to wag. Some of the tails were wagging very wearily now. They were heavy with involvement in the suppression of the Iraqi brothers intent on irritating the dog with their resistance, like a plague of fleas biting at every opportunity. Even the British tail was wagging with reluctance. The initial enthusiasm for the restoration of democracy in the Euphrates' lands had waned fast, and instead of the British wagging the American dog with a moderating influence, the American president had chosen to ignore what he, Samir, had hoped would be a voice of sanity. The British had often exercised moderation over the USA in the past, but the latter's incumbent president was tearing around like a pit bull terrier, oblivious to what the rest of the world thought or cared about. Pit Bull diplomacy might be just the thing in Texas but Samir knew that the rest of the world was tiring of it very quickly.

The Americans, with their big hammer philosophy, were on borrowed time and though he had come to admire much about the English during his university education in London, Samir had lost faith in their ability and freedom to voice rational opinions in the field of international politics. Freedom, that is, from the White House manipulations. Momentarily he pictured himself as a flea and the smile returned to his face as he thought of the degree of pain that even he could inflict on the big dog and its master.

***

141

Each CIPHERCAN-C2000 fax was built around a high quality Japanese, off-the shelf, heavy duty fax machine that from the outside would look at home on the desk of any busy commercial organisation. But there the likeness ended. Under the plastic covers it was a very different beast. A comparison of weight would reveal a new, heavy metal base and further metallic shielding that prevented any tell-tale radiation being emitted from the sensitive electronics within. The digital encryption process was state of the art and totally enclosed in a tamperproof module embedded into the main circuit board. Anybody messing with the module would destroy it without capturing any of its secret parameters. Samir thought that the C2000 was well protected against both electromagnetic monitoring and physical attack. Lesser equipment leaked signals like water through a sieve and these were easily picked up by standard test gear that could be purchased from any electronics shop in the souk. He'd tested this model but had not been able to detect any stray signal that might carry message information. Even with the limited equipment in his workshop he'd been able to monitor the radiation from the PC screen in the next office. If Bonetti had seen his own computer screen shot displayed on Samir's test monitor, on the other side of his office wall, he would have bust a blood vessel. Samir grinned at the thought and knowing of Bonetti's blood pressure problems considered that it might just be worth the effort some day. It was just like looking over his boss's shoulder. As it was, he had had to content himself with viewing the soft porn that Bonetti swept through from time to time, usually at the end of the day, after he'd made his dollar and was ready to ride the traffic jam conveyor home.

Often the stimulation would lead to Bonetti passing by the Lucky Palace bar just in case there was some tasty piece for him to take away for his evening's entertainment. On occasions, Samir had been dragged there too and whilst it was worth his while to tag along, his religious ardour was stronger than his physical desire and resisted easily the temptations of the flesh. The place and the people disgusted him, but it was a popular watering hole for many high fliers and many a secret had slipped inadvertently from their lubricated tongues. And it was Faisal's lair.

The navy's C2000s had the BASE algorithm and carried up to one hundred secret keys with which to cipher the messages that it transmitted and decipher the ones that it received. This was one of the big selling points that the Canadian company banked on. It meant that if there were another one hundred fax stations out there in the network, then each link could be protected by its individual key. Samir could remember when single key machines were on the market and how much simpler it must have been to tease out the one key that gave security to the whole of a network. Those days were gone however, and the use of a hundred keys posed many problems for the would-be eavesdropper. Even the super-fast computers of the America's NSA or Britain's GCHQ would have their work cut out to break into those in useful time. Of course many of his customers did not have the necessary planning skills to manage a network with a hundred keys and relied on a mere handful, or even on occasions reverting to a single key to encrypt all their top secret data. On some occasions when Samir had been consulted about the key installations, he'd just entered a very basic key, one that he could readily remember, for demonstration purposes, only to return some weeks later to find the same key active. He'd used this fact, that nobody in the navy took care to change keys regularly, to catch every fax message that was broadcast from the navy HQ. Whenever HQ had sent an all points broadcast fax to all the land stations by phone line, a copy appeared on Samir's own workshop fax, fully prepared with the very same key that was installed in the commander's machine. When the HQ transmitted over the high frequency radio to their ships around the world, then Samir picked it up and read it as if he was a navy captain at sea.

It had not been difficult to slip his own fax number in with the fifty or so genuine stations, whilst he had been left alone for a minute, when called in to troubleshoot a minor problem in the Jebel Ali main signal office. Then so long as his workshop machine had the same key as the signal office in HQ, he got whatever was sent.

With the HF radio fax transmissions it was even easier. During one of his many meetings with the communications security people, he had convinced them that their ships should practice radio silence in order not to give away their precise location to anybody caring to listen. Within the Gulf, he emphasised that if the Iranians were not listening then others would be. The threat from Iran was well established with their seizure of islands belonging to the UAE some years back. It seemed sound advice and the navy had adopted the method as standard practice. So, instead of a two way communication to check secret key compatibility taking place between two fax machines, as was the case of transmission over telephone lines, HQ just transmitted the radio fax without absolute knowledge that it had been received by the ships. There was no two way handshake. Experience alone told them that it would have been received, especially as each transmission was automatically sent at least three times. Of course any ciphered transmission could not be read by anybody without the correct secret key and for a long time Samir's machine had the same key. Just like inserting his own fax number in the HQ machine's phone list, Samir had selected a radio ID that fell within the range of the navy's IDs and installed the same ID in his own HF radio. For lengthy periods of time he was reading every broadcasted fax and in time, he became familiar with all the routines, all the dispositions and even the names of each ship's captain and senior crew members. When he crossed paths with them at the base, he felt it was like greeting family members, he knew so much about them. Sometimes he had had to bite his tongue so as not to give the game away, even though he would have loved to say, 'Congratulations on your promotion, sir.' 'How was Karachi?' or 'Did you manage to get the starboard propeller straightened out?'

It was just like a computer game to him. He would positively beam to himself when some particularly interesting news passed his way. He'd sit there, tugging at his greying moustache, a knowing smirk on his face, his dark eyes plotting the progress of every ship in the navy on some imaginary sea chart that he pictured before him. Being Muslim and an Arab and having nothing against the UAE as a nation, he never considered taking any action on the information that he captured. For himself, the satisfaction that he knew these secrets was enough, but Faisal had another idea, and told him that it was all about building the big picture. Every morsel of information was like a piece of a giant jigsaw puzzle and when they took Samir's input along with that of other brothers, the big picture was always developing. What did greatly interest both of them was the information that was riding on the back of the day to day UAE naval operations. It was news of the coalition navy's ships. Every so often Samir would see a reference to US, Australian and British ships that were moving around in the Gulf waters and he had seen for himself the regular visits that they paid to the UAE either for the crew's rest and recreation, taking on provisions, or docking for repairs. Jebel Ali as a deep water port, and Dubai, as a social and commercial centre, provided everything that a visiting ship might need whilst supporting the invasion of Iraq and deterring any other errant society having thoughts of imposing its own vision on the region. Neither Samir nor Faisal seriously believed that there was any military threat to coalition forces outside Iraq. The massive fire power available to the Americans and their followers imposed itself on all other nations in the region and it would be suicidal for any of the Gulf navies to shake more than a fist at the unwanted visitors. No, other navies could not stand face to face with these giants; but there were certain other organisations, indeed certain individuals who could.

Samir considered himself to be one of them.

***

After months of successfully monitoring the naval signals, Samir's machine suddenly fell silent. Nothing was coming his way. A change of staff at Jebel Ali HQ had recently brought to the front a clutch of new officers who were more diligent than their predecessors. He still had access to the base and the communications centre and he still drank "chi" with his contacts but the main problem was that the navy were changing their secret keys much more often than ever before. Maybe it was the American influence, maybe there were suspicions that somebody really was reading their mail. Perhaps they had a source of information. He was certain that his own actions had been discreet and extremely passive. Nobody, other than Faisal and himself, knew what he was doing. The more he thought about it, the more he was convinced that he had not been compromised. After all, he was still getting into the base and he was still having an influence on the use of keys, but it was becoming more difficult and it wouldn't be long before somebody decided that his services were no longer needed. Then he wouldn't be able to copy the secret key data. This was why he had set up the C2000 faxes in the workshop. To find another way in!

One of the problems that any network manager had was when a station lost its keys, for one reason or another. Or missed a key change or key loading. In such circumstances the only option was to transmit plain messages until a security officer went to load new keys into the offending machine. This of course was a weak link in any secure communications network and one that needed to be dealt with quickly before too much information became available to anyone listening. Samir wondered if there was a way round this. He could hardly pretend that his machine had lost its keys due to some failure, as the last thing he wanted was anybody snooping around his workshop investigating the matter. He remembered attending one of Bonetti's sales presentations and some wise guy in the audience had asked a question on the same subject of missing keys and how could this problem be overcome? Bonetti had given a solution, in fact two, but Samir could only recall one, and it was impractical in his situation because it would draw attention to his workshop machine. The usual procedure is that if a common key could not be found during the fax handshake protocol between the two stations, there was an option for them to communicate in plain. If this option was set up in both machines, then after three failed attempts to transmit in cipher mode the machines would automatically step to plain mode and the fax message would be sent in plain. Not only would the message be available to any eaves-dropper, the action would be reported on the HQ machine and probably invite an investigation.

He read and re-read the CIPHERCAN manuals, searched through machine's programming menu and he tried several program options on the two machines available to him, but none gave a satisfactory solution. His machine had to remain inconspicuous, transparent to the navy's security management, a silent, sleeping partner that attracted no untoward attention. He had to solve this problem and he had to solve it quickly. Bonetti was due back from Canada any day now and Samir couldn't carry on this research under his nose without questions being asked. Exhausted by the day's efforts, he rubbed his sore eyes and flexed a stiff neck which signalled that it was too late to make progress now, so he would have to sleep on it and try again in the morning when his mind was refreshed and alert, Insha'allaah. As he joined the red light traffic snake to cross the Maktoom bridge for home, behind him the neon's of the Lighthouse Drummer continued to beat out the city's pulse. It wouldn't be long before it missed a beat or two.

∗∗∗

Samir was back at his workshop early. The family being on their summer vacation back in Amman left him free of the usual responsibilities of school runs and hospital waiting rooms that ate away at his mission time. Sleep had not come easily but normally four or five hours was enough for him to recharge his batteries and his alert mind had already been working on the problem ever since he had risen from his morning prayer.

His flow of information direct from the Emirates' Navy which had been almost uninterrupted for the last twelve months and was being threatened by a tightening of security at the Jebel Ali HQ, an immediate solution evaded him. He had played through in his mind, the scenario of the HQ fax transmitting to his station, which may or may not have a compatible key with which to cipher the message. If his key was not the same as the key in the HQ unit, then it would

147

not transmit in cipher mode and would try to drop back to plain mode. This would inevitably attract unwanted attention. In the past he had had access to the HQ machine and had been able to influence the secret key input, copying them into his own unit. He had only rarely needed to break into the HQ machine, but now it was becoming more frequent. And in the future? – This was his concern.

He thought back to the initial installations that he had carried out and how he had filled the key memories with a very basic key of thirty two digits, all ones. He was surprised, when some time later, he had returned to the machine only to find that the key was still present, even though other keys had been entered afterwards. A hundred keys, in fact! Why hadn't that very first key been overwritten? There in front of customers, he had declared it as his mistake in programming. But it wasn't. He hadn't made a mistake, he just couldn't offer an explanation at the time and the incident had soon been forgotten. But *he* had not forgotten and he had never found an answer. Why was it still there, when another one hundred new keys had been entered?

Once more Samir powered up the two faxes. He would start again – from the very beginning. He opened up the case of the first fax and as expected, the hidden micro switch tripped, as it would if some invader was trying to get at the secrets held inside. With this signal, all the entries into the machine whether they be secret keys, merely operating parameters, or network telephone IDs, or radio IDs, would be erased. Everything was cleared and the machine was reset to its default state. He opened up the programming menu, using the default password and made his way through the menu to the key entry option. There he entered the first secret key with thirty two digits; all ones and checked for the key's signature. Like a footprint in the snow, once the person leaving it had gone, he could not be seen again, but the footprint indicated that he had been there. It was similar with the signature. Once he had entered the secret key, he could never see its data again. It was common security practice. All he could get back was the signature, a three digit code that identified the key's data without showing what the actual data was.

For the thirty two ones, the signature came back as 5E2. It was a hexadecimal code.

Samir turned his attention to the second machine and went through the whole process again. In the end, he once again checked the signature: 5E2. The same! And just to make sure all was correct, he transmitted a blank paper message from one to the other. Al-hamdu-lillah! Thanks be to God – it worked. The whole operation took fifty five seconds after the link had been established with about ten seconds of negotiation to check that the keys in both machines were the same and forty five seconds for the actual message transmission. Normal!

Trying to reproduce the very first experience, Samir then entered one hundred secret keys into both machines and tried again. Sure enough it worked, also normal! The only difference was the negotiation of the keys took fifteen seconds as the machines searched through their memories before they came up with a common key from the one hundred. On this test all the hundred keys were the same in each machine.

Now he wanted to check the negotiation time when the machines failed to find a common key, so he left the first machine as it was and then entered a different set of one hundred keys into the second machine, making sure that none were the same in the two machines. Once again he put a blank paper message in the first machine, dialled the number of the other and checked his watch to measure the time of the negotiation, knowing that it would fail; the second finger moved round and as it reached fifteen, the fax went through! – Impossible! Shit! Samir was amazed. He checked the key signatures again, going slowly through the hundred keys in both machines, and yes, he was sure, there were *no* common keys in the machines, yet the fax was transmitted, and transmitted in cipher mode. If Bonetti saw this he would explode and so would his customers.

Confused, he deleted all the keys in each machine and tried again to transmit in cipher mode. It failed! 'Thanks be to God,' he murmured as if being reassured about his sanity. The negotiation time was twenty four seconds before it dropped out and cut the communication.

Taking his time, he re-entered one hundred keys in the first machine and then one hundred different keys in the second. Once again he put in the paper and tried to transmit; He counted the negotiation time; nine, ten, eleven, twelve, thirteen, fourteen, fifteen, sixteen, seventeen, eighteen, nineteen, twenty … the transmission failed. Of course it should fail. – Damn! But the first time, it hadn't. What was different this time?

Samir beat the bench in frustration with his fist. He ran his fingers through his thick crop of hair and moved over to the window gazing sightlessly over the Dubai Creek, to the Deira region beyond. Slowly his eyes re-focussed and he was surprised to see that the sun was already quite low in the sky and dhows headed out from the port for other gulf destinations or beyond to Pakistan. The diner boats were preparing for their wealthy clientele whom they would pamper obscenely whilst cruising up and down the creek all evening. He'd worked through the best part of the day, without a break, missing the mid-day salah and having become aware of the tension in his body, sought some relief in a glass of 'Sulamani.'

Samir was still confused. On the one hand he was tempted to start all over again and try to duplicate the situation once more, yet on the other he had already done this. Once here, on his test bench, this very morning, and once before during the first naval installations, some two years ago. He had to trust his senses and his testing technique. He had to reassure himself that he had not made a mistake. There had to be something hidden in the machines, whether it be intentional, a software error or some programming residue left over from the original research and development that had been forgotten and left to sleep until woken by some accident or enquiring mind that delved too deeply into the operating system. He briefly thought that it could be a virus and if the machines had been computers, then it would have been one of his first considerations. But with a fax machine, there was no possible connection between the communications medium and the operating system. It just wasn't physically possible.

How could two machines with dissimilar secret keys, still

communicate in cipher mode? They couldn't. Not only he, but the entire CIPHERCAN engineering team would have designed and built the C2000 with that fundamental property in mind. Otherwise they would not be in business.

The mint tea dispatched, he returned to the machines. Maybe he had overlooked something. If he had entered one hundred keys into one machine and then the same hundred keys into the second machine, then the two machines would pick out any two common keys from the hundred. It was just a question of time before they reached agreement. This, in any case, was not quite the situation with the navy network. Each machine had one hundred keys but they were not all the same as in other machines. Instead they were configured so that for example if Jebel Ali called Amman, the machines would use, perhaps, key one, whereas if Jebel Ali called Muscat, then they would agree on say, key two, and so on. Bearing the real situation in mind, Samir left the same hundred keys in the first machine and knowing that the second machine had one hundred *different* keys, he deleted one and in its place entered a copy of one key in the first machine. He put the paper in, dialled the other phone number and waited ... It worked – the fax message went through. The key negotiation time was ten seconds!

If the same one hundred keys were installed in each machine, then he had seen that it took fifteen seconds to find the right one. To be sure, he wrote the results down.

a) 100 same keys in machine one and two = 15 seconds to find right key.
b) 1 common key out of 100 in each machine = 10 seconds to find it.
c) No common keys in machines = 24 seconds before drop out.
d) Only one common key (signature 5E2) in each machine = 10 seconds to find it.

He stared at the figures – certain that they had a message to tell him. What about the very first try, this morning, or was it yesterday?

Time had passed so quickly that two days had merged into one. His hand swept through the scraps of paper that had accumulated on his work top. The bench top light was needed. He found the first scratching – it read ten seconds!

So the option gave him the following:

After entering the first secret key (5E2) in each machine and then entering one hundred different keys in each machine, the negotiation time was – ten seconds. And it worked, even though there were no common keys in the hundred entered!

The ten second negotiation pointed to the fact that there was a common key, just one! But he'd entered a hundred very different keys and in each case their signatures, their footprints in the snow, were different…

Samir sighed heavily and rested his head in his hands, the muscles across his shoulders relaxed as his arms took the weight of his aching head and for a moment the stiffness of his neck muscles drew his attention to the fact that his body, like his mind had been stressed for longer than it could tolerate without objection.

Ten seconds, ten seconds? What was the significance?

Ten seconds, he repeated over and over again. Ten seconds for one key to be found?

Then it came slowly to him at first. Just a dim, barely perceptible ember of recognition, an instant when he knew there was an answer. But he had to freeze his thoughts, capture it before it was lost for ever. Retrace the flow of signals through the neurones in his brain, to that single fleeting electrochemical interaction that flagged an answer. He recovered that state and let it run again, captured it like a snap shot, a still frame in a movie, and started to tease out the reasoning. His head was covered in beads of sweat as he toiled with the beast that tried to keep it locked away. Ten seconds – one key – my God, his body was rigid with concentration, every cell was drained of energy as he fixed upon that moment.

His arms dropped from the bench to his sides and his head fell backwards across the top of the chair. He took a breath, so deep that it seemed to fill every cavity in his body. 'Allah Akbar! Allah Akbar he whispered, God is great! Thanks be to God!' He stood, filled with jubilation – He knew the answer, and he also knew that he didn't need to verify it. The C2000 didn't hold one hundred keys as it professed to! It held one hundred and one!

Red flashing lights filled the darkened room. The Lighthouse drummer, looking down on the creek dhows and diners, had started his evening beat.

CHAPTER 9

The Black Message

The Toyota pick-up turned off the Defence Roundabout and took the Sheikh Zayed Highway to the west, out of Dubai, and headed for Jebel Ali. The first ten kilometres of the highway had just been widened to five lanes in an effort to relieve the horrendous traffic jams that built up there every morning and evening. As far as Samir could see, the new constructions would just migrate the problem back along the highway to the World Trade Centre intersection, but on this occasion the traffic was down as it was the first day of the Arab weekend. The stream of trucks, cars, buses and the ubiquitous yellow taxis was steady and most drivers were content to go with the flow. Samir too had no reason to take his life in his hands and just eased along, taking in the view and plotting his activity over the next few hours. To the left were the new car sales showrooms, the Metropolitan Hotel and cinema complex, whilst to the right was the southern end of the ever spreading Jumeira suburbs. After a few kilometres, this gave out to the new apartment blocks that were beginning to tower above the desert and beyond them lay the chain of luxury hotels that tempted European winter sun-seekers with their warm seas, expansive sandy beaches, five star golf courses, shuttle bus services to every major shopping mall in the city and a choice of every restaurant fare that one could imagine. The pinnacle of hotel attractions was the Burj Al Arab – advertised as the world's first six, or was it seven-star hotel? Samir had heard that they even charged two hundred dirham just to have a look around the apartments that ranged upwards of a thousand dollars a night. Its new-world silhouette formed the shape of a ship's sail that was topped by a futuristic helicopter pad which permitted the more affluent of guests the option of a ten minute flight direct from the Dubai Airport. He couldn't for the life of him, think why this plateau of dusty, dirty sand was so attractive to the tourists who were flocking to the region, escaping the winter traumas of Northern Europe. There was no culture here and the beaches had been pegged out into squares of flat barren sand traps with hardly a palm tree to decorate the strip with a sign of natural life. A few miles inland and the scenery deteriorated even more and it was very difficult to find any sign of the classic sand dunes that adorned the travel posters around the world.

Each hotel on the beach laid out row upon row of sun chairs with shades and wooden walkways for visitors to move around without blistering their feet on the burning sand. What ambition was it to lie there cooking in the hot sun during the day and sweltering in the heavy sodden air that rose up once the sun had set? Gone were the natural sand dunes where his children used to play and where campers set up their tents for laid back weekends by the sea. They were replaced by the towels for the fat Europeans whose grotesque women hung their sagging flesh out for all to see. Samir could no longer tolerate the scene or the thought that all of this was sponsored by Arab Muslims, whose ideals and ethics were light years away from the sun-worshipping hordes that swarmed along Jumeirah. As he approached Jebel Ali Naval Base, he saw that a new inlet had been carved from the sand, allowing the sea in to form another man-made lake, which gave all the property developers an excuse to build more and more towers of apartment blocks. Beyond these, the builders had not been content to deface the natural coast line, but had recently started constructing The Palm Resort that was already emerging from the water, perhaps a kilometre out to sea. The Hard Rock Café slipped by as he moved into the Free Port Area, where Motorola, Acer, BMW and Jaguar had built rows and rows of warehouses and outlets. Opposite was probably the only green grassed area between the Persian Gulf and the Arabian Gulf, five hundred kilometres to the south east. It was the Emirates' Golf Club complex. Huge billboards announced the upcoming Desert Classic Golf Competition, with its grand prizes in the order of a million dollars or so. Then at last he began to leave it all behind as the cranes of the port came into view on the horizon. The port too had expanded and it was difficult to make out where the barrier separating the port from its neighbouring power station and desalination plant actually lay. But it was the port and that part occupied by the navy that was his destination now. He'd driven this route many times as part of his normal working duty, but for the first time he was nervous about the outcome of this particular visit.

He turned off the highway and drove northwards towards the coast and after a few minutes turned into the port. His pass got him through the first gate without any enquiry other than the regular search of the pick-up's contents. From there it was another five minute drive to the second gate, the naval port and HQ. As he drew up, there were just two vehicles in the queue awaiting the inspection of gate passes and the cursory search for weapons or explosives. A local Arab dressed in his white dish-dash was arguing with a guard about his apparent failure to get past the gate. The next in line was a beat-up old bus. It was the standard workers' bus carrying perhaps twenty labourers from the Indian subcontinent all dressed on their blue boiler suits bearing the orange logo of their esteemed employer *Clean Ops* on their backs. No two-day weekend for them, to be sure. As he waited patiently, he took a look around, and to the right hand side of the gate, maybe just 50 metres away, was evidence of a new structure. A sign board advertised, in Arabic, the construction of the navy's new training centre and a temporary message painted on an old cardboard box remnant invited site traffic to peel off the main road to take the dusty track over to the construction. Samir turned back to the confrontation at the gate. The local was pacing angrily, backwards and forwards berating somebody over his mobile phone. The bus had emptied its Bangladeshi passengers who had been beginning to stew in the late morning heat. Now they sat on the floor outside, taking shade from the bus. Samir thought he would have a look at the new building and pulled off the road onto the track.

It was a bit soft under foot so he had to keep within the tyre tracks of the lorries that had been depositing materials. The Toyota had enough ground clearance to ride over the central ridge, with ease. Part of the security fence had been taken down to allow the builders' vehicles access, so Samir drove in to have a look. There were a few workers around, mostly Pakistanis or Indians and none took any notice of the pick-up. One more dusty four wheel drive didn't arouse any concern. He had intended just to drive round and return to the gate after the confrontation had been sorted out, but as he threaded his way through the piles of sand, bricks and gravel, it became obvious that the far side of the site had direct access to the base. Al-hamdu-lillah, muttered Samir, he didn't really need to sneak in by the back door, as he had a gate pass and the signals people were expecting him. Having nothing to lose, he continued on into the base, making sure that he stayed out of direct view of the gate. No need to push his luck. Not just yet anyhow.

Once inside the base, he drove unhindered down the quay side, passing a couple of small patrol boats and a decrepit old landing craft that listed heavily to one side. It had been there for years and Samir had never seen anyone on board and it certainly hadn't moved since he'd been coming to the base. It was probably waiting for some crucial gear to be repaired and, as was usually the case, nobody had taken the initiative to follow up the service action and so, like other vessels, the hulk had become for all intents and purposes – like Samir, he smiled – part of the furniture. The English phrase amused him and he was happily relaxed now as once again he felt proud of his prowess with the colloquial language. Beyond, lay the serious fighting ships of the Emirates' Navy. The frigate Al Fujairah, the biggest vessel in the fleet, was tied up in her berth. Compared with anything else in the port, she looked impressive, but Samir, having spent much time on board, knew that despite the grand appearance, it had seen better days. Due to shortage in manpower, all the navy's ships were undermanned, and there being not nearly enough

Emeratis to fill the posts. Indian and Pakistani expatriates made up the bulk of the crews. At the time of its commissioning, flags had flown and trumpets had been blown in a grand fanfare to announce that The Emirates' Navy had arrived on the scene as a force to be reckoned with. Throughout the Gulf, different states, on seeing the American naval power and how it had been so influential in Desert Storm, just had to have a big ship! The Al Fujairah was again the centre of activity, with supply trucks making deliveries and a number of crew's personal cars lined up along the quay opposite the ship. It all suggested that she was about to sail. A rare excursion and one unlikely to take her out of sight of land. Samir sneered at their ineptitude.

The Jordanian considered, like many, the decision to buy the ship to be a mistake, but the positive side of the purchase was that they needed him. And they *really* needed him urgently today. Not on the ships, but at the signals HQ and that's where he pulled up, reached over to the back seat for his tool bag and briefcase before arranging the sunscreen on the dashboard so that the baking sun would not transform the cabin into a fifty or sixty degree furnace, when he came to leave.

The guard at the security office stood to meet him, 'Al Salam Alaikoum.' – Alaikoum Al Salam, was the response and both men leant forward to touch noses in a greeting of affection. Samir was part of the family.

'Chi?' enquired the guard.

'No thanks, business first,' he laughed. 'But sure, I'll have a tea when I have finished.'

'Insha'allaah' called the guard noisily, as Samir disappeared down the corridor toward the main signal office.

There had been times, not so long distant, when he had been able to walk straight into the machine room. It housed the banks of HF and VHF radios, telephones, communications computers and even a couple of old telex machines, each connected with racks of cipher units. Nowadays however, a few new faces of authority had appeared on the scene and his way through the iron door was blocked by a security key pad on the wall, at the side. It was a twelve digit terminal with a key pad that displayed the digits zero to eight in the first three rows of the matrix, with the bottom row also having three buttons, reading left to right, a star character, the nine digit and finally a bell symbol. Samir had had fun with them before by attempting to guess the four digit entry code. He'd seen various signal men punch in the numbers and of course remembered them for next time, because they never changed. If they ever changed the code, then he reckoned that nobody would be able to get in. He could imagine the officer changing it and then going off duty without telling the new watch. All hell would break loose until they'd have to call him back to get the correct password. On another occasion, the security officer had actually stood in front of him to hide the information that he punched in, whilst unbelievably mumbling out the characters as he had entered them. When Samir had next come to the entrance and typed in the correct door code, he walked in to be greeted by shouts of glee that triggered much laughter and admiration. It was schoolboy stuff and even now as he inspected the key pad, he could see that five buttons were dirtied by the many fingerprints that had been there. He was confident that he could also get in today as the four, seven, zero and nine buttons were discoloured along with the star entry button. He didn't know the full sequence of the four digits but it wouldn't have taken him long to go through all of them before getting the right one. Not today though. He had to be crystal clean today, so he pressed the bottom right hand button and heard a muffled bell from inside, followed shortly by the click of the automatic door release.

The hiss of radio static and the frantic chatter of printers and tape punches welcomed him, along with the rather stern faced captain who swung the heavy door open. The officer was however thankful to see who the visitor was and the tight lipped grimace gave way to a thin smile. It expressed his relief that the communications problem that had been bugging him, might soon be solved by the Lighthouse man. Samir had great confidence that he would have no problem in making the captain's day, for it was he – Samir who had generated the problem.

***

159

Under the Captain's command, there were two signalmen busy answering calls, collecting incoming messages, transmitting messages and dealing with the continuous flow of paperwork. He knew them both well, but for the sake of the officer, greeted them in a more formal manner than he would normally. The captain, a newcomer, was somewhat aloof, but at the same time polite in raising the subject of his early morning call to Samir's office. He drew the engineer over to the CIPHERCAN C2000 fax machine that resided on a bench in the corner of the windowless room. At the side, a small partition housed a desk and two chairs and a small hole in the wall, the shape and size of a slightly large letterbox, covered by a hinged metallic flap, underneath which was a strategically positioned in-tray. From time to time, a hand would appear through the flap to deposit a paper into the in-tray. It was the collection point where messages to be transmitted were deposited to await the signal staff's attentions.

By the side of the fax was a pile of sheets of flimsy, heat-sensitive paper, white on one side and almost totally black on the other. Just a thin strip of white showed down each side of the black central mass. Samir shook his head as he inspected the papers. They had arrived through the night, explained the captain. At first, just the odd copy, but then later, as a continuous stream, without a pause, until the entire role of heat-sensitive paper in the machine had been exhausted.

Samir made a second inspection as if to check an idea that had come to him. He was content to see that even the normal header, that usually identified the sending station and the transmitter's phone number, or ID, was obscured. He tugged at his moustache and after a pause, asked: 'Did it print out normally sometimes? I mean did you get some normal fax prints, from some stations, or were they *all* black?'

'They were all black!' the captain said sharply, casting a dark glance in the direction of one of the operators, who responded sheepishly and turned his attention to a different subject. 'So we don't know if they all came from one remote station or from several – nobody took notice of the machine's display.' The pointed criticism brought a hapless shrug from the offending signalman.

Samir sat at the machine and tugged at his moustache. Then thinking aloud, 'looks like a problem with *this* machine then.' He switched on the power but disconnected the phone/radio line. Then he took a fresh sheet of A4, scribbled boldly his initial S and entered into the offending machine, pressed the copy button and waited for the result. A few seconds later, out came the paper, perfectly white except for the large S. 'Fine.' said Samir. 'So if it's not a problem with the print mechanism, then it must be the interface.' He opened up the tool bag and picked through its contents, retrieving a small package of semi transparent, plastic bubble paper. 'It's a new modem,' declared Samir with authority. 'It will take some time to replace the other unit, but you'll be back on line, in say – an hour?

The captain was paying close attention and merely nodded his consent to go ahead with the repair.

Samir had succeeded in gaining access to the machine, but if the captain was going to continue to observe like the hawk that he was now, the crucial part of the fix would be impossible. The simulation of the fault had gone perfectly, like a dream, he smiled. It hadn't been at all difficult. The night before he had gone to his workshop's photocopy machine, lifted the lid and pressed copy, and there, thanks be to God, had emerged a totally black sheet of A4 paper. He had repeated this four times and taken one sheet to the C2000 fax and transmitted it, in plain mode, to the navy HQ station. To simulate a gradual breakdown of a component, rather than a single catastrophic event, Samir sent the single sheet a number of times. He then took the remaining three sheets of black copy paper and glued them, one by one, end to end so that he had a long black A4 paper. Next, he fed one end of the paper through the roller and scanning mechanism of his fax and brought the two ends together to tape the two loose ends by adhesive tape, in a firm bond. He had taken care that the adhesive tape had been attached to the white side of the paper, so that it wouldn't be evident at the receiving end. So he now had a continuous loop of black paper, slotted through his own C2000. It even blacked out the place where his station's ID and phone number would normally be printed. As far as the HQ station was concerned, the source of the message was anonymous. The only gamble was that the operators wouldn't bother to look at the HQ fax's display panel during the initial part for the transmission. Knowing the routine in the signals centre, lots of noise, messages all over the place and using the window of the dead of night, all made it less likely that the duty signalman would even care about the fax display. After all the sender's ID would be printed out on the copy of the received message. It always was, so why should it be different this time? Finally Samir had done something that he'd never done before, he dialled the HQ fax number, switched to plain mode and let the black message loop through his machine as its sombre data was transmitted. Predictably, as soon as the captain came on duty that morning, he was presented with the black message by a bewildered signalman. The very same signalman had switched off the HQ fax in the certainty that it had developed a fault. That had been a bonus. Samir knew that if it hadn't run out of paper it would have subsequently received *normal* messages and stored them in its memory bank.

The captain's next action had been to call the Lighthouse workshop. Samir had been ready. He'd spent the whole night snoozing in the easy chair, waiting for the call. Insha'allaah, God willing.

***

Still the captain observed every stage of the repair procedure. Although Samir had strung along the removal of the faulty module, opportunities at getting to the security housing were becoming fewer by the minute. He was struggling to come up with a valid excuse to unscrew the retaining fastener that would release the micro-switch that would completely erase all of the secret keys leaving only the hidden memory space for the initial default key that he'd discovered the previous night. The elaborate ruse of the black message to get to this stage of the infiltration was all going to waste. The captain had never taken his eyes off Samir and his testing. Whether it was devotion to duty or just a technical fascination, Samir was becoming increasingly disturbed. His nerves were fraying to such an extent that he was finding difficulty in holding his tools with a steady hand. Usually he would have been offered chi, or at least a glass of water to break up the session, but the men that would normally provide such relief were for once very much focussed on their daily tasks. He hadn't expected such a vigil. This was anything but normal. Not even a telephone call to distract the officer. Had this been performed in any other location, Samir could have been sure that his observer would have been disturbed by numerous calls to his mobile phone, but the screening of this room that prevented spontaneous tell-tale radio emissions also prevented the ingress of them. They were all cut off from outside interference.

Samir needed only a few seconds to unscrew the security housing retainer, lift it just a few millimetres for the micro-switch to trip, then say about ten seconds to replace the housing. After that, he would need to enter the access password into the C2000 keyboard, scroll through the menu, to *key input*, enter the thirty two digits, check for the signature to make sure that he'd entered the correct data, close the menu and then tinker with something else to make it look normal – say two minutes of freedom – that should be sufficient.

There was one chance that he could see presenting itself. As the paper roll was empty, somebody would have to find a replacement and it wouldn't be him. He wouldn't be able to roam around, looking in cupboards for the reload, so perhaps the captain could be diverted to this task. 'I hope that you've got a new roll?' asked Samir, looking up at his spectator.

Without moving a muscle, the captain barked a command, and one of the signalmen responded with 'Sidi – Sir,' and immediately left what he was doing to search for the paper. Samir cursed his luck. Now he had no chance to enter his own key. He only had one more tiny screw to put in place before he closed the outer cover and installed the paper and handed the machine back to Hawk Eyes. It was all for nothing.

The signalman returned with the paper which was wrapped in a sealed packaging to protect it from heat and dust. He was just about to tear open the packing, when the letterbox in the partitioned office rattled. A hand appeared, dropped an outgoing message into the tray, but the hand wasn't withdrawn. Instead it held open the flap and a voice shouted a single word: 'erselha'-urgent!

The captain motioned the signalman to take the necessary action and pushed him on his way whilst at the same time grabbing the package from his hand. Thinking perhaps that the repair was complete, the captain set about removing the protective cover from the paper roll. It was Samir's last chance. The cover was tougher than the captain had expected and he had to concentrate.

Samir took the opportunity. As he busied himself in the bowels of the fax machine, his left hand moved unseen to the security housing. The screwdriver in his right hand made a quick dart to the screw head and a quick twist was all that was needed to release its pressure. The technician's touch in the fingers of his left hand gripped the screw and, thanks be to God, it moved. A quick, hidden spin between the finger ends and Samir could tell that it was free. But now the captain had wrestled the paper from its protection and was waiting for Samir to close the outer cover. He still needed about a minute and he had the last cover screw in his hand. Samir tried to hide the tension, but the sweat that was breaking out on his brow did its best to betray him. Explaining that he was not feeling so good after a sleepless night, he raised his right hand, screwdriver still in its grasp, to draw the back of his hand across his forehead. His left hand, hovering above the open machine and still holding the last screw, let it drop – he cursed quietly – but audibly, as it fell, bounced and vanished through the ventilation slots cut into the base of the fax.

The captain, on seeing this, put the paper roll down and in only his second supportive action of the day, lifted the C2000 at one side so that Samir could peer underneath and retrieve the errant screw.

Magic! Samir couldn't believe his luck. As the officer lifted the fax, the security housing swung slowly open and they both heard the click of the micro-switch releasing all one hundred secret keys. The captain's explosive curse next to Samir's ear caught him by surprise and the two signalmen spun round to check the alarm.

Samir's eyes met the captain's. The latter apologised profusely thinking the key destruction to be the result of his own clumsiness. Seeing the retrieved screw in Samir's hand, he lowered the fax carefully back to the bench.

He was speechless, but after the long agonizing silence, Samir shrugged his shoulders and spluttered: 'It must have been loose all the time.'

The captain stared down at the machine in disbelief. Painfully, the flashing red LED on its front panel proclaimed the bad news. The key memory was empty. The cipher machine was unusable without them. Samir fixed the loose housing as the captain gathered himself together. Shaking his head in despair, he moved to the telephone and dialled the commander's desk. As the call went through, the Lighthouse man deftly replaced the C2000 outer cover and opened up the keypad with the default security password that all machines had, for such circumstances. In the background he could hear the officer being heavily chastised in the most vociferous manner. The captain responded in silence before replacing the handset and stood glumly awaiting the click of the iron door that would announce one irate colonel with the keys to the safe.

Samir busied himself with installing the paper roll back into its receptacle. The key board would remain unlocked for just another minute or so, but the officer was looking his way and, still believing the key clearance to be his own blunder, apologised once more. The signalmen smirked unsympathetically. Samir felt a moment of compassion. The keys would have been deleted anyway, even if the officer had not intervened, but it was not Samir who had lost them. The result appeared not at all contrived. Here, this man had carried out his duty, diligently as none had done before, yet not by his own fault, had given Samir and the Brothers of Islam access to the navy's most sensitive fax signals for some time to come.

A muffled noise from outside preceded the colonel's arrival. There was nothing muffled about the retributions that filled the bunker as the senior officer blasted the subdued captain. Whilst this was going on, Samir took advantage of the undivided attention that the navy men were giving to their commander, by stepping through the menu with the down cursor, to the *Key Entry* level. The colonel passed the metal key of the safe to the captain who inserted it into the lock and turned it to release the safe's dial mechanism. Then in a sublime moment, as Samir saw the captain stiffen as the colonel *read out aloud* the sequence of settings for the combination lock. Samir was so shocked that he almost forgot his own task, but he recovered with just enough time to enter the thirty two digits, all ones that constituted the hidden default key. After he had hit the enter button, the signature 5E2 was displayed for a moment, and then it would lie hidden, dormant for his later use, under the hundred secret keys that had just been retrieved from the signal office safe.

✳✳✳

Samir drove sedately towards the gate. The flagship was indeed about to cast off. It would soon be out in the Gulf, receiving commands on ciphered fax messages that only its commander and Samir could read. He should have felt elated, but the mental exhaustion of his efforts over the last thirty six hours allowed him only a tired lift of the hand as the guards waved him past. 'Shukran habibi,' – thank you my friends. 'Thanks be to God.'

✳✳✳

It was when the massif of Mont Blanc was slipping by forty thousand feet below, that the heavy drinking session back at Charles de Gaulle began to trouble his bladder. Before that, he had not needed to locate the bathroom, having been totally occupied in controlling his blood pressure, temper and body posture after the tornado take off. Hakim, on seeing the shirt change from a light pastel blue to something much darker, had supplied him with numerous cooling towels to help his charge control the profuse sweating. It was getting to the state where Bonetti was having trouble sitting with himself. Even the cabin boy, dressed immaculately in white and beige, was noticeably staying as far away as possible from the Italian. For Hakim, the length of the Lear was just not long enough. If he could have opened a window to let in fresh air, he would have done it. Bonetti took the hint. If even a bloody Packy found his body odour objectionable, then he really must stink like shit. 'God damn!' he blasted.

The son from Chianti country blushed once more as the claustrophobia started to kick in again, and the body temperature rose proportional to his discomfort. With this in mind and the distended bladder giving more aggravation, Bonetti looked around for the toilet. There were only two doors in the cabin, one went through to the cockpit and the other, had he been able to open it, would have quickly deposited him close to his birth place, on the hills of San Gimignano. Turin would have been all his.

'How long is the flight?' Bonetti shouted to Hakim.

'About five hours!' came back the reply.

Bonetti looked behind him, just to make sure that he hadn't missed another door. He hadn't. 'Does that mean I can't have a bloody sheet or pees for another four bloody hours?'

'No sir,' replied the cabin boy, looking at his watch. '...... We have to refuel in Cyprus.'

'And how long does this over rated sports car take to get to Cyprus?' The eyes were bulging, demanding an answer.

Hakim suppressed the laugh, forcing himself to put on a stern face. Enjoying the moment, he lingered just to see the Italian squirm a *leetle beet* longer, before replying 'That would be three – three hours sir!'

Bonetti exploded! – struggled to his feet and set off for the cockpit door. Whether it was intentional or not, he couldn't be sure, for he couldn't see how the pilot could have known that he was heading for the cockpit. Yet his approach just happened to coincide with the Lear starting a climb to the next height. As the aircraft nose went up, Bonetti went backwards. Hakim turned away and from his tiny fold-down canvas seat, gazed in feigned oblivion down on the Golfo di Genova.

Bonetti, once he'd restored balance and confidence in the fact that the Lear was not going to leap around again, strode purposefully to the front and ripped open the cockpit door. 'Leesten here meester Top Gun! – Get this plane on the bloody ground now! er...' The wind was taken from his sails by two brown faces simultaneously turning to greet him with the broadest of smiles, each revealing two rows of perfectly white teeth. The captain took off his headset. The head of jet black hair wobbled slightly: 'and what can we be doing for you, my good sir?'

For God's sake, Bonetti thought to himself. I'm surrounded by a plane full of gay, bloody Packys. 'You have to land. I need a pees!'

The head wobbled again. 'Oh no Sir, we cannot be doing that. It is not on our flight plan.'

'Well it's certainly on *my* bloody flight plan!' 'If you don't put this God forsaken plane down then I'll open the door and pees in the damned Mediterranean.'

'Oh no Siree, there is no need for this.'

The smile was still there. Perhaps it's painted on, thought Bonetti and the head wobbled again. Bonetti couldn't be sure if it was a wobble in the negative or if it preceded something positive.

'What I am meaning to say my good Sir, is that we carry suitable equipment for our good Sir's condition.' The toothy smile and head wobbling hinted at a solution to the passenger's disquiet.

Bonetti was half expecting a length of rubber hose to be pulled out of the hat. But the pilot continued, shouting beyond the big frame that was blocking the door – 'Hakeem! Please show our good Sir how to use the commode!' and waved his right hand in a limp, but graceful gesture to indicate that Bonetti should retire back to the main cabin.

Hakim stood, ushered Bonetti back from the cockpit and then bent down to a seat that opposed the main cabin door. He removed the seat cushion and pulled a lever that lifted the whole arrangement to the standard toilet sit up position. 'If Sir would be in need of accessories ...' He opened a sliding door to the side that revealed a roll of paper, wad of paper towels and a bottle of water '... for washing, sir!' he added, seeing Bonetti's puzzled look.

Bonetti was close to death anyway but he could see that even if he was a normally proportioned human being, it would have to be a contortionist show to perform without a major mishap. For one of Bonetti's bulk, it was going to be a Herculean effort. He weighed up the strategy that would suit him best, and then turned to look at the cabin boy and then at his fold down seat.

Hakim read his thoughts: 'And there is a curtain for Sir's privacy.' He reached up and drew the plastic curtain across the full width of the cabin and retired to the other side, leaving the good Sir to his own devices.

Bonetti prepared, but in a final gesture of protest, turned to bang on the cockpit door to announce that if Meester Top Gun didn't keep the bloody plane steady for the next ten minutes, he'd fill his toy-boy cockpit with recycled Chianti.

CHAPTER 10

The Red Message

Twenty two thousand, five hundred miles above the Indian Ocean, Mercury was listening.

*****

Samir's first fax that day was not ciphered. It came from Toronto, to announce Bonetti's intended arrival in Dubai. Samir had been expecting the confirmation and had already made provision for the Lighthouse limousine to pick him up on arrival. He had already been informed by Sheikh Hamed, that Bonetti had been invited to fly back with the Lear Jet which was due to come back to Dubai from Paris anyway. Typical of Bonetti to be in the right place at the right time, thought Samir. The man was always exploiting his contacts for personal gain. With disgust, he could imagine the self important Italian boosting his already inflated ego, by rubbing shoulders with royalty as he took another step toward his goals of riches and power.

It had seemed a generous gesture by the Sheikh, but in truth the Sheikh needed the CIPERCAN director to oversee his project of securing the communications for the coming DUBEXAIR exhibition. As the local sponsor of the Canadian organisation in the UAE, there were exciting financial possibilities ahead. CIPHERCAN had emerged as a major player in the field of secure communications, and whilst their main marketing target had previously been with military organisations, Bonetti was eager to exploit any niche that was there to be exploited. Sheikh Hamed did not particularly like

Bonetti as a person, but he kept his reservations to himself. What he did like was the man's dynamism, commercial aggression, experience in dealing with the military and his role as a brain-stormer. Now under the Sheikh's own umbrella company, Lighthouse, they made strange bedfellows, but as long as the security of the Emirates and Lighthouse could benefit from the arrangement, then he had to accept the situation. He could not, with any conviction, refer to it as a partnership, but whilst the business goals were being met, Bonetti's antics and opinions could be tolerated. The mitigation was that Bonetti's sole ambition in life was to make money and as long as that remained his singular motivation, then he was a dog with a loud bark, but little bite. There was however another factor in his favour. The man was a constant source of entertainment. You could love him or hate him, but you could not ignore him. The Sheikh had no doubts whatsoever that should the Italian overstep the line, he would be out in a flash. The big players in this southern gulf state didn't suffer fools gladly.

Bonetti was on his way. His office and projects awaited him. The new project was the import of the latest ciphered fax machine from CIPHERCAN, the C2000. The Canadians had marketed this as the first player in the new generation of fax machines, and Bonetti, with his usual effervescent enthusiasm had promoted it successfully in the face of much competition, and it had to be said, in the face of some criticism. Competitors had offered more sophisticated solutions, mirroring the headlong race into the IT communications that had gained momentum over the last decade. They had pooh-poohed the CIPHERCAN proposal as old fashioned, even pedantic. But they had over played the advanced technology card, and in doing so, frightened the life out of the system integrators and security administrators. Bonetti had done his homework well. He knew that the DUBEXAIR organisation did not have the technically experienced personnel to implement the security of high tech hardware. The difficulties were compounded by the facts that time was short, due to the communications security only being considered as an after thought, and also that it had become clear that the intended network spread far and wide across the world. Bonetti's *simple as possible* solution had thus won the day, and he had topped it off with the announcement that CIPHERCAN had implemented the successor to the BASE encryption algorithm, in the C2000. For Bonetti and CIPHERCAN, it was the second step into the Middle East market and an opportunity to explore the commercial niche.

Having a local sponsor was a crucial factor in gaining this foothold and Sheikh Hamed had all the contacts that a foreign company could wish for. The fact that he was also heavily involved in promoting Dubai as an international exhibition centre par excellence, and hence his interest in the autumn's DUBEXAIR, was also useful. The Sheikh knew everybody who was important to know. He also had a great deal to gain from Lighthouse's success in this project, and a great deal more to lose if it wasn't a success.

✳✳✳

Samir's second fax that morning stopped him in his tracks. It was ciphered and it came from the Naval HQ. It was not the first ciphered message from the navy, since he'd introduced his own key into their hidden key memory. It was, however the most important. It had been transmitted by HF radio – to all the Emirati ships and remote ground stations, not to mention of course the Lighthouse workshop. Samir read it three times before its contents really began to sink in. The navy was expecting a visitor. He'd seen coalition ships in the port before. It was a regular stop-over place for ships either on their way to patrol the waters at the head of the Gulf, or on their way home after their tour of duty. But the largest ship that he'd seen in Jebel Ali had just been the regular troop transports and marine assault craft – plenty of smaller stuff, like mine-hunters, patrol boats and destroyers. Now the Americans were deploying yet a third carrier group to The Gulf! Tehran would be incensed. Samir made a mental note of the details and shredded the fax.

✳✳✳

172

That morning things were different. Samir didn't like the changes. He'd got used to the peace and the freedom that he'd enjoyed over the last two months, but as soon as he entered the lift, the stench of cigarettes had announced that Bonetti was back. Samir's mood deepened at the thought: the noise, the papers strewn everywhere, the bad language, bawdy jokes and the never ending ring of telephones. Bonetti didn't need a telephone. When he was on the phone, the whole building was party to the call. Bonetti would bellow and curse at some poor listener hanging onto the other end of the line. Anybody in earshot got the full force of the blast. Even when his latest tart called to see if he wanted her for that night Bonetti would embarrass everyone on the floor with the lurid details of either what special bedroom adventure was expected, or be informed by the crude report on last night's romp.

As soon as Samir stepped onto the fifteenth floor he could smell the coffee and, if all the other signs could be ignored, then the constant flow of espressos to Bonetti's office could not. The coffee he didn't mind, but the cigarettes he did, and even if Bonetti wasn't smoking when he came in to see Samir, he could still smell it on his clothes and on his breath. Fortunately the Italian's sojourns into the workshop were rare. This was not Bonetti's domain. He was a business man not a mere techie, as he would always be happy to point out.

The one positive thing about having Bonetti back was that he'd be sitting at his desk bashing the keyboard with two fingers, rattling out Emails to his customers, colleagues and the few friends that he had. This was good compensation for all the discomforts that Bonetti brought with him because with Bonetti came information. It wouldn't be long before Samir's video monitor, with its signal generator, amplifier and antenna were looking over the Italian's shoulder. From now on Bonetti's news was Samir's news.

It was a pretty crude and simple affair and constructed with hardware that could be found in any electronics workshop. There was no need to hide any gear, nor any need to justify its presence even if Bonetti could recognise an electronic eaves dropping kit if he should fall over one. But others might, and the evidence of some

planted bug would immediately point the finger at the prime suspect:
– him?

A single brick thickness of wall separated the two offices, but there was no direct access between Samir's territory and Bonetti's office, except, that is, for the air-conditioning ducts that traversed the whole floor above the under-slung ceiling. It was here that Samir had found the opportunity to run a cable up through the ceiling tiles and then along the inside of the air duct to the ventilation grill in Bonetti's office. The location of the grill was critical and although Samir could receive a signal from Bonetti's computer screen via the first grill, it was of such poor quality that he could rarely read it. It was also unstable that his monitor screen would roll, just like the old cine films did when the film speed and shutter were not synchronised. He'd had to be patient, but this was one of Samir's greatest virtues. Bonetti did work hard, he had to grant him that quality, and for weeks after his arrival, the man never seemed to leave his office. But at last, when its occupier had been back in Canada, Samir had struck. In less than five minutes of access time, he'd removed his shoes, skipped up on a meeting table and loosened a screw that helped fix the grill to the ducting. The back of that screw had connected the wire carrying the tell tale signals back to Samir's workshop. He had then gone back to his own office and removed his own grill so that he could pull the loose wire back in his direction, until the loose end fell onto a second grill of Bonetti's ceiling. Samir went back into the other office, stood gingerly on Bonetti's desk and on seeing the cable end lying on tip of the grill, loosened one corner and fished the cable down. He made a quick loop of the bare conductor around the corner screw and then fastened it in place. It was invisible from the floor and when he was satisfied that his operation had not left any trace, Samir went to complete the alterations in his own den. That was all he could do until Bonetti came back and switched on.

***

He hadn't had to wait long for the opportunity to test his spy net. It was the first time that he'd actually been struck by that word. He never seriously considered himself as a spy. It was just a simple technological interest, a challenge, just to see if he could do it. To invade somebody's secret thoughts. Initially he had not even considered using the information. But when he casually mentioned the experiments to Faisal, the Egyptian had taken it up enthusiastically. Then slowly, over a number of weeks, he had awakened in Samir the idea that he would be doing a great service to Islam if he were able to pass on any information that could support his religious brethren. The bait had been cast and Samir had been hooked and reeled into the cause. Samir would never admit to himself that he had been totally indoctrinated, but the satisfaction and at times – elation were exciting. Professional pride also played no small role in the decision and when he started to access some of Bonetti's data, these gems drew him deeper and deeper into the tradecraft. Faisal had told him that this was Allah's purpose for him. If he was doing God's work, then what better purpose could his life have? There were other elements that lent argument to Samir's recruitment into a deeper clandestine role. The invasion of Iraq by the so-called coalition was foremost. Everyday, on every newscast of every TV or radio channel, he saw the American and Jewish infidels destroying the lives of everyday people like himself. And he had seen, thankful that they were safely at home in Amman – his own family's image, in the blood soaked, broken bodies of countless children and helpless women, torn apart by the invaders from the West. So it went on and on, all based on the fabrications of the despotic American presidency. Conversely, Samir abhorred the Hollywood show that certain Islamic groups broadcast to the world. No real Muslim could ever condone the butchery of kidnapped individuals, especially civilians. His father had bred into him that all people were God's people, whatever their religion, race or colour. Tolerance was what was widely proclaimed in the Koran. The knowledge that his own subterfuge was not focussed on civilians or innocents, but on the military and particularly the American forces, was of great comfort to him. Faisal, it had to be said, was more radical, but apart from that they shared many common sympathies.

175

Payments were also of some influence, although he certainly considered them as a minor one, not motivating him in the slightest. They did not in any way represent a reward. The money he received went a long way to fund the education of his children and open up their prospects in the future. Samir was totally satisfied that this was a noble cause. Finally, if he had any remaining doubts at all about justification, his intense loathing of Bonetti and all he represented, left him with no uncertainty that the Faisal's path was a moral one. In the end it had been an easy decision.

✳✳✳

Predictably the first task of Bonetti's morning routine was to bellow at the office boy about his coffee. Bonetti himself admitted that it wasn't until the second espresso and the third cigarette that he felt that he could function at even a basic level. Once the Italian had drowned his tremors in coffee and surrounded himself in a fog of cigarette smoke – Samir thought him like a reptile, needing the warm sun on its back before it could move, then Bonetti was in full flight.

The second task was to log on to the internet and download mail replies to the commands that he'd sent the previous evening.

Samir had been waiting with suppressed excitement for that very moment. He'd not been able to sleep for several nights anticipating his coup. And he was not disappointed. As cover, he had many pieces of test gear running at any time, but of pertinent interest on this morning, was the video monitor, its amplifiers, signal generators and, in the next room, the key component – the grill. It was this metallic matrix functioning as an antenna, the collector of the signals inadvertently emitted from Bonetti's pc screen, that was crucial component in the exercise. At first, his monitor had just registered white noise, electronic noise that would have produced a hiss in any speaker or earphone, had they been connected. On the video screen, the picture was one of chaos and randomness as individual pixels were excited by the loose electron gun. But as Samir played with the

176

amplifiers, filtering out the noise, a discernable picture started to emerge. He was intent and breathing shallow, as if he feared it would further disturb the captured signal – A touch here on this dial, a slow rotation of the next to increase the gain – It was there! – Samir could see the computer desktop that was staring, at that very moment, into the bloodshot eyes next door. It flickered and rolled and broke up into the random pattern again. Samir's calm hand hovered from dial to dial, to tease carefully out the stable picture. At last, the final adjustment of the signal generator that controlled the monitor's video time-base was synchronised with the screen's horizontal scan, and the picture came to a halt. Samir had been expecting some signal, but the quality was better than he had dared to hope. By normal TV standards it was lousy, but he could read every word and recognise every icon that appeared simultaneously in front of Bonetti. Even the Italian's mouse was identifiable, albeit grainy, as it moved to select an application. Samir was in business.

It was a release, a relief, not unlike a physical emotion, almost sexual, giving the same sort of satisfaction. Samir felt elated and powerful. In possession of sensitive data from Bonetti's computer and the navy net, he could really have an impact on world events. He didn't need a gun, he didn't need a bomb, he had something far more powerful. He had access to information.

***

Most of Bonetti's mails were general run-of-the-mill business exchanges with reports, prices and proposals, intermingled with junk that he deleted without bothering to open. There were a number of personal mails, notes from his brother and some other friend that were encrypted as far as Samir was concerned, because they were written in Italian. After a day off, there were some twenty mails to be checked and Bonetti waded through them. Some were simply read and then binned, some were read and stored and others warranted either a response which Bonetti bashed out in the usual two fingered manner, or were forwarded. Samir wondered if the man ever used more than two fingers in any aspect of his life. He smiled at the thought and at *his* own capture of English humour.

There was one last mail that remained but Bonetti had either missed it or was intending to go back to it. For some reason, he suddenly went to his favourites web page, that of the Il Tempo newspaper. Ah yes, thought Samir as he saw the list of the Italian football results. Then Bonetti went to the Juventus page, no doubt to find some explanation of their surprising defeat in the previous night's game.

But he hadn't overlooked it. He was saving it to the last – for his undivided attention. Samir peered closer, eager to see the contents. It was from CIPHERCAN, judging by the source address, and when Bonetti double clicked the mouse, the note wasn't opened as Samir had expected to see. Instead, another window flashed open, demanding a response to the Yes or No virtual buttons. The rest of the text was very grainy and difficult to make out, partly because the grill receptor didn't pick out the red coloured wording. He needn't have fretted, as the response to Yes was a more boldly written statement: – Decryption Started! Samir's attention was immediately grabbed. Progress of the decryption was painfully slow, and Samir was beginning to wonder if it had locked and would fail to open the secret data that it presumably contained. Judging by the passage of time it must be a large document, or contain pictures. Momentarily, he speculated that it might be more porn shots that Bonetti received from time to time. It would have been exciting for Bonetti, but certainly not for Samir. But no, it wasn't porn. The document suddenly burst open and he could see a detailed letter, with large blocks of text interspersed with rows of mathematical formula. After a few minutes, he heard a stream of crude expletives from the other side of the wall. It just served to heighten Samir's interest, but the document was difficult to read, and there was so much of it. Neither did the lines of calculations mean anything to him. He prayed for some method of storing the message but he wasn't using a computer, just a monitor. He didn't even have a camera on hand with which to capture a few screen shots, so all he could do was to scan through the document quickly and get the gist of what it had to tell Bonetti. Fortunately, Bonetti was also taking some time to digest the news, and Samir had time to read most of each screen as the Italian scrolled through the individual pages.

The first two pages were on the subject of software updates for the C2000 fax and a list of the functions that would be modified. Samir was just quickly catching the general information. He might be getting the full detail later, from Bonetti himself, because he was certain that it would be his task to carry out any instructions relayed in the message. But then, two thirds of the way down, his heart stopped. They'd found the key memory fault! He tried to read on, but the picture rolled as synchronisation of the picture scan was temporarily lost. Samir was desperate to get it back before Bonetti scanned further down the page. His fingers flew frantically from dial to dial. Resisting the onset of panic and the loss of the whole session, he forced himself to take his time. This eaves dropping set-up was as crude as they come and inherently prone to disturbances and interference. He had to draw the display back with the sensitivity of a surgeon performing a delicate procedure. In the back of his mind, he was already thinking of how he could possibly overcome, or disable the software correction that CIPHERCAN were bound to implement. It came back – Bonetti was still there – Just a few seconds, please, Insha'allaah.

He had it, but couldn't believe it. They'd found the memory problem in the Canadian laboratories, but had decided that it was most unlikely that any customer would discover it. Ha! little did they know! And as it was an expensive task to eliminate it, the research and development department was recommending that no action be taken! No wonder Bonetti had erupted. If that became well known, then he was in for a great deal of aggravation from his customers. Should it be discovered, then it would probably mean a mass recall of already distributed machines and all that entailed. On top of that, there would be a catastrophic loss of confidence in the company, which in the worst might even cause it to fold. Confidence and trust were paramount qualities in the communications security business. However on the other side of the wall, Samir was delighted, his little game was still in play.

Such was his relief that he missed the next couple of pages as his concentration lapsed. When he next looked at the screen, Bonetti had moved on. Samir quickly scanned the whole page that was now displayed to at least get the general idea, if not the details. It was largely mathematical and beyond Samir. But he stuck with it and understood that it was discussing algorithms. NAMES was mentioned and that meant something to him. He recollected from his readings that it superseded the earlier BASE algorithm. Ok, so the new machines, the C2000s, for the DUBEXAIR project were equipped with the latest, i.e. NAMES. He was expecting that, and from the first part of the mail, he had already become resigned to the fact that the memory problem would have been removed. There was no mention of it here, or at least he didn't see any, because Bonetti scrolled down to the next page before Samir had had chance to read it.

There again were some lines of mathematics and a report. It had been written some time ago as the date of the original mail, and the identity of its author were still attached. The date was too grainy to make out except that Samir saw that it was from earlier in the year. It was written by a man he had never met, but often heard of. He had read at length, of the sudden death of Doctor Peter Goodwin in the technical journals scattered about the office. He looked on. After a page of complex formula that even Samir recognised as relating to probabilities, there was a summary. Once again his eyes scanned quickly down the page in case Bonetti moved to the next page. But he didn't. It was the last page and the Italian left the screen as it was. Samir had time to read it twice without it being removed. The way it was written made it difficult to digest but it was certainly written in anger. Goodwin was obviously not a happy man when he wrote it. Samir understood that, but the reason for the fury was not so easy to discern. There was silence from next door. Bonetti was not moving around, nor was he on the telephone, so he must still be at his desk. Still studying the final page. Samir would have given a lot to be able to see what was registering on his face.

He read again. It looked as though Goodwin had *proven* that SQUIRREL was a more secure algorithm than NAMES, and he was planning to reveal it at the COMSEC conference. Now it struck him! Of course Bonetti had been there during his last trip to Canada. He must have known about this before. He must have been at Goodwin's lecture. But this was further bad news for CIPHERCAN. If what Goodwin had revealed here was true, then the new machines were carrying a flawed algorithm. And if their machines were carrying a flawed algorithm, then *all* the cipher machines that were exported from the North American continent – Samir's mind raced as it dawned on him – were inflicted with the same fault. But why, if Goodwin had revealed this at COMSEC, were CIPHERCAN and Bonetti in particular, still selling the C2000 if it was known to be compromised? This, after all, was the vanguard for their new generation of machines. Even more interesting was the question: why was anybody buying it? He'd read that NAMES was the successor of BASE, that the latter was the subject of much speculation. It was old and it was reputedly weak. That was the generally accepted opinion. So what did that mean for NAMES? In a strange way, Samir felt regret about seeing the message. Not the fact that he'd been able to look over Bonetti's shoulder, but that before the message, it had all seemed quite straight forward. Now, having read it, he was confused.

Samir turned off the monitor. He didn't want anyone, especially Bonetti, coming in unannounced and seeing what he was up to.

***

Samir was beside himself with delight. The impact of his discovery was still being digested and he was pacing around his workshop like a caged lion. He wanted to tell the world, and if he did, it would certainly bring down Bonetti and thus give him personally, great satisfaction. But of course, he recognised that the real value of what he knew was precisely what the rest of the world didn't know. If the NAMES problem became public knowledge, then it would have no value to The Brothers,

181

whereas if he kept it quiet, they might have the opportunity to exploit it – to gain access to half the world's communications. NAMES was a universal algorithm being implemented in software and hardware alike. It was rapidly being installed in voice encryption, data encryption, fax communications and computer security. His estimate of fifty percent of the world's communications using the algorithm was not far wrong, as indeed it had been accepted as the industry standard, and was already an off-the-shelf product. Of course there were other companies marketing private or proprietary algorithms but CIPHERCAN was not one of those. As far as Samir was aware, there were only four people who knew about the NAMES problem: Himself, whoever had forwarded the report, Bonetti, and the genius who had discovered it, Doctor Goodwin. Goodwin – Goodwin, but Goodwin was dead. What a man! What a mind! Since Samir had read of his death in a company newsletter, he had so wished that he had had the chance to meet him. To discover how he thought, and how he reasoned, what his feelings were about religion? A real thinking man, like himself, he pondered briefly before his modesty put things more into perspective. Now, he felt powerful! The power of secrets! It was amazing, an extraordinary feeling. He felt like a child capturing his first frog from the garden pond and like a child, he wanted to share it with everyone, to tell them what he'd found. So exciting! But then he knew that once it was shared, this feeling of knowing, knowing everything, would be lost and every child would be able to capture a frog from the pool. Quite a conundrum, he smiled. A secret is only secret when it is not known. Anyone who says he has secrets doesn't have any secret at all. Yet, mused Samir, what is the point of knowing a secret if it cannot be used? Without acting on that knowledge it is of no benefit to anyone. Apart from, of course, the one who holds it and selfishly keeps it just for his own satisfaction. Just like life, he thought, only valuable for a fleeting moment in time, when it is in the hand and then slowly, but inevitably losing it, like sand slipping through the fingers. For the moment however, Samir enjoyed the treasure that was in his hands, knowing full well that in time his secret too would slip through his fingers.

Sipping his tea from the cup in one hand and with the prayer beads of celebration in the other, Samir gazed out of his window across the sweltering city. The Creek was just a misty haze. It was often difficult to realise what the weather was like outside when he was cocooned in the luxury of air-conditioning. Yet he only had to touch the window glass with the back of his hand to feel the scorching heat. Not as warm now as it was over the last three months. September was still hot, around forty at midday and still humid when the sun went down, but the winter knocking on the door would be welcomed by all. Thanks be to God, he murmured.

Three people now in the know, but it would have to be four. Samir realised that he would have to let it go. Others could use it far more effectively than he alone. Faisal would be delighted, he was Samir's sole connection with The Brothers and letting the euphoria of the moment get the better of him, he decided to tell him right away. He just had to share the news. He picked up his mobile and dialled Faisal's number. It was switched off, or out of contact range, came the system supplier's response. Samir smiled as he punched in the text message: *Have a gem in my hands. Thanks be to Goodwin – Sami.* Again the English twist of humour made him chuckle.

✳✳✳

Once the elation had ebbed a little, some of the consequences of what he had discovered began to trouble him, and the more he thought about it, the more he began to realise that holding secrets was not wholly fulfilling. There were also some disturbing elements. After all, he was the latest in the line in knowing about the NAMES dilemma, and, of the three, one was dead – Murdered! The other was Bonetti! It was for a blind man not to see a possible motive behind Goodwin's murder. Unless he was very much mistaken, CIPHERCAN, and therefore Bonetti, would have lost everything should Goodwin have fulfilled his promise to go public in Toronto. But it was also obvious that it was only with the knowledge of what Goodwin was intending to reveal, that suspicions could be cast on

183

the Canadians and their director. Otherwise it was not so clear cut. In addition to the financial catastrophe that the Canadian company would have suffered had Goodwin still been alive there was one other organisation that would have profited enormously from Goodwin's silence. Samir sneered with hatred as *NSA* crossed his lips. The Americans! The National Security Agency. How surprising – the world's self appointed policeman!

***

Cameron had been expecting it, and now it had arrived, it had brought with it a complex of emotions that ranged through pride, honour and nervous apprehension. It had been inevitable, but he wished that it had not come and that he could be allowed to just get on with his everyday life and not be thrust back into the limelight. He had been there before, and whilst many in his shoes craved for the fame and fortune of a successful sportsman, Cameron Cameron was a very reluctant hero. He played golf because he loved to play golf. He loved the environment in which it was played and he loved the people who played it. There was just one draw back – he hated competition. Competition brought another dimension, an unwanted one as far as he was concerned. Stress! How unfortunate that the one thing that he was really successful at brought along so much excess baggage, namely the media, sponsors, crowds, exhausting travel and separation from his lovely home and the two women in his life. Three if he had to count the old battleaxe.

His mother had been dead for a few years now, but she had left her mark on him a long time ago. Domination had been the name of her game and when he heard that the British navy had a warship sailing under the name of HMS Battleaxe, Cameron thought that it must have been named after his mother. God bless her soul! God bless all who sailed in her! Anyone close to his mother needed God's blessing. If only she had been born a few generations earlier – in the time of Bonnie Prince Charlie – The Duke of Cumberland's army would have been routed at Culloden, and highland history would have been a whole different story. If only the Scottish red haired dreadnought going by the name of Annie Cameron had led the clans.

Anyway she hadn't been there – and as it transpired, her best gift to the Scottish people had been something far less dramatic than beating the English just up the A7, on the infamous hillside battlefield: her son. Cameron Cameron, Scotland's best, and it's most reluctant golfing hero of modern time. That his mother's overbearing personality had conditioned him to become more or less a recluse, was, for the tartan hordes, most unfortunate. The Scots' inferiority complex was carried eternally, in their genes. The nation always craved for a star and success. Something – anything – anybody! that would give them an excuse to explode into wild celebrations. In Cameron's memory, such outpourings of patriotic joy had been few and far between. So rare, he mused, that the recent tendency had been for the Scots to celebrate before the big game, just in case there was little to celebrate after it. Ha! Therein lay the problem, he smiled.

Cameron had given his supporters occasional cause to cheer. He'd represented Scotland as an individual and as a team player when it was required. It *had been* required that he represent Europe in what was regarded by many as the ultimate honour and the ultimate challenge, The Ryder Cup. It was also the ultimate stress! – And hence the source of his worst nightmare.

***

That he hated the attentions of the media was well known, but for all that dislike it had ironically given him his greatest joy and his greatest supporter: Brigitte Blondaux Cameron. She hated the acronym BBC but tolerated it when her husband was in one of his teasing moods. It was worth it just to see the wicked smile on his face. Of all professions for her to hold, she was a journalist!

God, not another one of them, he had silently whispered to himself when he found out. In those first moments, she had not made it known and although he professed to be able to smell them

185

from several miles away, on this occasion he hadn't. Heavily disguised by the Channel, he later declared. She didn't hold a microphone and she wasn't carrying a note pad, and she didn't appear to have a tape recorder in her bag, nor was she accompanied with a man carrying an iron parrot with a cohort in tow carrying a stuffed cat on a stick. For once, the TV crews had left him alone at a corner of the beer tent to descend on some other poor unfortunate carrying a big trophy. She hadn't approached him, but just appeared when the others had drifted outside. Being left alone with a woman usually brought a tremble to his knees with immediate paralysis of vocal chords. Under similar circumstances he would have welcomed the timely interruption of some autograph hunter, or a waiter bearing a tray full of canapés, but none were around. To have excused himself for a faked need to visit the gents would have been too obvious and even insulting. Play the course, he remembered, not the man. Man she was certainly not. Pretty she was – most certainly. Big, dark brown eyes peered from beneath the fringe of natural blonde hair that hung heavily on each shoulder and across her generous breasts. Enormous looped earrings, pert nose, and a long loose dress gave a suggestion of gipsy, as did her tan. The tan must have been tropical because that sort of tan did not come locally. Ireland had never professed to be a sun-bleached land and true to form, the greens of Kilkenny had been well watered over the whole competition. It was the dusky complexion and the plunging neckline that threw his stuttering conversation a lifeline. Play the course!

'Now where in the world did you pick up a sun tan like that?' he had enquired, doing his best not to let his eyes drift to the south. That she was French became immediately apparent from the heavy accent. When she had told him it was the result of living on the French Riviera, he groaned, wishing that The Irish Open could have been held under the Mediterranean sun rather than under the ubiquitous Guinness umbrellas that seemed to be an essential part of the scene whenever he was there. She'd flashed a row of white teeth an instant before she had had the time to hide the laugh behind a long fingered hand. The ice was broken, and when he conveniently recollected that he had once enjoyed strolling and dining on the tree sheltered avenues of Aix en Provence, her eyes gave more delight. It was indeed her hometown. Not in fact, as she had initially generalised, on the Cote d'Azur. The relationship was sealed with drinks and then dinner at the hotel. She was impressed by his reserved humour and later confided that he had a sinful glint in his eye. Cameron could not politely explain where the eye glint came from, but that it persisted throughout their marriage, told its own story.

It was only later that she revealed the dark side of her life – she, with great remorse announced that she was a journalist! 'Quelle horreur!' he had blurted in his worst possible Scottish/French accent. Thereafter he became a self confessed Francophile and immediately forgave all journalists of all their inherent shortcomings, well female ones that is – and then after some consideration thought that he had gone a little too far, so further qualified the statement by declaring that the pardon only applied to French ones.

✳✳✳

So it had been Brigitte who had borne the invitation through from a series of enquiring telephone calls from his agent. He'd been sitting at his desk in the pro's office wading through the day's post and handicap certificates, when the sight of the red MGB pulling into the car park caught his attention. She'd had the hood down and despite the head scarf; her long hair was all over the place. It didn't matter; she looked elegant and stunning no matter what the occasion, a wedding, a dinner, or simply tearing weeds from the garden. Madame was just at home in shorts, jeans, swimsuit, or evening gown with stilettos. She often called by for a coffee when business at the shop was not heavy. Not that she ever needed an excuse to share some new idea or merely to bring the post. On this occasion she walked past the practice green with a sense of purpose, an envelope clutched firmly in hand. It always seemed that the scent of her perfume arrived before she did, as if to announce the approach of her ladyship. In any case he was up, with arms held to greet her to be followed with a peck on both cheeks as if they had not met for weeks, rather than shared breakfast a couple of hours ago.

They both knew the contents of the envelope and both had mixed emotions about the invitation. She was excited, a chance to travel, sunshine, fine restaurants, shopping and the likelihood of meeting some interesting people. She loved the summer life in Aviemore, but she had to escape the cruel winters and here was a good opportunity to do just that. But! She knew the stress that another high-profile competition would bring to her husband, even more so after the debacle at The Country Club, Brookland, Mass. in 1999. He was good, and like the best, a natural. Seemingly excelling with little effort and modest to the third degree about any success that came his way. Success did come his way, quite often too. Yet for himself, he didn't need to win. Cameron's reward was in just being there. Every time he walked out onto a golf course, he offered his thanks to God and blessed his good luck in having the freedom to be there in such beautiful surroundings and earning his living doing something that he could never call his job. That was his complete ambition. Nothing less, nothing more, and something that he could live with very nicely for the rest of his days – thank you very much.

The problem with being good was that the rest of the world wanted a piece of it. Cameron was most happy, playing with his friends and sharing their despairs and mirth in the club bar afterwards. On the occasion that wagers were laid, then a bottle of single malt was enough to give the game a serious edge. Beyond that, he recognized, it did become a job. This was when the sponsors, manufacturers and the cursed media came knocking. Even the most well-meaning writers clamouring for an interview, trying to gain an insight into his inner self, what made him tick, to what did he owe his success, disturbed him. Ha! How disappointed they were when Cameron confirmed his own belief that he was quite shallow, of little interest to anyone let alone the thousands who might pick up some glossy sports magazine. He was just there because he enjoyed doing what he did. His bloody mother was the worst of them all. Annie

Cameron, warrior extraordinaire! She had spent the early years of his life berating him for his lethargy and placid view on life and then elevated him to the nation's hero when she realised that his serene demeanour was the major ingredient in defining him as a top rank golfer.

Annie, Queen of Scots! Would that the present day Elizabeth had incarcerated her in some cold, dank tower before commanding the axe man to separate her ginger locks from the rest of her body? The day they buried her, he didn't attend. But he did catch a glimpse of the descending casket as he drove past the church, in his golfing attire, on the way to the afternoon's round. He'd seen the image of her head on every tee and his playing partners were in awe at the ferocity with which his driver connected with the *Top Flights*. Cameron Cameron was a powerful man and he hit the ball a very long way, but never as far as he did on that day. He had never lost so many balls on a single round before. – But the ghost was not yet laid.

She had enjoyed the trappings of her boy and the media followed suit. Suddenly he had become public property. The media were to blame for that – promoting him as Scotland's best hope, Britain's brightest star, and even Europe's best bet in the Ryder Cup. For a while, the momentum of his natural instincts had carried him through, but the hype had been getting to him more and more until eventually it had all boiled over in Massachusetts. After that day he had declared himself null and void. No more aeroplanes, no more crowds and no more competitions!

CHAPTER 11

Mercury's Ear

The place haunted him still. As a young adventurer he spent many of his childhood days turning the pages of a tattered *Times Atlas*, discovering far off lands and people. Puala Seribu! Many a time his attention had wandered from that dreary classroom, from the tedious mathematics and the soporific lectures on the chemical bonding of giant molecules, to the boundless, unfettered space and freedom of the blue sky outside. His mind had been carried under that same blue sky to every pencil mark on the atlas that identified places that he just had to visit. On Monday, he would be in Peru; Tuesday he'd be on Sugarloaf Mountain taking in the beaches of Copacabana and Ipenema, Wednesday, trekking through the Canadian forests with Thursday spent crossing the Kalahari and he'd be in Indonesia by Friday. He lived for Friday. He always kept the best till last, something to pull him, entice him through the rest of the week. Sometimes he would spend Thursday on the Russian Steppes, in the middle of an icy winter, just so that Friday would be even more appealing than usual. He'd even enacted out the drama of Thursdays by dressing in his winter gear. His mother had looked on in dismay when he had run to catch the school bus, labouring under a heavy duffle coat with scarf, gloves and cap, whilst the others were in their sleeveless July outfits. All this, so that on Friday he could throw it all off and be free as a bird, to land on some tropical island in a different universe. Thirty years later and he was still a Friday man.

His teachers, seeing his flights of fantasy often asked: 'And where are you today, young Ashley?' His father, being a slave of the

Yorkshire coalfield and steel mills, had often asked the same, but with his own childhood dreams smothered in wars, grime, poverty and ration cards, there had been no escape. That his son should carry those same hopes and fantasies, jealously annoyed him, and so they were dismissed as castles in the air. 'Some chance! You'll come down to earth one day, and the sooner the better my lad.'

Mike often thought that his father was a man who was always in the wrong place at the wrong time. It wasn't his fault that he never had a chance to realise his dreams, and Mike hadn't needed to ask about them. He'd seen in his father's eyes the recognition of what he'd missed and he didn't want his daydreaming son to remind him of the lost years. It was an eternal pain, hidden deep in his soul and in his body, like the cancer that would eventually extinguish the last lights of his life. Even when the careers officer had interviewed him the day he was set free upon the unsuspecting world, the youngster's dreams, which he'd blurted out as the pointless interview was about to come to an all quite predictable conclusion, were looked upon in disdain. He remembered the timidity of his own shy, childlike parting response. He should have kept quiet, gone with the crowd, accepted what was expected of him and assumed his position in the working society. Just like all the others. Other kids, waiting in line, had giggled and tormented him for wanting to be different. In later years, he had relived that moment as a pivotal moment in his life – perhaps *the* pivotal moment. He was petrified to be seen as a rebel, nursing fostered ideas that were not his to have. So he locked them away from the rest of the world and had only drawn them from deep within his soul for occasional moments of private absorption. Ideas that he secretly relied upon to carry him high above the day-to-day drudgery of the less imaginative.

To have spoken out of turn and spontaneously release those inner secrets, letting the pent-up passions burst from him like lemonade gushing from a shaken bottle, later horrified him. Perhaps he'd recognized it as a last chance, his final desperate plea for help? Speak now or forever … He'd half expected the corporal punishment that seemed to go with all acts of individuality, but the careers officer, perhaps seeing in the young Ashley what he had seen in himself at that age, beckoned him back to the seat from which he had just sheepishly slunk. Now the man played the role of a priest listening to the young boy's most profound confessions. The other boys, sitting in line behind, had hushed their humour and ridicule and waited, unsure about what next and uncertain of where their allegiance should lay. To a boy, they regretted the conditioned reflexes that suppressed their own ambitions. Was he speaking for them too?

'Whatever gave you such grand ideas, young fellow?'

Ashley hadn't said a word, but had delved into his bag, and after a frantic rummage round, pulled out a brochure. It was an early marketing document that he'd requested from one of the engineering oil companies. The remnant of some now long elapsed class project. The heavily thumbed pages bore evidence of long hours of study. Most striking were the pictures – photographs of colourful, sleek ships, palm trees, shining oil terminals and silver sanded beaches, all set under a clear sky of azure blue.

The advisor had taken it and flipped through the colourful pages to view the evidence for himself. Meanwhile Ashley had let his gaze wander out of the library window, over the school field, to the smoke and flames of the dark, grim heritage of the iron foundries filling Sheffield's Don Valley. He was already a million miles away. The careers man, who'd, spent his own working life finding ten thousand joiners, a thousand plumbers, shop keepers, hairdressers, and condemned countless urchins to the black holes of the local coal fields, looked up at the schoolboy and followed his gaze to the steel mills beyond. After a moment of introspection, a sad glaze had come over his eyes. He handed the booklet back and said, 'God bless you on your way, son.'

***

The thousand islands of the Sundra Straights separating Java from Sumatra were exactly the place. They *were* Friday. Puala Seribu, literally a thousand islands, was the most enchanting place he could ever wish to be. And the bride on his arm was the most enchanting person he could possibly wish to be with. He had stood hand in hand on the silvered coral sand with his wife of just a few hours, looking across the crystal sea that lapped at their feet. Amidst the tranquillity and the emotions that flooded him that day, he'd caught a fleeting glimpse back to that now distant sunny afternoon, in that school library where he'd declared to the world that he would go his own way and live his dreams. He wondered where the boys who sat in line, were now. He'd felt a tear swell in his eyes as he thought of his father's, and his grandfather's endeavours through the dark ages of war and toil. There but for the grace of God …… He wished that, for a moment, they could share this, his dream as it now came true. He prayed that, in their lives, they had perhaps, unrecognised by himself, lived at least *some* of their own youthful dreams.

✳✳✳

The most pleasant chapter in his life had the most appalling postscript, and it had been brought painfully back to him, by Clements's call. The murder of his young wife, and the death of Goodwin had something in common. How Fitri had been caught in the bombing of the Indonesia Hotel in Jakarta had been clear. She had just been an anonymous passer-by. Like the thousands of others, who, in going about their innocent day to day lives, had strayed into the obscene theatre of indiscriminate radical attacks as they targeted the most vulnerable of this world. But, how Goodwin's death had been linked to the same movement, albeit one of the multitude of Al Qaeda franchises, had not been immediately made clear to him.

Project *Symphony* had been reopened, not that it had ever been closed after his gruesome findings on the Ontario lake. Its passive status within MI6 had suddenly been elevated to one of immediate action. Ashley had been summoned to the safe-house meeting with Clements and his communications expert going under the unlikely name of Jeremy Zup. After the brief, formal introduction, Clements sat back and let Zup lead with information that he had.

'Without beating about the bush! Let me give you a brief overview of what we have found.' Zup's boyish face peered out from behind his school boy spectacles. The fresh face, slim body and soft voice and the way he graphically conducted every syllable by the exaggerated flow of hand movements, led Ashley to conclude that he was undoubtedly gay. Ashley smiled quietly and cast a quizzical glance at Clements. From his grim reprimanding glare, Ashley took it that Mr Zup was worth listening to and after an apologetic nod to Clements, he focussed his attention on the young expert.

Whether or not Zup had noticed the peripheral exchange, he gave no sign of it, and with a nervous push to move his spectacles further up the finely cut nose, continued with his briefing. 'I suppose that you are somewhat familiar with er – the function of GCHQ and Menwith?'

'In general terms, yes. In detail, no,' answered Ashley.

'Well, er, without revealing too much, – Her Majesty's Government has a technical facility, sharing common resources with certain friendly nations, with the goal of, er collecting certain information, which is of interest to Her Majesty's Government.' The index finger paused to reposition the spectacles once again before continuing with a wave that somehow seemed to be connected to Her Majesty's Government.

Ashley could not resist another peek in Clements's direction but once again the stern rapprochement that was reflected back left him in no doubt that he should give the specialist due respect. It was a chastened Ashley who settled into the discussion.

'We have some skills and assets that we share with er, our friends. They represent a number of systems that are useful in detecting, recording and decoding er, signals and messages. Probably you have heard of ELINT, SIGINT and COMINT?' Zup gestured with his hand to ask if Ashley knew, and the eyebrows lifted to ask if he needed more elaboration. A nod of accord was enough to ease the engineer on his way. After another spectacle realignment and a glance at the small card held in his left, the right hand continued in conducting the Halle Orchestra as Zup continued into the meat of his dialogue. 'SIGINT is short for Signals Intelligence, which er, includes ELINT and COMINT. ELINT is electronic intelligence that is gained from non-communications signals such as radar and the telemetric control of missiles, but COMINT is er, let us say in my field of er – interest.' Zup's hand scribed a vertical cut to emphasise that the two *INTs* were separate entities, and then curved to touch his own chest in an action that would have impressed a Roman Catholic priest blessing the crowds outside the Vatican. On this occasion, Ashley resisted the look to Clements. He could feel the commander's eyes aimed, loaded and ready to fire, had he done so.

'Communications intelligence is all about analysing the signal source and destination as well as the message contents er, such as we see here.' Ashley obviously couldn't see the message contents as Zup was waving it around in front of his face, but took it that at sometime in the near future the card would land on the table in front of him. For now Zup continued, 'This particular message er, – came from Mercury!'

Well, here *was* a surprise, Ashley couldn't resist. 'Where else?' he muttered, as if Mercury could be the one and only source of all signals.

Zup, oblivious to the agent's humour, once more repositioned the bridge of his glasses: 'Mercury as you may know or not, as the case maybe, was the Roman mythological character responsible for carrying messages between the Gods and er … er…' The hand flapped faster.

'- er general public?' offered Ashley

Clements rose to his feet and turning his back on them went to check the weather situation at the window.

'- Is er, a satellite component of a joint effort by the US, Australia, New Zealand and ourselves to monitor various communications media. You would be surprised how much HMG actually contributed to the launch and upkeep of the network.'

Ashley nodded that he would be surprised, 'are we talking about Echelon?'

'Strictly speaking, No!' replied Zup sharply, 'but if you are – er, Joe Public, then yes, you could say that.'

195

Ashley conceded that he was JP all the way.

'As I was saying,' Zup looked at him sternly though the school glasses, 'Mercury is a part of the Vortex constellation of geostationary satellites that give us access to communications being transmitted in er, the VHF and UHF bandwidths,' and added for clarification: 'line of sight.' He continued: 'This particular satellite has a thirty eight meter dish, its ear, so to speak, and is located at er, close to twenty thousand miles above the er – Indian Ocean. It collects signals either directly, as can be the case in either radio or GSM transmissions, or from their network base stations.'

'What, from twenty thousand miles?' exclaimed an incredulous Ashley.

'Oh yes, it's no problem at all!' replied Zup, in equal dismay that Ashley could have possibly doubted that they had the technology. His enthusiasm triggered Zup to continue: 'GSM base stations can transmit several hundred watts of radio signals and from a distance of thirty six thousand, if you prefer metric? Kilometres over the Indian Ocean. This is well within the reception spec of our geostationary birds such as Mercury. If you have any doubt, then you might consider the NASA communications with the Voyager spacecraft: From a few light weeks – that's several billion kilometres away, Voyager, designed in seventies technology, talks to earth with a twenty-eight watt transmitter!' He paused to let the enormity of the statement sink in. 'Yes – er, and we in turn download the monitored signals from Mercury, via Pine Gap near Alice Springs, Fort Mead in Maryland or here in the UK at Menwith Hill in Yorkshire. Which, actually, is where I am based?' Zup made an exaggerated sweep of his hand to indicate that Menwith Hill was located somewhere outside, behind the rock garden, and then very firmly pushed the glasses back in place to signal that, that was that!

But it wasn't. 'And the message was …?'

'The message was from a GSM telephone located in the United Arab Emirates er, it was a text message.'

'And … it said?'

Zup looked down at him and after a long thoughtful pause, said,

– 'Thanks be to Goodwin!' and handing him the card, softly repeated: 'Thanks be to Goodwin!'

Ashley sat back heavily in his seat, pursed his lips and crossed his arms. He nodded slowly as he looked eye to eye at the Menwith man and, after a few seconds of silent digestion, they both turned to Clements.

Clements, who had lit his pipe, fixed his gaze on Ashley, 'Would you be so kind as to tell him how you found the text – please Jeremy?

'Well, er yes, as you wish sir. – "The Echelon system," and I must use quotes there, as the existence of such a system has never been officially acknowledged, is capable of listening to, and monitoring almost any GSM phone call or SMS message transmission in the world.' He hurried to add: 'Obviously, it is totally impractical for us to detect every single call, listen to it and analyse it. Therefore we prime the system with filters, of er, various types with various subject matter triggers. In this case, we were asked, by *Symphony*, to look for messages that might refer to the gentleman by the name of Peter Goodwin.' Zup, for the last time, waved towards the card with a graceful sweep, '… and after nine weeks of looking, there you have it!'

For a moment Mike was taken back to the Canadian lake where he had discovered Goodwin's corpse and once again, the sympathy and sadness welled up over him. That sympathy had now been accompanied by anger. A desire for justice and revenge was growing in him, just as it had after he lost his Fitri.

Clements interrupted his thoughts, 'Unless you have any further questions for Jeremy? ……

'No. – Not at all. Thanks. It's been *most* interesting,' replied a stunned Ashley. And belatedly added a congratulatory: 'Well done! great job! – Jeremy,' conceding, with a slight reluctance, that it had been indeed, a job well done.

Clements stood and Zup knew that it was time for him to leave. His task was complete for the moment and he didn't want to know any more. They exchanged handshakes and Jeremy Zup whipped his jacket off the back of the chair and, like a bullfighter with his cape' swept it with some flamboyant drama over his head and hung it loosely across his shoulders. Suitably robed, he moved for the door, opened it and stepped out into the hall. He was just about to close it behind him when Ashley fired one late question. 'Where did you say the call was from – and its destination?'

Zup stopped, peered back inside, and sliding his index finger up the side of his nose, answered with raised eyebrows, 'I didn't,' he smiled. – 'But it originated in Dubai – and it was destined for Dubai! Just a simple local call.' And with that, the Menwith man was gone.

CHAPTER 12

Emirates

The Hook of Holland slid by through the thinning cloud and once the autumn sun had risen sufficiently to disperse the threads and tails of cirrus, it promised Western Europe a fine Indian summer's day. But it wasn't one that would be enjoyed by Ashley, although it wouldn't be the lack of sunshine that he would miss. The Emirates flight was destined for the United Arab Emirates, on the southern shores of The Persian Gulf.

Flying south for the winter, mused Ashley, as the airbus approached its cruising height. The front page of The Telegraph revealed that the Bank of England was under pressure to reduce its interest rate as the housing market showed signs of stagnation. The Iranian president had made another sabre rattling speech, threatening the world with a new unfettered source of nuclear weapons. The American response was immediate and equally threatening as yet another naval carrier force was earmarked for The Gulf. Ashley wondered how on earth they could cram any more fighting ships into such a confined sea. Middle East tension was building all the time and here he was heading right into the thick of it.

An alert chimed to announce that seat belts could be removed. The cabin staff was quick off the mark and he could hear the tinkle of glass as the inevitable drinks trolley was prepared for the roll down the aisles. Most of the business class passengers had been hushed, oblivious to the pre-flight procedures and even take off – awareness still largely dormant after the early morning start. Ashley had been in a similar mode but the stewardess at the front of the cabin caught his attention as she went about the karaoke animation of identifying the nearest escape exits and floor level lighting to guide one to them. He'd seen it – perhaps five hundred times, at least on the occasions when his head had not been buried in the morning newspaper. But on this occasion, the graceful flourish of arms and the beaming smile radiating from Miss Singapore was worth his audience for the few minutes at least. Compared with the usual robotic display, this presentation reminded him of a priest casting incense over his congregation. In-Excelsis-Deo, he wanted to chant. Delightful – and somebody showed their appreciation too, as a singular clap of ovation woke the rest from their lingering moments of slumber. The stewardess's smiled broadened further as she and nearby passengers turned to identify the source of applause. Ashley found to his great surprise that they were all looking in his direction and he suddenly realized that in a moment of rare abandonment, he had been the guilty party. Conscious of the attention, he quickly dipped his head back into the newspaper and hid in the sports pages as if to deny his very existence. The clatter of the trolley rescued his embarrassing moment and suddenly a new enthusiasm spread through the cabin. It reminded Ashley of his first studies in psychology, most of which he missed, going AWOL to lead the college cricket eleven in the summer and then the football team in the winter. All he could remember from those dim and tedious lectures that he *did* attend were the antics of Skinner's rats and Pavlov's dogs. He could readily relate them now to his fellow passengers in whom the expected clatter of glass and cans elicited the autonomic surge of adrenalin and induced salivation. Pavlov would have been proud.

***

The seven hour flight was neither here nor there, not short enough to do without entertainment and yet not long enough to sleep through it. In this way, Ashley preferred the long haul flights to such places as Hong Kong, Jakarta or KL, where he could enjoy a few pre dinner drinks on departing Heathrow, have an extended dinner, watch an in-flight movie and drift into a dreamy slumber as the flight crossed the Himalayan roof of the world, before turning southerly to South East Asia. At that point the sun would be rising and the smell of breakfast cooking in the galley would be triggering yet another Pavlovian reaction.

***

She was Singaporean Chinese, the stewardess that is. He should have guessed and her generous smile was matched by the equally generous serving of whisky and double helping of pretzels. As she passed on, pushing her wagon of delights before her, their eyes had met in a fleeting, but Ashley felt, a meaningful exchange. It was a moment that drew him back into the recent depths of his emotional winter from which he had just painfully dragged himself.

Ashley was jolted out of his nightmare; God knows how many of those had haunted him in the past. He had thought that they were now just a thing of the past, but even though time had eased his winter into the background, it still crept back from time to time. Chill drafts of the past caught him unawares, pulling his mood down until he managed to realise what was happening and snap out of it before it overwhelmed him again. In the two years since he had lost her, he had struggled through the days, occupying his time as much as body and mind could tolerate. Looking to survive until the night came and he could hide in his sleep. Sleep that hardly ever came, or if the exertions of the day did mercifully exhaust him to the point where he would simply collapse on the bed, he would wake, expecting the day to already be well under way only to find that dawn was still many hours distant. He dreamt often, mostly reliving the rendezvous at Cengkareng, the newspaper accounts of the explosion and imagery conjured from his imagination of what his she must have gone through when the terrorist bomb had torn her delicate body apart. By far the most tormenting was the recurring visions of the wonderful times they had together. The times they made delicious love and those of waking up with her in his arms, her long hair stretched across the pillow as she slept peacefully assured by his athletic physique. They were so vivid that he often stirred thinking that her death was in fact the dream and that now he was awake, all was well. Any minute now and she'd be stepping out of the shower and prancing past him with her towel shyly held to preserve her modesty and at the same time seductively enchant him. Cruelly the vision would last just a few seconds before reality set in and once again the dreadful truth would dawn upon him. There was a yet another whole new day in front to torture him. It would be just like the last one, and the next. There was no escape, no relief.

***

The flight had landed without incident or delay as the evening twilight had surrendered to the onset of night. Dubai was at its busiest as its populace emerged from the sanctuaries of air-conditioned villas and apartments, to seek out a table in one of the city's legion of multi-ethnic restaurants, or join in the headlong rush to the mall to spend easily made Dirhams. Even on the final approach Ashley could see that the place had taken on a completely new identity since his last sojourn here. Every highway seemed to be lined with shopping malls decked in Gucci and Rolex splendour and, from the snakes of tail lights, the only thing between their passengers and an empty wallet was the stagnant traffic.

'Welcome to Dubai, Mr. Ashley.' Ashley turned from the baggage carousel to face the source of softly spoken words. The tall, finely-featured Arab was dressed in the ubiquitous white thobe and guttrah. The white spotless head gear contrasted sharply with the Arab's dark eyes and short trimmed, black beard. One heavily haired hand rested on the bar of a baggage trolley whilst the other was extended towards him in anticipation of a gentleman's greeting.

'Good evening sir,' was the only response that Ashley thought suitable to the moment. He was unsure of the identity of his escort and half expected the man to identify himself as a hotel representative, but then this escort was on the wrong side of immigration and the heavy yellow gold neck chain and shining titanium of the Breitling Chrono Avenger, were well outside the financial reach of a hotel meet-and-greet representative.

Recognising the questioning eyes and element of caution in the way that the English man had responded, Colonel Ali Abdullah retained the firm handshake a little longer than a foreigner might expect, and confidently, with a touch of arrogance about the smile, looked Ashley in the eyes and introduced himself. Ashley returned the smile, feeling immediately comfortable in the man's authoritative presence and in the recognition of his contact from the Ministry of the Interior. Both men firmed the handshake and then released with a respectful touch to the breast bone. Reminiscent of the traditions of the east, thought Ashley.

'How was London? – the flight?' and before Ashley could reply to either, 'How many pieces of baggage are we looking for?' followed in the most eloquent English that couldn't fail to impress him. Ashley wondered if a blind man passing by could have identified himself as the native English speaker, or the state security man who now busied himself in directing a maroon jacketed porter, to pick out Ashley's bulky red case and load it onto the trolley.

'Two!' was the hastened reply, as Ashley caught sight of the second toppling from the chute onto the carousel. Ashley noticed a chalk mark on two surfaces of the somewhat battered Samsonite as the diminutive Asian porter wrestled it onto the waiting trolley. Ashley purposely left all the hotel and airport security stickers in place, so that primarily he could easily identify his bags amongst the host of other Samsonite or Delseys. Of equal importance, was that nobody else could credibly mistake one of his bags as belonging to them.

Dispatching the porter with dismissive wave, Col. Ali Abdullah took up the trolley and headed for the customs desk. Ashley anticipated that they would be stopped because of the tell-tale chalk marks on his case, heralding an interest in its contents. Just as he was sure that they would be stopped, he was equally confident that nothing clandestine would be found by the most thorough search.

However, he need not have been the slightest bit concerned as the Colonel breezed through the aircrew exit with Ashley in close attendance. It was as if they had been invisible to immigration and the hovering customs examiners. Without a word, they marched out through the electric doors that slid open to spill them out into the hot and humid night. Within seconds Ashley's brow was perspiring and he could feel sweat collecting beneath his arm pits and a warm stream started to trickle down his spine painting the dark blue polo shirt with indigo patches. Ali strode through hordes of greeters awaiting Air India to disgorge its flock of cheap labour from Mumbai. Ashley thought of Moses parting the waves of the Red Sea as he followed in his host's wake, but kept it to himself. An expensive white Mercedes awaited them directly by the curb outside the arrivals hall. The status of the vehicle's owner was made apparent to all by the lustrous sparkle of chrome and expensive enamel which were sufficient to ward off most of the crowd. The symbols of affluence and authority were clear for all to see. The odd body that threatened to venture too close was quickly dispatched by a sharp bark from the attendant driver. Ashley was somewhat surprised when the squarely built chauffeur strode round from his guardian post to introduce himself and shake Ashley's hand with a firm imposing grip. Ashley would recognize later that this fellow was not the run-of-the-mill driver as the man ushered him into the back seat of the limousine and easily lifted the heavy bags into the rear. Ashley noted that he had slight limp as he settled behind the wheel. Colonel Ali took his place by his side and gave a polite respectful command to indicate the next destination. Ashley settled with slight but growing embarrassment. The sweat of his travel and arrival mixed all too heavily with the sweet perfume of his host and the pervading bouquet of new leather and carpeting textures. He yearned for a shower to refresh himself and clean clothes to give him comfort in the illustrious company in which he had now found himself.

Ali turned to say that it was a pleasure to meet him, that Commander Clements sent his regards and that there was nothing on the agenda that couldn't await the next morning, and that he felt sure that a good night's relaxation would leave him alert to the task in hand.

CHAPTER 13

The Lucky Palace

Bonetti was high as a kite. The bar was always busy at weekends and none more so than on Thursday evenings. Expatriate office staff and engineers escaped their chores early to wash away the week's accumulated stress, exchange gossip, scandal and jokes with their associates. The stop-over for a few beers was easily justified as the best way to beat Dubai's turgid traffic jams, when speeds never rose above single digits. The Lucky Palace had many delights to offer its clientele.

Much to Samir's disgust and his initial amazement that such places could exist within an Islamic state, the bar was heavily populated by ladies of the world. Mostly Oriental but mixed with a cocktail of African and Balkan states, their sole role in life being devoted to the entertainment of the LP's guests. At first the presence of an occasional lady of the night had caused quite a stir, but the steady influx of new talent had ensured that the 'Palace' had rapidly become a popular place where guests and hostesses packed its lounge every weekend. The term 'Chinese Take-away' had taken on a whole new meaning. It was definitely not included in any tourist itinerary that guided the sun seeker tourists of the Jumeira around the more illustrious of the Emirate's venues. But like many such establishments the world over, it had become a favourite haunt of thirsty expatriate workers and as much a centre of commerce as the financial trading houses just across the creek. It generated its own line of peripheral trading. Sooner or later every oiler, soldier, business consultant, financial expert and airline pilot, or some other visitor of dubious reputation had thrown a smile and mock salute to Salim the doorman. He dutifully handed out temporary membership cards, valid only that day and waved them through its doors into the boisterous, bachalian arena of pleasure. If one had a reputation of high standing before entry, then one certainly didn't have it after being spotted by some lecherous business associate secluded away in one of the bar's darker corners. Countless transactions were carried out in the Lucky Palace, some of them of a genuine mercantile nature and some of them of a more seditious nature. Whatever the deal, none were struck in confidence! Here no secrets were secret for long. The walls had ears and the scanning eyes of the palace's customers were sometimes not what they might at first seem. Gossip was rife, mostly propagated by the maidens of the night, many of whom were content to reveal all or recant all for the price of a Pizza and Bacardi and Coke. Cross a palm with silver here and you could get the next winner at Longchamps or the revelation of the winning tender for a squadron of F16 fighter aircraft. Some were simply hookers, but others were surprisingly gifted and explored the more subtle niches to make a living – namely the supply and manipulation of information! Bonetti had crudely labelled them en masse as the *Shanghai Shag*, drawing a humorous parallel to rhyme with Chiang Kai-Shek that amused none but himself. Samir himself, for all his reluctance to associate himself with satanic trade, found, much to his surprise, that some who had cautiously approached him, were indeed blessed with high intellect. Explaining their immediate plight in a variety of desperate circumstances. Failed businesses back in China, divorce and abandonment by despotic husbands, not to mention the occasional family fortune lost over a quiet game of Ma Jiang. There but for the grace of Allah, go I.

There were times when his distaste was moderated by compassion. Must be a remnant from his childhood upbringing, he thought. Here was a den of perfect spies. A Mata Hari at every table. Over the years many a glib tongue, lubricated by alcoholic narcosis, had let slip pertinent details of commercial and military dealings into the Palace's ether. Unguarded communications were seized upon and recorded by an alert opportunist and sold for a dollar to the next client at the next table, or in the next bed. Samir was forced to acknowledge the commercial instinct and entrepreneurial skills that were inbred, particularly in the Chinese. If there was a dollar, or a dirham to be made, you could make a safe bet that the Sino sisters would be exploiting the sector better than any other.

Samir's first appearance at the door had caused something of an embarrassing confrontation, for entry was strictly limited to *members only* and as Samir looked every bit the Muslim conservative that he was, his way was barred by the ever present brick wall that went by the name of Salim. The doorman was ex-special forces and reputedly only came into this role after falling out of the back of a C130 freighter with a dodgy parachute. That he ever lived to tell the tale said a lot about his physique. As wide as he was tall, bull necked with legs like tree trunks and arms as thick as Samir's thighs. Salim was a force to be reckoned with and no one with any notion of self preservation exchanged a cross word with him. On the few occasions when some boisterous oilman fresh from his offshore rig had passed more of his hard earned money across the bar than was wise, Salim would ease himself into the melee, place his vast arm around the offending shoulders and subtly persuade the intoxicated friend that it was time to go. With the assurance of a prize fighter and the patience of a chess master he would escort the now more-than-willing companion outside to the taxi rank, and with the single barked command. 'Go!' – dispatch him into the night. Where some of these evacuees spent the night was anyone's guess and a subject of much conjecture, but as long as peace in the palace was maintained, nobody cared a toss. Salim, whose permanent limp was the only telltale of his *bounce* from ten thousand feet, was a much respected character and certainly one to be kept on your side of the fence.

Samir had not passed the test of looking like a *Palace* member and it was only on the intervention of Faisal that he was allowed into the inner sanctum. As a prospective member, it was suggested. In contrast, Faisal looked resident, undoubtedly meeting the qualifying criteria with a characteristic blood-red nose and cheeks to match.

His face gave overt evidence of the many hours sitting on his own corner stool, directly under the illuminated Smirnoff sign. The sign that he extinguished every time he entered before drinking countless draughts of neat vodka, washed down with the occasional swallow of Apollinaris water. Faisal was normally Samir's sole reason to visit *The Palace*. On this occasion however it had been Bonetti's effervescent exuberance that had cajoled him into joining the party. Samir consoled himself with the knowledge that he was there to serve his Islamic brothers and them alone. In sharp contrast, Carlo Bonetti was there with the intention of celebrating. And when Bonetti celebrated, everyone celebrated.

Faisal, his long thinning hair strategically stretched across his wide bald dome from one ear to the other, was attired in what seemed to be the only contents of his wardrobe. Brown leather shoes carrying half the dust of the Dubai desert, the well worn signature suit of off-peach, green shirt and a dark tie of uncertain colour that carried a hieroglyphic logo to testify that he was, or claimed to have been at some time, the curator of the Egyptian National Museum of Antique Artefacts in Alexandria. When Samir had first introduced the two, Bonetti, based on first impressions, had made the aside that it was more likely that Faisal was one of the museum's exhibits rather than its curator. It had of course been intended as a murmured pun to bystanders, rather than a face to face jovial exchange with Faisal himself. Whilst it had drawn a round of guffaws from the rest of the group, Faisal was one not blessed with the slightest sense of humour. The grim curvature of the lips let all but Bonetti know that, in no uncertain terms, Faisal's attire and appearance were not subjects for general mirth or discussion. If Bonetti had noticed the hint, he showed not the slightest acknowledgement and chose to reinforce his good nature and friendship by administering a jollifying, but excessive slap to Faisal's rounded shoulders. The Italian had already turned to the bar – grabbed the rope of the bell to announce to all within, that the next round was on Carlo Bonetti. One bar sceptic was quick to notice that Bonetti's timing was exquisite and that he had just, by chance, caught the last order for happy hour, after which all drinks went for twice the price. This was of no concern to the *Shanghai Shags* or the *African Queens*, all of whom emerged out of the woodwork to vociferously claim their free drink of the night.

The proclamation that there was a wealthy or foolish fellow, or both, in house, prompted a sudden bovine migration of would-be masseurs or mistresses to the Bonetti/Faisal corner and Samir, who had been as static as a shop-window mannequin, was brushed to one side in the stampede. Bonetti had names for most of them. One unfortunate with the build of a cart horse with mane and teeth to match was inevitably christened *Horse*, her sister of similar stature, *Dobbin*, another with a pronounced nasal appendage had been adopted unkindly as *the Gnu*, and yet another who always dressed completely in black was known throughout as *The Black Widow*. Not to forget, of course *The Jolly Green Giant*.

Not all the herd were parading their assets so overtly, however. One girl had distanced herself from the others. Prim, short cut hair and modestly dressed in jeans, denim shirt, short boots and sleeveless denim jacket to match. She only needed a Stetson to impart an image of what might have been seen in some saloon bar of cowboy days. *Jessie Jane* was perched with some elegance, and it had to be said with more than a touch of arrogance atop her tall bar stool. She was probably of Chinese extraction with perhaps a hint of Korean about the shallow bridge of her nose and dark brown, elliptical eyes. Even Samir was of the opinion that this one was in a class of her own. He somehow had the impression that she was not there of her own volition. He continued to sip his orange juice and quietly observed as Bonetti's party snowballed.

***

Surely Bonetti could not continue swilling down the lagers as he had been for the last hour? Cost however would not be a consideration. He'd just lined his pockets from the backdoor sale of four of the fax machines that had already been paid for under the DUBEXAIR contract. Samir, who'd actually been the middle man in pointing

210

Bonetti in Faisal's direction, had received a commission of nearly a thousand dollars. Once again he contented himself with the knowledge that another half year's school fees for his son in Amman had been met. Yet at the same time it pained him considerably knowing that Bonetti had pocketed twenty times that sum. That Faisal had been the customer and that the hardware was destined to benefit the cause of his *Brothers of Islam,* justified his participation. Little did Bonetti know that some machines had already been smuggled out of the country without any concern for the formal export paperwork and compulsory *end user certification.* Faisal had contacts everywhere and even at that moment, as Bonetti stood in front of him, one C2000 was being installed in Peshawar whilst another awaited Samir's installation in Faisal's home. For the first time ever, The *Brothers of Islam* had their own secure communications network, giving them ciphered messaging beyond the reach of the best cryptanalysts of the western world.

***

Back into the party Bonetti, the now much dishevelled Italian was beginning to feel hungry and not being particularly attracted by any of the ladies milling around, thought it preferable to order a couple of pizzas at the bar. Better than be seen taking one the whores on his arm to a more salubrious restaurant in the city. The pizzas arrived in quick time and a feeding frenzy began. Bonetti had never been so popular although only he and Samir knew that it was all funded from Faisal's account. Faisal was not a party animal and sat in his usual corner quietly rejecting the numerous promises of affection and offers of every conceivable style of massage that the imagination could conjure up. The flamboyant Bonetti was a different story though. He had his arm around every girl in turn and each *Bella Donna* took her turn to seek his attention in the hope of later seeing the inside of his apparently bloated wallet.

Samir had remained in quiet discomfort observing the scene from a distance and apart from the early feline enquiries as to his plans for the night did little except observe and drink his orange juice. Soon after arriving he had intimated that he wished to leave but both Bonetti and Faisal had insisted that he should stay a while longer – Bonetti, because he wanted to see his engineer's religious dedication tested by either the alcohol, or a woman, or hopefully both, and Faisal was always coaxing Samir to get even closer to the Italian. All too predictably, Bonetti had made a seditious whisper in a Chinese ear to the effect that the quiet guy on the other table was lonely and in need of company. Sure enough a few moments later Samir would felt a tug on his arm followed by a self invitation to slide in beside him.

'Were you flom?'

'I flom Jordan. Where *you* flom?' At least Samir got some humorous satisfaction from imitating the halting English of the unwanted conversation.

'I flom China.- Wot your name? – my name Angel'

Not wishing to be impolite and also realising that some attention to his new *friend* added to his credence for being here, Samir responded with as little information as possible 'Samy.'

'Samee velly hansom – you working Dubai?'

'I just stay here for short time,' he lied.

'Samee like China lady?'

In all the brief encounters that he had that evening, the conversation format was the same, apart from the occasions when the lady had a good command of the English in which case he became a little more enthused and condescended to engage in some common topic. In the end though, the goal was the same. 'Yes, China lady beautiful,' he had lied sometimes.

'Gambay, cheers!' was the next step in the routine and Samir, as every other fellow in the bar, was required to clink glasses in a toast to either oriental or african beauty.

By now his escort would be growing in confidence and Samir growing in impatience. 'Wah I nee, Samee,' would be accompanied by an enquiring smile and flutter of eyelids.

Samir wondered how any woman could possibly fall in love with a complete stranger, in an instant, and then with a different stranger the next night. But he could never think of a suitable repost.

'Samee likee take a lady tonight?'

The idea of taking a whore home for the night, or at any time for that matter appalled him. A shake of the head was the most reasonable response that he could muster.

'Why you no likee me, Samee.?'

Now it was getting difficult and he was beginning to regret being drawn into the unlikely alliance. Unused to this sort of scene, his predicament was reflected in his facial colour and he felt the heat generated by his discomfort bring the first beads of sweat to his brow.

'I give you lovely time – maka Samee velle 'appy tonight.' And a small hand would make its first barely detectable contact with his thigh.

Close to vomiting in revulsion, he brusquely swept the invading fingers from his leg as if they were cockroaches. He turned sharply to the girl – Angel, he remembered, met her eyes with his and he paused, took a deep breath and with his temper rising rapidly was about to object in a violent manner. The fear and concern in her eyes caught him by surprise and quickly tempered his anger She was human, his father would have told him. She's here, doing this because she has no other option. It's dangerous and unpleasant work, sleeping with any stinking, drunken lout who happened to have a dollar in his pocket and who may beat her or pay her, as was his whim, after her reluctant service. Angel was probably the sole support for her family and children of an all too common broken marriage. Her mother, back home in Dalian or Shenzen, will be proudly telling her neighbours of her daughter's fine clerical position in some smart business office, earning enough money to support the home and put the children into the best school in the province. Had she known that the pride of her life was assuming other sorts of positions selling her body to any who would take her, the wizened old mother would have died of shame. Instead of the company apartment her daughter was living in some rat hole of an apartment room shared with half a dozen similar girls. Angel, like so many others, had paid some unscrupulous agent a fortune on the premise of a decent job, with just reward, company health care and annual flights home, only to be dumped on the steps of Dubai airport, to fend for herself in a very strange land, with a very strange language. Samir bit his tongue. Tolerance Samir. Islam preaches tolerance, his father had told him. If he had forgotten much over the years, this fundamental was still a salient teaching permanently engraved in his mind.

'Angel, you are very nice lady – beautiful. But I have wife and family at home and my heart is there. – Sorry.'

Angel, for the first time paused in her otherwise incessant gum chewing – smiled meekly and then offered up her glass. 'Gambay!' and was gone in search of easier prey.

✳✳✳

Uproar drew not just Samir's, but everyone's attention to Bonetti who was now definitely looking the worse for wear. Divested of his jacket and his loosened tie hanging noose-like around his neck, Bonetti was re-enacting some past drama. He was leaning over the bar, his head resting on the overhead woodwork alongside his left hand, face red with effort and mouth working overtime in explanation of some plight that he had found himself in. The Bonetti association bellowed their support. Samir was horrified when the Italian's free hand went to the front of his trousers. He shook his head in disbelief. His employer was reliving the flight of the Lear Jet, once again. The bar's clientele eager to enjoy Bonetti's portrayal of his high flying embarrassment, fell about in great swathes of laughter. The pandemonium had attracted the attention of Salim, who limped into the room to check for the root of the disturbance. Mercifully for all, Bonetti was content to sway around and demonstrate his newly acquired skill of peeing from on high, without further explicit revelations from what remained of his clothes. The moment over, and satisfied that the local decency laws were not in danger of being infringed, the doorman returned to his post. Bonetti recovered what remained of his poise, took up his beer and turned round to acknowledge the fervent applause with a wave of the hand – Bonetti the actor. Bonetti the emperor.

It was during his acceptance of the ovation that the Italian's eyes had cause to hesitate as they swept over the evening's drinkers. Samir followed his interest. Jessie Jane still sat high on her roost, demure, but the pursed lips and raised chin spoke of arrogance and challenge. She hadn't moved throughout the whole episode. Her drink untouched, she hadn't smiled, nor spoken to anyone. Samir had the impression that she wasn't there for anyone. Anyone else but Bonetti perhaps?

***

Bonetti had returned to the attention of his cohorts. Faisal had distanced himself from the entourage and was engaged in his own conversation with his usual drinking partners, beneath the darkened Smirnoff sign. A few seconds passed before Bonetti turned once again. Jessie Jane remained at her post, unmoved and uninterested. Bonetti quizzed her with a frown and raised his eyebrows. Samir was sure that she'd seen the Lighthouse man's body language, but maybe the language barrier stretched beyond the verbal for she gave no recognition of the communication. Bonetti turned full-square to her and peered higher to get a clearer view across the crowd. At last he seemed to have caught her attention as she turned her head slightly to meet his gaze. He beckoned her to join him with as subtle a tilt of the head as he could manage. The girl averted her look and ignored the crude invitation, or was it command? He'd *never* seen anyone ignore Bonetti before. Generals, executives, sheikhs and ministers had never been seen to snub Bonetti. Maybe they hated him at times, but Samir had never seen any of them ignore him. Yet, here was this whore refusing to give the slightest acknowledgement of his advances. This was going to be interesting thought Samir.

Bonetti turned his back once again, obviously miffed. It was not within his script to be seen as the fish taking the bait, especially if

215

the bait happened to be some tart in a third rate whore house.

It was a full five minutes before curiosity got the better of him. Resist as he might, the pretty young woman had suggested a touch of class that was certainly out of place in this den of sedition. Unlike those still hanging on his arm, she was obviously not an easy pull. Her confidence and pride, not to mention the easy, seductive deportment, was proving to be too much of a challenge, even for Bonetti. The interest had been aroused and he was compelled to seek her out once more. His pulse quickened and even though the heavy drinking had dulled his senses, the sap was definitely rising.

She'd gone! The stool was empty – Bonetti had missed his chance and he felt weak at the knees in disappointment. Molly, aka Jessie Jane, had slipped off the pedestal and was making her exit through the crowd. Bonetti caught sight of her as she approached the swing doors. Just at the penultimate moment, she half turned her head to catch the briefest glimpse of Bonetti's craning head. Salim pushed the door open and closed it after she had sailed through, stepping as a Dior model might promenade down a Parisian catwalk.

Bonetti whisked his wallet from his back pocket planted out a generous estimate of the evening's entertainment in the barman's hand and took a few hurried steps for the exit. He turned on his heel, returning briefly to grab his forgotten jacket, and then forced his way through the throng, in hot pursuit. Hooked! observed Samir. Well and truly hooked.

CHAPTER 14

All Square

Flight Lieutenant Gul grabbed his helmet, stormed out of the ops centre and strode across Sweihan's tarmac apron oblivious to the shimmering heat and the noise of the external power unit that supplied his helicopter. His fiery glare matched that of the mid-day sun but his expletive incantations were drowned out by the start-up whines of the other aircraft. It was plain to see that ground crew would do well to get his bird into the air without hitch or drama. Gul mounted the cockpit through the door, and flung his briefcase behind the co-pilot's seat. Its other occupant had prudently followed the captain at some distance, uncertain as to where his allegiance should lay. Faraj and Gul had been a team for several years now, but the end was in sight. The skill and experience of his Pakistani captain would be severely missed, but he wouldn't miss the arrogance and belligerence. The writing had been on the wall for some time and the UAE government's declaration that it intended to localise its armed forces had spelt the career end for many accomplished expatriate serviceman. Already the air force's support staff had been trimmed of the vast majority of its Indian subcontinent engineers. First went the chaff, or dead wood that nobody missed, but as months passed, the red line moved up and even senior, more valued airman were relieved of their posts and waved back home to Islamabad or Karachi. Governmental statistics showed that there were enough locally bred helicopter pilots to fly the squadron's helicopters and so, men like Gul, who had been the country's aviation pioneers, had bluntly been informed that *their* time had come. And so it happened on that morning. The squadron leader had quietly caught Gul from the hangar and escorted him to his office. It had been with great reluctance that he had had to hand over the document that gave his best pilot just three more months of employment and a plane ticket home. The promised golden handshake was anything but golden. Faraj had mixed emotions as they went through the pre-flight routine one more time. He, as all of his fellow Arab flight crew companions, knew that government statistics were false criteria for drastic decision making and that numbers meant little to their military commanders who had to make the system work. In the face of pressure from their political peers, they had clung on to their expatriate officers for as long as possible, knowing full well that they formed the cream of both their engineers and aircrew and that the vast majority of local replacements were just not ready for the task. Still, it did mean that in all likelihood he would be promoted, even if it would be beyond his present capabilities. That was his ambition in any case and it would be a lifetime's achievement to sit in the command seat. It was expected of him and although he aspired to the rank and prestige, the responsibility would weigh heavily on his shoulders. Decision making was not his major forte.

Gul waved away the ground staff, throttled up the engines to lift off a metre or so and then taxied the Super Puma out onto the runway. A final visual check of the wingman's aircraft position and an 'ok' from the tower left Gul free to lift the helicopter into the hot, dusty, desert air.

***

Flying Officer Faraj cast his eyes around the desert below him. The daily routine took them from the in-land base to cross a flat plane of desert scrub land which then suddenly changed into a juvenile forest. At that point they would alter course to the north for the Gulf coast. A few years ago, nobody, least of all *he*, ever dreamt that the terrain between the capital Abu Dhabi and its illustrious neighbour Dubai could be anything but desert. But drillers had found a vast subterranean reservoir, albeit of brackish water that wouldn't be potable for the human population without prohibitive expense. Yet it was found to be well capable of supporting certain strains of vegetation. Within a few years, saplings had been planted by the tens of thousands and there, for all the sceptics to see with their very own eyes was the UAE's own fledgling forest. And now it extended for miles! Whether or not its growth would lead to a full forest in the European sense of the word, one that might even lead to climate change, he could not guess. Even as it stood, it was an impressive sight to any Arab eyes and just went to show what miracles could be achieved with the stupendous wealth that flowed from under the waters of the Persian Gulf.

A few miles further up the coast a forest of a very different type was sprouting. This too was man made.

Their flight plan that morning took them up to the coast before heading north east towards Jebel Ali. From there they were to fly off the coast line, up to Ras Al Khaimah and then back again. They would pass just north of Dubai and Sharjah on both legs, keeping well below the flight paths of both civil airports, before cutting back inland across the desert once more and back to Sweihan. It was a standard patrol and a routine that they had followed many times. Faraj wondered if it served any real purpose at all, other than just showing the flag and keeping their airtime above the minimum required. Anyway it was more interesting than the countless circuit-and-bumps that most aircrews carried out around the airbase just to maintain take-off and landing statistics. Insha'allaah, he was spared that mind-numbing schedule on *this* morning.

Despite the mundane schedule they did in fact have a purposeful mission to patrol up and down the coast, keeping an eye on the shipping and to investigate anything untoward. Typically, their presence would inhibit unlawful oil discharges in the tanker channels and discourage illegal fishing or smuggling. Since the climax of the second Gulf war, naval traffic had dropped off as many coalition ships had eventually headed home to the region's relief. Once again however trouble was in the air and once again there were a lot of big ships around. The American fleets were an awesome sight as they headed up and down on their Gulf patrol with occasional maintenance and re-stocking visits to the ports of Dubai and the naval base at Jebel Ali. The helicopter patrols were especially keen to scrutinize the dhow traffic. It came as a surprise to many foreigners that there were hundreds of these ancient craft still plying their trade between the UAE, Iran and Pakistan, not to mention the cluster of off-shore islands. Some of these were subject to territorial disputes, as there were many ill defined borders around this part of the Gulf and the Straits of Hormuz. Faraj himself had no doubt that numerous of the traditional wooden vessels carried contraband and he was equally certain that most of all the drugs which found their way onto the streets of the UAE were smuggled in by this manner. From time to time, they would drop down to wave height and get up close and personal to give the over-laden vessels a closer inspection. Typically the cargo would be covered by tarpaulins weighed down with old tyres and hawsers stretched across the bulging hold. Some carried engineering equipment and even vehicles for export and occasionally one of the more wealthy seafaring captains would carry his own battered four-wheel drive on board. Although the helicopter crews could not intercept suspect traders, they could identify the vessels, their origin and destinations, and if suspicions *were* aroused, call up the local coast guard to make for assistance.

Gul took the Puma down low to thunder across the sand dunes that backed the beaches and then climbed above the ocean to two thousand feet turning eastward towards the tower blocks of Jumeira. In recent times there had been a new focus of interest and as they approached Jebel Ali they could already see through the dusty haze the new territories emerging from the mirror-like-sea. Millions of tons of rock and sand were being dumped on to the sea bed. Both Gul and Faraj had been astounded at the speed at which the new islands were formed. At first just a few isolated sandbanks broke the surface followed by the formation of a backbone chain as the islands as were linked together defining new territories. Whole mountains had been shifted from the southeast to be dumped into the shallow sea forming a complex array in the shape of a vast palm tree, called quite simply, *The Palm*. Now it was well into the final stages of development with the construction of high end villas, luxury apartments and five star hotels for the millions who were being enticed to spend their dollars on the Gulf's southern shore.

Gul had been of the opinion that, in the first place it could not actually be built, and secondly, that few people would be rushing in to buy the plots at such exorbitant prices. Gul had been wrong, *very* much so, he had latterly acknowledged. All things were possible in Dubai. What he'd failed to see was the promise of year-round-sun, shopping and golf! European winters drove many from their cold northern climes to the sun soaked beaches and the golf courses that had sprouted like mirages from the desert wastes. The Med and Florida had been the traditional hunting grounds of the winter sun seekers and now Dubai had marketed itself as a new and exciting alternative. Yet the success had by the real estate offices and web pages bursting at the seams with prospective buyers meant little to him now.

The air force *had* given him a good life and since his first arrival as a loan officer from Pakistan Naval Aviation, he had given them his best years. After the probation period, he had been fully integrated into the UAE forces and had been witness to the geneses of the helicopter squadrons and even emerged as one of its best pilots and instructors. His value to GHQ had been recognised when he had been selected to lead a team of aircrew to France to test fly the new generation of Super Pumas, and then to undergo pilot training at the Eurocopter facility just outside Marseille. He'd taken the task very seriously and overseen the training of his subordinates with a watchful eye. The French were not always easy to deal with and were often downright stubborn when it came to the grey areas of services and support. Gul had been equally stubborn and defended his employer's stance most vigorously. He'd excelled there as both a pilot and a commander. His reputation had earned him promotion and an extension to his contract, at a time when others around him were being terminated. And now as the government mandate to repatriate the remaining foreign aircrews came into its most clinical phase, he, the best of the best would be on his way home in less than three months. Now that the coup de grace had finally arrived, Gul took it as a personal affront and Faraj witnessed his bitterness at first hand.

His *normal* captain would have caressed the Puma around the skies as if it were a woman, which is exactly what the helicopter was to Gul. He was a devoted admirer and often referred to it as his only love affair. Faraj suspected that if he could have taken it home, he would have slept with it. Today was different however. The gentle hands had become aggressive and he literally threw it through every manoeuvre as if he hated the bitch. Faraj was not unduly alarmed, the Super Puma was built to endure the worst that the elements could throw at it, that was why it was *the* first choice chopper for the coast guards and offshore rig pilots the world over. The first officer knew of the circumstances and he knew that nothing he could say would appease his irate captain. He just sat back and observed as Gul took out his frustrations on his beloved lady – soon to be divorced.

✳✳✳

Two thousand feet below, Molly had slipped quietly through the French windows onto the villa's patio. She stretched in the damp morning air and breathed deeply to clear her lungs of the stale sweat laden atmosphere of Bonetti's bedroom. The AC had been cooling but it had not been able to clear the Italian's body odour and the reek of cigarette smoke from the previous night had clung to his clothing. She bent at an outside water tap to splash cooling water on her face washing the slumber from her eyes as the warm freshness of the early desert day started to invigorate her mind and body. She stepped barefoot around the pool to face north and the open view to the sea – stood feet apart – arms out stretched and let her head tilt back pausing for a second or two before bringing her hands together high above her face. She was oblivious to the throb of the helicopter passing directly overhead as she slowly brought her hands down to point her fingers to her chin and then let them slip further down to her chest in a prayer-like supplication before letting them fall to her sides. A few moments of quite meditation and then she was ready. Her arms came up, extended in front of her at shoulder height with palms facing the ground. Slowly she bent her arms, brought her hands inwards, towards each other, and then lowered her arms so that the palms of her hands rested in front of her thighs. She shifted the weight of her body onto her left foot and moved the right to point to the east and then her right hand up to her shoulder before sweeping her left arm to the right side of her body as if holding a large invisible ball between her arms and right hip. She leant to the east, transferring her weight onto the right foot and gracefully swept her right hand in a downward curve that took it closely past the left hand, letting it come to rest, once more by her thigh to complete the *Grasp Sparrows Tail* form. Already she could feel the chi moving through her body, released by the intrinsically beautiful movements as she followed the routine. A succession of hieroglyphs cleared the energy channels of her body and the nervous system that controlled the forms. From the *Sparrow's Tail* to the *White Crane Spreads its Wings*, the *Needle At The Bottom of the Sea*. Each one addressed to a different point of the compass and each one exercising a different part of the body and mind and was repeated in the poetic melody that was Tai Chi. The morning humidity was slowly being burnt off by the rising sun and as the sun climbed in the dusty sky, so did the temperature. Beads of sweat had formed on Molly's brow and damp patches had spread through her white pyjamas by the time she had moved through *Crossed Hands* and then finally pivoted from the west to face north and conclude her ritual. She stood silently for a few moments, letting the outside world creep back into her life.

She had not heard Bonetti rise from the dead and take a seat on one of the basket chairs by the patio table. He had been woken from his hangover by the beat of the helicopter blades as they drummed pulses of air through his painful skull. He wondered how it could ever recover from the latest abuse and as on most mornings after, he felt like shit. Only his own well practiced routine of a glass of water followed by a coffee flood and the nicotine injection from four cigarettes would transform him into something of use to the world. He was well into the coffee and nicotine by the time Molly had realised his presence, if one could possibly call it a presence. She had stripped off her pyjamas that had clung to her perspiring skin and with hardly a splash, plunged into the pool, gliding under the water to come up for breath at the far end before turning to face the new man in her life. She looked back at him, sitting sprawled across the poolside chair, still dressed in the crumpled white shirt and black trousers that he had pulled on some twenty four hours ago. The night's heavy drinking had precluded any change of attire or shower, so the sweat, alcohol, and cigarettes still pervaded the air around him. Attempts at sexual intercourse had been feeble and perfunctory and it had been to her relief that the big man had succumbed after just a few pathetic gropes and bear hugs, to fall into the anaesthetic of heavy sleep. Now she looked upon him in disgust and wondered how she could survive with this pathetic figure of a man. The money would have to be good – very good.

Bonetti was returning her gaze and it wasn't difficult to see that she was not impressed with his opening romantic overtures. It was he who had crudely christened her Jessie Jane to the amusement of all, but now the ribaldry of the night seemed long timed past. It was only now that he had asked her real name. At that precise moment, Bonetti hated himself and wondered briefly if he might seek relief from his hangover by following the Tai Chi opera that he had just witnessed. The mystique of this oriental practice did look the sort of thing that he needed to escape the fetters of the body that he was cursed with. Yet in his present condition, standing on one leg whilst waving his arms around did not immediately strike him as the easiest thing to perform at that moment. Another cigarette was a safer bet to steady the shaking hands.

***

Jebel Ali was busy, mostly with tankers, freighters and the tenders of the bigger vessels that were anchored off shore. The navy base was less crowded with only a couple of smaller patrol vessels and landing craft tied up. What caught the eye though was the capital ship of the Dubai Navy: the *Al Fujairah* which was a little dated but had been refitted with the latest trappings of modern warfare and was now firmly established as the pride of the Gulf Fleet. Both Gul and Faraj were aware however that the ship spent little time at sea and for most of the time could be seen tied up opposite the base HQ. It was apparent that the navy also suffered the same crewing shortages as did the helicopter squadrons. Gul guessed that prior to the mass repatriations most of her crew had also been from the Indian subcontinent. Still she was an impressive sight and undoubtedly a deterrent to any would be aggressor.

Further east came the new skyline of Jumeira, its new glittering, palatial hotels lining the beach front that would be paced by the latest batch of sun seekers. As the Puma flew overhead, both the early swimmers and the construction workers of the *Palm Islands* who had been labouring in the same morning's humidity, looked skywards to catch sight of the helicopter. Beyond *The Palm*, came the real star of Jumeirah – the Burj Al Arab, the signature building of Dubai. Rising over three hundred and twenty metres above the sea and beach, *The Burj*, as it was locally known, was the first seven-star hotel in the whole Gulf region. Its stunning architecture, a figure of the utmost opulence, left the vision of it indelibly etched in the memory all that'd had seen it. Flying at an altitude of six hundred metres, Faraj had the impression of being within touching distance of the futuristic, sail-like, glass and steel sculpture. They passed on the landward side level with the helicopter pad that stretched so dramatically from near the top of the main tower. It seemed to invite the Puma to visit, but the imposing height and precipitous drop to the sea, were enough to prompt anxiety even amongst the most experienced aviators.

Gul would have loved to fly lower and pass so close to the hotel front in order to give some breakfasting millionaire a more dramatic early morning call to that which had first awakened him. Just for a second, Gul considered it – a buzz – in every sense of the word. It would be his first and last one though, as by the time they had got back to base, the military police would have been waiting on the Sweihan tarmac to welcome his return. Gul let a grin pass under his face mask at the thought. Ha! That would shock the bastards. Almost worth the loss of the paltry pension that had been offered that morning. Professionalism made sure that the helicopter continued its projected course. If only Faraj had known what thoughts had triggered Gul's fleeting moment of silent humour!

Off to the north and completely lost in the haze were the foundation structures of yet another startling man-made archipelago known as *The World*. As its name implied and like *The Palm*, it was a series of man made islands constructed with mountains of excavated rock laid down to represent an atlas view of the world. It too was to be adorned with lavish villas and apartments. If that was not astonishing enough, Gul knew, that even at that moment, construction had commenced on two further Palm Island developments being laid down a few hundred metres off the Dubai shore line. A few minutes later, it was Dubai's own commercial deep water port of Port Rashid that passed silently below. The unmistakable outline of the QE2 lay moored, awaiting transformation into yet another luxury hotel. Then on to one of the few natural navigable channels in the region, the Dubai Creek. It was into the Creek that many of the dhows and smaller ferries passed on the final part of their journey to deposit their cargoes within easy reach of the souqs and innumerable small business warehouses.

Further to the east, the coast would take them past Sharjah, Ras Al Khaimah and eventually to the Straits of Hormuz: The narrow passage into the Persian Gulf for all its oil tankers, commercial traders and the naval might of the Americans. The strategic importance of Hormuz was lost on no one. Just to the north were the islands of Abu Musa and Tunb, which were at the limit of the UAE's territorial waters. In reality the actual oceanic boundary was ill defined and remained very much a bone of contention. Whilst the UAE claimed sovereignty of the islands, the Iranians had unilaterally occupied some, whether as threat of future expansion or as a defensive measure, nobody was quite certain. It caused great unease amongst the UAE leaders. Gul had flown many missions in the area and conceded that they were quite tricky outings. On the one hand, they had to show the flag and monitor the sea lanes with vigilance, but on the other, to stray beyond what was unilaterally declared by the Iranians as their perimeter would provoke an aggressive response that might lead to a serious diplomatic incident. The width of the Straits of Hormuz was only fifty kilometres or so, and of strategic importance to not only the UAE, Oman and Iran, but all the nations at the head of the Gulf. Gul felt that the present stalemate would continue to exist. With such powerful American forces in the Gulf, the Iranians had no intention of giving Washington the slightest excuse to intervene. The Arabs, despite fervent claims to the contrary, were not in a military position to exercise any belligerence of their own. For the time being they preferred to let sleeping dogs lay. Gul found that he didn't care any longer and was surprised to find that his own ethics would not be troubled if the Iranians took it upon themselves to occupy a few more of the contentious islands. Without him and the other expatriate expertise forming the pillar of the UAE's armed forces, they were a toothless organisation. The shift of his allegiance was as sudden as it was irreversible. The Puma swung round and headed back the way it had come. The cockpit mood had become one of tension and disquiet. Neither man spoke, but despite the din from the engines and the deafening beat of the rotors, the change was tangible. Faraj had become filled with a growing apprehension. Strange he thought how the two pilots could communicate without any physical exchange between them. Sweihan airbase couldn't come into view quickly enough.

CHAPTER 15

Desert Meat

Although it was well past midnight, Ashley's mind and body were still in a different time zone and the day's lack of physical activity, had left him wide awake. From the lofty perch of one of the Sheraton's penthouse suites the path along the Creek seemed like the likely place to burn off some of the excess energy. At the same time it would offer a few quiet moments for Ashley to get some thoughts together about the task ahead. The misted apartment windows should have hinted that it would be a rather less comfortable way to pass the time than he had imagined. The resident Philippino band was rendering a melodic *Blue Bayou* when he stepped through the hotel's automatic doors. The fog of humidity hit him like a wall of water. The summer was past its worst, but even this late in the year as the sun went down, so the humidity soared. The lack of any breeze did not help and within seconds, Ashley's shirt was sticking to his body. The normal midday temperatures were in the order of forty plus, and he guessed that it couldn't be far off that peak now.

He turned out of the lobby entrance and walked past the concierges busily attending to arriving and departing guests. The Dubai hotels were always busy no matter how obscene the hour and Ashley had to weave through the late surge to follow a jogging path across the cultivated garden. Lawn sprinklers were adding their own water vapour to the already heavy atmosphere. As he moved away from the building, Ashley had the sensation that he was not alone. In daylight, the inside of his sunglasses were like wing mirrors enabling him to catch glimpses of the scene behind him without any hint that he was watching his own back. But at night, shop windows or reflections from parked cars were useful sensors. In this case the dark glass cladding of the hotel gave a broad panorama revealed nothing untoward. As he moved further through the hotel gardens, the residual heat that the tarmac and buildings had absorbed during the blistering daylight hours diminished. He turned left and strolled up the creek side trail. Over on the far western side of the water, the residential area of the city was at last showing signs of easing into slumber. But on his side, the towering blocks of hotels and apartments gave no indication of reduced activity. Neons and lasers flashed into the night sky and traffic was still heavy on the highways. Across and over his left shoulder there was one particular luminous exhibit that attracted his attention. High up on a nearby tower an animated electronic drummer was beating a drum. The figure was somehow out of place here, rather antiquated and perhaps belonging to an older generation than the more blatant illuminations of the modern era. As Ashley moved along the path, a second lower display came into view. It caused him to halt in mid-step – *Lighthouse* – so this was it! He had inadvertently discovered Bonetti's local lair. He paused to scan up and down the windows, in search of a clue as to whether or not the Italian was at that moment busily cooking his books. Then remembering the local time, he dismissed the idea that the man could be still working. A glance behind showed the track was clear.

He continued the saunter as the path took him to the road side and across the side streets that led to the jetties lining the creek. Here the pace of life had eased, though there was some movement amongst the shadows as vessels were either tied up or departed. It was the dhow harbour. In practice there were many scattered around the emirate, but when one spoke of *the* Creek Dhow Harbour, this was it. The air was full of complex smells, a mixture of diesel fumes, engine exhausts and cooking. Crews either bought food from the dock side stalls or rustled up their own delights from a primus or charcoal grill. Amongst the myriad of exotic aromas was one that excited him, bringing back memories of times gone by – Kretek! –

Somebody was smoking Kretek – cloves! Very popular in Indonesia but uncommon here, he would have thought. He peered into the night to perhaps catch a glimpse of some Javanese vessel, but dismissed the idea as dark shadows moved to and fro. Most dhows were quiet and just riding the swell of the river, but down one of the jetties, deck hands were unloading one particularly darkened boat. Heavy stuff, judging by the slow progress that the labourers were making in transferring bundles onto the back of a Toyota pick-up.

Ashley hesitated, his curiosity instantly aroused. There was no conversation. Had they noticed him? In the dark, he had made out four dim shadows, but now only one was left on the dock side. The others had merged into the shadows or gone below – conceivably their task completed. The moment was frozen, his senses suddenly become alert and the wet hairs on the back of his neck bristled. The creek water had always been lapping against the wooden hulls but it was only now that he heard it. Loose rigging slapped against the multitude of masts. The waves from a passing vessel disturbed the dhows and he could hear the groan of taut ropes as the hawsers held them tight to the jetty. His curiosity got the better of him. He *had* to investigate – but as he stepped towards the Toyota, vibrations in his pocket alerted him to an SMS reception. It carried a single word: *symfony*! Ashley was mystified and sensed urgency in the message's brevity and miss-spelling. Once again he glanced around at the now deserted quay. It was deathly quiet – too quiet. For once prudence overcame curiosity and he reluctantly decided to move on. The SMS diversion, was it timely or purely coincidental? Ashley rarely accepted coincidence, but the moment ebbed away as his growing suffocation became increasingly intolerable. The humidity was causing his sinuses to swell so much that he had to breathe through his mouth. The cool, refreshing aircon of the hotel promised instant relief, so after a cursory glance back towards the quay, he sought the sanctuary of the Sheraton.

Still puzzled by the anonymous text message, he searched the shadows for a possible source and at the same time his thoughts returned to the other matter that was troubling him – Goodwin –

how was Peter Goodwin connected to this hot, steamy metropolis?

The journalist's hesitation on the harbour side *had* been noticed and it *had* brought a frown of concern to the brow of a sweating Samir as he nervously oversaw the transfer of missiles, mortars and Kalashnikovs. Fearing intervention, he had continued with the transfer in the best air of normality that he could muster whilst his cohorts slid out of view. The Dhow from Karachi had evaded all the attentions of the coast guard and helicopter patrols, but these were the trickiest moments, and for one heart stopping minute Samir feared that they had been compromised. The other men had hidden behind the pick-up, and from where he stood, Samir caught the glint of a knife blade. He suddenly wondered what in God's name *was he* doing here. This was a very different world that he was entering, people were in danger, someone was going to get hurt! He was finding himself being completely overtaken by events. Events that he, of all people had triggered. Insha'allaah. Samir looked up at the Lighthouse building and thought for an instant that he had seen the drummer miss a beat whilst overseeing the harbour drama, but knew that it could only be his imagination. His own pulse which had been thudding in his ears started to ease and as logic prevailed, his confidence gradually returned. He twisted around to tie down the tarpaulin covers, now that the boat had been freed of its illicit cargo. His brothers slept silently below. Over the next twenty-four hours they would gradually disperse so as not to attract unwanted attention and lodge themselves with compatriots, posing as labourers or cleaners. The time for their other professional skills would come later.

It was a pivotal moment for the Jordanian. Beforehand Samir was the jealous keeper of secrets, other people's secrets, and lived in that role with the sublime satisfaction of knowing what others didn't. Now that he had shared his grand secret a great void had opened up in his life. The sensations of power, of reason and importance were lost. Suddenly he felt terribly vulnerable as others took control.

✳✳✳

The garden sprinklers once again burst into life.

'Thanks be to Goodwin!' – Just what did that mean? Just exactly what linked Bonetti and his technician, Samir, with Goodwin? And what did they know about Goodwin? Undoubtedly Bonetti provided a link between Goodwin, CIPHERCAN, Lighthouse and Samir, and therefore it was probable that whatever had been revealed to Samir had been somehow passed on through the Italian. Bonetti could, despite all the investigations that had failed to find Goodwin's murderer, still be the culprit. A precise motive for the death of the cryptologist had never been clearly determined, but the timing of his disappearance and the secrets that he locked away in that vast memory certainly pointed a finger at CIPHERCAN and Bonetti.

***

The crescendo of the final lines of Leonard Bernstein's *New York* flooded the lobby from the bar beyond, greeting Ashley as the concierge moved to open the door. He was immediately grateful to feel the cool air and breathed in slowly and deeply so that it could ease his blocked sinuses. The clammy shirt took in the chill of the *aircon* but as he moved through to the bar, it was the dish-dash of an Arab who had followed him in, that caught his attention. The bottom of the white robe was drenched and stuck to his legs as the figure limped across to the bathrooms.

It was an exhausted Ashley who took a large gulp of cool refreshing beer. The sequin clad singers had wound up their performance in the gusto demanded by the final *New York, New York* and the bar's late drinkers were beginning to drift away. The cooling beer was getting to the important parts as the journalist considered a different sort of symphony.

***

The questions that Ashley was turning over in his mind, and the few answers that surfaced, urged him to seek assistance – local assistance and none was more informed about the security environment in Dubai than its own Ministry of the Interior. They, after all, Clements had told him, were not only his sponsors in the Emirate but they also had all the resources. When it was all said and done, were it not for their help, MI6 would not be here. Whether or not there was much to glean from them, Ashley was not sure, but he at least felt that it would be courteous to involve them, at least to keep them informed. As it transpired, it was not Ashley's decision. The hand-delivered message that arrived on the morning after his midnight promenade pre-empted his own call for conference. The authentication of the message was never in question as Ashley immediately recognized the courier, Sheikh Ali's chauffeur. And it was the very same fellow who picked him up that evening in a standard Dubai taxi. Ashley wondered if this fellow had been appointed as his personal minder, or observer. The quiet confidence and overt muscular presence seemed rather out of place in the elegance of his white thobe and guttrah, but if he needed a minder, then he filled the bill most adequately.

***

The taxi was for show only. Soon after they left the Sheraton, Ashley was invited to change vehicles at one of the city's multitude of shopping malls. Minder parked the taxi and as they came to rest alongside a four wheel drive, its rear door was pushed open and a beckoning hand appeared from within. Minder climbed into the front passenger seat and the Land Cruiser moved off into the traffic stream. Perfume and polish filled the cool air with an expensive aroma as he was welcomed by Colonel Ali Abdullah who lifted his regal hand to indicate the perpetual jam of crawling traffic. 'We will find a more quiet place to enjoy the evening and give you some experience of something er, let us say, a bit more in the Arabic tradition.' And added, as an afterthought: 'I trust you find the hotel both comfortable and ideally located?'

Ashley confirmed his satisfaction and wondered if, by location, Colonel Ali was referring to its proximity to the Lighthouse tower, or the dhow harbour, or both? Apart from the background of Arabic music and the occasional exchange between the driver and the Head of MOI sitting beside him, the rest of the journey passed off without much further conversation. Ashley was happy that someone else was driving, as he drew comparisons with the rush hour M25 back in London. It left him with the conclusion that everywhere was the same, there was just no escape from grid lock. But he was mistaken! It wasn't long before the driver using local knowledge and some belligerence, had got them out of the city, heading south towards the Hajar Mountains. They moved faster into the night now as buildings and the signs of suburban life were left behind, but on more than one occasion had to brake sharply.

'Camels!' explained the driver and sure enough the headlights caught a herd of them crossing the road without a hint of urgency or fear.

Ashley felt the need to break the silence. 'It seems that camels only have two speeds, dead slow and stop!'

'Not at all my friend,' smiled his host. 'Camel racing is big business in this part of the world – and let me assure you, these creatures can be fleet of foot, or rather – hoof,' he corrected. Minder wound down the window to bellow some Arabic curse at the hump backed pedestrians, but without any noticeable effect. The warm stench of animals infiltrated the Toyota and Minder cursed again before winding up the window. The offending beasts carried on their pedantic way, showing not the slightest hint of offence or acceleration.

'Kabir Mushcula – big problem, very dangerous!'

Ashley commented satirically, if he was referring to the smell or the sneer of fearsome teeth that had been the animal's sole response to their meeting.

The Colonel chuckled and, not sure if Ashley was jesting, informed him, 'Yes those too, but on the road is what he means. Many a driver has lost his life hitting stray camels in the night. They are so tall that when hit by a car, the legs just buckle and the body of the camel comes flying through the windscreen.

'Death by suffocation or bad breath?' enquired the Englishman, with a sly grin on his face.

'Mabruk Mr. Ashley, you have a good sense of humour. Insha'allaah, you will never find out,' laughed the Colonel.

The Land cruiser turned off the road onto a dark desert track. They bumped along for a kilometre or so and then, as they crested a rise, Ashley saw lights ahead. There was another vehicle already parked up, with headlights blazing and a number of smaller lights apparently defining their destination. The driver moved into four wheel drive as the depth of sand on the track began to slow the vehicle and caused it to slew from side to side. But they were there now as the Land cruiser drew up besides the first vehicle and switched off the power and lights. Having pinpointed the rendezvous, the driver of the other car also switched off, so that other than the cooling noises from the hot engines, they were immersed into a shock of silence under the moonless night. As they alighted, the group congregated around the Colonel and exchanged greetings. Each man in turn approached to shake hands, embrace, touch noses and effect kisses to both cheeks before making way for the next.

Alsalam Alaikoum – Alaikoum Alsalam, the master's entourage adding the assidi – sir, in acknowledgement of his position. Immediately the Arabic formalities were completed, each of the men moved forward to greet Ashley. He was surprised by both their friendly embrace and their respect in addressing *him* as assidi. He was left with the feeling that they were all well aware of his purpose for being in the Emirates and exactly whom he was representing. Uncertain about the next stage in the protocol, Ashley hesitated, not wanting to put a foot out of place, but his hosts, aware of his awkwardness, invited him to take his place. A large square of carpets had been spread across the shallow dip between the sand dunes. Ashley kicked off his shoes as he took his place sitting crossed legged, facing the others as they joined him in the square. A cushion was strategically placed for each of the assembly as a prop to lean against. The two drivers took up their secondary role as waiters and moved amongst those seated to serve dates and Arabic coffee from an ornate jug. Ashley, being served first as the official guest, waited until the others had received their drink. They all waited until the

Colonel raised the shallow cup to his lips and then followed suite. The rich aroma of cardamom filled his nostrils but the hot cloudy liquid stung his lips so that he had to wait for it to cool before taking a sip. Driver one waited close by for an immediate refill and Ashley felt obliged to rush his drink so that his attendant could move on to the next man. Conversation was shallow but polite and Ashley had the feeling that they were waiting for something or for somebody else, to join them. It seemed an age, but eventually the reason for the interval became apparent.

Triggered by some unseen signal each man rose to his feet and as Ashley made an effort to follow, the Colonel leant across towards him with a sweep of his arm, invited his guest to remain as he was. 'We have prayer time Mr Ashley; it's time for the Isha prayer. Please relax, you will not disturb us – and then we will eat.'

'Thank you sir, but it's years since I spent this long sat crossed legged. If I don't move now, I might never recover the use of my legs.' Ashley rose too and with slight embarrassment, moved away from the carpets and left the Arabs to face north-west to Mecca, the holy city.

The Englishman made a slightly exaggerated show of stretching his legs and moved as silently as possible to the perimeter of the sandy bowl in which the camp had been laid. The men stood in a line side by side behind the Colonel. It was he who took the lead in the prayer routine. Sitting astride the crest of the highest dune Ashley took the time to view the surrounding terrain. The blackness was intense. There were no immediate man-made lights surrounding the camp, but to the north, the city glow of Dubai filled that part of the night sky. To the south, it was darker still. No evidence of any population there, nor to the east. With Dubai behind him, Ashley looked up into the heavens where stars decorated a cloudless sky. He was startled by the clouds of bright stars and as he turned, it was not difficult to pick out Venus and Saturn, and the outline of Orion was well defined. The inevitable humidity of the autumn evening was adding to the twinkle and distortion, but he could well imagine that on a winter's night a decent telescope would reveal many stellar

236

delights. He had rarely seen such a spectrum through the clouds of an English winter night. The flashing lights of high altitude aircraft were threading their way amongst nature's evening show.

In the hollow, Ashley had felt the increasing humidity, but up on the dune the hint of a breeze coming down from the nearby mountains refreshed him. He was thankful to be able to breathe more easily and the perspiration on his brow dried. Such a contrast with the climate of northern Canada. There the air was cool, clear and perfumed with pine leaves. Where every vista was a colourful embroidery of nature. The sounds were also different. Here on the south-eastern tip of the Arabian Peninsula, the desert was whispering as grains of sand caught by zephyrs, flowed over each other. The lakes and forests of North America were an adagio with a background hum of insects and birdcalls producing a symphony of sound. The haunting call of the loons completed the orchestrations. Symphony? Ha!...... another orchestration came to mind and with it came a chill that made him shudder, even on that warm desert evening – It was the raucous call of alarm – the call of the gulls as they wheeled around in the sky above taking turns to dive on Goodwin's sad waterlogged corpse. In all the horror of that discovery, the empty eye sockets were the single most tragic and shocking image that he had ever witnessed. That, and the steel wire garrotte, that had almost severed the cryptologist's head.

***

Following the simple and apparently innocuous text message, plucked so dramatically from the ether by Mercury, Ashley at last felt that there was an answer to be found. And that the answer was close at hand. It had become a personal thing, and Clements in his wisdom had not only recognised the impact that Goodwin's gruesome demise had had on his young accomplice, but had cultivated it. The seeds of intrigue and enquiry had grown into a passionate desire to point the finger at the Cambridge man's murderer.

There was hardly a smoking gun and the only obvious motivation to silence Goodwin lay with CIPHERCAN and its leading light, Carlo Bonetti. He had been in Toronto at the time, so he had the opportunity. But what exactly was the motive? The method of dispensing with Goodwin was not beyond anybody of reasonable strength, but somehow Bonetti did not strike him as being the type to get his fingers dirty. Generating the plan was more likely to be Bonetti's role. Conducting the play, yes maybe, but actually carrying out the grisly deed was beneath the Italian's dignity. If Bonetti had a killer instinct, it was in the world of business and high finance, not one that involved physical brutality. The question remained – would he kill for big money?

The usual investigations by the RCMP had uncovered no evidence that could positively implicate either Bonetti or CIPHERCAN. The company had a reputation of integrity and of being a highly professional organisation. These were its most valuable assets in an industry, where competitors were only too eager to exploit the merest whiff of scandal. Goodwin was inextricably linked with CIPHERCAN and his death had inevitably tarnished the company's image. The CIPHERCAN board of directors had issued more than one statement – each to appease its now dubious customers and to point out that the company had nothing whatsoever to gain from the loss of its senior cryptologist. Quite the reverse.

Indeed, CIPHERCAN *had* suffered a major blow. First and foremost, it no longer had the mathematical services of one of the most brilliant scientists in the field, but also its previously blemish-free reputation was now under scrutiny. And it was this wound that was being so viciously exploited by its rivals. Rumours were rife and spread readily by the opportunists in the industry, and broadcast by hungry journalists who acted like a pack of hyenas, seizing upon any morsel of suspicion from which to foment a new eye-catching headline.

Yet the pertinent questions remained: why and who? An answer to the first would surely give a strong indication to the second. In the meantime, Ashley had only two factors known to him that could provide an insight into the events in Canada. One was that Goodwin was about to contentiously make revelations about the newly adopted global algorithm, NAMES, and the other was the *Thanks be to Goodwin*, message from this fellow, Samir. From this simple statement, it was plain to see that Samir had discovered something quite fundamental about Goodwin and that implied some knowledge about the algorithm. The source of this revelation had to come through Bonetti. This was the prime reason for Ashley to be, at that moment, sat on top of a sand dune on a humid evening witnessing the conclusion of the day's Islamic vespers.

The most immediate issue, as far as Ashley was concerned, was to establish what exactly was of interest to the UAE intelligence fraternity, and what they knew that he didn't. The cessation of his host's incantations to Mecca had brought him back to the present and he was eager to exchange some ideas, information and assess opinions garnered from a different viewpoint. His keenness to pursue the matter was tempered by the appreciation that local protocols were to be observed. The MOI had shown its respect for their guest in inviting him to this conference with all the trimmings attached. In this setting, Ashley recognised something of his own strategy in getting the best out of people. Information flowed more readily from a mind at ease rather than one stressed by explicit examination. Spying, after all, was about watching and waiting. Now *he* had to wait a little longer.

***

A flurry of activity broke out below as the Arabs finished their prayers. Pitchers of water were produced for the washing of hands. Colonel Ali called to Ashley that he should join them. The two of them sat on one corner of the square whilst the others busied themselves preparing the food. Minder came round again with the Arabic coffee, which he served from a traditional brass samovar. The piping hot cardamom was difficult to swallow quickly and Ashley felt once more, a touch embarrassed that Minder stood in patient attendance behind them, in case a refill was required. The

Colonel took his time and then signalled with a shake of the cup that he had had enough. Ashley took the cue and also declined a refill from Minder who collected the thimble sized cups and retired to leave them to their discussions. Once again Ashley felt the discomfort of the humidity, and fuelled by the hot cardamom started to perspire heavily around the neck and head. Ali Abdullah sensed Ashley's impatience and put him somewhat ease by saying that the subject would be more comfortably discussed after the evening meal.

The drivers now doubled as waiters and brought three large platters of food from the first vehicle. One plate carried Arabic bread and an array of pickles; the second a massive pile of rice and the third when the aluminium foil had been removed, revealed the piece de resistance – a complete roasted goat. It certainly smelt more appetizing than it looked, and Ashley was quick to feign the delight of the others who had squatted around to join the feast. Unfortunately for the Englishman, the creature's skull faced directly his position and every time he reached across to pluck some meat from its carcass, he was forced to overlook the toothy leer. The others tore at the goat, ripping shreds of the most tender of morsels from the skeleton with their bare hands. 'Allow me,' spoke the Colonel, as he leaned across and plucked a portion of darker meat from the rib cage and then put it on the small plate in front of his guest.

Ashley was startled that someone else should serve him with their bare hands, but rightly took it as a mark of respect. The inner parts of the beast were still very hot, so care had to be taken, but the rice had cooled such that he had no difficulty in taking a handful of it and like the others squeezed it into a ball before popping it into his mouth. All of this done under the watchful eyes of the locals to see if he could cope with eating Arabic style, and more importantly following the Islamic requirement of only using his right hand to carry food to his mouth. He generally managed to avoid too many pickles, especially the purple ones, which nearly took his head off when he first bit into one, but the Colonel would insist on serving him the best choice.

In surprisingly quick time, the goat had been reduced to a mere skeleton. Not that it had ever looked like *The Fatted Calf*, if any of the live ones he had seen were anything to go by. Both eyes and the tongue had disappeared, eaten by whom, he did not question, but was just thankful that nobody had plucked either to lay at his place. The khobza, as the meal was locally defined, was washed down with cans of cold Pepsi. Ashley was grateful for the drink and also for the cool condensation that collected on the can. His right hand, by the end of the meal, was a mass of sticky rice that became even more adhesive as it cooled into super glue. Ashley was not impressed as it welded all his fingers together in one glutinous mass and added to the discomfort of sitting crossed legged for an hour or so. The last time he had done that was back in his school days, and now that the time had come to move around, he was doubtful if he could ever straighten his knees out, let alone walk again. So it was a much-relieved Ashley who stood with the others and took his turn at the water barrel to wash off the rice and filaments of goat from his hands.

'Mabruk!' smiled the others, content with his ritualistic performance as they cleared away what remained of the meal.

The whole evening had tired him and although he was sure that it was not his host's intention, he felt himself like the well-tenderised goat when the time came to discuss serious matters. Ashley longed for the cool air of the air conditioner. True, the air had cooled as had the sand which retained little heat from the blistering daylight sun. But the humidity became heavier as the night wore on, the only relief being the occasional puffs of wind that stirred the sand.

Minder passed around serving *sulamani* mint tea in tiny glasses and another round of Pepsi, whilst his nameless companion arranged sheesha pipes for one and all. The charcoal had been previously prepared. For Ashley could see the glow of heat as it was loaded onto the silver foil of each pipe in turn. He felt that it would not be the right time to refuse on account of his being a non smoker. To his relief however, his host informed that they were smoking nothing more than an apple mixture that night. When all were seated, the Arabs took obvious pleasure in the deep inhalations of aromatic smoke. Ashley had never smoked in his life, but the first tentative breath was rewarded with a rich aromatic vapour cooled by the water through which it bubbled when he drew on the pipe. Other than the pleasant taste, he felt no sense of narcotic effect except from the moments of peaceful silence that surrounded them as they sat under the stars. The pleasing bubbling of the *hubbly-bubblys* invoked a feeling of bonhomie although Ashley was sure that each of his new friends was, as he was, gathering their thoughts together for what would follow. The Colonel took a particularly deep breath and lent back on his cushion slowly and, apparently with some reluctance, expelled the smoke in the direction of Orion. It was the signal for the serious debate to begin and the drivers and the others making up the party fringe moved some distance away to chatter, cross legged and take turns to stroll around the camp perimeter. This left Colonel Ali Abdullah, Minder and himself at one corner of the rug.

***

'Mr Ashley, if we could get down to business now?'

'Of course,' nodded Ashley.

'I've known Commander Clements for many years. We were at Sandhurst together. I spent two years under his tutorship on intelligence work and we have confided in each other a great deal ever since. But of course, strictly on matters in which we had a common interest. In this day of threats from terrorism we share a good deal of information. Particularly the fruits of surveillance whether they be from simple manual observation, or electronic intercepts. However, we here have little background knowledge of *Symphony*. If you would be so kind as to fill us in.' Ashley wondered if *us* including the whole of the MOI or was it just Minder and himself who needed to know? 'Then we may be able to help you more than we have done so far.'

Ashley was never one to divulge a great deal about anything, but Clements had indicated his confidence in his Arabic associate and that was good enough for Ashley. Even so, there were limitations to what he felt comfortable in relating to the Colonel. Besides a fair proportion of what Ashley had, was either just supposition or simply a gut feeling. He didn't also wish to cloud the subject with vague allusions that might mistakenly influence the MOI's own theories and their possible reactions. The last thing he wanted was somebody else jumping in and stirring the already muddy water. Nevertheless, he needed the Colonel's people and technical resources, even if they were just watchers, or minders. It was reassuring, if not useful, to have somebody minding his back, but a poor minder was just like carrying a flag around to announce his otherwise unnoticed presence. Wherever possible, Ashley preferred his own company which readily enabled him to merge inconspicuously into everyday life. Journalism opened many doors and gave him the right to ask the pertinent questions that others were not qualified to. Officially he was here to monitor the events surrounding DUBEXAIR. *Janes'* were expected to be there with their journal recording the new aviation hardware and security innovations, sales, and opinions. *Janes* was read by everybody in the industry as the world's gospel of military development. In the upcoming exhibition, he would lose himself in exactly that role, but for the moment he had to observe the build up and the people involved in it. That included Bonetti and his CIPHERCAN people.

***

Ashley felt comfortable about describing the events in Toronto and Canada, without actually reliving the gruesome findings in Temagami. This was after all already in the public domain. The discovery of the *Thanks be to Goodwin* message was also known to the Arabs.

The Colonel and Minder sat passively listening to the confirmation of what they already knew. When he finally raised the issue of Lighthouse, he not only sensed increasing interest but also saw reinforcement of this on the Colonel's furrowed brow. Until that moment, the Colonel had studied Ashley's face intently. His brown eyes glinted in the lantern lights, catching every facial innuendo, seeking to penetrate the Englishman's defences for any reservation, or shortfall.

The only thing that Ashley omitted to elaborate on was the discussion that he had had on the Toronto waterfront, with Goodwin's protégé, Steve.

There was a grave silence when Ashley concluded. Just the sand hissing slightly as it moved under the impetus of a draught from the mountains beyond. The Colonel's thoughtful eyes, hidden in shadow, continued to bore into Ashley's mind as if expecting more. Ashley returned the gaze, himself wondering what information *his host* had to offer. It was like a gunfighter standoff at some oriental Ok Coral, with neither wanting to give way, nor take the next step. Ashley felt himself being examined, his very integrity being brought into question. The Arabs couldn't expect him to divulge everything that he knew. It was the nature of the game. A silent negotiation before both parties' cards could be laid on the table. The silence continued, as did the optical examination. What did they know? Ashley could see why Clements held the Colonel in high esteem, but Ashley too was a master in this game. His ability to dismiss compromising elements from his mind, replacing them with freely available specifics was like dropping a protective firewall behind his eyes. Ashley had told the truth. If it had been otherwise, then the Colonel would most certainly have discerned it. What the latter did discern however was that Ashley had been frank and surmised that there was little else to come from his guest.

Just as the man from the MOI had been observing him, so *had* Ashley been watching and waiting. As he was mentally summarising what Ashley had told him, the Colonel momentarily relaxed, dropping his guard, letting his gaze shift into the night. In that instant Ashley knew that the locals were keeping something from him! That *was* interesting! What did they know?

***

'Mabruk, Mr Ashley, enough of the mind games,' he conceded. Minder stirred in relief of the break in the intellectual hiatus as

Colonel Ali went on to say. 'What is of immediate concern to us, is the security of the exhibition and ultimately the security of our state. The eyes of the world are on Dubai, Mr Ashley. We have emerged from the Bedouin lifestyle to develop the most advanced society of the Middle East, if not the entire world. We have one of the world's best airlines, a city that boasts a skyline second to none, a commercial centre that has attracted the investment of billions from the financial sector and tourism blessed with sunshine, sandy beaches, horse racing and a clutch of classic golf courses that the very best search out to play. Add to these, the most prestigious military and aviation exhibitions that one could either visit or exhibit at and you can see that we have a lot to lose. Dubai holds an undoubtedly tenuous position as the leading state of the Middle East and all other nations look to emulate or surpass it – and *all* of this achieved in little over a decade.

He continued. 'Terrorism has, most fortunately, largely passed us by, but we are not blind to the threat and we keep a very close watch to maintain our peace and progress. However, we have neither the resources nor the experience to maintain this watch on our own and so we have sought assistance from supportive and trusted nations. Without doubt, our most trusted partnership is that with Britain and to a lesser extent with the Americans. Britain and the UAE have a unique relationship that has grown in strength from the days when the British instigated and defended the then Trucial States from the jealous desires eyes of our neighbours, namely Saudi and Persia. Since *nine eleven* and the bombings in Madrid and London, our organisations have come closer together. Today, the exchange of information between the two of us has unearthed what appears to be a new threat which, on the face of it, is common to both our nations. However, just exactly what that threat is and who its perpetrators are, remain to be seen. So Mr Ashley, we are delighted to welcome you here as London's advisor in this common cause and I, on behalf of our ruler and people, will offer whatever we can in bringing the issue to a satisfactory conclusion.'

Ashley nodded slowly, acknowledging the alliance. Perhaps a formal speech of acceptance on behalf of Queen and country was expected, even warranted, but Ashley kept it personal. 'Ali Abdullah,' risking his preferred informality – 'We don't really have any precise information about what exact threats *do* exist. Goodwin's death was a pretty serious development. – We can't prove anything, but there's a lot of conjecture about who might be responsible. Just how this affects the UAE and the region we can but speculate. A great deal of uneasiness also persists regarding CIPHERCAN and NAMES. Until the interception of the Goodwin text, there was no apparent connection with the UAE or Dubai. Even now the link with Lighthouse and this fellow Samir is not clear – this is the reason I'm here – to investigate this link and whatever might lay beyond it.'

'So this is the extent of what you know?'

'Yes – It all went quiet after Toronto, nobody wanted to touch it,' and as an afterthought, Ashley added, 'too many people were too nervous about the truth rearing its ugly head.'

'Too many heads on the block?'

'Ha!' Ashley chortled. 'Maybe, but I have the feeling that it is not quite as simple as that.'

'So in your opinion, Goodwin's murder was job related? Not just a sad coincidence of his being in the wrong place at the wrong time? Insha'allaah.'

'Insha'allaah,' echoed the normally silent Minder.

'What is your next step?' enquired an intense Colonel Ali Abdullah.

'I need to know more about Lighthouse, its personnel and contracts, and especially everything that you have on Samir. – Then we have to find out what in heaven he discovered about Goodwin. Why he sent this message and what it meant to his associates. I guess that I need to have a look at his computer and his communications – not forgetting Bonetti of course. He is still very much number one on my list!'

The Colonel thought for a moment, rubbed his stubbled chin, and then responded. 'Whatever the Jordanian and Italian are involved in, I am sure – no! – I am *certain,* that Sheikh Hamed, the owner of

Lighthouse, is *not* aware of it. He is directly related our royal family and he is one of the main sponsors of the DUBEXAIR exhibition, and in fact it is he who chairs the Dubai Exhibitions Council. Hamed has too much to lose should things go wrong. I know this man – he is a good Emirati and has done much for Dubai.'

'Well, I have no reason to believe otherwise Colonel Ali.' Ashley reverted to formality, sensing that he had become annoyed by the fact that a relative of his might somehow be implicated. Choosing his words carefully he added, 'I think that in these circumstances it is best if we keep him er – in the dark as it were. We don't want to give any warning, inadvertent or otherwise, to Bonetti or Samir. If they have an inkling that they are under investigation, then it will make our task all the more difficult.' The word danger was on his lips but whilst he didn't speak of it, it did occur to him that, for the first time, there *may* be a hidden personal menace. After all, Goodwin had died.

'We are in agreement then – about keeping things low key. From our part we have to have a serious look at what, or who might be a target and who might be plotting.'

Ashley took in every word. He found it surprising that the Colonel was so eager to assume that there was a threat to the UAE. From what *he* knew, the only indication that there might be a risk to the region was the fact that the Goodwin intercept had originated here. It was the cryptologist's murder that brought him to Dubai. The link with CIPHERCAN and Bonetti was obvious but that with Lighthouse and beyond was tenuous to say the least. So how could Colonel Ali Abdullah so readily extrapolate a threat from such meagre information?

⁂

A gust of wind stronger than before stirred the sand and flipped over one corner of the carpet square. Ashley looked towards the cars: the little group of attendants and drivers had risen from their conversations. Their chatter had ceased and their attentions were to the eastern sky. One of them turned to return to the hollow and approached the Colonel. 'Sidi – shimal – mushkula!'

Ashley noted the sense of urgency even if he didn't follow the Arabic warning of a shimal – a sand storm. Sure enough, when he looked directly above him, Canis Major could be clearly seen, but when he panned across to the east, the stars were blocked out by clouds. Looking back towards Dubai, the city lights still cast their glow into the night sky but the colour of the glow was changing by the minute. He didn't need Ali Abdullah to translate. They were leaving, and leaving quickly. Even in the short time that it took them to pack the carpets, the sand had been whipped up so that it hissed eerily in the otherwise silent night. The remnants of the meal were thrown to the scavengers. Foxes, feral cats and lizards would make short work of what was left of the goat and rice.

Once back on the road, the four wheelers made good progress, but the shimal was catching them and by the time they had gained the outskirts of the city, the flying sand had reduced visibility to just a few yards. The driver took them back to the shopping mall car park and Minder indicated that they would re-use the taxi for the last leg of the journey back to the hotel. It only took seconds to transfer but in that time Ashley had to pull his shirt over his face to protect his nose and eyes. The sand was stinging his exposed flesh as he waited momentarily for Minder to unlock the taxi. Minder himself had wrapped his head gear across his face and Ashley had to admit that the Arabic robes were the ideal attire for this evening.

CHAPTER 16

Eye Opener

The American patriotic mentality came to him as a high-on-the-Richter-Scale shock. He'd always considered the Scots fervent supporters of any cause which came their way. None more so than when they were exiled on some foreign soil and when flag waving became so important in identifying the highlands as being their native soil. But the Americans were something different. They just *had* to win. They were expected to be the best, their newspapers and journals had elevated their golfers to such a high plain that anything other than a complete whitewash of the opposition was regarded as an absolute failure. The unfortunate culprit would be condemned as number one on the nation's most hated list. He had seen the immense, extraordinary pressure under which his American counterparts were playing. He himself struggled to carry the yoke of his own supporters' burden, but the Americans? The pressure was so extreme that he had to give them credit for just being able to hit a ball off the tee, never mind keeping it on the fairway, or actually sinking a put to win a hole.

In the past, Ryder Cup galleries, whether they had been European or American, had been praised as being both knowledgeable and sporting – like himself, just enjoying the grand occasion. But at Brookland, that all went by the way. Nobody had come up with an explanation as to why things were different, but different they were. True, the Americans were on a roll. The last day started with the home team being five points behind, but in the morning singles, the Americans had eaten away at the European lead, to pull level by lunch. So when the pairs assembled for the afternoon and final leg of the competition, the ascendancy was with the home team and the steam rolling of the morning had whipped up the supporters into a feeding frenzy. Cameron remembered the noise and the incessant chanting of: *U-S-A, U-S-A* that lifted the home team and at the same time tested the visitors' nerves to the limit. Despite the tension and patriotic fervour the European team had got their act together somewhat, and hit back at the Americans to claim and share a few more points so that when Cameron's round came, it all hinged on his penultimate game.

A wall of sound had greeted them as they walked to the first tee. Any observer, who spared a moment to think about how the two contestants felt as they stood on the tee, must have appreciated the super-human qualities that professional golfers must call upon at times like that. Cameron had never enjoyed the crowds and on any day he would have preferred to be a million miles away, back in the solitude of the Highland courses. But he had been playing high quality golf throughout the season and his friends, family and fellow Scots expected it of him. And now Team Europe needed him to pull through. He'd never played JC before although their paths had crossed during the American tour competitions. As a Native American, JC had become something of a cult figure in the last few years and had earned the title of *Él Presidente. JC for president!* Was a common call from members of his race. And the same was often seen on the flags and banners that inevitably followed his every game. So the favourite on that day, both in the betting shops and on the course, was bound to be the Hopi Indian. Quite amazing that on the one hand, Native Americans were often despised, yet on the other, all that was forgotten or forgiven when such individuals as Jaycee flew the flag for the good *ole* US of A. In any case Cameron liked the man, and whilst they were fierce opponents, the pleasant companionship of the two was plain to see.

The excited throng snaked its way around Brookland as Cameron and JC battled out the second last round. Cameron had been well prepared for this and after a session of consultation with his psychologist guru, his beloved *BBC*, he had spent most of the morning on one of the practice greens. There he had mentally blocked out the commotion that was building around the place and slowly became more and more focussed on the task in hand. As the time for his game came closer, the crowd and atmosphere had been pushed into the background, so much so that by the time Cameron stood on the tee the noise and clamour had been filtered out to leave him in a state of isolation. It was almost as if he were wearing earmuffs, so little did the din penetrate his defences. Even the compulsory smiles, waves and handshakes had been relegated to the autonomic senses so that his focus on the course was complete. Only the gentle, supporting tones of his caddy were allowed to enter the no-go area. JC had a similar attitude and strategy, although he was much more flamboyant than the Scot, as was inevitably demanded by the Americans and especially fostered by the media.

The round progressed well with each golfer having his own successes and an equal share of missed chips and putts. It was a high standard that delighted the gallery following the course, not to mention the millions glued to their TV screens on either side of the Atlantic. As the afternoon wore on, other games had been brought to conclusions that put new pressures on both players and galleries of the remaining contests. Much as the American team strove to satiate their supporter's voracious appetite for victory, the Europeans clung on with equal tenacity. Cameron, oblivious to the outside world, focussed entirely on playing the course. He meticulously lined up tee shots, went through his swing routine and calculated distances whilst at the same time observing the wind direction and the texture of the grass and sand in occasionally visited bunkers. Crucial to his game were the way in which he approached the greens and his putting once there. The Scot had gleaned much from the practice rounds, analysing the nap of the close cut surfaces and searching for subtle contours that were hidden to all but the expert eye. They were in perfect condition and had been prepared to be fast and true, giving a lot of confidence to both men when setting the crucial parameters of line and strength. Putt after putt had been sunk in what had become a contest within a contest and the crowd loved it. It was going to the wire as if the whole thing had been written as a drama script.

The sixteenth had come and gone and as they assembled around the seventeenth tee, the swarthy Indian led by a single hole. He only had to tie the seventeenth to be sure of sharing a point. Winning the hole would mean that his point would give the USA almost certain victory and possession of The Ryder Cup for another two years. Both players were tiring and not just from the physical heat, but also from the concentration and mind control demanded by the occasion. The marshals had done a good job in controlling the massing supporters. Even so, some individuals felt that they had to contribute to the American effort in their own, small way. A growing number had succumbed to coughs and sneezes at opportune moments. Cameron had almost become accustomed to it and, as the round progressed, the unfair agitation when he was into his tee shot swing had gradually increased to unacceptable levels. Even JC had beseeched his followers to grant his opponent the expected courtesy of silence at that crucial moment.

Outwardly, Cameron had not flinched, and his policy of playing the course had carried him above all the mind games and ultimately kept him in the competition. Yet underneath the calm façade, fatigue of not just this round but that of the entire four-day competition, was undermining his self control. As greater energy was being channelled to deal with the heat and physical aspects of the game, less remained to control the psychological demands. Whilst his game remained almost faultless and confidence was still high, Cameron's concentration was beginning to waver. The deluge of taunts and interruptions had begun to penetrate his defensive shield and were fraying the edges of his temper. The mental isolation that had been built during his preparations was slowly becoming more and more invaded. Suddenly, the Scot began to feel the warm breeze in his hair and his olfactory senses smelt the pine trees as if they had never existed before. His hearing had become the most sensitive organ in his otherwise tiring body and he heard everything! Every whisper, every cough or sigh of every body around him. It was deafening.

The Indian was going through the same process, as did any athlete. Trying to suppress the excruciating pain of the final push when the finishing line came into view. The difference between these contestants was that JC didn't hear the heckling, or interruptions, simply because when *he* was in play, there weren't any. Cameron did his best to hang on, but now he was not playing the course any longer. He was playing against a class golfer *and* the rest of the American nation gathered around the tee.

Physical power, coupled with growing antipathy for the increasingly animated gallery, gave him a long straight shot from the driver. Whether JC was affected by the occasion or not, Cameron had not the inclination to consider, but the American's tee shot fell short of his own by some distance. The expectant crowd quietened as if to acknowledge that the game was not quite over, after all. This respite allowed Cameron to gather himself for a final effort and his self-belief returned so that when he came to play the lofted approach shot over the water hazard separating the fairway from the green, he played it with his usual assurance. From the moment he struck the ball he knew that it would be safely on the green, if not close to the hole. JC had fallen short again, just off the front edge but it was only after the long walk around the hazard that Cameron's advantage became apparent. The Scot was only two yards from the pin and much to the gallery's anguish; their favourite's ball lay some twenty yards from the hole, just a few inches off the green.

Momentarily, the weight was off the broad shoulders of the man from Aviemore and all the pressure had been transferred to his opponent as they approached their respective positions. The tumultuous reception that both golfers received reached new levels, although undoubtedly the vast majority of vocal prayers were for the local hero. Even Cameron who had crawled snail like back into his protective shell, could sense that the American tone was anxious as JC inspected his options from every angle. Cameron had squatted behind his own ball and seen that there was a slight gradient to consider. Despite that his remaining putt was not difficult. Relieved, he marked his ball, lifted it for the caddy to wipe, and stood to one side as JC deliberated with his own caddy about his own line.

The crowd hushed as JC approached, took a few pendulum like swings with the putter, before addressing the ball. There was absolute silence. JC made minor adjustments before setting his ball off up the hill. It was a firm hit and Cameron could see already that it would come close if the direction was right. The Titelist surged onto the green and mounted the first level with little evidence of slowing or deviation. It crossed to the second level and was now visibly slowing. The crowd urged it on – still four or five yards to go as it hit the final slope to the crown of the green. With the pace falling off quickly now, the ball at last began to follow the contours. JC and his caddy were pursuing in the line of the ball's progress. It was going to be close, but the ball's energy had almost been exhausted. Somehow it found the slightest of dips, which teased it to the side of the hole. The crowd willed it to go on – just another roll. Just another roll! It obliged, caught the edge, and with painful slowness ran the rim of the hole to spiral down – and in. JC leapt into the air and the roar of the massed spectators reached every corner of the Brookland estate. At that instant the sheer volume of the cheer announced to everyone around the course that the cup was won or lost, even though the vast majority had not been able to see it with their own eyes.

Cameron respected his opponent. JC was an excellent golfer, arguably the best in the world at that time, and he knew that the American would be close, but to put the ball in from that lie and over that distance required something more than skill alone. Whatever it was, the American had it.

The gallery had been on tenterhooks all day, had now become a different beast. The gradual up-welling of emotions had in that instant become all too much and suddenly all restraints were broken. The gallery disintegrated into a mob, breaking through the marshals' cordon, each man and woman intent on un-fettered celebration, and each individual finding it necessary to shake the hand of their hero. To this end, there was a wild stampede and the vain attempts of the course marshals were swept aside. Upwards of a thousand onlookers raced onto the green and danced jigs of joy on its manicured turf.

Many were horrified – marshals and team members aghast, as were the majority of the spectators, but the damage was done. The animals had shown great irreverence for the game itself and thoughtlessness for the opposing team, and destroying the seventeenth green beyond repair.

Eventually, when the chaotic celebrations had subsided enough for Cameron to continue, he returned with reluctance to where his ball had last come to a halt. What had been a relatively flat, even surface before, was now pitted and scarred like the surface of the moon. Even Cameron's marker had disappeared so that the marshal had to be called to advise exactly where the Scot's ball should be placed. It wasn't the scene that Cameron had looked over just a few moments ago. His senses, training, and professionalism told him – play the course – not the baying hyenas, who were poised for yet another invasion. Cameron took his time; the shock of events had completely destroyed his concentration. Never in his life had he been witness to such desecration. What had happened, he immediately took as a personal insult and it would be one that remained with him for the rest of his career. But Team Europe needed him now.

It was a disgusted and shell-shocked Cameron who replaced the ball in its designated spot. He took his time to assess the position and gather his thoughts – viewing the line from all angles. It was desperate. The crowd was baying for more success, the final victory and the entire European team that had gathered in support of their beleaguered team-mate were angry and anxious by the turn of events.

To Cameron, it was not any longer about winning or losing, but about humanity and the ethics of the game of golf itself. In the present circumstances, apart from the actual putt itself made so complicated by the distressed surface of the green, there were other issues that were passing through his mind. One of them was that if he missed this putt, the Americans would again plunge onto the course to acclaim victory, as the final game following on behind was already theirs. For the life of him, he didn't want to give them that satisfaction, yet in this state of trauma, he could not guarantee being able to sink this ball and take the competition to the eighteenth.

Play the course Cameron. Play the course.

The mantra came back to him. Cameron squatted behind his ball, oblivious now to everything around him. He was focussed once again. He stood, the crowd hushed a little, he took a deep breath and walked towards his ball. But the course had been changed. *They* changed the course! – It was not what it had been! Millions saw him bend and without pause, pick up his ball and walk off the green – back to the clubhouse and into infamy. Cameron Cameron had conceded, The Ryder Cup was lost, yet in his own mind, he had a victory.

✳✳✳

Cameron had left America, howled down by the American public and castigated as a coward by the American media. Though he relived those tense moments many times, he never talked about it with others, team mates or friends. After much introspection, he was still certain that he had done the right thing. His only regret was that in the heat of the moment he had forgotten the customary handshake with JC. It had inevitably been taken as a personal affront. It was only after his wife had pointed it out that Cameron realised his error and after the event's formalities had died down, he sought out the Indian to offer his apologies. JC had said little except to declare that he never considered that there was any animosity between them and it *had* been a great game of golf. A warm embrace followed which cleared the matter between the two of them.

For many months Cameron was true to his word, and declared the next twelve months as a sabbatical. A sabbatical at home with his wife and family. Nothing else mattered, as nothing else troubled him – except for the nightmares, that is.

Time passed. The phone began to ring with more frequent calls from his agent and local Scottish event organisers sought him out to attend charity functions. Slowly Cameron began to accept the outside world again, and vice versa, so that he was invited to play in national tournaments. Invitations that he became more inclined to consent to, as his convalescence continued. The Americans however were slow to forgive and forget. His name was synonymous with Brookland and *that* could not be easily forgotten.

***

It was never his intention to play abroad again, but two things led him to reconsider. One was the invitation that he now held in his hand. It bore the postal stamp of the UAE, the United Arab Emirates. The other was a newspaper cutting containing an article written around an interview with his old adversary Jaycee. The article related much of the American's origins, his family and tribal upbringing as well as his rise to be cause-celebre for the North American Indian minorities. Their own El Presidente. This was interesting in its own right, but what caught Cameron's attention was one of the final paragraphs, which talked about his golfing successes. The Ryder Cups were inevitably mentioned, being for any golfer – the ultimate event in any career. JC had then identified Brookland as the one event that stood out in his mind above all others. Cameron had expected to read on about the success of the USA team in capturing the trophy in one of the most nail biting competitions in the history of the game. But JC mentioned nothing of triumph; his focal point was purely on those infamous events on the seventeenth hole. Anxiety crept into Cameron's heart as he read on, he didn't really want to be reminded of it yet again but against his objections, Brigitte pressed him to read on.

JC had stated that it was the greatest regret of his sporting life, that he had not had the guts to follow Cameron's example of picking up his ball and then declaring the hole tied. If he could have turned the clocks back, he too would have conceded Cameron's putt as a 'given' and then also walked off the green, side by side, with him.

Since that interview had been published, with what was considered another interpretation of the never ending enquiry, there had been a growing consensus in The States that far from being the coward that he was initially branded, Cameron had acquired a growing band of supporters. They had come to admire his dogmatic stand in the face of extreme personal pressure. That article's interview had concluded by stating: That the whole American golfing circus was *still* plagued by, what was now infamously called, *The Seventeenth Event*, and was testament to the fact that after all this time, it *still* remained a thorn in the American side – and would continue as such for many years to come.

Therefore it transpired that the Cameron *pick-up* had been more devastating to the American dream, than if he had actually sunk the God damned putt!

✳✳✳

'What made you move into biometrics?' asked Ashley, nodding to the door whilst pulling a fresh notepad from his briefcase.

'Eet ees the latest technology of access control. And we are a company that rides on the leading edge of technical innovation. As you, yourself have noted the iris scanner, so do our customers and eet leaves them with a sense that we at CIPHERCAN take our role in the field most seriously. If they thought that they could just walk in to our offices, then they might think that also they could walk into our communications.' Bonetti was switched into sales mode and took a deep breath as if to continue.

But Ashley saw an opportunity open up for him. 'So what we see here in the Lighthouse building – I mean to say, the security of your offices, is rather just for show, let's say, impression, rather than actually protecting what data you might have,' he looked around at the glass cupboards, 'in your files?' and then turned back to his host.

Bonetti's eyes were small and piggy, but the thick spectacles enlarged the whites, lending great emphasis to the response. 'Oh, not at all! my friend.' He lent forward to take the espresso and looking Ashley in the eye. 'Of course we have a *lot* of confidential material here and we need to protect it.' He sat back into the leather chair which squeaked expensively under the shift of his one hundred and twenty kilos, and lifted the coffee to his lips.

Ashley had not been sure when in the interview to hit him with the pertinent questions. But there at the very beginning, the scanner had been the perfect trigger. Perhaps it *was* safer to get the important stuff done and dusted before getting immersed in the bulk of material for his column. Then hopefully by the end, the Italian would have forgotten that the critical questions were ever raised.

As it was, Bonetti was drawn in, and all too eager to underline his own significance in both the roles of CIPHERCAN sales director and security manager for the exhibition. Ashley had not recorded anything on his note pad, so as to imply that they were still in the opening gambits and not yet into the information that Ashley was really after and let his host continue.

'The explicit show of security is most useful in itself, and also we 'ave many competitors who would love to get their hands on details of our contracts for commercial reasons, and at the same time be very interested to steal our technical know-how. So *all* of our offices around the world have security devices to keep snoopers out. Then, on the other hand, at this moment we 'ave to consider the exhibition. We are now just a few days away from the opening of the most influential display of aircraft, both commercial and military, for – the last decade,' Bonetti decided.

Ashley would have loved to continue with the access security a while longer, but Bonetti had drifted into the main theme and so he started to scribble on his pad. To interrupt again might just have aroused suspicions. Better to let the man continue with what he wanted Ashley to tell the world, rather than pursue the wrong line.

Bonetti downed the dregs of espresso and accelerated with boyish enthusiasm into the subject of aircraft and related sideshows. He reeled off a list of airlines that were looking to expand their fleets. Ashley wondered where they got financing for some extraordinary purchases. Indian Airlines, not by any means the world's favourite, had a mandate to spend a phenomenal seven billion dollars on refurbishing and replacing their fleet. Qatar, now, was flexing its muscles as it emerged from relative seclusion on the back of the discovery that the tiny Gulf state was sitting on vast reserves of petrocarbons. How Qatar Air could make inroads into an already highly competitive sector was beyond Bonetti, and for that matter Ashley. But there they were, attending the exhibition in large numbers with the rumour that they were in the market for twenty new 787s, the Boeing Dreamliner. Then the UAE's own fledgling airline Etihad, which Bonetti was knowledgeable enough to translate into *United* for the journalist, was itself purchasing an average of one airbus every month. Emirates, the region's most successful carrier was emphatically making known its intentions of remaining the prestige Arab airline. So it was no wonder that every manufacturer of civilian aircraft on the planet had long ago paid their many thousands of dollars to reserve a stand on which to woo these big spenders. As one would expect, Boeing and Airbus had the biggest representations on the tarmac to show off their leviathans. Neither Bonetti nor Ashley had actually been on the Airbus 380, and both had shared excitement at the possibility of getting on board to have a privileged VIP view. Ashley was not sure that his application for VIP status or his press corps badge would be forthcoming. Either was necessary to enable him to get up close to the *birds*, as Bonetti called them. As of course Bonetti was certain to have VIP status and the Italian made a promise to see what he could do for the journalist. Then he could be sure that CIPHERCAN, and therefore naturally himself, would figure favourably in the magazine's special edition.

If the likes of Boeing were expecting to leave with bulging order books, then smaller players like the Brazilian Embraer, Bonetti had reminded him, were expecting to sweep into the commuter carrier sector. Each manufacturer was pushing to exploit their particular market niche.

Bonetti left him in no doubt that it was the civilian market that was going to dominate the aviation scene in the near future, but that didn't mean that the likes of Saab, BAE, Illyushin, Northrop, Boeing and Dassault would not be flying their Viggens, Hawks, Typhoons and Mirages in noisy and breathtaking flybys throughout the week.

Bonetti rattled them off as if he knew each of them from personal experience.

Ashley, inundated with aircraft names, held his hand up to slow the man down, so that he could capture each and every one. The Italian paused and took the time to fetch a cigarette packet from the desk, extract a single Ellesse and then light it with a flame from the table top lighter bearing the emblem of *Eurocopter*. 'And of course there are helicopters for all seasons' - remembering the freebee that had come his way courtesy of the French Puma builder.

Ashley had just asked about the static support exhibitions. Those with missiles, aero engines, ejection seats - even cabin crew uniforms to show, when he saw Bonetti's attention switch to the slightly open door. 'Moll, that you girl?' he demanded, peering in the opposite direction. The doors opened a little and Ashley was surprised to see a young female peering through the gap. Bonetti was up sharply and the blush illustrated that he was embarrassed by the interruption. 'Oh yes, of course. Sheet - Sorry darling, forgot it was Tuesday.' He moved back to the desk, walked around the back and disconnected something from the computer. It was only when he returned to the door that Ashley could see that it was a set of headphones and mike.

The intruder pushed open the door a little further to receive the headset and in doing so, revealed herself in more detail. Asian, short dark hair, large doleful eyes set aside a pert, bridgeless nose with an arrogant chin held high conveying a sense of aloofness. Ashley couldn't help thinking that she reminded him of what a wood elf would look like. Something from Tolkein. Fascinated, he looked on as Bonetti flustered around, telling her that he was busy and that she might use the computer next door, in Samir's workshop. The elf cast a short glance in the Englishman's direction. It was only there for a second, maybe two, but it was sufficient to leave Ashley with the feeling that he had been assessed in some subtle way. He half expected to see pointed ears as she turned silently away and without having spoken, or made any acknowledgement to either man, she disappeared from view.

Bonetti, on impulse, made as if to follow but merely stepped into the corridor to call after her, 'See you in the Palace later!' and appended a hesitant 'dear,' as an afterthought. Ashley was not sure if it was a command or a question. The big man, so familiar for his bellowed instructions to all and sundry, seemed suddenly vulnerable, even timid. He turned back to his seat and explained: 'Voice over IP. She wants to call her family – Beijing.'

Again he had hesitated, and Ashley struggled to hide his amusement that the diminutive imp might have some underworld power over the Italian ogre.

Ashley shrugged: 'You were saying,' – Bonetti took a few more seconds to get back in synch, 'about the static part of the exhibition?'

'Si, of course,' searching for the correct language. 'Trent – a full size sectioned model of the new Trent engine, the power plant for the Airbus 380, by RR. Wonderful exhibit. Typical Rolls Royce effort, of course.' Bonetti was back in the present having suddenly remembered the script. He continued to elucidate with increased animation as if he needed to emphasise his regained composure. In renewed confidence the big man settled into an impressive list of supporting teams and even paused to retrieve a plan of the exhibition to show where each and every exhibitor had their plot.

'And with all of these giants of the industry attending, one would expect them to be supported by senior government figures and even, dare I say, perhaps – heads of state?' Now Ashley judged it time to probe deeper. Distant alarm bells rang.

Bonetti was removing the silver cufflinks from his shirt – miniature figures of Concorde, no doubt another freebee from some BA or Air France representative seeking a minor favour. 'Absolutely! – Presidents Bush and Blair, our own Prime Minister Berlusconi, Musharraf, Chirac and probably the Chinese premier.' But Bonetti couldn't remember the name and besides, they were too numerous to mention individually.

Ashley briefly mused the pun of Blair's reputation by referring to him as being presidential with a smile, but was immediately distracted as Bonetti rolled on; expanding on how the presence of world leaders raised the profile of events like DUBEX. He gazed across at the dark glass of cupboard doors and a reflected movement drew his attention. He could see the image of Bonetti's desk top monitor. The screensaver dissolved and then painted a new image. The Vatican emerged from the remnants of the Bay of Naples. The tumblers of Ashley's mind had been clicking round ever since his meeting in the desert on the previous evening. Rapidly at first but then slowing, until now, they stopped – giving a moment for Ashley to unlock something unknown to him. He suddenly understood what was troubling the MOI, and especially Colonel Ali. One just had to cast an eye down the list of exhibitions and attendant dignitaries to see why he had been thinking in terms of a threat. Was it just the Goodwin story that triggered it, or was it information from another source? Was it just a fear based without any fact whatsoever, or was it credible and supported by …?

'You must need light Meester Ashley?' Bonetti clicked on some lights as the sultry dusk gathered outside. No wonder the computer monitor's image of Rome had been so bright.

The interview had ground to a halt, for the moment exhausted of interesting material. Bonetti had at last tired whilst Ashley had ample data to add to his coming review of DUBEXAIR. Ashley folded his journalistic tools away and they rose in unison. Bonetti suddenly became most apologetic, knowing that Ashley appreciated Italian wine and that he hadn't thought to offer him *any* liquid refreshment. In recompense he suggested that they retire to one of the Dubai bars to put the matter right. Besides, as Bonetti went on vociferously, it was *that* time of day.

From Ashley's point of view, it was encouraging that Bonetti should make the suggestion with apparent spontaneity, and if this was as it seemed, then he had taken the journalist at face value. So they agreed to meet – where? 'At the Palace!' declared Bonetti without hesitation, and seeing his guest's puzzled look, went on to explain the location of his favourite bar.

All agreed, they moved towards the door, but again the computer monitor pulled him back as if it had something to tell. 'Sorrento!' advised the Italian. But it wasn't the steep cliffs and azure blue sea that caught his attention. Ashley had seen them before, when he had first entered the room but had then been disturbed by Bonetti's later entrance. Around the flat top screen was the usual cream frame with its built-in speakers. Scrawled in light pencil across the top of the frame, were collections of figures, jumbles of numbers and texts. Could it possibly be that CIPHERCAN's security manager couldn't remember web pages or email addresses – or were they passwords?

Bonetti gathered his mobile phone from the desk and they left together. As Bonetti closed the door, Ashley leant inquisitively to inspect the security scanner. The Italian, rebuked him. 'Not so close, my friend. It scans the iris and not the retina,' and with boastful confidence invited him to try it. Ashley, both amused and inquisitive, peered into the glass eye of the scanner so that he could see his own eye in its reflection. After five seconds, the blinking LED indicator steadied to red.

'There you see!' he laughed proudly. 'No chance, amico mio.'

***

The dust from the previous night's storm had settled out of the atmosphere, leaving patches of sand on the roads and pathways. As it was only a few hundred metres from the Lighthouse tower to the Sheraton, and the humidity was reasonable, Ashley decided that a little evening exercise was needed and strolled back to the hotel. He used the time to take in what he had gleaned from the meeting and formulate a basic plan for the next few days. If he was going to make progress on the Goodwin affair and further investigate the apparent fears of the local MOI people, then he was going to need some help. Furthermore, if the information that he needed was to be found in the Lighthouse offices, it would almost certainly be protected by the latest IT encryption then he would certainly need a helping hand.

On arrival back at his suite, he stepped out on to the balcony to make a ciphered phone call back to Clements. In addition to his request for back up, Ashley was hoping that Clements might exert some pressure on the MOI, to release what other information they might be withholding from him. Ashley normally would make such a call from somewhere other than a hotel room where there was the possibility that the conversation would be eavesdropped – hence the move outside. He took the GSM out of his pocket and selected the data channel that had been assigned to members of his group. After a moment's hesitation, he stepped back into the room. If the MOI people had in fact bugged the place, it might be *convenient* if they *did* overhear the ensuing discussion. They would certainly get the subtle hint that MI6 were aware of their reluctance to divulge all of what they knew. Tipped off that pressure might soon be coming from above, they might be a little more forthcoming than they had been. So he stood on the cool side of the window this time, and facing the illuminations of the Lighthouse building, Ashley went ahead with the call to London. Once the handshake between the two mobile phones had automatically selected the cipher key to use, Ashley reported the situation to his superior, anticipating that his conversation might be heard locally by microphones but secure in the knowledge that the electronic airwaves would be protected against any monitoring, even by Echelon. Had Samir been able to use the same technology, then the Goodwin message might never have been intercepted.

Clements had just listened patiently to his roving reporter's monologue, mainly responding in the affirmative to the request for assistance. Ashley closed the link and stood for a moment to reflect on the promise of immediate action. Only then did he notice that he was, in fact, staring at the Lighthouse drummer beating out his message to the city's evening traffic on its turgid flow to the suburbs.

Ashley switched on the television in order to catch up with the world news, but when the picture finally materialised, it was the local Dubai news channel relating the arrival of a new container ship at the Jebel Ali port. Only when the picture showing it passing a local dhow did Ashley realise why such a common every day event should be newsworthy. The perspective relationship with the local wooden craft and the container indicated in no uncertain terms, that the latter was truly massive. After he had struggled to find the remote control, he heard that the MSC Rachele, at three hundred and thirty metres it was one of the longest ships in the world. Amazing! He would like to catch a glimpse of her in real life. He made a mental note to search it out if he could find the place and the time.

***

Ashley was there first, but the Lucky Palace was already full with office staff seeking to drown the sorrows of the day and catch the big football game on the bar's large screen. The bar maid came to take his order just as the football got under way and five minutes later there was a gentle tug at his elbow as the pint of John Smiths duly arrived. Ashley, seeing the waitress's hands full, lifted the glass and its beer mat and the slip of paper, which he took to be the receipt from the tray. As happy hour prices were advertised until just a few minutes after his arrival, he inquisitively checked the price to see if he had beaten the deadline. At twenty Dirhams, he gathered that this was not his lucky day, but in addition to the usual cash register printout were two words, lightly pencilled in over the account details. *Faisal, Smirnoff!*

He screwed up the paper and threw it in the nearest ashtray and took a long swig of the dark, cool beer before setting it down on the high table. He had already looked around to see if Bonetti had arrived, but now he glanced around with a new objective in mind. There were a number of illuminated signs around the walls, all advertising the benefits of the bar's ales and liquors, but he didn't notice any Smirnoff poster at first. A burst of excitement and applause drew his attention back to the big screen in time to see an action replay of the first near miss of the evening. The second near miss was there right next to the left hand side of the screen. Hidden by the bright lights from the football match was a Smirnoff bottle mounted on the wall. The fact that its illumination had been switched off made it difficult to see. Ashley joined in the excitement of the other spectators who were intensely analysing a penalty claim. But he wasn't looking at the penalty, he was looking at the short, light-suited figure, perched on a bar stool under the vodka display. Oblivious to all the football fever around him, Faisal was stirring the contents of a large brandy glass with a swivel stick. If this was a terrorist, or an Al Qaeda go-between, he certainly didn't look the part. A man of less than modest stature, in fact a bit of a weasel, Ashley considered. About fifty to fifty five, sixty five kilos, one metre sixty, with a small poky face which gave him more of a European look than Egyptian. However the most outstanding feature was his almost totally bald dome, which carried a few strands of hair that emanated from somewhere around his left ear and stretched across the full width of his head to disappear in the opposite side. So this was Samir's contact! Ashley felt almost disappointed that his adversary didn't fit the archetypical villain, but then neither did Samir, and in all fairness, he couldn't himself claim to be in James Bond's image either. If Hollywood only knew.

But here came a man who did fit the part. Bonetti's girth didn't necessarily fit comfortably into the lower half of a pin stripe suit, but if ever a producer was looking for actors to star in a sequel to *The Godfather*, he wouldn't need to look further than the ebullient Italian. The noisy entrance into the bar had announced his arrival to all and sundry. There couldn't have been more fuss if royalty had arrived thought Ashley with a wry smile. Much of the commotion was due to the fact that Bonetti purposefully stopped directly in front of the big screen, to calmly light up one of his slender cigarettes. When the football supporters voiced their wrathful abuse, Bonetti simply stood there, feigning absolute ignorance. He prolonged their agony by taking a long drag on the Ellesse and turned to face the crowd with a two finger and cigarette salute, before moving at his own pace to the bar. Carlo Bonetti felt *exceedingly* pleased with himself. Faisal and the Italian were poles apart in both physique and manner, yet neither filled the standard objective of being the *grey men* professed by the training manuals on intelligence and espionage. Everybody knew Bonetti; It didn't matter whether it was in a bar or an aeroplane, if Bonetti was on board, everybody knew it. Faisal was the extreme opposite. Indeed, the likeness to a weasel fitted him well. He was not a *grey* character by any means. His seclusion in a dark corner was countered by the high contrast of his light suit and the reflections from his head. The weird appearance, and the fact that he rarely spoke to anyone, other than a barked command to some suffering bar attendant, drew distaste from those around.

Ashley feared that Bonetti would join Faisal in conversation and then draw him into it. Ashley wanted to stay in the background. But he needn't have worried, for other than the briefest of nods to his one-time customer, the Italian joined everyone else in ignoring the Smirnoff figure for the remainder of the evening. It was Ashley's companionship he sought. Aware that excessive drinking lowered even the most guarded of tongues, Ashley, determined to follow the *ears only* policy, had set his threshold night's alcohol intake at very low. It was a practised art where Ashley became the polite listener, avoiding any contrived enquiry aimed in his direction.

With other targets, it might have proven to be a quiet, even boring intercourse, but as he suspected, Bonetti needed no prompting. After a couple of glasses of Chianti he spoke loudly and authoritatively on any subject under the sun. Inevitably within the present environment, football was the initial subject of discussion and the Italian was as enthusiastic as the supporters in the bar, when their heroes took the lead. Bonetti even claimed that he had at one time or other been on Juventus' books, though Ashley could only ever imagine that it would have been in a goalkeeping role. Nonetheless, once a common interest had been established, both men relaxed into the convivial atmosphere. Bonetti was even more buoyant than normal, but it was not until the half time pause for more drinks orders that the reason for his high spirits was made clear.

'Mikey, mio amico. Any chance you mighta playa golf?'

Ashley confirmed that he did indeed knock a ball around the park when the opportunity arose. He was half expecting Bonetti to invite him for a game. But that wasn't the case. It was the Italian who had been invited. Ashley had caught *some* news of the Desert Classic Pro Am competition to be played here in Dubai, but other than the fact that his old friend Cameron was down to play, it had been lost to him.

'Eet ees a charity competition, to be played on the famous Majlis Course down in Jumeira this next weekend. Ashley was all ears. 'Many big people to play!' continued Bonetti with his cigarette hand flamboyantly emphasising the importance of the game.

'In that case, *you* must have been invited? ...' Ashley couldn't help but interrupt Bonetti in full flow.

Bonetti faltered, lost for words took time to digest Ashley's input as either pure sarcasm or over-the-top patronisation. For a second or more, he studied his new found friend's facial expression for clues as to the intended inference. Detecting the slightest curl of mischief at each end of the mouth – he erupted into a bellowing laughter. 'Bastard! These Ingleesh, all bastards!' he announced to all around. Everyone in earshot paused in their own private conversations to nod in agreement. The Italian's shoulders convulsed and his face quickly took on the same colour as the wine in his glass. He struggled to regain his composure, so that he could continue with the story. 'Yes, I play,' he spluttered. 'I want to play with Ingleesh champion – Cameron!'

Truly impressed, Ashley corrected. 'The Scottish champion.'

'What you mean?'

'Scottish – Cameron is Scottish!'

'Oh sheet, I make a beeg mistake.' Bonetti's bulging eyes displayed his horror.

Ashley considered that he had saved Bonetti some considerable embarrassment in informing him of Cameron's true nationality. The Italian made a mental note of the fact.

As the conversation carried on, it emerged that with the likes of Cameron and Americans such as Jaycee being involved, it was indeed a beeg competition, as Bonetti had put it. It soon followed that although a number of local amateurs of good standing had put their names into the hat hoping to draw one of the top names. Beeg money amateurs of lesser repute had bought into it. Ashley could well imagine the many calls of foul play that would be voiced when the draw was announced, but in all fairness he thought: if it was for charity, why not raise the impact with the *beeg* money coming in from the likes of Bonetti?

In a moment of sublime inspiration, Ashley thought of a way to further endear himself with the Italian. 'My friend, if I were to say to you that I just *might* be able to fix it for you to play with Cameron – do you think that you might *just* be able to fix a VIP pass to the exhibition?'

Bonetti froze, glass raised to his lips – his eyes nearly bulging out of their sockets, and for a moment he really believed Ashley's offer to be genuine. But then his face relaxed into a lecherous smile, 'mio amico – you tease me – how you can fix these?'

'I tease you not Carlo!'

Now Bonetti saw that behind Ashley's grin, there was a confidence that belied a mere bar room boast. 'Go on my friend – I am all ears – ees it possible, no?'

'Very much so,' Ashley dragged it out, enjoying the moment immensely and also the moments when he and Cameron would share the story over dinner sometime in the future. The Scot would *never* forgive him. But the thought painted an even wider grin across his face. 'It so happens that your Ingleesh champion, as you call him, is a great pal of mine – dating back many years.'

'Yes ok – cut the crap you bastard – can I play with him – or not?'

The Italian would have sold his mother at that moment, but the VIP pass was all that Ashley could wish for. 'Just look at the draw tomorrow.'

'Sold!' Bonetti bellowed in such delight that everyone turned abruptly to the screen, fully expecting to see a goal scorer wheeling away from a famous strike. Bonetti couldn't order the next round of drinks fast enough – and fringe friends inched closer to be included. In other circumstances, Ashley himself would have loved to spend a day watching the golf, especially with such big names on show; however *Symphony* was calling the tune. Bonetti had been more than useful in helping to organise *insider* meetings over and above the usual press tours. Ashley wished to avoid most of the tedious and time-consuming presentations and with a VIP pass he could spend time with his primary targets that would provide him with the bulk of the material for next month's issue of *Jane's*. As far as Symphony was concerned, his personal success to date was that he had achieved one of his initial goals in getting close to Bonetti. However, the easy manner in which the latter had accepted him into his environment troubled Ashley. Either the Italian had something to hide, in which case he was an actor with considerable talent, or if Ashley was to take him at face value, the CIPHERCAN man was simply a man in the wrong place at the wrong time. Here in Dubai, Bonetti had given no hint of any subterfuge whatsoever, yet the certainty that he had been involved with the death of Goodwin remained with Ashley. Perhaps Bonetti was *really* the master of the double bluff and it was him playing Ashley on a very long line, rather than Ashley playing Bonetti.

Faisal's departure went largely un-noticed but Ashley caught it in the corner of his eye. Throughout the whole evening Ashley had sought a point of observation from which his attentions would have gone unnoticed. He'd been able to watch the Egyptian from the very first ID, either through the various mirrors around the room or the polished metal of the many pieces of decorative bric-a-brac adorning the bar's walls. He'd shown no interest whatsoever in the football match that had now come to its noisy conclusion, yet slunk off from his darkened stool the precise moment that it had finished. Ashley counted a dozen brandies with ice cubes. Faisal had stirred his drinks continuously through the night and spoken to no one apart from a snarled riposte whenever some uninformed lady of the night had been desperate enough to offer her services. Hardly had he exited through the swing doors, before a member of the bar staff walked by to switch on the Smirnoff sign, bringing an abrupt relief to the deep shadows of Faisal's den.

When and how she had emerged, Ashley had no inclination. He was just angry with himself that she appeared at Bonetti's elbow without him seeing her approach. At first he had mistaken her for just another of the girls, hiding in Bonetti's bulk. It came as a surprise, and not an unpleasant one at that, when he recognised the elf from Bonetti's office. Making Internet calls to Beijing, he remembered. Now *here* was a grey player. Certainly not in her sexual appearance or arrogant carriage but certainly in the way she drifted effortlessly in and out of events. She avoided eye contact, except for the briefest of glimpses when their eyes chanced to meet. Ashley was once more struck by mischief of her porcelain face. It stirred something from the distant past.

CHAPTER 17

Pipes Aboard

Nothing had changed at Jebel Ali since his last trial run. Normal traffic through the security gate was the usual slow process of negotiation between guard and visitor. Samir cruised slowly up to the back of the queue to observe operations. Regulars were generally allowed through without much delay and vehicle searches were cursory. He slid by the rear of the queue and dropped off the road to the right to follow the construction track that fed building materials and heavy plant to the new training centre. The builder's sentry emerged from his wooden shelter but immediately recognized Samir and waved him through with a perfunctory flip of the hand. Had he taken the time to investigate the load in the back of the Lighthouse man's Toyota, he would have seen it packed with regulation black plastic PVC water pipes, the like of which were to be seen in piles all over the site. Samir waved back and shouted the usual amicable greeting to his new found friend, bought the day before with a new Swiss Army knife carrying enough gadgets to keep the man happy for a month. Samir wouldn't need a month. Two more trips like this and he would have all that was needed safely inside the base.

Getting his materials into the base was one thing, but unloading and stowing them safely until they were needed was a bit more difficult. It was late in the afternoon and by this time most of the base's operations had finished for the day leaving only the duty personnel and a few sailors manning the boats that would be setting sail for patrol within the next few hours. Samir needed to buy time and headed for one of his safe houses where he knew that he would be welcomed with tea and idle conversation. The rice, lamb and vegetables that he carried with him would also help them pass the time until darkness had fallen.

***

The base mosque heralded the oncoming night with the prayer call. It was Samir's signal for action. Office staff poured outside and wended their way to the wash house to perform their ablutions before entering the mosque's main hall. Samir followed his comrades out of the signal's mess room, but instead of heading for the mosque, picked his way through the crowd milling around waiting to take their turn to wash. He got back to the Toyota and headed towards the base entrance but pulled off onto a little used quay. He brought the Toyota to a gradual halt opposite a half sunken landing craft that had been gathering dust for a decade or so. It was moored in the remote spot many years ago and left to wallow in decay as the harsh environment took its toll on the un-serviced vessel. The lack of illumination was another factor why Samir chose this as the location for the cache of weapons that he was to build up over the next two days.

He switched off the engine and lights, and sat in the cab for a few moments to let his eyes get accustomed to the dim light outside and then took a slow cautious look around before getting out of the cab. The Jordanian's heart was pumping quickly now. He was still not used to physical subterfuge. After long discussions with Faisal, he had reluctantly accepted the fact that he was the only man who could gain access to the base without attracting attention. It had to be *his* vehicle and *his* face that turned up at the builders' entrance. A stranger showing up, even in Samir's pick-up would have invited unwanted questions and even a moderate search of his load in the back would have revealed the true purpose of his illicit entry. He had argued that he was a man of thought and skilled in information gathering and not one to be crawling around in the dark, hiding the smuggled weapons, under the threat of physical violence and capture.

Faisal had agreed and stated that they already were indebted to his courage and innovation. They had sought an alternative, another way, but much as they brainstormed, Samir himself could see only one option. It had to be him. Finally he had accepted that it was God's work and that the whole success of project rested on his narrow shoulders, and despite the raw fear of discovery and possibly death it would be a worthy sacrifice. Martyrdom awaited any who fell whilst furthering the cause of Islam, Faisal had told him. Besides he had been assured that he would not be anywhere near the assault when it took place. And in any case, who could possibly suspect that someone like Samir be complicit in a military action against the UAE navy?

And so he found himself walking around the Toyota as if inspecting some technical problem or other, whilst at the same time observing all around him for any sign of movement or unwanted interest. Only the clicking sounds of the cooling vehicle and the muffled chanting from the distant mosque broke the silence. Samir dropped the back of the pick-up and reached across to lift off the spare wheel and then carried it around to the seaward side. Then he opened the passenger door and retrieved a jack and four legged wheel brace. Once again he surveyed all around him before kneeling to start the removal of the passenger side front wheel. The wheel was removed quickly to be replaced by the spare that he had picked from the back. He half tightened the wheel nuts and then slowly released the jack so that the car sank onto the spare wheel. As he expected, the tyre flattened under the weight of the Toyota. For the fiftieth time Samir squatted low behind the front end and once more scanned the scene around him. In the distance, prayers had concluded and the steps of the mosque were busy with exiting worshippers. He could hear their chatter, relaxing now that their religious obligations were over for the day. They returned to their evening duty shift but the main thing occupying their minds now was food, followed by copious tea drinking and eventually, sleep.

Seeing that he was clear to start the main task of the exercise, Samir collected a number of sacks from the Toyota and jumped down onto the hull of the landing craft and spread the sacks around so as to deaden any sound of movement of metal hitting the deck and then climbed back onto the quayside. Once again he moved to the pick-up and slid out one of the plastic pipes, prised off a protective cardboard end cap and took the three metre tube in his arms, moved so that the open end of the tube was overhanging the quay. A quick glance around told him that he could continue, which he did by lowering the open end. Gently he increased the angle until he could hear, and feel the contents of the water pipe slide and then fall into the landing craft. A dull thump from the darkness below, told him that the weapons had found their cushioned target. Samir replaced the empty tube back into the Toyota, then de-capped a second, took it in his arms and similarly let its contents slide into the depths of the landing craft. Twenty pipes contained deadly packages and Samir had disgorged half of them without hindrance. It was all too easy he thought, maybe the job is not so bad after all. Perhaps it was the gradual swell of confidence through his body that caused the lapse in vigilance. Had he been totally alert he would have seen the vehicle before he was caught in its headlights. Like a hare on a dark country lane, Samir was trapped, frozen in its beams, unable to move a muscle. His heart stopped for a second and then came the urge to run, or to hide. His pulse quickened so that the blood vessels around his temples threatened to burst. He needed time to think, but this was not some technical problem of one of his cipher machines, where he could take his time to trace signals through its circuit boards. This was out in the wild, when animal instincts of speed and brute force carried the day. Fight or flee impulses had long been suppressed by Samir's habitual make up, so the inability to make a spontaneous decision left him rooted at the tailgate of the Toyota.

Momentarily the oncoming car had to change direction to avoid one of the numerous obstacles, perhaps one of the water hydrants that littered the quay. The instant of darkness released him from the hypnotic trance and the panic eased. For a moment he'd completely forgotten the back-up plan but the preparation of the puncture now left him in a good position. He moved round to the front of the car and squatted by the front wheel. By the time the mystery car had drawn close, he was well into the routine of changing it. The mix of physical exertions and stress, not to mention the humidity of the autumn evening soaked his shirt in sweat. Samir was happier to be doing something with his hands and as the car closed and drew to a halt alongside, he managed to stand with a feigned grin of relief. Help had arrived. The driver was hidden in the shadows, but he wound the window down and released a surge of Arabic music into the night air. 'Alsalam my friend! What's your problem?'

'Mafi mushkula,' no problem, shouted Samir above the din of the music, hoping that the still hidden figure would elect to head off home without further investigation. 'Just a blown tyre – will have it off in a minute – no problem – thanks anyway.'

The music stopped, and to his alarm, the curious visitor opened the car door and rose to see the damage for himself. Samir moved round the pick-up to greet him, wiping his hands as he went and offering the inevitable handshake. To his relief, he recognised the man as civilian clerk, from the signals office, so at least he didn't have to explain his plight to a naval officer. Even so, he hoped that the fellow wouldn't linger whilst Samir completed the wheel change. His prime task was not yet completed and he needed ten minutes of solitude to unload all the remaining tubes carrying weapons.

'Oh yes, I see – must have been a nail.' The clerk was satisfied to peer into the dim light, to see the airless tyre on the ground and its replacement ready to be bolted in place. 'Perhaps you need more light? I can bring my car round so that you can see better.'

Samir was horrified at the thought, 'Thank you, no it's fine, I can see ok – nearly finished anyway.'

The man paused and then hitched his white thobe above his knees and squatted as if he wanted to continue the chatter if not to physically assist in the wheel change. Samir bit back the frustration and resigned himself to put the spare wheel on the empty wheel hub, praying that the man would disappear and leave him to his task. Mercifully, music once again struck up in the cab of his helper's car.

But it wasn't from the radio, it was from a mobile phone. The helper rose and went to answer the call. 'Insha'allaah, habibi!' – God willing my darling,' was all that Samir could hear of the conversation. The call was brief and obviously from a woman. 'It's my wife. She needs the car to go shopping. Are you sure everything is ok here?'

'Thanks be to God, everything is good,' said a much relieved Samir. He rose to offer a hand, but withdrew it when he realised it was dirty from his toils. The man excused himself and returned to his vehicle. Samir breathed more easily than he had done for some time.

The helper stood at his door and took one more look around and seemed surprised at the location where he now found himself. 'What brought you down here? It's just a graveyard for boats.'

Samir had squatted back to the wheel, so the helper could not see the grimace on Samir's face. Inspiration came to his rescue, 'I needed a piss!'

The helper chortled, pulled the driver's door closed and yelled Ma is-salaama. With a wave that Samir didn't see, the helper drove off towards the gate accompanied by the Arabic music that propelled him home.

Samir stood to search again that he was alone and when it was clear, he stepped to the back of the pick-up to continue emptying the contents of the tubes.

Ten minutes later, he too was on his way. The landing craft once more was carrying weapons. Samir felt a rush of elation at the thought of completing his mission. He drove with the windows down and switched on his own radio to let the local music reinforce his buoyant mood. In his relief, he had forgotten one thing – the tubes! Shit! He still had the empty tubes on board. In the heat of the moment he'd forgotten to drop them off, but he was already at the construction site gate. – Too late to turn around without attracting attention. As it was late evening now, the builder's guard had lowered a wooden boom across the exit forcing Samir to stop until the little man came out of his hut to see who the late worker was. It was the same guy who had been there earlier and on seeing the familiar face at the wheel of the Toyota, he raised the boom. As Samir edged forward, the guard glanced into the back of the pick-up and then shot a inquisitive glance into the cab. 'You take pipes back?'

'Wrong size,' shrugged Samir. 'I'll be back tomorrow.'

CHAPTER 18

Code-breaker

Ashley got back to his room late and exhausted as the climate still got to him. The evening had been both revealing and pleasant, apart from the smoke from the Lucky Palace. His stinging eyes added to his fatigue. A cool, refreshing shower was the highest priority. Already the aircon was clearing his sinuses of the dust and humidity. It had been almost impossible to breathe outside, when the humidity came up after sunset.

He stood under the cool cascade for a full fifteen minutes, letting the full force of fresh water wash away the grime and sweat from every pore of his body. Soon the benefits of the aquatic therapy spread to massage the muscles of his weary limbs and invigorate his tired mind.

As new life infused through his body and the mental chaff washed from his head, his thoughts returned to the message – the grubby folded paper that had been surreptitiously handed to him as he left the bar. By the underhand manner in which it was transferred to him, Ashley took it that he should secret it away until such time when he could open it in privacy. Only when sat alone in the taxi, did he retrieve it from his pocket quite expecting an invitation from some lady of the night offering her phone number in the hope of being of some service to him?

Either Clements had really pulled out the stops in pressuring the locals for more assistance, or MOI really *had* been eaves-dropping his call that afternoon, for there in type print was the note:

GSM text message from Samir to Faisal

Date: xxxxx Time: xxxxx
Bootlireiadhiptalqeaiabphbootlireiadhiptacipwdoop
Ivieruteetqkitliebkbdpwibrqpaeibhywbdtipkfeqtliea

At first, having read the word *boot*, under the light of passing street lamps, he took it to be a simple typed message, but when a prolonged illumination allowed him a better look, he found that first word was indeed the only understandable part of the whole. Not being able to make sense out of the two lines of continuous text characters, Ashley turned his attention to the top line – so he had been right, His gut feeling that Colonel Ali Abdullah had been withholding something from him had been borne out. And there it was! Without delay, he refolded the paper and put it into the breast pocket of his shirt. He leant backwards so that he could look up through the back window and could relax a little whilst amber and neon lights escorted him home, only tapping his pocket once with his fingers, as he left the taxi, just to make sure that its contents were still secure.

Safely in his hotel suite, Ashley withdrew the note from his pocket and spread it flat upon the desk, before switching on the lamp and throwing a pool of light onto Samir's secret writing. And there it remained whilst he enjoyed his rejuvenation in the shower.

Once the caressing foam of shampoo and shower gel had been rinsed away, he towelled and wrapped himself in the heavy dressing gown that the hotel hung behind the bathroom door. In three strides he was in the kitchenette and within a few seconds the espresso machine was charged with Columbian Gold. Feeling and smelling a different man, Ashley moved to the desk and settled into the deep leather chair, leant forward and took the paper in both hands. His suspicions about the text were confirmed. It was not, he was certain, written in the plain text of any language that he knew of, and the omission of any punctuation whatsoever, made it obvious that it was written in code. Anything encrypted must hold some secret.

It had been many years since Ashley had carried out any code breaking so he had to spend some of the time trying to recollect the exercises that he had gone through after the service induction course.

The big fear was that the cipher had been carried out using a one-time-pad. This would mean perfect encryption – a process that could not be broken. The source would take his plain text and, character by character, add to each a second character from a randomly produced alphabetic list – the key. The list would be at least as long as the message, so there would be no repetition in the ciphering process. The only possibility of reading a message encrypted in this way was by the receiver having possession of an identical copy of the same key. Each key was printed out on a pad of paper, similar to the ones found in any stationer's with each leaf of the pad being destroyed after use by immersion in water or by digestion. The simple glory of it was that no key was ever used again: The method was unbreakable. Any statistical test would reveal a set of purely random characters, or numbers, making it infeasible for even the best computers to attack it successfully.

In the case of this particular message, or ciphertext as it is known in the trade, the first *t* would have been produced by two plaintext characters: say H + L, they being the eighth and twelfth characters of the alphabet, to give twenty, which designated *t* as the ciphertext. The intended recipient would take his own key list, read from it the letter H and perform the modulo addition to retrieve the plaintext character L. The complexity, which any cryptanalyst was faced with, was that plaintext A + S also produced twenty, as did B and R as well as a mass of other combinations, as they were in the real life one-time-pad encryption.

Had Samir encrypted his message by a one-time-pad, then Ashley would not have been sitting at his desk anticipating a long night of analysis ahead of him. He would have headed to the mini-bar and ensured a heavy sleep by adding a few whiskies to the early evening's swill. As it was, his second read through the body of the ciphertext highlighted a degree of repetition, and even in his slightly inebriated state, he could identify telltale patterns. No such patterns would have been evident with one-time-pads. No! Samir had been using a substitution cipher: Mono-alphabetic or Poly-alphabetic was *not* clear at that moment. It could also be a Vignere or Caesar's cipher, or some bastardisation of either, and Ashley guessed that it was ciphered by hand. He relished tackling the challenge at first hand.

The hiss of high-pressure steam announced that the Columbian Gold was ready. He would need all the caffeine-based motivation to keep him wakeful through what was destined to be a long shift. Once the coffee was perched on the far corner of the desk, Ashley cleared it of everything else bar the light. He then prepared his tools, and any observer, expecting an assembly of advanced computers and the like, would have been disappointed with Ashley's collection of coloured pens, pencils, an eraser and an A4 squared writing pad. His only electronic aid was his crossword solver. He never liked to use it, for solving crosswords that is, but there were times when his sweated brow succumbed to a puzzle setter's excesses, in which case he would allow himself a peek in the hope that he might learn something for the next impossible clue. It wouldn't be a useful word source on this night, but it was the *only* source of English language statistics that was readily at hand.

***

His first action of attack was to copy the message body onto a sheet of squared paper. He did this with a red pen, writing down each character in italics and extending the list into four lines with enough space below each line for edits. As more and more data was produced, Ashley knew that it was essential to be methodical and disciplined. He had to keep things in order and not risk the loss of clues, or become confused by variations in style or fail to distinguish between ciphertext, plaintext and temporary versions of both. Even a short message could produce mountains of scrap paper and eraser dross, not to mention a mountain of plastic coffee cups.

He grouped letters into five, with a space in between. This was a common strategy to make the analyst's task a mite easier when a long list of characters was segmented into smaller, more manageable groups, then checked for any errors. Errors at this early stage would become compounded as the night wore on, and hours could be lost in retracing one's steps. When he was satisfied the list to be a true copy, he counted the characters: ninety-eight with nineteen spaces. He duly recorded this at the end of the line and then moved to the fax machine in the corner of the room to make eight extra copies of the ciphertext.

bootl ireia dhipt alqea iabph bootl ireia dhipt acipw doopi
vieru teetq kitli ebkbd pwibr qpaei bhywb dtipk feqtl iea = 98+19

Table One

Group 1					Group 2					Group 3					Group 4					Group 5				
b	o	o	t	l	i	r	e	i	a	d	h	i	p	t	a	l	q	e	a	i	a	b	p	h

Group 6					Group 7					Group 8					Group 9					Group 10				
b	o	o	t	l	i	r	e	i	a	d	h	i	p	t	a	c	i	p	w	d	o	o	p	i

Group 11					Group 12					Group 13					Group 14					Group 15				
v	i	e	r	u	t	e	e	t	q	k	i	t	l	i	e	b	k	b	d	p	w	i	b	r

Group 16					Group 17					Group 18					Group 19					Group 20				
q	p	a	e	i	b	h	y	w	b	d	t	i	p	k	f	e	q	t	l	i	e	a		

Ashley considered stage one completed: He had the pure database material and only arranged it to facilitate an analytical attack.

Stage two would represent the first steps in the analysis, and Ashley thought that he should consider other factors about the message in order to get an overview about it, rather than just plunge straight in with a formal statistical attack. He already knew quite a bit about *bootli*, as he was beginning to call it. Its source and its destination were reasonably well defined, but there was the chance that it might just be a message fragment from one leg in a relay that the MOI or Echelon had managed to catch. There was also some further background information that might give an insight into solving the riddle. Every germ of information was valuable, but one of the main difficulties was distinguishing between what was relative and useful and what was simply chaff. He took a short break to muster up another coffee whilst plotting a useful strategy. He wouldn't expect much chaff in a hand ciphered message. Samir wouldn't have time for cosmetics.

Once again the smell of roasted coffee beans alone was invigorating as he spread his nostrils and took in the rich aroma. Who needed heroin when one had fresh ground coffee beans to sniff. *He* got a kick out of the coffee even if nobody else did. He smiled to himself and steaming cup in hand, moved to the window on the Dubai night. There before him was the very den of intrigue with its guardian, the electric drummer. His metronomic beat counting down the time. A countdown to what? he wondered, suddenly aware that just maybe, time was indeed running out.

Ashley tried to put himself in Samir's position, running through once again what possible links he could have with Goodwin? What information about the cryptologist had made him so excited and why should he wish to share that information with the likes of a greasy character like Faisal – and why send it by SMS – and why cipher it? Had Samir's profile identified him as a violent man, an Islamic radical even, then he would have attracted the MOI's attention long ago and therefore appeared on *Six's* black list. But no, the Jordanian was just another expat engineer making a living for his family. He had a good reputation from his employer and a spotless police record, not even a bloody parking fine. Like the majority of the population, Samir was a grey man, and that made him dangerous if he really had more than a passing interest in the Goodwin saga. The single blot on his standing as a good citizen was his connection with the Egyptian, Faisal. Now *there* was a shady character. Lots of suspicions and lots of rumours, yet nothing tangible to pin on his chest. Faisal just seemed to drift around in the background of so many stories. A bit of an Arabic Bonetti, wheeler-dealer, but what else? Ashley could not put his finger on it, but having seen in the flesh at the bar, he sensed that the man carried his own dark cloud with him. Was there a way to get inside him, find out what made him tick? He had not attracted any of the bar girls around him, which was a pity as that might have been an opportunity worth exploring. For the moment, Ashley put it to the back of his mind but there would need to be some answers to the questions he had just posed. Perhaps *bootli* would provide some clues.

He was assuming that this message was in English, for no other reason than the first one was in English. Surely Samir, being resident in the UAE, would have Arabic on his phone, as would Faisal, so why not communicate in their common natural tongue? But then again, how would *Thanks be to Goodwin,* translate into Arabic? Not too well he supposed. The little play between God and Goodwin was interesting and exposed a sense of humour in his target. Ashley wondered if it was just a one-off pun, or was it a trait? And if the latter, then maybe, just maybe, the *bootli* text was in the same style? Nothing concrete, but something else to bear in mind.

The drummer and empty coffee cups reminded him that time *was* passing, but now he *had* a strategy in mind and returned to the desk and the papers that awaited his attention. Stage two was complete; he was to go for the substitution cipher.

✳✳✳

One of the most noticeable features of any language was the frequency of alphabetic characters that appeared in dialog so Ashley set about to determine the character count of *bootli*, listing on a fresh piece of squared paper, the ciphertext characters. He wrote these in italics to easily distinguish the cipher text, and in ink – to identify it as absolute fact, not supposition!

Table two:

a	b	c	d	e	f	g	h	i	j	k	l	m	n	o	p	q	r	s	t	u	v	w	x	y	z
8	8	1	5	10	1	0	4	16	0	3	5	0	0	6	8	4	4	0	9	1	1	3	0	1	0

Without looking at the crossword solver, he knew that E was by far the most common character in the English language. From table two it was easy to see that the ciphertext *i*, was likely to represent a plaintext E. It was also easy to confirm that a one-time-pad had not been used because if it had, the distribution of letters would have been almost even.

Statistics were often very misleading, especially when they had a limited sample size, and in terms of cryptanalysis this message was too short to be conclusive when it came to letter frequencies. He would have preferred a longer message in order to give the database a bit more authority. What you see is what you get he mused, and still felt that if this was a basic substitution encryption, then *i* was far more significant than any other character. He would go with this for the time being and track back if things didn't pan out later. So he went through the table and substituted all ciphertext *i*'s with plaintext E's in table three.

Ashley then drew yet another chart, which he called *The Pot*. This *Pot* was where he collected the result of each step of the cipher attack and where he tried to reconstruct Samir's alphabetic substitution. From *The Pot* it was possible, if his analysis was successful, to get an insight into what key Samir had chosen even before all the logical processes had been exhausted. If he was really lucky, a predictable pattern might emerge so that he could make an educated guess at the complete key even if he couldn't work out every individual character.

Table three:

b	o	o	t	l	i	r	e	i	a	d	h	i	p	t	a	l	q	e	a	i	a	b	p	h
					E			E				E								E				
					E		T	E				E						T		E				

b	o	o	t	l	i	r	e	i	a	d	h	i	p	t	a	c	i	p	w	d	o	o	p	i
					E			E				E					E							E
					E		T	E				E					E							E

v	i	e	r	u	t	e	e	t	q	k	i	t	l	i	e	b	k	b	d	p	w	i	b	r
	E										E			E								E		
	E	T				T	T				E			E	T							E		

q	p	a	e	i	b	h	y	w	b	d	t	i	p	k	f	e	q	t	l	i	e	a
				E								E								E		
			T	E								E				T				E	T	

Turning back to the character frequencies, he recollected that T was the second most popular character in the English language. Consulting the table two data, he saw that ciphertext *e* was the best candidate for plaintext T. But this was where the lack of material, i.e. the limited message length, became a problem. The parity of the frequencies of ciphertext characters *a,b,e, p* and *t*, made it too close to call. There appeared to be little option but to try each one in turn and eliminate those that didn't fit well. Ashley ran his hand through his hair. Shit! This was going to take time. Perhaps he should fire it back to London. There *really* wasn't enough material for him to work on but he diligently pencilled in the plaintext T's into line three of table three, determined to follow the logical routine.

He looked at the result in his table. With two characters entered, there were no salient points that immediately attracted his attention, except that he was pretty confident about the E. What he did notice was that there were three TE's and a TT. These he knew as bigrams, pairs of letters, and they too had a frequency component in any Latin-based language. This is where the crossword solver came in handy, for it did carry some frequency tables for bigrams and trigrams as well as the most common words. Ashley accessed the bigram table and searched for TE. Its relative index was 805, whereas the most frequent bigram was TH with a relative index of 3000. Ashley thought for a while, disappointed that TE was fairly common in *bootli*, and seemingly too frequent when considering the bigram table. Seeking support from the TT, he found that its index was, surprisingly, 500! even less than TE.

In his newspaper crossword experience, there were usually two hidden pointers within a cryptic clue. Here the statistics did neither conclusively support *e* being plaintext T, nor dismiss it. It was almost a toss of a coin decision whether to continue with this suggestion. He looked back at the table to make one more check for a second clue. What could Samir be writing and how would he write it? – Then came a moment of classic crossword inspiration. Sometimes a clue would remain hidden all day, defeating every attempt to break it. Yet after a break, a night's sleep, he would next day look at the offending clue – and immediately recognise the obvious answer. Now he didn't have time to reflect on every clue, but in a typical cryptic crossword attack, lateral thinking often found the answer.

First came the idea about sentence structure and a suggestion of a smile creased Ashley's mouth. He confirmed his suspicion from table three and the smile broadened. It couldn't be TE! If it were TE, then there would be only one possibility of THE occurring in the entire message and that would be in the fourth and fifth groups where *a* would have to be H. But then *e,a,i,a* would give an unlikely plain text of _THEH_. Not impossible, but sufficient to throw enough doubt for Ashley to dismiss it, for the time being, and move to the next likely ciphertext for T.

Ashley remembered the stories of the code breakers of Bletchley Park, who regularly broke into the Nazi communications ciphered by their ill-fated Enigma machine. One of its weaknesses that allowed a way in to the cipher, was that the machine never ciphered a plaintext character with the same ciphertext character. Now, at this juncture, Ashley was faced with the same dilemma. Statistics indicated that the next most likely substitution for plaintext T, was ciphertext *t*. He wondered if Samir was familiar with the history of WWII code breaking, and in particular the Enigma operation. He doubted it, and even so it would be foolhardy to dismiss the possibility, without some attempt to justify that *t* might equal T. Samir surely wouldn't be so careless, but was he experienced enough to see the flaw? So he went for it and erased the T's in line three and replaced them under the columns that were headed *t*.

Only one TE bigram, in line 4, plus a new one: ET in line 3. According to the bigram frequency table ET had an index of 850 and so was not expected to be common. Ashley was reassured to see that it wasn't. Sometimes negatives can be positive, he chuckled to himself.

Table Four

b	o	o	t	l	i	r	e	i	a	d	h	i	p	t	a	l	q	e	a	i	a	b	p	h
						E		E				E								E				
			T			E		E				E		T						E				

b	o	o	t	l	i	r	e	i	a	d	h	i	p	t	a	c	i	p	w	d	o	o	p	i
						E		E				E					E							E
			T			E		E				E		T			E							E

v	i	e	r	u	t	e	e	l	q	k	i	t	l	i	e	b	k	b	d	p	w	i	b	r
E											E			E								E		
E					T			T			E	T		E								E		T

q	p	a	e	i	b	h	y	w	b	d	t	i	p	k	f	e	q	t	l	i	e	a
				E								E								E		
				E							T	E						T		E		

He should have seen it before and mildly cursed himself for missing one of the most obvious features about *bootli*. He *had* seen that the first three groups had been repeated but the significance had been lost on him. Not only was the ciphertext repeated, but it must be the case that the code mixed with the plaintext was also the same. In other words, there was no shift of the code during this part of the message, it simply repeated. If Samir had used a one-time-pad, this characteristic would certainly not have appeared. Ashley's initial strategy of doing the simple things first was fine, but a little more observation of the *bootli* text would have added some logic to his decision-making. However, it was reassuring to know that Samir was an amateur! Message repeats, indeed any repetition whatsoever, gave the analyst a chance to get a foot in the door. Ashley was growing confident that he was on the right path and that he could at least break some of the message if not all. It was surprising, he thought, how much a secret message divulged about its source. In this case, even though he had almost no computer power available to him, such as would be found in the GCHQ and the NSA institutions, he had prised the door of *bootli* open with some very basic analysis.

Encouraged, Ashley turned his attention back to his table three. A second feature announced itself. Looking at the first two groups, if he ignored the space between them, *bootlireia* overlapped to give a *tli* run in the middle. This of course was there again in the second line with the same two groups. In fact, looking through the entire message, there were four incidences of T_E. It didn't take much inspiration to see that these represented the plaintext word, THE. And it followed that ciphertext *l* was probably plaintext H. With no hesitation, Ashley was now working with enthusiasm, putting both H and T into his line three and then changing his mind to enter them into line two

He was so confident with the result that he immediately entered both characters into what he called *his pot*. *The Pot* was where eventually the Holy Grail, the secret key would evolve.

Of the few characters he had in hand, he was most confident about the E. He wasn't confident however, that the single character frequency tables were capable of defining many more plaintext letters, because of the dearth of material on which to compare them. If he had computing power he could have run a brute-force attack, which would have eventually come up with solutions. But for the moment that was out of the question. Instead, he focussed on the E and its ciphertext alias, i.

Table Five

b	o	o	t	l	i	r	e	i	a	d	h	i	p	t	a	l	q	e	a	i	a	b	p	h
			T	H	E			E				E		T		H				E				

b	o	o	t	l	i	r	e	i	a	d	h	i	p	t	a	c	i	p	w	d	a	o	p	i
			T	H	E			E				E		T			E							E

v	i	e	r	u	t	e	e	t	q	k	i	t	l	i	e	b	k	b	d	p	w	i	b	r
	E				T			T			E	T	H	E								E		T

q	p	a	e	i	b	h	y	w	b	d	t	i	p	k	f	e	q	t	l	i	e	a	
				E							T	E						T	H	E			

From Table three, he discerned that there were several bigrams worth some attention. He arranged, *ip, ia, ie, ir, ib* and their possible plaintext decryptions, into a matrix according to their indexed probabilities and gave it a label: Table six was born.

Table Six

Col. 1	Col. 2	Col. 3	Col. 4	Col. 5	Co. 6	Col. 7
Cipher text	Index	1800	1200	1100	1000	850
4 *ip*		ER	ES	EN	EA	ET
3 *ia*		ER	ES	EN	EA	ET
3 *ie*		ER	ES	EN	EA	ET
2 *ir*		ER	ES	EN	EA	ET
2 *ib*		ER	ES	EN	EA	ET

Ashley deleted out the ET column as he was already pretty sure that T had been found. This reduced the possibilities to four columns in table four. Then he took one of the spare copies of table three, entered the E, H and T components into line 2 and then in line 3 transposed all the *ip's* with ER and therefore all *p's* to R. Nothing excited him about R, so he moved along table four and inserted S's in column four of table three for every ciphertext *p*, in line 3 – then repeated the process for N in column five, and A in column six.

In the groups 3, 8, 18 a possible trigram was formed by each inclusion and therefore he was unable to throw out any of them, so he repeated the process for the *ia's* and *a's*. and after another negative search through the table did the same for *ie's* and *e's*.

Once again there were no real patterns that stood out, but he didn't like the results for the twelfth group, which gave some doubles that were not easily going to fit in to any English dialogue. It seemed from this group that *e* couldn't be A and therefore *ie*/EA was scratched from table four.

Table Seven

b	o	o	t	i	i	r	e	i	a	d	h	i	p	t	a	l	q	e	a	i	a	b	p	h
			T	H	E			E		E		T			H					E				
					E	R	R	E	R	E	R	T				R		R	R	E	R		R	
					E	S	S	E	S	E	S	T				S		S	S	E	S		S	
					E	N	N	E	N	E	N	T				N		N	N	E	N		N	
					E	A	A	E	A	E	A	T				A		A	A	E	A		A	
					E	P	P	E	P	E	P	T												

b	o	o	t	i	i	r	e	i	a	d	h	i	p	t	a	c	i	p	w	d	o	o	p	i
			T	H	E			E		E		T			E									E
						R	E	R			R						R				R			
						S	E	S			S						S				S			
						N	E	N			N						N				N			
						A	E	A			A						A				A			

v	i	e	r	u	t	e	e	t	q	k	i	t	i	i	e	b	k	b	d	p	w	i	b	r
E					T			T		E	T	H	E							E				T
	R					R	R									R						R		
	S					S	S									S						S		
	N					N	N									N						N		
	A					A	A									A						A		

q	p	a	e	i	b	h	y	w	b	d	t	i	p	k	f	e	q	t	l	i	e	a
			E							T		E							T	H	E	
	R											R				R				R	R	
	S											S				S				S	S	
	N											N				N				N	N	
	A											A				A				A	A	

Group two gave a lot of possibilities. - too many, but the last two groups gave a clue. He couldn't easily think of a word that ended; THERA, THESA, THEAN, THEAR, THENA, THESN, THESR, but there were possibilities for THERS and THERN. The words NORTHERN and OTHERS, even BOTHERS, were but a few. He could even extrapolate to get BROTHERS from the last two groups, although this meant accepting RR in group 12.

Seeking either support or elimination for this trial, Ashley looked back to group 2 where the ciphertext *i, r, e ,i, a* – gave a major part of some hidden word. He methodically carried out a process of elimination. THE *had* to be fixed, and therefore it followed that the second *i* must also be fixed to E, and if it was correct then *r, e, i, a* would almost certainly represent the start of another word. On that premise, Ashley made a list of all possible combinations of the plaintext characters R, S, N, A, P and with some relief only found RAPS, NAPS, AREN, PREN and PRES to give reasonable suggestions about what might follow, but of these, only the last three took in E as their third letter. Besides – because of the *ee*/AA in group twelve, he had already decided that *e* could not be A. That meant group two would be EAREN, EPREN or EPRES.

If Ashley smoked, then this would be the time to light up, take a stroll or wander out onto the balcony and watch the late night birds driving home after their bars and restaurants had closed their doors. He was depressed now. After the initial breakthrough, his confidence had soared, but things had not subsequently fallen into place as he had hoped. He was sure the answer was there, and he *had* made progress, but it seemed that no matter which angle he attacked from he always came to the same brick wall. He was tired, but knew that with his mind racing through combinations of letters and numbers, tables and charts, that sleep would not come easily. He had also a growing concern that time was becoming a critical factor and that unease was in fact pressuring him to get *bootli* decoded, and decoded quickly. In these circumstances a clear, logical mind was what was needed for an efficient analysis. It slowly dawned on him that he had deviated from the path. The message had produced a hurdle. Perhaps Samir was not the amateur that he thought just a few hours ago. Ashley stood from the desk, pushing the chair back with his legs as he rose and stretched. He was still in the bathrobe and whilst the body was warm, the aircon had chilled his naked feet and legs, to the point that they were giving him pain which had gone un-noticed because of his efforts on the code breaking.

The coffee had been strong and was giving him the discomfort of a gnawing heartburn. His shoulders and neck ached from the crouching over his papers. His head throbbed with a low-key hangover, and now to cap it all he was suffering almost from frostbite in the lower extremes!

✳✳✳

Aware that the silence in the room had become charged with his tension, the code breaker sought to change the environment by turning on the hotel's in-house music channel. Television would have been far too distracting. The classical channel was playing Shostakovich – The Gadfly. He remembered the soft, undulating airs as the theme music from the television series, *Riley Ace of Spies* which had fascinated him some twenty years ago. It had entranced him at the time and whenever he heard this title music, he was transported back to his postgraduate days and the tiny first floor apartment on a leafy avenue he shared with his first real lover – the gorgeous Lizzie. Latin looks with a Latin temperament to match, a cocktail that could only have sown the seeds of one type of relationship – a passionate one. No – it must have been fifteen years ago. But it wasn't the memory of those steamy nights and late lazy Sunday lie-ins that now brought a broad smile to his lips. It was the irony that, here was Ashley, doing pretty much the same sort of work as Sidney Reilly had done for MI6 in Russia in the twenties. Mellowing, Ashley clung to every chord of the passage and hummed it through in as a melodic and emotional accompaniment as he could fashion. The London Symphony Orchestra had risen to the occasion and a tear moistened Ashley's tired eyes.

Symphony! – The word brought him back to the present with a shock that raised his pulse to an elevated level. The image of the leafy Sheffield apartment, Reilly and Latin nights, was replaced by that of the desert city night. The electric drummer had taken on an air of portent and Ashley had to look twice to make sure that the drumbeat had not quickened.

***

Ciphertext 'ee' giving RR in group twelve, was *the* problem. In normal text it didn't make sense when sandwiched between T's, but when observed from two different points of view – from the last two groups and from group 2, each came up with the same answer, 'ee' gave RR. Despite the sceptical gut feeling, he had to proceed with the logic. There had been a danger of him losing it before his interlude so he focussed once more to follow the trail through.

He decided to give it another go and took out another spare table three sheet, kept the first line as fixed, and then transposed 'r' for P, 'e' for R and 'a' for S. They all fitted well with table four and they gave PRES in group two and THERS at the message end, so he transposed all three characters in *bootli*.

Table Eight

b	o	o	t	l	i	r	e	i	a	d	h	i	p	t	a	l	q	e	a	i	a	b	p	h
			T		E			E			H	E		T						E				
						P	R		S						S			R	S		S			

b	o	o	t	l	i	r	e	i	a	d	h	i	p	t	a	c	i	p	w	d	o	o	p	i
			T		E			E			H	E		T			E							E
						P	R		S						S									

v	i	e	r	u	t	e	e	t	q	k	i	t	l	i	e	b	k	b	d	p	w	i	b	r
	E				T			T		H	E	T		E			H					E		T
		R				R	R								R									

q	p	a	e	i	b	h	y	w	b	d	t	i	p	k	f	e	q	t	l	i	e	a
				E							T	E		H				T		E		
		S	R													R					R	S

It was time to check 'The Pot' to see what effect these latest inputs might have on his reconstruction of Samir's alphabet.

The Pot

```
a  b  c  d  e  f  g  h  i  j  k  l  m  n  o  p  q  r  s  t  u  v  w  x  y  z
S           R           E     H                     P     T
```

There was no obvious pattern in *The Pot*. The cipher wasn't a simple shifted alphabet, although the periods between E and H, and from T to the end of the ciphertext alphabet would accommodate the intermediate plaintext letters. It might have been just coincidence that real words were beginning to form, but in this line of work, coincidence was not easily accepted. Continuing with the momentum, Ashley moved the plaintext line 2 letters from line 2 into the fix of line 1.

Table Nine

b	o	o	t	l	i	r	e	i	a	d	h	i	p	t	a	l	q	e	a	i	a	b	p	h
		T	H		E	P	R	E	S			E		T	S	H		R	S	E	S			

b	o	o	t	l	i	r	e	i	a	d	h	i	p	t	a	c	i	p	w	d	o	o	p	i
		T	H		E	P	R	E	S			E		T	S		E							E

v	i	e	r	u	t	e	e	t	q	k	i	t	l	i	e	b	k	b	d	p	w	i	b	r
	E	R			T	R	R	T			E	T	H	E	R							E		T

q	p	a	e	i	b	h	y	w	b	d	t	i	p	k	f	e	q	t	l	i	e	a
	S	R	E								T	E				R		T	H	E	R	S

Then it was time to update Table four in view of these findings.

Table Ten

	Index	1800	1200	1100	1000	850
4 ip		ER	ES	EN	EA	ET
3 ia		ER	ES	EN	EA	ET
3 ie		ER	ES	EN	EA	ET
2 ir		ER	ES	EN	EA	ET
2 ib		ER	ES	EN	EA	ET

Ashley felt that he was getting somewhere, and as the pace of discovery accelerated, so did his efforts. Table four was almost complete and it only remained to determine the relationships of ciphertexts *ip* and *ib* with EN and EA.

As *ip* was the more common bigram of the two, Ashley aligned it with EN which had a greater frequency index than EA. The new proposals were added into line 2 of a new latest copy of Table three.

Ashley was stunned. 'Shit!' he shouted down at the pile of papers littering the desk. It was a mix of sheer elation at *finally* getting something from *bootli* and, at the same time an awareness of the gravity carried by the message. – There, it was obvious! The first three groups gave A_ _THEPRES_ _ENT SH.

It was there for all to the see: A _ _THE PRESIDENTS H _. 'My God!'

Working feverishly now, Ashley added the newly found letters, I and D into the latest Table three, and from that he could see that he had won an AND in group five.

Table Eleven

b	o	o	t	l	i	r	e	i	a	d	h	i	p	t	a	l	q	e	a	i	a	b	p	h
			T	H	E	P	R	E	S			E		T	S	H		R	S	E	S			
A													N									A	N	
										I	D													D

b	o	o	t	l	i	r	e	i	a	d	h	i	p	t	a	c	i	p	w	d	o	o	p	i
			T	H	E	P	R	E	S			E		T	S		E							E
A													N						N					N	
										I	D													

v	i	e	r	u	t	e	e	t	q	k	i	t	l	i	e	b	k	b	d	p	w	i	b	r
	E	R			T	R	R	T			E	T	H	E	R							E		T
																A		A		N			A	
																	I							

q	p	a	e	i	b	h	y	w	b	d	t	i	p	k	f	e	q	t	l	i	e	a
		S	R	E							T	E			R			T	H	E	R	S
N					A								N									
										I												

Then Ashley quickly added the new letters to *The Pot* to see if Samir's alphabet and key were exposed yet, whilst humming Shostakovich in increasing volume as he progressed.

The Pot

a	b	c	d	e	f	g	h	i	j	k	l	m	n	o	p	q	r	s	t	u	v	w	x	y	z
S	A		I	R			D	E			H				N			P		T					

Could that be SAMIR heading the ciphering alphabet? He asked himself – in which case *c* would give M. Ashley searched for a ciphertext *c* in *bootli*. – Second line, group 9.

MEN, it gave MEN!

And then the second line crumbled. Ashley had it – ALL THE PRESIDENTS MEN!

He was euphoric, ALL THE PRESIDENTS MEN – The Watergate movie – it starred Dustin Hoffman and Redford, Robert Redford – RR? Could there be another relationship there? It was like a cascade of flood water breaking over a dam and now falling so easily into place. But he couldn't see how the RR fitted in, as much as he sought an answer. Still now he could add more letters into the Table three and directly fix them in line 1.

Table Twelve

b	*o*	*o*	*t*	*l*	*i*	*r*	*e*	*i*	*a*	*d*	*h*	*i*	*p*	*t*	*a*	*i*	*q*	*e*	*a*	*i*	*a*	*b*	*p*	*h*
A	L	L	T	H	E	P	R	E	S	I	D	E	N	T	S	H		R	S	E	S	A	N	D

b	*o*	*o*	*t*	*l*	*i*	*r*	*e*	*i*	*a*	*d*	*h*	*i*	*p*	*t*	*a*	*c*	*i*	*p*	*w*	*d*	*o*	*o*	*p*	*i*
A	L	L	T	H	E	P	R	E	S	I	D	E	N	T	S	M	E	N			L	L	N	E
							I																	

v	*i*	*e*	*r*	*u*	*t*	*e*	*e*	*t*	*q*	*k*	*i*	*t*	*l*	*i*	*e*	*b*	*k*	*b*	*d*	*p*	*w*	*i*	*b*	*r*
	E	R	P			T	R	R	T		E	T	H	E	R	A		A	I	N		E	A	T

q	*p*	*a*	*e*	*i*	*b*	*h*	*y*	*w*	*b*	*d*	*t*	*i*	*p*	*k*	*f*	*e*	*q*	*t*	*l*	*i*	*e*	*a*
N	S	R	E		A	D		A		I	T	E	N			R		T	H	E	R	S

'Now the coup de grace,' smiled Ashley aloud. 'Back to *The Pot*. What is in *The Pot*, I wonder?'

The Pot

a	*b*	*c*	*d*	*e*	*f*	*g*	*h*	*i*	*j*	*k*	*l*	*m*	*n*	*o*	*p*	*q*	*r*	*s*	*t*	*u*	*v*	*w*	*x*	*y*	*z*
S	A	M	I	R			D	E		H			L	N		P			T						

That was it! Samir had used his own name to act as a key to the cipher. Samir had just gone down in Ashley's esteem. Fancy using your own bloody name! That might not have been your first mistake but it certainly was your worst, and the next was?

Ashley scratched a pencil line under *The Pot* to give the final *pot*.

The Pot

a	*b*	*c*	*d*	*e*	*f*	*g*	*h*	*i*	*j*	*k*	*l*	*m*	*n*	*o*	*p*	*q*	*r*	*s*	*t*	*u*	*v*	*w*	*x*	*y*	*z*
S	A	M	I	R		D	E		H			L	N		P		T								
		B	C		F	G		J		K				O		Q			U	V	W	X	Y	Z	

The next was that: 'Your name just wasn't long enough my friend!' he laughed. Samir had used his name to shift the substitution alphabet along and then fill in the missing letters of the alphabet, without re-using those that made up his name. The trouble with that was there for all to see. The last six letters ciphered themselves. It was plaintext and even if the message had been more complicated, statistics would have eventually weeded out the likes of U,V, W, X, Y and Z. It was just a matter of time.

The simplicity of the key and cipher system meant that it would be easy for both transmitter and receiver to set a predetermined series of keys that would cipher each message in a different way. Ashley would have put a lot of money on the next key being FAISAL, becoming FAISL when omitting the duplication of A. 'Too simple my friend – classic.'

ALL THE PRESIDENTS HORSES AND ALL THE PRESIDENTS MEN
WILL NEVER PUT
RR TOGETHER AGAIN WEATONS READY WAITENG BROTHERS

Relieved as he was, Ashley read through the message several times. Even though it was clearly deciphered, there were still some oddities that needed to be addressed. WEATONS, WAITENG BROTHERS and RR departed from the expected. Ashley checked back through his workings and found that he had made a mistake in transposing r for T in group 15, instead of giving a plaintext P, and WEAPONS!

Ashley's delight in deciphering the message was rapidly tempered by the news that the MOI had been right to be alarmed. He turned his attention to the last two words. Perhaps there was another mistake. But after another quick check, followed by a longer one, he could not clear it. The message deciphered correctly did read WAITENG BROTHERS. As it was, he thought that it could be referring to ENGlish brothers, but the more he considered the idea, the more he became convinced that it was WAITING.

Ashley was shocked. How could such an apparently mild mannered family man like Samir get mixed up with weapons? That an attack was being prepared was now pretty conclusive, but by whom? and against whom? Knowledge of RR seemed to be crucial, but it had been a problem the whole way through – and which president was involved? There were still answers to be found.

On finding that he had made at least one mistake in the deciphering, Ashley spent more time checking through the processes again, hoping that one would be found to settle the problem of RR. But other than start the whole task again, he could find no mistake and no way into its meaning. And PRESIDENT? Which president? He was exhausted now and his mind had slowed so that it was difficult to concentrate for more than a few seconds. Once again Ashley rose and looked out over the Creek and its Dhow harbour, and beyond that to the Lighthouse building with its drummer. Further than that, he was able to discern the eastern horizon and the faint traces of the new dawn. Switching his train of thoughts back to Samir and his message, the use of the pun of the old English nursery rhyme was hardly surprising, given the first message. Ashley's immediate question was: why had he changed *King's* men to *President's* men?

Ashley lay down, stretched out on the bed exhausted, intending to ponder this latest riddle, but sleep came upon him immediately the moment he closed his eyes.

CHAPTER 19

Stefan Larchey

All that Ashley knew about the arrival of his promised support from Clements was that he went by the name of Larchey, initial S for Stefan, an associate of Goodwin's and to expect his arrival courtesy of the MOI on the Monday evening. What he didn't expect, when he answered the doorbell, was that he would come face to face with an old acquaintance. The last time Ashley had seen Mr. Larchey was when he stormed off from the harbour-front restaurant in Toronto. Steve, as he had introduced himself had left in a pique of ill temper and though, on this occasion, the two greeted each other with polite recognition, Ashley felt that Stefan Larchey hadn't come to Dubai of his own volition. At the first opportunity Ashley surreptitiously called up Clements to complain about his choice, only to be told that Stefan Larchey actually came with Goodwin's very own recommendation. Young and headstrong he might be, but he was the best of the rest. *The* very best.

Minder had stood behind the newcomer and politely waited for the two Englishmen to get through their initial greetings, excused himself and carried into the suite an aluminium chest containing Stefan's hardware. Although he was invited to stay, the MOI man offered his thanks but assured Ashley of his immediate availability should it be needed then quietly left the room. Larchey put a finger to his lips, took a sheet of paper from a hotel notepad, and scribbled a few words before silently handing the note to Ashley.

Yes initially, our walls did have ears, friendly ones, but I was promised that they cleared them out. Even so...'
Larchey simply nodded.

Still feeling somewhat worse for wear following the late night code breaking, but aware of the circumstances under which they parted last. Ashley sought to break the ice with an invitation for dinner. However Stefan had other ideas in mind and said that he was here to help bring Symphony to a successful conclusion, and would prefer to get straight onto the task in hand. Ashley compromised by ordering room service food for the two of them, and getting into his briefing of the mission status from his point of view.

The meals on wheels arrived with Minder taking on the role of deliveryman; and each took ample portions of the buffet and immediately returned to the small circular dining table.

'Now I see the situation at first hand, I deem my major role here being to attack the communications between both Lighthouse users and whoever they are communicating with,' the cryptologist opened. '*My* personal goal would be to establish who murdered Peter Goodwin, but in view of the new threat, as identified by yourself, Commander Clements insisted that our efforts should be aligned to solving this local problem first.'

'I see,' Ashley paused, carefully choosing his words before continuing, 'There is no doubt that if we're going to get to the bottom of this, your analytical skills represent the best, and perhaps the only option available to us. I am pretty sure now that we have the confidence of the local guys. The MOI people are giving all assistance possible, after their initial reluctance that is.'

'What do you see that reluctance being due to?' asked Stefan, his abruptness still apparent.

Ashley, once again, was treading carefully. The last thing he needed was a loose cannon on board. Team spirit was going to be paramount over the next few days. He considered his response for several seconds before speaking. 'Two things Stefan. First and foremost, these people are proud people, proud of their heritage, but also proud of the dynamic progress that the UAE is making. They are going through tremendous growth, making their mark on the world, and having a fundamental impact on the region. The country's growth rate has stretched their resources to the limit including the security forces which are still fledgling institutions. MOI needs to justify its existence to the powers that be. They *need* to get it right first time; hence *we* are in the game.

'This leads me to the second reason which, I think – is purely and simply that they do not know who to trust. For all their overt statements of support for their fellow Arabs, the Gulf nations still don't really trust each other when it comes to the crunch. The Middle East remains very treacherous ground and just as Saddam had envious eyes for the riches of his neighbour Kuwait, so there are others who are resentful of The UAE's enormous wealth. And there are still others, conservative religious zealots, who regard Dubai in particular, as rapidly departing from their own ideals of Islam. They would love to see it brought back into the fold.' Seeing that Stefan was patiently taking all of this on board, Ashley continued: 'After the American intelligence debacle in Iraq, it doesn't leave many options when one is looking for help on matters of national security. Happily the British alliance with its belligerent coalition partner from across the pond has not tarnished its image to the degree that one might have come to expect. Besides, we have a long traditional alliance with these people – an association that goes back, even before the time of the formation of The Trucial States. That was, as it is to this day, a relationship that goes beyond the political and military posturing that we see so much of. Still, I am sure it was only when the Government and the MOI began to realise there could be a very serious problem brewing, that they came to us. – The catalyst was the Goodwin intercept!'

'So now they are shitting themselves?' It was a statement to himself rather than a question seeking an Ashley opinion.

'There are a lot of very nervous people out there and many a Sheikh is having sleepless nights.' Ashley tempered. 'You've obviously been putting together some kind of strategy, Stefan. What exactly do you need from me?'

Having eased the tension a little, Ashley now wanted to give his reluctant companion his head, realising that he, himself would have to take on the dirty tricks, leaving the mathematician to delve into the darkness of his own ethereal world.

'Clements recruited me for *Symphony* because he thought that I was close to Goodwin's way of thinking and might have some insight into what was troubling him about NAMES. I have to find it – this is my task. Your friends, Samir and Bonetti, it would appear, have some *inside* information, so it would be worthwhile to explore the possibilities of getting our hands on that. If, and it's a big if, they know precisely what is wrong with NAMES – Knowing this, I feel that there's a good chance of getting into their communications – and finding out what's really cooking.'

Stefan Larchey made it sound so simple. But Ashley was a touch more sceptical. If Goodwin was the only one to fault NAMES, he couldn't follow the justification for this young fellow's upbeat optimism. But Goodwin *wasn't* the only one – somebody else knew, which was precisely why Goodwin was dead. Was it Benjamin Franklin who said: '*Three men can keep a secret, only if two of them are dead*'? Ashley couldn't remember, but wondered if it would *only* be two and could have added – '*and if it is to remain a secret, then all three must be dead.*'

'As we only have the two SMS messages, one must assume there are alternative communications between Bonetti, Samir and Faisal – and others –' Ashley added, 'will probably have been by word of mouth, or by the ciphered fax machines that they all have. However we haven't been able to monitor *any* faxes between Bonetti and Faisal. On the other hand Bonetti has been faxing all over the world, and *all* of them – every single one, has been ciphered.'

'You said *two* SMS messages?' Stefan reined him back quizzically.

'Yes – of course, it came to life whilst you were travelling. My apologies.' Ashley wrote the message down on a hotel notepad. 'It was sent by Samir to his partner, Faisal.'

Stefan took it and studied the rhyme. 'This guy must be reading Sherlock Holmes' stuff.' After analysing it several times he asked. 'And who the hell is RR?'

'Ah, now that *is* interesting, because I've been asking myself the very same thing! Originally I suspected that there was a mistake in either the coding or decoding of the message, because there were other discrepancies which were certainly errors, but there is no feasible alternative solution for RR.'

Stefan raised his eyebrows. 'It must be American?'

'Now, why do you say that?'

Impatience began to show itself in the cryptologist's tone, 'Because if it referred to anything English, it should read, "All the Queen's horses and all the Queen's men."'

Ashley had also surmised that before, but he was happy for another opinion. 'That would indeed seem to be the case,' he paused, seeking to play the role of the devil's advocate, before posing, 'yet, in these times, people are increasingly referring to Britain as a republic, and Blair's autocratic leadership making him its president!'

'Do you really think that this fellow Samir is that close to British society and the topical concerns of the British people?'

'I think that this fellow, as you call him, should not be underestimated, and yes, I *do* think that he has his finger very much on the British pulse. If that were not the case, then where and why does he make use of English nursery rhymes and British humour? The man is intelligent, dangerous, he's an Arab, he's strictly Muslim, but he thinks like an English man – and is evidently proud of it. If he is a terrorist, then he represents the most elusive and dangerous type, the type that our security forces fear most, that is one of our own, or damned close to it.'

'So what is the link with RR, if he is referring to a British target?'

'Well, that's the million dollar question, Stefan, and the only thing on the table at the moment is that Rolls Royce is here at DUBEX, and here in a big way. Some big players in aviation reckon that the new Trent engine is either the make or break factor for the company. The future of Rolls, and perhaps the whole British aviation manufacturing industry is on the line. Here and now!'

'I can't see an attack on Rolls Royce as being the sort of target that, say, Al Qaeda, would see as being so prestigious as to advance their cause.'

Ashley's immediate response would have been to voice his

disagreement, but to do so would probably alienate Larchey even further than he already was. It was vital to keep the man on his side. 'On one side of the coin, I would agree. To bomb Big Ben, would certainly have a massive impact on the British people and on the face of it and represents the ideal target. On the other hand, they've already done something similar on nine eleven. It would be seen by many as just an action replay, whereas an attack on one of the salient manufacturers in Britain would illustrate just how diverse and therefore more credible Al Qaeda, or its franchises, would be seen to be. It wouldn't be lost on them, or the British people, that Rolls Royce is still a major British icon.'

Larchey was still sceptical, but certainly less aggressive in his argument. 'In my opinion, going for the likes of Blair, or Bush, would be where my money would rest. These two men represent the prime targets.'

'Maybe you are right, but we mustn't also forget what an attack of that magnitude, no matter the precise target, would mean to Dubai or the UAE! Just get in a taxi and drive around Stefan, it will open your eyes. It's an education. The development in Dubai especially, is absolutely incredible. The oil revenue from the UAE fields is in the order of $150Million a day! And a high proportion of that is going straight back into the state. Investing for a future when there is no more oil in the ground.

'There we are in agreement. Perhaps it's not the target of an attack, but *where* the attack is, that is the fundamental issue?'

Ashley silently breathed a sigh of relief. Larchey was still on board and they were, on the whole, in agreement about where a strike might come. The working relationship was made healthier for its lateral opinions and the apparent unification in its mission.

***

'So there has been fax traffic between Samir and Faisal.'

'Yes – also ciphered. And also between both of them and a station in Pakistan – Islamabad, to be precise.'

'Ciphered?' asked Larchey.

'Ciphered.'

'They all use faxes with NAMES, I expect?'

'Not all: Samir only has an older CIPHERCAN machine that is pre NAMES. All the rest have new machines with the latest algorithm. So messages to and from Samir must be ciphered using the old algorithm, BASE,' informed Ashley. 'So the newer machines are compatible with the older versions.'

'Yes, the two algorithms were capable of working together, and I remember that it was exactly this backwards compatibility between them that troubled Peter Goodwin. This is where he favoured his own SQUIRREL algorithm.'

'Wouldn't that be natural? – his preference for his own algorithm, I mean?'

'No, not at all!' responded Larchey harshly, as if he personally had been offended by Ashley's supposition. 'Peter would never have been so arrogant. If he offered SQUIRREL to the industry, then you can be damned sure that there wasn't a hole in it. It would be more than his life's worth if some analyst had found a backdoor into *his* algorithm – it would have been the end of him.'

My God, he thought, they are all the same, these bloody crypto freaks, so damned superior. He wanted to take the man to task by pointing out that his beloved Peter *was* dead. It *had* been the end of him, and it *was* almost certainly linked with SQUIRREL, NAMES, or BASE, but he bit his tongue and nursed the irate mathematician back on course. He let a few seconds pass to allow the heat to dissipate before asking, 'Stefan, how can we attack this compatibility problem that Peter may have found, or rather *did* find?' Adding the '*did*' at the last moment, to placate the man even further.

Stefan either missed it, or chose to ignore what he might have construed to be another slur on his hero. 'What I need is – a) A copy of a ciphered fax message between Samir's and Bonetti's machines, b) A copy of the same message sent in plain mode. And c) A copy of exactly the same message sent between Bonetti and Faisal – essentially, the actual ciphertext that would be transmitted in a) and c).

Ashley could see the reasoning behind these demands. A ciphered message between the Samir and Bonetti machines would have to use the old, inferior security algorithm BASE, in order to be compatible. The same message ciphered by NAMES, as it would inevitably be, between Bonetti and Faisal, would indicate the difference between the algorithms. The very same message transmitted in plain would also display a different pattern.

The two men looked at each other over the remains of the buffet dinner. No word was spoken as each took in the enormity of the task. Larchey was sitting back in his chair, his long legs crossed and fingers drumming lightly on the tabletop. His lower jaw was set high in a pose of blatant superiority, so that he looked down his nose at Ashley. The latter quite rightly read the challenge that was being silently presented to him. With elbows on the table, hands clasped together in a pyramid to support his own chin, Ashley looked the younger man directly in the eye and then let his gaze change focus, still eyeball to eyeball, but now right through the cryptologist. Whereas Ashley was considering the means by which he could collect the vital information, the cryptologist had the mistaken impression that it was *he* who was being investigated. Ashley sensed the discomfort of the man opposite him, but let the state persist for what seemed a considerable time. It was only when Stefan's body posture changed, retreating palpably from his *higher than thou* attitude, that Ashley let the faintest of smiles grow from his lips. At last, he broke the silence. 'a and b should be possible but as for c, there is no record of any fax communication between Bonetti and Faisal. Besides, I am now convinced that Bonetti has nothing to do with any threat to the UAE. It simply doesn't make sense for him, or for Lighthouse. Both have an awful lot to lose should somebody pull the rug out from under the Emirates boom.

Another argument is that if the two don't have ciphered communications, then they are most unlikely to have the same ......' Ashley stopped in mid sentence, momentarily lost in thought.

'You were going to say – secret keys?' prompted Stefan, wanting to be in on the puzzle.

'Indeed I was. But that may not be *quite* the case.' Suddenly Ashley became animated, he sat upright and with the edge of his hand chopped out, karate style, on the table, each point of what he had to say. 'Somewhere, in our conversations Bonetti distinctly told me that he was coming to Dubai to manage the fax network for DUBEXAIR – and I wouldn't mind betting a small fortune that he is managing Faisal's network too. It's not so easy to distribute keys and parameters without some kind of training. I really don't think Faisal has that know-how. He is definitely a non-technical man.'

'But if he can't manage it, and they wanted to cut Bonetti out of their communications, and *I* certainly would, then there is only one man who could.'

'Samir!' they both exclaimed together, and for a moment Ashley thought that they were going to celebrate with a high five but Larchey managed to suppress the emotion before any serious damage was done to his reputation.

Collecting himself, he went on to underline what they were both thinking. 'It could be that Samir, certainly the man in-the-know about security and encryption, has *all* the keys for Faisal's net. He's the man to target rather than Bonetti. But shit! It would really help my number crunching if we could get at least one copy of a known message ciphered with a known key and then collect a copy of the ciphered text as it was transmitted.'

'OK Stefan, here's the plan. – I'll try and access Samir's fax and computer, and maybe Bonetti's too, if the opportunity presents itself. We are, after all, still hunting Goodwin's killer. If Samir is in control then he must have the keys somewhere just in case he has to recall them. In any case, I'll try to exchange faxes between the two machines as you ask, and in the meantime perhaps you can have thoughts about the algorithms, and your number crunching. That leaves us with just the one hurdle – how to get a copy of a known NAMES message with Faisal's key?'

***

310

Ashley didn't consider himself as one to climb up the side of multi-storey buildings, or swing from a trapeze through someone's plate glass window. This was for desperate men on desperate occasions. Although pressure was building to get some results, it was imperative that no warning should be given to Samir and *his Brothers* that their communications were being monitored. So the subtler approach, the better, and it was towards this end that he approached Colonel Ali Abdullah for assistance.

The MOI man was delighted to be brought into play and the only problem was that Ashley had to temper the man's enthusiasm so that the secrecy of Symphony was maintained. In the first instance, he was not sure what in fact the MOI could achieve. But thinking of the need to nurture the relationship he considered it only polite to involve the local people in some small, yet significant way. After all, the continuous presence of Minder and his willingness to help on the simplest of tasks was a signal of Ali's support as well as inevitably providing feedback of events to the MOI. As it was, they excelled. Ashley's immediate problem was gaining access to the Lighthouse offices. Given time he could have managed the entrance codes at the main entrance and the keypad guarding Samir's office, but the biometric eye scanner was a problem that needed addressing in a different manner.

Passwords were vulnerable to attack in many ways. The fundamental problem being that they could be copied, shared, and detected in a number of different techniques. The result was that, unless they were very closely controlled and guarded by the owner, they didn't always identify correctly the person trying to access a facility. Knowledge of the password by anyone was enough. Security was trivial when only passwords were used. Real access security only came when access was based on something known, something possessed and something you are. Hence the emergence of biometrics as a security technology. Even so, fingerprints, voice monitoring and the like, were not the perfect answer that the man in the street came to believe. In choosing eye-scanning, Ashley was not sure that Bonetti really had sensitive data to protect other than the normal commercial material. It may be that he was just interested in being seen to have the latest toys on the market? From casual observation it was difficult to see whether the eye scanner was actually scanning the iris, or the retina, but his little play outside Bonetti's office at the interview had solved that problem. In either case the iris scanner would have been the best bet. Scanning the retina tended to be personally invasive, with people being very reluctant to allow lights to be shone into the depths of their eye. In comparison, Iris scanning was less unpleasant and also gave better security. It identified the user with almost the same unique certainty as would the monitoring their genetic code.

Ali Abdullah promised that he would get the access codes for the external door and Samir's, but that he would have to consult with his expert team as to how to find a way to open Bonetti's door. In less than an hour Minder had knocked on his door and whispered the two door panel codes into Ashley's ear. Impressed by the prompt response, Ashley had asked his guardian as to how they had been come by in such a short time.

'A sweet swallow sang,' Minder had grinned with intrigue and fair amount of satisfaction that he, on this occasion, knew more than both Ashley and his spotty associate.

The eye scanner was however causing some consternation and it was only the next morning that Ashley was called to conference. Once again, Minder used his own personal taxi to pick him up at the hotel and whisk him out to Jumeira where Colonel Ali Abdullah was waiting, parked up by one of the last stretches of free beach on the coastline. As the taxi drew up alongside, the darkened glass rear window dropped down to reveal the bearded head of the Colonel.

'A walk on the beach, habibi?'

'Why not?' replied Ashley, feeling reasonably comfortable in the early sunshine made tolerable by the light offshore breeze.

The Colonel wrapped his flowing white guttrah across his shoulders and invited the Englishman to join him as he led the way onto the firm sand left by the receding tide. Ali Abdullah's convivial manner quickly became more serious. 'We believe that there are two options to get past the Bonetti device. The first would be to scan your eyes on one of our machines and then get at the database of Bonetti's scanner so that we could insert your iris data. In this way, it would accept your scan at the door. At first we wanted to go with this idea, but as you can probably surmise there are at least two drawbacks. One, that we have to hack into the database and the other is that if we didn't want your data to reside there as a telltale afterwards, we would have to go in again to remove it. That's two invasions, in addition to yours.'

Ashley nodded – it would have certainly been the easiest option as far as he was concerned. The last thing he wanted when breaking into target premises were complications. As simple as possible was the golden rule, and being able just to walk up to the scanner, peer into its lens, press the enter button and simply wait for the door to click open for him, would have been ideal. 'No chance to hack into it through the Internet, for example?'

'No. It's simply a stand-alone device. That's a positive in one sense, because that means that there would be no record of an entry for anybody to check on.'

'You're going to tell me that the second option is the only one viable.'

'And for you my dear friend, it's the difficult one.' Ali smiled sympathetically.

'Go on, give me the bad news.' Ashley's was resigned. His rueful grimace gave away the tensions and frustrations building up inside him.

'It's not all bad news habibi. The reverse procedure would be for us to fabricate a copy of Bonetti's iris, put it on a contact lens, which you could then use on the occasion of your entry.'

'And the good news is?'

'That we already have Bonetti's scan data.' Ali, feeling very pleased with himself, let a smug smile spread slowly across his face. He turned to see Ashley' response, proudly lifted his head and turned to scan the blue sea and the Palm Island construction in the distance. 'All administrative personnel who will have access to the restricted areas at the DUBEX exhibition will need to have deposited a reference eye scan prior to the exhibition. – We took Bonetti's last week!'

'So you think that you have the ability and the facilities to reproduce Bonetti's iris, put it on a contact lens and make it realistic so that the scanner will recognise him instead of me?' asked Ashley doubtfully.

'I can see that you are sceptical habibi.'

'Well, yes – it did cross my mind,' he admitted sarcastically.

'My friend! Once there was the time when the world's richest and most influential people sought medical treatment in London, Los Angeles, or some Swiss mountain clinic when they were in need of life saving treatment. Nowadays, they come here.' Ali raised an arm to describe, in a sweeping arc, the tower blocks of the world's newest, sophisticated city. 'We not only have everything, and can do anything, we also have the very best surgeons and specialists to do it.'

Looking at the plethora of high-rise buildings sprouting from the Jumeira desert – he could easily count a hundred major constructions, all attended by a thousand tower cranes. Impressed, Ashley nodded in reluctant belief: 'ok, let's do it!'

They turned, and Ashley immediately felt the rising heat of the sun on his back. Moisture had gathered on his forehead, and the hair around his temples and neck were already dark with sweat. They walked in silence back towards the waiting cars. Ashley was surprised at how far they had walked. Beyond the cars loomed the Jebel Ali power station. Its builders could not have foreseen that what was once intentionally a remote location, out of the public eye, had now become an unsightly intrusion at the edge of the new playground for the rich. Farther still, he could just make out through the persistent haze, the cranes and derricks of the port. The Colonel was strolling, hands clasped behind his back, guttrah head-gear blowing in the light calming breeze. His head was down either lost in thought or observing the imprints of his sandals in the drying sand. Ashley looked across towards him, but his attention was grabbed by a huge bulk out to sea. At first he assumed that it was just a part of the Palm Islands construction but when he concentrated on it, he eventually recognised it as the stacked deck of a container ship. It dawned on him that there was the very ship that he'd seen previously on the local television station. '*The Rachele,*' he recalled.

'One other thing you should know Mr. Ashley. -The American president nor ex president is *not* intending to visit the UAE in the near future.'

***

It was immaculate. He had never seen The Majlis course in better condition, but then it had been some three years since he'd played at The Emirates Club. Nothing much had changed about the course itself but the enormous building complexes around it were more imposing. Skyscrapers by the dozen and the huge shopping malls of Geant and Carrefour seemed to cover every square metre of vacant ground. His wife had been restless all the evening before, itching to get out and spend the dollars that she'd hoarded for just such an opportunity. The organisers had promised a bus pick-up that very morning, but she preferred her own company when embarking on some serious shopping. She would join the other golfing widows for lunch. That also she was looking forward to. She had made some casual friends in the group. Happy as she was, living in the Scottish Highlands, expeditions like this had been too few and far between during the days of Cameron's self-imposed exile. It was good to be back on the circuit.

Cameron stood on the first tee, waiting for the previous group to move beyond the range of his driver. The morning practice round had suited him well so that he could acclimatize a little before the serious event started on the morrow. The forecast had been for a mercifully cooler period than it had apparently been prior to his arrival. Buggies were on offer, but the Scot was feeling fit and wanted both to get the legs and lungs working after the restrictions of the evening flight and check the terrain from close up. His one regret was that his allotted partner had not turned up. The Italian, he assumed from the name, was seriously tied up in the organisation of the other big event of the week, evidence of which had been all too clear to see. Flags, banners, and massive posters all announced one thing – DUBEXAIR. It hadn't meant much to him before, but as the city's hotels were filling up with aviation's best boys, the more esteemed of the golfing fraternity had been offered individual villas. Each in luxurious seclusion with a pool and fully serviced by maids and drivers. They both appreciated being out of the hustle of packed hotels and apart from a compulsory excursion or two to the malls, breakfast and dinner by their own pool were quintessentially much more desirable. It would have been useful to practise with this guy Bonetti, just to workout some sort of strategy, but he had called the desk to say that he'd be there to join the professional for the back nine. At least, thought Cameron, the local guy would be familiar with the course *and* according to Ashley's phone call, fully acclimatised to the conditions. Little did he know that at that very moment, Bonetti was bellowing into some poor outfitter's ear about their utter failure to stock quality attire for the golfer of somewhat more generous proportions than those of the normal sportsman! As usual, the Italian had left it until the last minute, and it was typical of him that he was more intent on looking the part rather than actually playing it. Hence the morning's dash, although no one *ever* dashed around Dubai, to search out the best that Calloway had to offer. If the world's sporting press and TV cameras were there, they were going to see Bonetti in his prime. The evening's formal charity dinner would be a great time to mix with some of the heroes of '*the leetle white ball*,' as he would call them, and could he *really* miss the opportunity to impose himself on such a scene, rubbing shoulders with the elite?

Bonetti was on cloud nine. His communication security measures were in place and functioned flawlessly in the build-up to DUBEX. Further business was bound to follow. The Lighthouse and CIPHERCAN logos were everywhere around the airport's exhibition halls. On top of that the crowning glory. The chance to play golf with the world's best in one of the world's most prestigious competitions. On one of the world's best courses and all in front of the international media and television cameras. He sat back in the cool luxury of the company limousine thinking of the night before. For the first time in a long time, a very long time – he'd actually enjoyed sex. Not in recent memory had the promise been fulfilled. Usually the excesses of Chianti, having first raised his interest and bravado in acquiring a partner for the night, would contribute along with the prostate, the blood pressure and diabetes, in bringing about the all-too-familiar failure at the all-important time. Not last night however. This girl was different. Bonetti's Moll was something special. With his bulk, the usual position was out of the question but when she sat astride him, the lithe gyrations of her small tight body excited him to a new level. He smiled contentedly to himself as he remembered her small, pert breasts in his bear like paws, the devilish – no, it *was* a lustful expression on her impish, Asian face. Her groans of ecstasy were not those of a faked orgasm, and my God, was he an expert on those? In the end, all the inhibitions were shed and he surrendered blissfully to her control. Afterwards her damp, warm body had lain across him and not wishing to disturb her, he had let her sleep the whole night on his human pillow. As the morning grew late he rose to shower without waking her, but the noise of the water jets had done just that. He was both surprised and elated when she slid back the curtain and joined him in the delight of cool cascades and perfumed gel. He smiled with even greater content as her silence added to her mystique. She hadn't spoken more than a dozen words since that first encounter yet he was utterly captivated. Words couldn't express how fine the world was today. It was a good time to be Carlo Bonetti – and the Tai Chi was not to be missed. Golf could wait a little longer.

CHAPTER 20

Cracker

Click! – He was in. The first pass code from the MOI was correct. The door sprung open a centimetre or two as the latch was electronically released. Ashley pushed it just wide enough to slip inside and stood his ground for a moment to enable his eyes to become accustomed to the dim light. The Lighthouse lobby was initially dark and shadowy, but soon the ambient light from street and neighbouring buildings provided enough illumination for him to start. He rounded the receptionist's empty desk and the decorative privacy screen behind it, to enter the corridor. Ashley's pulse was hammering away at his temples and he made a conscious effort to control his breathing and slow down his actions. It was easy to make mistakes under these conditions. Take your time, he told himself. Samir's workshop was the first in line, with Bonetti's ten metres beyond. Here little light was available forcing Ashley to reach into his pocket for his laser pointer. A simple but powerful device, the kind used by teachers and lecturers to guide their students through educational presentations. On this occasion the highly focussed beam picked out Ashley's targets without broadcasting his presence to any outside observer. It was far easier than a torch and gave a pool of dim red light only where the beam struck a surface. The first target was the keypad guarding Samir's door.

Simple things first – Bonetti's office would have to wait. Somehow the MOI had also gained knowledge of the pass code for Samir's door, and it too was correct. Hardly had Ashley's finger hit the fourth button when this door too clicked open, swinging slightly on its hinges to give him the freedom of the Jordanian's lair. Ashley breathed a sigh of relief and his pulse slowed considerably now that he was over the second hurdle. Even though Minder had assured him that nobody was working a late shift, Ashley knew from experience, to expect the unexpected.

He eased Samir's door open, peering around the perimeter of the door frame before stepping inside. It was standard procedure to make certain that there were no obvious telltales left to indicate that Samir had had a late night visitor. Once reassured that the way was clear, Ashley bent to insert a wedge in place under the door and moved over to the workbench taking in the exact position of Samir's swivel chair, the location of all tools and stationery on the work surfaces and especially that of the computer mouse. It would have been tempting to use digital camera shots as references, but without resorting to flash there just wasn't enough light.

A number of LED's were blinking, signalling the status of various pieces of electronic test gear were alive, but idle. His primary task was to search for files that might contain computer passwords and subsequently the details of any secret keys used to protect his fax network. Any information found about Peter Goodwin would be a bonus.

As Ashley settled to begin his attack, he looked up to the window and cast a glance outside, no longer surprised to see the main arteries of Dubai still streaming with traffic even at this late hour. It was his own reflection in the glass that caught him by surprise and particularly the hotel's shower cap that he'd pulled over his head. It made an amusing sight, but it worth his while to take some basic precautions against alien hairs being found by Samir when he returned to his duties on the following morn.

His second precautionary measure was less obvious, but the surgeon's gloves simply kept the surfaces that he touched free of his fingerprints. Ashley was confident that neither Samir nor Bonetti had the slightest notion that they were under clandestine observation, but it was a situation that he endeavoured to maintain. One careless mishap would give the game away.

His third tool he now withdrew from the jogger's back pack. It was a large black trash-bag borrowed from the hotel kitchen. He had already torn a hole in the closed end of the bag and stretched it so that he could slide it over the computer's monitor leaving the open end hanging down behind the keyboard. Apart from a simple pen and small note pad, the only other items he carried were a CD case and an electromagnetic coupler with a battery powered recorder. It was the CD case that he removed first, setting it down on the desk and then taking the CD to insert it into the computer's drive tray. He checked that the trash bag was still in place and pressed the power button. The sudden hum from the computer seemed alarmingly loud in the otherwise silent room, drowning out the street noise from outside.

The computer boot-up program got under way but didn't get as far as the normal demand for a user password. The MOI people had promised this password too, but it had not been forthcoming by the time he had to make his move, so Stefan Larchey's software box had been rifled for the password cracker.

It never ceased to amaze him how little care *Joe Public* took in protecting their data. Whether it was from the belief that they had nothing to protect, that nobody could possibly be interested in their material, or just in sheer laziness, people adopted the weakest and most obvious passwords to protect their secret treasures. In ninety percent of cases, people took on family names, pet names or lovers' names, and a little bit of research revealed all of these to any seriously interested party. Of the rest, those who had trouble remembering their more ingenious passwords actually wrote them down and kept them close at hand for fear of being shut out of their own system when memory failed them. Ashley strongly believed that Bonetti was such a case in point. The pencil scratching around the TFT monitor frame in his office, he was pretty sure, were various access codes to different accounts and web pages. How could people be so naïve? Here was the fellow investing serious money and time in installing sophisticated security for his office, yet not able to observe the simplest, though most crucial steps in protecting it.

No such give-aways around Samir's computer though. There had been times when Ashley had thought Samir's efforts were merely those of an interested amateur. He did grant him a degree of respect; he was not naïve and did put barriers in the way to his confidential information. Hence the use of Cracker. The CD was already running. It carried a password cracker that searched through the target computer to find the hidden files which carried Samir's ciphered passwords. On finding them, the program halted so that Ashley could elect to launch one of three types of attack. There was the brute force attack whereby the cracker raced through all possible combinations of six to eight keyboard characters and ciphered each with the same BASE algorithm that was used to protect the user's genuine password. Once the two ciphered values were in agreement, you had a correct copy of the password in your hand.

His second option was a *dictionary attack.* The CD carried the entire contents of the Concise Oxford English Dictionary and in a similar process to the brute force attack, the Cracker clocked through the complete dictionary in *very quick* time. If the user's password was in the English dictionary then Cracker would find it. It was just the same if the attack were to be carried out in German, or French or even Mandarin – the assailant simply used the dictionary in question. Statistics however, pointed to names dictionaries as being the best bet. First names, family names, nicknames, pet names; you name it and Ashley's CD would have it, and if Samir used Arabic names, then so be it, these too were not a problem.

It was the names attack that Ashley set in motion. He had tucked his head under the open end of the trash bag, so that the screen illuminated the computer keyboard and nothing else. The rest of the room slept in its background illumination, giving no indication to the outside world that serious overtime was being carried out at Lighthouse that night. The program displayed the captured password, albeit ciphered, and in another window the plaintext names from the dictionary flashed across the screen.

Aaron-aarti-abdenace-abdol-abdul-abdulkaf-abdullah-abdur-abhijit-abhiram-abraham-abrar-acacia-adam-adel-adi-adib-adine-

adrianne-adrien-adrienne-aeneas-afrid-aggie-agnes-ahidee-ahmed-ahmet-aileen-aimee-ajai-ajay-akhil-akiko-alain-alamgir-alan-alastair-alayne-albatros-albert-alberto-alejandr-alena-alessand-alex......

In trial runs, the typical search time was in the order of about four minutes, but under real conditions, the process seemed painfully slow. Ashley knew that it wasn't the computer that was slow, but the speed of his own mental operations being enhanced by stress and adrenaline that made the cracker clock almost pedestrian. He wanted to be in and out, in minimal time. Any lengthy problems to be solved would only permit a cursory search and then further assessment later. Yet so much was at stake that there was pressure to remain there until all the questions had answers. Clean and speedy was the objective. For the moment it was out of his hands. All he could do was sit and watch the names go by;

birgetta-birgit-bizhan-bjorn-blaine-blair-blake-blss-bob-bobbi-bobby-boleslaw-bong-bonnie-boon -boozie-bor-rong-wen-boris-boyd-brad-bradford-bradley-branisla-brat-brenda-brendan-brenden-brent—bret-breton-brett-brian-bridget-bridgett-brinkley-bromberg-bruce-bruno-bryan-bryce-bryn-bunny-burke-burton-busalacc-butch-byoung-byoungin-byungho-cadat-cadweld-cal-caleb-calendar-calvin-cameron-c amilla-camille ....

Ashley jumped out of his skin! A telephone ring from reception startled him so much that he could feel his pulse once more throbbing in the arteries of his neck. He became further alarmed when the call was answered. '*Shit!*'- He swore under his breath and rose silently from Samir's chair to the door. It was still ajar, resting on the wedge as he had left it. There was no light coming from the front desk area, but he could distinctly hear a woman's voice. He was not alone! Holding his breath he listened, just catching the odd clear word of the dialogue. '...... please leave your name and contact number after the tone......' Ashley cursed himself for the unnecessary distress. It was just the company answer-phone. Disgusted with himself, he returned to the monitor.

...Keith-kelley-kelly-ken-kenji-kenneth-kenny-kent—kenton-kenzo-keshav-kester-ketan-kevin-khanh-khayroll-khoanh-khoi-khong-khong-

me-khoon-sa-khosrow-khueh-khueh-ho—khurshee   kian-kian-tat-
kiang-kiang-sh-kianusch-kiat-kieu-kim-kimberly-kimmo-kimon-king-
kinson-kip-kiran-kirk-kirsten—klaus-knute-koichi-koji-kok-kia-kongjoo
-konrad-korda-kraig-kris-krishna-krishnam-krista-kristen-kristi-
kristin-kristina-krystyna ...

Still not finished – it was taking a lifetime. Ashley nervously checked his watch and was surprised to see that less than three minutes had elapsed since he'd started the cracker. Surely the program would start to pick up the first characters soon.

...lynette-lynn-lynne-maddie-madhu-madhusud-mady-magdalen-
maggie-mahbuba-mahesh-mahlon-mahmoud-maia-make-makoto-
manahil-mandy-manfred-mangesh-mani-manish-manohar-manoj-ma
non-manuel-marc-marc-pau-marcel-marcella-marci-marcia-marcio-
marco-marcus-marcy-marek-margalit-margaret—margarid-margarit-
marge-margie-margo-maria-marian-marianne-marie-marietta-marily
n-marina......

The moment he started to relax and concentrate on the cracker process, Ashley jumped out of his skin again! This time the phone ring was loud and close, very close! He whipped his head from under his trash-bag screening the instant that Samir's fax machine came to life. Ashley cursed again, but once he saw the fax accepting the transmission, he breathed again and moved across to see what the message contents were. The printout too seemed to take an age, but when it came, he was disappointed to find that it was the fax world's equivalent to computer spam; The Beach Hotel was delighted to announce the opening night of its new Indian restaurant – The Taj Mahal......

'Great stuff,' he muttered. 'Perhaps you have a table for one in an hour's time. Better make it two hours!' Ashley's frustration increased when he moved back to the computer. Cracker had stopped. In one window remained the ciphered password, whilst in the other was displayed a single character – R. The cracker had run all the way through its names list and just spewed out the first letter. On the face of it, he was left high and dry, but Ashley had seen this program work numerous times before, and work with great efficiency. So what was different? It had not found the second character. The one draw back, it seemed, was that if it didn't find a character, then it would *not* progress through the remainder. It had to find each character in sequence. Ashley paused, rose from the seat once again and tried to clear his racing mind. He gazed sightless – out, at the opposite building. Had he been switched to receive observations of the real world, rather than forcing his mind to run through the computer graphics, he would have seen the reflection of the Lighthouse drummer engaged in his endless tattoo.

If Cracker didn't show the second character, then it meant that this specific character was not alphabetical – at least not English – nor of the Latin alphabet either. Ashley looked down at the keyboard. There was no Arabic text. Therefore, he surmised, the second character must be other than any alphabetical symbol. He moved quickly back into the seat. His fingers were flying across the keyboard now, with instructions to Cracker that it should now include the control characters, numerals, punctuation marks and the other keyboard symbols that he could think of. Then he ran Cracker again, but starting it from the letter Q to save time. In no time at all the plaintext *R???????* came up as the first letter and then the program continued.

...... willy-wilson-win-winfred-wing-wojtek-won-wong-wonyun-woobin-woodrow-wooiyi-wun-wun-jou-wuntsin-wynne—xavier-xi-xiao-xiao-gua-xiao-lin-xiao-wei-xiaobo-xiaogang-xiaoli-xiaomin-xing hao-xue-xue-jun-xueqing-yael-yan-yang—yanjun-yaomin-yaser-yee-yeng-yeon-yeong-yeong-sh-yew-shin-yezi-yi-yi-bing-yiannis-yigal-yihua-yingsha-yishun-yogesh-yoichi-yolanda-yon-yon-chun-yonah-yon g-yongdong-yongho-yonghwan-yongsam-yoshiaki-yoshio-youcef-youhanse-young. Without a pause it raced on into the new additions that Ashley made in its search objective.

R0?????? a zero!, Ashley smiled, and a few seconds later *R0b?????* and then soon after that – *R0b1????* In no time at all he had it – *R0b1nRe).*

'You bastard Samir! – I know you now.' Ashley momentarily forgot his circumstances and voiced his content aloud. The clever bugger uses a password he can *never* forget but makes it difficult to crack by inserting numeral and symbol substitutes in the place of similarly shaped alphabetic characters. Hence Ashley surmised that the end bracket represented the character D. – Robin Red Breast! – My God Samir, what is it with you and the English language? Ashley was almost chuckling with the success. He removed the cracker CD and rebooted the computer ... and glory be – when it demanded a password, *R0b1nRe)* opened up Samir's entire treasure chest. Ashley, sweat beginning to trickle down from his temples, checked the watch again – shit! Twenty five minutes had passed, and as yet, he had no data to take back to Larchey.

File by file, Ashley imposed a routine discipline as he scanned down through the Jordanian's material. His first efforts drew negative results. Searches for the name *Goodwin* brought up a big zero as did *RR*. Both were big disappointments. There were a multitude of files and documents relating to Lighthouse, as well there should be. Documents and technical manuals on the operations and maintenance of the company's equipment. Of some interest was an excel sheet that listed all the fax equipment that Samir had installed, with serial numbers and locations but alas, no key data. But then, just as despondency was beginning creep in, he found a file hidden away within a tree marked *Personal,* a file named ominously – *Brothers*! With a sense of nervous expectancy, Ashley opened it up. It revealed a long list of word documents and one excel sheet. Here *was* the critical data.

***

He was forty five minutes into the mission and now came the time to tackle Bonetti's door but he had to prepare for the fax test first. He had closed down Samir's computer and repacked the trash-bag into his back pack and took out the electromagnetic coupler and recorder. The coupler was made in the form of a small clamp which he fastened around the telecomms cable connecting the fax to the phone socket in the wall. This was done in seconds and then Ashley checked the room to make sure that there were no disturbances to the layout so that he could make a quick departure once the final action next door had been completed. Moving to a vacant space on Samir's workbench, Ashley laid out a handkerchief and removed the surgeon's glove from his right hand. One more time he delved into the back pack to locate and remove a small bottle with an integral dropper. Similarly he withdrew a small plastic container that held a contact lens with Bonetti's iris imprinted on it. He opened both containers and set them on the handkerchief, taking great care in not spilling their contents. The light level was poor, and if he lost the contact lens, then all else would be lost with it. He took the laser pointer from his pocket and holding it in his left hand, shone it on the bottle and dropper. He slowly squeezed the rubber bell of the dropper and then released it to draw up a few drops of *Tropicamide* fluid. With his eyes wide open, Ashley allowed just a couple of drops to fall into the left eye and immediately screwed the dropper back in its place. He waited for a few minutes for the pupil-dilating mydriatic to take effect and then, satisfied that his iris was starting to dilate, gently dabbed his finger into the contact lens receptacle taking the lens onto the tip of his second finger. He rested his right arm on the bench top and he bent forward to stare into the thin, transparent plastic. Slowly, he brought his head down to meet the hand. In practice, this was not so difficult, but now in the poor light and with a hand that trembled like a leaf, it was a whole different scenario.

At the crucial instant, Ashley stiffened involuntarily. Yet another phone rang but this time it came from next door – Bonetti's office. He muttered aggressively, 'Jesus, don't these people ever bloody sleep?' He hesitated, then heard the electronic handshake of a fax unit and once again, took a deep breath and held it as he tried to apply the contact lens. It stung him slightly until the eye watered. Closing it and blinking carefully, he was satisfied to feel the lens in place.

Fifty minutes had passed as he made his way to Bonetti's door using the laser pointer to illuminate the way and then to locate the eye scanner. Ashley bent before the scanner. When Bonetti had demonstrated the device, it had worked instantly to unlock the door latch. Ashley stared into the lens, steadied himself and held his breath. The blood vessels in his temples pulsing heavily. He pressed the enter button and waited for the green light and the now familiar click of the latch. But after two long seconds of delay the only response that Ashley got, was a red light signalling its rejection. 'Shit!' Ashley swore under his breath as frustration grew. The stress was enormous. He was running dangerously out of time and as yet had achieved nothing. Duplicating and embedding iris details into a contact lens was still very much fringe technology and Ashley had been immensely sceptical about the MOI's insistence that it could be done. Yet Colonel Ali had promised him with great confidence that it *would* work. OK Mike, take it one at a time – no panic – stay cool!

He tried again with his head rotated a few degrees to see if it made any difference. – It didn't – annoyingly the red rejection signal blinked on and remained on for about five seconds before switching to its off state. If it failed three times then the door would be automatically locked for another hour. God forbid that to happen, he thought.

Resisting the urge to rush into another immediate attempt, Ashley waited a further two minutes, thinking perhaps that his own eye had not dilated sufficiently to leave the Bonetti iris pattern clear of interference from his own. The time passed slowly as he watched the luminous second finger trace inexorably two circuits, during which time he kept his left eye closed so that what little light was available didn't interfere with his relaxing iris. In the silence he picked up the sounds of the sleeping building, the hum of the 'ac' and the perpetual clamour from the streets outside. To make absolutely sure that it was fully open, he lingered a further thirty seconds, resisting the temptation to dive in again. When he felt that he could wait no longer, he turned back to the eye scanner and once more bent down so that his eye was perfectly in line with it. Sweat was seeping into both eyes now, but he resisted the autonomic blink response and his stress was so acute that he could hear the arteries in his neck throbbing. He held his breath and with a prayer to any God who was listening, pressed the enter button. The delay seemed endless and even when the green light flickered on, it seemed to do so with great reluctance. Thanking all Gods in attendance, Ashley still held his breath but eventually the entry light was followed by the regulation click of the electronic latch. Ashley exhaled an enormous sigh of relief. Miracles do happen! He grasped the door in his gloved hand just in case it tried to close again, then squatted to push a second rubber wedge in place to keep it open.

It wasn't there! Bonetti's computer had gone. Ashley checked and checked around the room again, but there was no doubt – there was no computer to work on. The monitor was there but the laptop had gone. So was the chance of finding out what Bonetti knew about Goodwin – and what Goodwin knew about the NAMES algorithm. It seemed that Ashley was destined to go home empty handed. The whole exercise had been frustrating, and Ashley found himself fighting his own growing anger. This exercise was fast becoming a farce and an anxious voice in his head was telling that it was time to quit – to get out now!, before he was discovered! Ashley considered running for all but a fleeting second, but then his innate determination kicked. He hated to walk out empty handed at any time but the thought of having to face Stephan Larchey's arrogant grimace when he broke the bad news, spurred him on into a do-or-die mood. It was backs-to-the-wall time. With that enforced motivation, he refocused and moved over to Bonetti's fax machine. A received document lay in the in-tray, no doubt the one which had disturbed his contact lens insertion. Ashley took it and found it to be the same as the one that had been transmitted to Samir's fax – the Taj Mahal restaurant opening event.

Stefan had asked for a copy of a simple document, even a blank white sheet sent between the two Lighthouse faxes would have sufficed, but now a new idea dawned on Ashley. Their one big problem, or rather his cryptanalyst's big problem, had been how to obtain a copy of a ciphered fax, a known document being exchanged between Bonetti's and Faisal's machines. It was difficult to instigate a genuine transmission between them, a ciphered one at that, especially as they didn't normally communicate at all. But the Taj Mahal had unwittingly presented a solution. A solution that was not completely devoid of risk, but one that was certainly worth taking. Simple things first though.

Ashley took the Taj fax page and fed it into Bonetti's machine, pressed the button to send the message in plain mode and then dialled Samir's number. The ringing in the workshop next door seemed to be loud enough to wake the dead, but late night calls appeared to be the norm in the Lighthouse building anyway. After three rings, the two machines entered into their electronic handshake and after a few seconds, the Taj invitation was on its way once more. Sensing a signal on the line, Ashley's coupler kicked into action and proceeded to catch the entire message of electronic signals flowing down the line and storing them in its memory. Ashley was happy to see the message go through without a hitch. Once the transmission had been completed, he fed the same paper into Bonetti's machine, pressed the cipher button this time and repeated the operation. Once again the fax went through without a problem, the only observable difference being the slightly prolonged handshake as both machines exchanged key data. Once they verified that each had the same values, then a green LED flashed to confirm that the massage was indeed ciphered. As before, the coupler attached to the phone lead of Samir's machine had started up, this time recording the ciphered message.

Ashley returned to the Jordanian's office and retrieved the copies of the faxes that he had sent, and replaced the original one back in the in-tray. Having finished in the workshop, he packed his bag with the bin liner, notepad and the CD case then disconnected the coupler from Samir's line, before placing that too in the bag. He checked that the computer had shut down correctly, placed the swivel chair to match its initial position and stood back to recall a visual picture of the office status Goodwin would have been proud he mused, as Ashley satisfied himself that all was just as Samir had left it. One last look back, and then he closed the door and moved into back into Bonetti's room. He'd now been in the premises for well over an hour and whilst he now felt at ease moving around, even confident since he had had some success. But! the longer he stayed, the greater became the risk of discovery. He'd almost finished.

It took only a few seconds to clamp the coupler in place on the phone lead of Bonetti's machine and set the Taj Mahal paper into the fax and pressed the cipher button. From memory, he dialled the fax number of Faisal's machine. The call was answered and the two machines stepped into their key agreement routine. Ashley held his breath, praying that secret key and phone number list on the excel sheet that he'd just found on Samir's computer was still valid. Once again, time seemed to be suspended, but it was only the statutory handshake period of a few seconds before the flier was drawn into Bonetti's fax. He sighed with relief. Things were going his way now. They *had* found a common key and fifty five seconds later, the paper was spewed out of the machine accompanied by a loud beep to signify that the call had been terminated. He'd finished! – not exactly as he intended – because once again he'd missed out on the Goodwin scenario. But he had met Larchey's goals and *that* alone gave him *great* satisfaction. The only one fear he had, was if somebody in Faisal's office or wherever his machine was located, took it upon themselves to inspect the source of the Taj message. Bonetti's fax number would be there in the header of the message for all to see. However, Ashley thought it more likely that, as with the vast majority of spam material, it would be binned immediately without any reference to the header.

The vibrations of the mobile phone brought an abrupt end to the now budding sense of satisfaction. He pulled the phone from his pocket and keyed in the keyboard password to retrieve the message. 'Expect visitor in three minutes!'

Once again Ashley swore and not for the first time that night wondered if Dubai ever slept. But he was finished and just in time. He checked that everything was stowed safely in his bag, returned the initial copy of the Taj Mahal into the Bonetti fax in-tray, and once again took a few seconds to recall the initial office layout when he entered. Satisfied that everything was in place, he left the room, pulling the door closed behind him. The corridor was in darkness but his still distended iris enabled him to make his way to the reception without delay. Once in the relative light of the front office, he found it necessary to squint as the extra light gave him some pain in the left eye. Still two minutes left to get onto the staircase. No real problem, he was on the home run yet Ashley's heart was racing again with the sudden burst of physical action. Someone had obviously driven into the underground car park and had been seen by Minder who had judged three minutes as being the time for him to abort.

Ashley was already out of the office entrance and about to close the door when, to his horror, he remembered – Shit, the CD! He'd left the cracker CD in Samir's drive. If Samir found that – and it was inevitable that he would – then the shit would hit the fan. With no alternative, Ashley jammed his hand in the closing door and then darted back inside, closing the door behind him. Perhaps ninety seconds remained before the lift would open and deliver its passenger onto the Lighthouse floor. Ashley moved quickly to Samir's door. By now his iris was almost back to normal, but still more dilated than his right eye which would take probably thirty seconds to become acclimatised. There was no time to rummage through his bag for the laser pointer, so he peered closely at the finger pad and with an extreme effort not to rush things, Ashley gingerly pressed the four buttons in turn. Eighty seconds, and he was into the workshop, moving to the computer.

With the power off, the only chance to open the disc drive was by means of a pin pushed into the eject hole that give access to the CD tray emergency opening function. Desperately he searched on the workshop table tops for anything thin enough to penetrate the hole. In the poor light it was an almost impossible task.

Seventy seconds or less and Ashley would be caught red handed. As a last resort, he thought of hiding in Samir's office in the hope that the visitor would only be paying a cursory visit to the office. But, it might even be Samir himself who was about to board the elevator in the basement.

Less than a minute to get out of the place yet there were no obvious tools or pins around, not even a paper clip, just a selection of screws all of which were far too thick for the purpose.

In desperation now, Ashley considered breaking open the disc drive door as a last resort. The drummer's flashing lights from outside were merging into a continuous glow, casting dancing shadows around the room. – Grotesque shadows that mocked him as they cavorted around the walls in celebration of his impending downfall. A bright reflection caught his eye from the desk top. It was a chrome stapling machine.

Ashley punched it hard and was relieved to feel the resistance of a loaded machine. It took him a few more precious seconds to find the ejected staple. Eventually his fingers, still in the surgeon's gloves, found it and he just had enough feeling to straighten the bent staple out.

Thirty seconds left and he fumbled at the eject hole. Ashley prodded here and there until eventually the disc tray slid open. He withdrew the cracker CD, stuck it his pocket and firmly pushed the tray closed. A quick body swerve around the forgotten chair and he was back out into the corridor. He closed Samir's door and held it there until he heard the latch click to lock it in place and then moved swiftly to the main office door. He hadn't time to look at the fingers of his watch but estimated that he was into the last twenty seconds, no more.

Back out of the reception, he pulled the main door closed and once again lingered until he was sure that the electric lock had caught it. Ashley turned and sprinted towards the lift and staircase. Approaching the lift, he could see that it had just passed through the sixteenth floor and was going to stop at his at any second. With no time to get past the lift to the staircase, Ashley looked around for a bolt hole. Only one door was close enough to try, he dashed for it and wrenched at the door knob. It wasn't locked. He dragged it open. It was a tiny broom cupboard, maybe a metre square, absolutely packed with a cleaner's trolley and its cluster of brushes. Just room to stand – he dived in at the very instant that the elevator bell rang to announce its arrival. Hardly had he closed the cupboard door before he heard the lift doors open and its passenger step out into the hall. Ashley froze, perched precariously over the trolley, fearing that any movement would dislodge one of the buckets or cleaning brooms stacked all around him. He held his breath as the footsteps approached and then receded down the corridor, heading with certainty for the Lighthouse entrance. Whoever it was, they were in a hurry. It wasn't exactly a run – but a quick, positive pace. Ashley was thankful for that – every muscle in his legs and back was already aching from the unnatural position that he held. Perhaps somebody calling in to reclaim a forgotten package or mislaid wallet or mobile phone. Or a worker returning home on a late night flight. Ashley waited before easing the door open, just enough to check that the corridor was empty. All clear – the lights from the Lighthouse reception flooded out through the glassed frontage into the corridor. The stairs were just ten metres away and Ashley made for them in double quick time. Down and out into the darkness of the early morning and clammy air that clung to his already sweat drenched body. Hot and sticky it may be but the clammy air meant a lucky escape!

CHAPTER 21

Fairways

The Sheraton Penthouse had been turned into a computer laboratory. There were printers, terminals, servers, and laptops everywhere, all coupled together into a makeshift LAN by a spaghetti of cables and power supplies. Stefan had purloined two massive white-boards that were perched precariously on the back of the sofa and balanced against the wall. When Ashley had returned to the room after his Lighthouse foray, the cryptanalyst hadn't even noticed his arrival until the smell of fresh coffee from the kitchenette had once again spread through the room. Even then the tousled head never lifted from the churning screens of his computers. For the very first time since Symphony was instigated, Ashley was aware that he was not the one making the decisions. He'd done all he could in providing the tools for Larchey to carry out his analysis. Now he felt that he had handed over control and no longer had the destiny of the project in his hands. It was with ill ease and considerable frustration that he sat down on the one vacant easy chair and sat passively observing the intensity of the mathematician at work. Symphony had inevitably become a team effort. He acknowledged that. But it didn't make it any easier now that he found himself sitting on the bench.

***

Bonetti had started well in the early morning. The inevitable early morning humidity had been burnt off by the rising sun and by the time it came for Cameron to get their match under way with a driver from the first tee, it was like playing an English course in the middle of summer. Cameron was a big man as was Bonetti, but the Scot's height was well balanced by the muscular square shoulders, strong arms and sturdy legs that told of much exercise in the gym and countless kilometres of golf. In sharp contrast however, most of Bonetti's bulk lay around his midriff and was built on the excesses of good pasta and Chianti. The Italian's exercise had for years been restricted to the climbing in and out of his golf buggy that carried him around the weekly club competitions. Not in living memory had the Italian walked around the full eighteen holes of any golf course. So it came to him as a bit of a shock when he and his partner turned up for the pre-game practice and found that the only assistance in transport for the day was a lanky Indian caddy. Pride got the better of him and though he feared for the state he might finish the day in, if indeed he finished at all, early bravado replaced his apprehension.

Cameron in his time had suffered at the hands of many an unlucky draw that landed him with all manner of partners in these Pro-Am foursomes. It was, by far the easiest format to play when there was such a mixed bag of skills bundled together. Two players playing the same ball with alternate shots was both efficient and at times hilarious, if one had a sense of humour that is. Some of the die-hard professionals thought it beneath their station to become involved in circuses like this, but sponsors wanted their pound of flesh, and God knows: didn't they pay for it. For Cameron, it was a challenge and being more at home with the artisans than the crème, it was usually became a pleasant distraction from the more serious circuit competitions. One thing that Cameron did enjoy about the format was that he often had to play from parts of the course that he wouldn't normally visit. His long launched tee shots usually meant that he rarely dropped into the fairway bunkers, but with Bonetti's swing largely inhibited by the pasta belt, the next two days would see Cameron using clubs that he had rarely used before. His main concern was that after just two days in the country, Bonetti was more acclimatised to the heat than he was. The early perspiration on the Italian brow however, didn't bode well for later, when the sun reached its zenith. One thing was certain however, Cameron would be seeking out the agent provocateur. Mike Ashley had a lot to answer for. No wonder there had been a sly grin on his face when he had persuaded the Scot to request the Italian as his amateur partner. Cameron had wondered what was in it for Ashley. He was looking forward to some serious debate once this was all over to discuss how Ashley was to compensate for all the credits that Cameron had amassed in granting this favour. The warm spirit between the two had survived everything since Jakarta. – Bonded for ever by the death of Fitri.

For Bonetti it was a relief that Cameron was the one to start from the first tee. The cluster of officials, media and supporters would have been too imposing for him, and Cameron had taken it upon himself to step up and relieve the Italian of possible trauma. As it was, the mammoth drive that left the gallery gasping in awe required Bonetti to make a simple 140 yard shot to the green. After what seemed an age of preparation, Bonetti had struck the shot cleanly leaving his champion a 15-yard putt to birdie the hole.

Cameron should have compensated more for the dew still clinging to the finely cut grass and left the ball two feet short from the pin. So it was left to Bonetti, still nervous from the attentions of the gathering supporters, to address the ball and claim the first par. He hadn't banked on these numbers in the gallery, thinking that once under way they would be left largely to themselves. Try as he might, he couldn't put the fact that there were a thousand pairs of eyes watching his every move. His partner, ever the professional, eased him into it with a suggestion that one ball width to the left of the hole would be the line to follow. Somehow, Bonetti's putter conspired to hit stronger than was necessary but the ball rattled into the back of the hole and dropped home. The apparent boldness of Bonetti's putt raised a few eyebrows and the warm, spontaneous applause alleviated his anxiety, paving the way for his normal effervescence to surface through the fog of nerves. The Bonetti grin returned and he even had the audacity to acknowledge the applause with as casual a wave as he could muster. Bonetti was on the ball!

***

336

In the penthouse, Stefan was also on the ball, but unlike Bonetti, he had no concern for whoever might be watching. Unlike the Italian, surrounded and scrutinized by public gaze, the cryptanalyst had no problems in singularly focussing his attention on his collection of computers, white boards, pens and papers. Even if there had been a noisy disco party next door, Ashley was convinced that he would be totally oblivious to it. In this environment, Ashley felt like an intruder in his own castle and paced the thick pile carpet, back and forth like a lion in its cage.

Until the mathematician arrived, he had been in sole control of Symphony. Even Clements had left him free to explore whatever he thought necessary, without the impositions of the ivory towers in Whitehall. Useful inputs had been forthcoming from both Clements and the local MOI, but the strategy had been left to the man on the ground. Now Ashley saw that things had changed and that he was almost entirely dependant on Larchey. The tousled haired, loose limbed, intense figure was bent over his monitors, scribbling feverishly the latest outputs on paper and white board. Larchey's etchings were in a code of their own and though Ashley could read the figures and symbols they were still a meaningless jumble that needed a translator to reveal their significance. The only man capable of that translation was on his own planet. Reluctantly Ashley thought it necessary to remain as transparent as possible.

The previous night's investigation into the Lighthouse stronghold had, in the end, produced unlikely, but better-than-expected results. Bonetti's missing computer had left many questions unanswered. The fax operations had however been most fruitful, – the timely Taj Mahal fax had been a fortuitous vehicle, to say the least. What neither he nor Larchey had anticipated, was gaining access to the secret keys and contacts that Ashley had found on Samir's Excel sheet. *That* had been a bonus.

✳✳✳

'The thing that I find most surprising,' Stefan's sudden interjection, woke Ashley from his own thoughts, 'is that Samir and his group have a ciphered network,' he turned from his labours, paused to look Ashley in the eye, – 'but they never seem to use it!'

'Perhaps they find it more secure to use pigeon post.'
Ashley had answered in jest, but the cryptanalyst's response was far from jocular. 'Yes I was thinking along those lines.'

Ashley waited, expecting his colleague to elucidate further – but it didn't come. Larchy was back, lost in his own world of figures and formulae. He was left to ruminate on the inference alone. Why wouldn't the Brothers want to communicate with an encrypted network? he asked himself. At a time like this, one would expect a flood of messages between the different groups of The Brothers, but neither MOI, nor Echelon, had come up with a single transmission. If they had somehow discovered that Ashley had been snooping around the Lighthouse data banks, then he could understand the dearth of communications, but the monitors had registered nothing for a week – so his break-in last night could not be a factor. Perhaps they *had* an inclination that their lines were being tapped. That was a possibility, and the more he thought about it, the tighter the muscles in his gut became. His apprehension grew even more when he considered the other possibility – that they were not communicating because they had no need – they were ready!

'What was it that Samir wrote in his first SMS message?' Stefan was still bent over his screens. Lines of numbers were scrolling up on all three of them.

'Have a gem in my hands. Thanks be to Goodwin, Sami.' – Ashley knew it by heart. He had gone over it time and time again. Its significance had woken him regularly from even the deepest slumber. That chance capture by Mercury had brought them all together, here and now. But nobody knew why? Yet they were no nearer understanding it than when Zup had so eloquently revealed it in Clement's office.

'We need to know?' Larchey was reading his mind.

'No – In the time I had to search through his computer, I could find no reference to Goodwin.'

'Checked emails?'

'Checked emails – and deleted ones.' Ashley didn't like the suggestions that he might have missed something, but he appreciated that the brainstorming was useful, even if the exchanges were frosty, they were inquiring.

'If whatever it was that stimulated this text was not an email and not on his computer, then don't you think that he might have picked it up by some other means?'

'Such as a telephone call?'

'Or perhaps overhearing something said over a phone.'

Ashley remembered the volume of the phone ring in Bonetti's office whilst he was plundering data from Samir's computer. 'Maybe, he overheard Bonetti – on the phone?'

'Bonetti certainly knew more about Goodwin than Samir *ever* did. At least at that point in time.'

Ashley rose and walked to the window, but he saw nothing of the desert city. Instead, his mind was replaying the moments of his first discussion with the Italian, a million miles away, in Toronto. Then, as now, Ashley felt that Bonetti must know something about Goodwin's work on the algorithms. He remembered his sudden reluctance to pursue the conversation and the bad vibrations that came from Bonetti's comrade on the CIPHERCAN stand. Of course Larchey himself was actually there, chasing down the elusive Goodwin.

There was a long pause. Stefan Larchey stopped whatever he was tending to at the desk, stretched his long legs out and leaned back over the chair, his hands clasping the back of his head.

'It's the algorithm – it's NAMES! It's *got* to be something about NAMES,' they echoed. Each coming to the same conclusion at exactly the same moment in time.

'Samir *knows* what Goodwin discovered about NAMES!'

'...... And that's why he is not using it to cipher their message – because he bloody well doesn't trust it!'

✳✳✳

Cameras flashed and a dozen microphones appeared as if from nowhere. Everyone knew what was on the lips of the President of Rolls Royce, but as he mounted the small podium on the Rolls Royce stand accompanied by Sheikh Ahmed and Prime Minister Blair at his side, the media world waited with baited breath. The TV cameras blinked their readiness and their news anchors paused to catch the speech.

'Your Highness, Prime Minister, ladies and gentlemen, and members of the press.' Ashley noted that as usual, the media was lowest in the hierarchy. 'Over the last few days, here at the DUBEXAIR, airlines of the Gulf region alone have placed orders for new assets that number in excess of one thousand aircraft.'

Applause erupted and as the President turned and nodded to Sheikh Ahmed, it was obvious that these opening lines and the applause that followed were meant as a mark of appreciation for the Sheikh's efforts as patron of the exhibition.

'As the senior representative of Rolls Royce, I am delighted to announce that of those thousand aircraft that will rise to the region's skies in the next few years, almost eight hundred of them will be powered by the engines of Rolls Royce.' There was an audible gasp as the audience grasped what these figures meant to the workforce back in the city of Derby, UK. A second round of further applause, more sustained than the first, brought beaming smiles from the Rolls sales team.

Once the applause had died sufficiently, the President continued, 'Of those eight hundred aircraft, twenty five percent will be a mix of the new generation aeroplane, namely the Dreamliners and Airbus 820s. Rolls Royce is delighted to announce – that *all* of these aircraft will cross these skies with contrails from the 75,000lb thrust of the Rolls Royce TRENT 1000 engine!'

On cue, spotlights were beamed onto the life size model of the TRENT and a fanfare of '*Thus Spake Zarathusa*' blasted dramatically from the loudspeakers. Cheers and rapturous applause raised the roof as Ashley accepted that this was indeed a great moment for the company. They had beaten off the American giants, at least for this market niche, and this vote of confidence would see the company through to the next generation of power units yet to appear onto the drawing board.

Impressive as it was, Ashley's real focus of attention was on Minder and his MOI staff who were intermingling with the excited crowd, each watchful for the slightest sign of trouble. The presence, under the same roof, of Rolls Royce and a President and a Prime Minister was too much of a coincidence to ignore. The MOI had been intensely interested. Security at the entrance had been noticeably tighter even though all of those granted entrance were by invitation only. Having been witness to the unprecedented scene of technological and commercial success, Ashley's initial scepticism that Rolls Royce could be a target of terrorism, was slowly being replaced by a growing concern that, along with the toothy grin of Premier Blair, it could well be in the sights of Samir's crowd.

Blair had now taken the podium, and the security men immediately raised their alertness. Ashley couldn't think of a more opportune moment for an assassin's attack. He was sure that Blair, at least, would be aware of some kind of threat, but less certain that the RR people had been informed. As it transpired, it seemed that there were more MOI people in the crowd than genuine visitors. Ashley found himself casually scanning the audience rather than attending to the numerous plaudits being voiced from the lectern. Who has the gun? He smiled, not to anyone particular but in the recognition of the fact that under such circumstances, even the most innocuously looking character suddenly sprouted horns and every unkempt, unshaven profile identified a classic terrorist. The only furtive characters around were the MOI spotters. They had become imposing, enough to alert anyone holding malicious intentions. Ashley had seen enough, it wasn't going to happen. Not today, at least. Bearing in mind what the invitation card that had been thrust in his hand said, they would all be seeing each other again soon. Rolls Royce had a further announcement too – its celebratory reception on the evening of the following day. All invited. Prawn sandwiches and champagne at The Burj.

CHAPTER 22

Bunkers and Birdies

So that was it. Seen as a goodwill gesture and the last honour that his commander could bestow on him, Gul's final flight for the UAE armed forces was scheduled for the following evening. On any other occasion, the chance to fly the very latest Super Puma would have excited him beyond compare, but Gul's anger and frustration precluded any feeling of elation or gratitude. The mission was prestigious to say the least, for he and Faraj were to take acceptance and delivery of the first component of the new squadron. It was to be a showpiece event during the closing stages of DUBEXAIR. Their orders were to formally take the handover of the machine, in front of the UAE Armed Forces Commander, then take off from the exhibition pad, perform some very simple manoeuvres over the airfield before making a high speed, low altitude fly past. Gul and Faraj would then deliver the new helicopter to its new base at Sweihan. On arrival there, Flying Officer Gul ur-Rehman would receive his discharge papers and an envelope bearing his paltry severance package. The following day he would collect his flight ticket, a single economy one-way flight to Islamabad, together with sufficient funds for him to travel home to the Peshawar valley by bus. It was hardly the reward the country's leading helicopter pilot might have expected. After 20 years of devotion to the service, they were kicking him out as if he was a mere street-cleaner. He could visualise all too well, the disappointment, even disgrace, of his family who had always been very public in their broadcasts of his rank and heroic exploits around the world.

The gratuity, if he lived on the basic necessities would see him through the next three months, if he were lucky. After that he was on his own. The money he had been sending back to his family had enabled them to build their own two-storey town house, so accommodation would not be an immediate problem. What *was* a problem was that his premature and unforeseen departure from the UAE would leave him well short of the funds required to push his son and daughter through their final years at university. That, and the task of providing for his ageing mother and all the expenses that her perpetual medical treatment incurred, left in him in a dark cloud of despair and failure. Somebody would have to pay. Insha'allaah. Allah would take care of them. In that he was most confident.

***

Cameron could see that Bonetti was dead on his feet. Gone was the grin, gone was the apparently endless stream of coarse jokes and dialogue, and gone was the swagger that had ridden on the early successes of the round. Now on the tee of the final hole of the competition, Bonetti could just about stand. Every thread of clothing was drenched with sweat although he had got to such a state of dehydration that even the ever-present perspiration on Bonetti's brow had dried up. His face was almost as red as the new, fine silk shirt and he felt every beat of his tired heart as it struggled to push blood through the constricted arteries. The heat was by no means excessive, but the humidity had been high all day. This, and the fact that the Italian had not walked seven kilometres since he was a teenage scout, had taken its inevitable toll.

Cameron had expected it and watched his partner deteriorate as the round went on. There had been moments when he had seriously considered retiring from the competition. But to give him his due, Bonetti would not hear of it. With his body failing rapidly, pride alone had driven him on. Bonetti could not be seen as a failure, it just didn't go with his make up. In the last quarter of the game, he

343

had ceased to concentrate on the game itself. All of his efforts were consigned to the task of taking the next step. Just to get home and collapse in the cool aircon of the bar was Bonetti's sole target of survival. Everything else had been put on automatic. The tactics and intricacies of the game were out of question and the scorecard had become quite irrelevant. It had been left to the wiles of his caddie and the skill of Cameron to get them through the final holes. Both had conspired so that when it came to Bonetti's shot, he only had to hit a ball straight to leave Cameron in the clear and free him to strike powerfully for the greens. This left few options for the Scot. There were no opportunities for him just to lay-up safely. That was Bonetti's role. Cameron had not only to hit the greens first time, but get so close to the pin that even his exhausted partner could not fail to sink the putt. Bonetti afterwards joked that he could see so many balls and holes when he lined up a putt, that he was sure to hit one of them squarely.

Now from the eighteenth tee came the ultimate test. The Majlis course, as did all great golf courses, had an awesome finishing hole. This one was 547 yards long, dog's-leg left, and a lake of a thousand fish that imposed itself on the weary golfer no matter from which angle he chose to attack.

The scoreboards confirmed the whispered rumours he'd heard about Jaycee's clubhouse score. In normal circumstances Cameron always stuck to his strategy of playing the course. Not the opponent. But in normal circumstances he didn't have to worry about an amateur partner and a partner who was closer to the morgue than to the bar in the 19th hole.

To win, they had to beat his old adversary from Brookland, and to do that, he and Bonetti had to finish in par.

The foursome's format demanded that one player teed off from the odd numbered holes, leaving his partner to start from the even numbers. As Bonetti had not been confident enough to drive from the first tee, amidst all furore of the milling crowd and clicking cameras, it was now left to him to take strike from the last. If Bonetti had been overwhelmed by the attentions of the gallery at the first tee, then with perhaps treble that number now waiting expectantly for him to step up, the Italian might have shrunk from the awesome task. As it was, Bonetti's semi comatose state conveniently isolated him from the environment of hustle and bustle.

Everything came mechanically as he focussed on the priority motions of walking and breathing. So when he stepped up to the tee, the only aspects that concerned him were the ball and the tunnel vision of the long fairway stretching out in front of him. There was no choice of club for him to make. Following the briefest of discussions with Cameron, Bonetti's caddy had thrust a middle-range five iron into his hand. The strategy, not that Bonetti had the slightest awareness that there *was* a strategy, was that with a bit of luck, Bonetti might be capable of hitting a medium length shot somewhere onto the fairway. Cameron could not trust him to hit long and true at any time and certainly not at this late stage. Had the Scot been the one to hit first, there was a good chance that he could have cut the corner of the left-hand dog's-leg, but anything extraordinary from the Italian was out of the question. Keep it simple Cameron had whispered into the ear of his ailing partner.

Bonetti steadied himself and the gallery hushed expectantly. He hardly looked up for the line, his sole focal point being the ball on the tee. He drew the club back into the swing but in his exhausted state he allowed the *whole* of his body to swing back with it. The swoop forwards and down onto the ball was the recipe for disaster, and in his determination to at least strike with strength, Bonetti took the tee and a huge swathe of turf with it.

The spectators groaned and offered a sympathetic applause, for it was obvious to all that the big man was not in good shape. Cameron's eyes followed the ball like a hawk and as the crowd's attentions were switched to the opposing team, he followed it into the light rough on the right of the fairway. It was short, of that there was no doubt, but as to the state of its lie, he could not discern from distance.

The lake that encroached from the right protected the green and shepherded all but the bravest to take an easier route around it. It presented a dilemma to Cameron now. Bonetti's ball lay down in the moderate length grass. Had it stood up, then he would have gone for the big hit over the lake. That would have then given them three shots to get down. As it was, any attempt from his present position to clear the water needed a superb strike and anything short would leave Bonetti with the awesome task of getting over the lake.

Cameron elected to play the course, no need to panic. He would play to the left of the lake, onto safe ground, and depending upon the length of his shot, Bonetti would simply have to skirt the fringe of the water, getting onto the green or very close to it. That would give them two shots to get down and win the competition.

In the event, Cameron used his upper body strength to clear the rough and place a long shot into the target area. This left Bonetti with a straight forward shot from 120 yards, to the green and leave Cameron with the first putt. All being equal, if the Italian played anything reasonable, they were in with a chance to close with a par.

'Just keep it out of the water,' muttered Cameron.

The gallery hushed as Bonetti prepared. Once again the tired body swayed, weight shifting from back to front, as if to *throw* the ball forwards. If his ambition was to avoid the water then he succeeded. He was immediately relieved to see it clear the lake and leave the thousand fish undisturbed. However as the ball soared tee'wards, the hook began to take effect. The initial hope of being close was soon replaced with a new anxiety. Both caddies and Cameron had seen the erratic swing and knew from that moment, that it was just a matter of how far and how much.

Bonetti watched the graceful but misguided trajectory. 'Get down – get down. Getta down you leetle bastard!'

But the ball was destined to veer into the crowd gathering around the 18th hole, or worse!

Bonetti cursed, taking care to do so in his native language, so that the sensitive souls within earshot might not understand, but none had to be a linguist to translate. Bonetti buried his club head in an angry thrash into the grass, and set off to find out how much damage he had done, without daring to glance in his partner's direction.

'Just get me out of this,' he pleaded to anyone who cared to listen.

Cameron set off at a brisk pace, eager to see what sort of trouble the Italian had left him with. By the time they reached the green, the gallery hummed with speculation. Watching from the elevated patio of the clubhouse, Jaycee, Él Presidente' watched their approach. He could see what they couldn't. Cameron was faced with an impossible lie. Cannoning off some poor spectator, the ill-fated ball had plugged itself under the lip of a bunker. He couldn't see how even a man of Cameron's strength and skill could get out of this bunker by hitting in the direction of the hole. He must come out either sideways, or even backwards. The trophy was as good as won.

Bonetti dared not look. Disconsolate, he remained some distance from the location, but could still read the expression on Cameron's face and hear the sympathising groans of the Scot's supporters. Cameron was taking his time, viewing the situation from every angle, desperate to get Bonetti onto the putting surface for a last-chance putt.

His decision was made. Playing the course at this point would not bring success. It was a time for inspiration and innovation and Bonetti was more than a little surprised to see his partner line up as if to play sideways out of the bunker. In fact he was lined up to hit out back towards the lake. Bonetti expected a *leetle* chip.

Cameron was indeed facing the water. It was not more than twenty yards away, and all too ready to claim any miss-hit. The big Scot shifted his feet in the sand so that they were planted as firmly as he could make them. The face of the sand wedge was almost parallel with the ground.

Once again the crowd hushed as it awaited the final drama. Cameron took an age to settle – then moved into his back swing that brought the club in a scythe like manner, to cut deep under the ball. Everything was lost to view in an explosion of sand

***

'We need to get closer. We can't just wait for something to happen – by that time, we'll be too late – and God knows what disaster we might have on our hands.' Ashley was begging to get impatient.

Time was passing by, and still he was not certain of the identity of RR, nor of the president whose men wouldn't be able to put him together again. Blair *had* been warned of an impending threat. As a result, he would not be spending the nights on the mainland. The British destroyer HMS Glamorgan was anchored off Jumeira. As a precautionary measure it would be the Prime Minister's residence for the duration of his visit. Physical defence of his lordship was hence left to the navy and a squad of marines. Ashley had no doubt that there would be a team of SAS deployed on board too. So they could consider that the threat to the *British President* to be considerably reduced. The local security forces, including the MOI, were naturally still on full alert. There was nothing unusual about that. With so many dignitaries and delegations attending the exhibition, the security scene was just as one would expect. The increase in personnel and military hardware on the streets and around the airport and its exhibition halls, was noticeable. With such a show of force, both Ashley and Larchey were in agreement – that an attack on the airport less likely even though it stood out as a prime target. Having experienced an incident free day at the exposition, their next cause for concern was the occasion of the Rolls Royce prawns and champers party. Perhaps that was one less RR to be concerned about.

Larchey was once more totally engrossed in his three computers and merely grunted to acknowledge that he was still present in body if not in mind.

The fact that Samir and his group had not been communicating either by SMS text message or by fax, ciphered or otherwise, left Ashley with a sense of foreboding. In the history of warfare, radio silence usually meant one thing – that all preparations were complete and an attack was imminent! Both Samir and Faisal had been under loose observation and as far as could be ascertained, neither had stepped out of line. Samir had cruised through his daily rounds and Faisal had only been seen outside his home and office on the occasions of his evening visits to the Lucky Palace. His routine was exactly as it had been on every working day since anyone could remember.

Unless he could get them to communicate, Stefan's industrious efforts would reveal nothing about the Brothers' target, or targets.

'What if we dropped something really significant into their laps – something *so* significant that they couldn't possibly ignore it?'

Larchey ignored him, as if he wasn't in the room. The first computer had come to a sudden halt.

Ashley moved to observe the screen, feeling that he ought to show support for his colleague by his closer attention, even if it was with some reluctance. Larchey at last sensed that he was required to comment. 'It's only the correlation between the data of the plain fax you sent and the actual data that was transmitted,' he waved theatrically at the second screen. 'And this is performing the same analysis of the ciphered fax – the one using BASE – between Bonetti's machine and Samir's.' Pre-empting Ashley's next question, the cryptanalyst flicked his head to indicate the third screen, in a motion that would have drawn applause in any football match, 'and that is, let us say, reading Peter Goodwin's mind.' Stefan Larchey condescended to turn and face Ashley. The furrowed brow emphasised the mystique of his ultimate exercise before he returned to his beloved statistics as if to say, no more questions!

Ashley failed to be impressed as it became more obvious that Larchey was working on different priorities to the ones demanding his own considerations. 'Let me remind you that our first objective is to tackle the most immediate problem. This is what we agreed upon! – It's pretty obvious that Samir and his friends are in the final throes of launching some form of attack – here – and now. The fate of Goodwin is without doubt something that we need to solve, but *that* can wait.'

Larchey froze – and then signalled his own impatience by taking a deep inhalation that Ashley could see as a preparation for a verbal outburst. Still seated, he spun round. The red face and hands-on-hips attitude said it all.

But Ashley took the moment to deflect the angry barrage that was about to be propelled his way. 'Just remember that I was there! – I was with Goodwin and saw the manner in which he died. It is not an image that I can expect to clear from my mind, even if I should live another hundred years. So, my friend, you can rest assured that if anyone wants to resolve the murder of *our* friend Mr. Peter Goodwin, that no one, and I repeat *no one*, wants that more than I!' Ashley jerked his thumb to his chest to emphasise the point.

The severity of Ashley's tone caught Stefan unprepared. He had not known Ashley to be so forthright, or even capable of it. And it left him with a problem. His own aggressive stance offered him no way back without being seen to be submissive.

Ashley was not in the mood to help his colleague out of the painful corner into which his arrogance had put him. Instead he left the analyst to dangle like a fish on the hook. It was Ashley's turn to stand defiantly, with hands on hips, leaving Larchey in no doubt that if he wanted a fight, then *he* was ready for it. The kitchen wall clock counted loudly. The mental squirming also brought no relief, so the mathematician sought a way out of his dilemma. One that saved face whilst moving to a condescending position. He ignored it.

'Exactly what sort of prompt were you thinking of? – that might illicit a suitable response, I mean?'

Ashley relaxed a little, not sure if they were yet out of their own bunker, and opened cautiously with: 'At this moment in time, any response would be of interest. But what I was thinking was to farm them with something like a fundamental change in Blair's program – for example. Give them the information that the PM is moving his base off shore.'

'Don't you think that might be seen as a warning that they've been rumbled?'

'Yes, there *is* that danger. But even so, if it averts an assault, then at least we will have erred in a positive way. To do nothing at this stage is to invite whatever they are planning to be thrown at us.'

'A bit like kicking the sleeping dog to see if it's dead, or not?'

'Exactly. I think that it's time to take the initiative.' Ashley was relieved that Larchey was back on board. Their personal crisis had been dispelled to the history books – for the moment!

'So we let it out that Blair will not, in fact, be staying at The Burj Al Arab, or the consulate and see what happens?'

'We move the goalposts and then see if that brings about a change their activity.'

***

Bonetti secretly stubbed out the cigarette as he suddenly became aware that the spotlight was on him. The exhaustion was still with him, but whether or not it was the few draughts of tobacco, or just the magnitude of the moment that relegated his physical demeanour one of secondary importance. What *was* important was that Cameron had rescued the situation. From a position of impossibility, the bold wedge shot that Cameron had executed as an artist might have swept a brush across a canvas, had left them with a tough position, but still in with a chance. He was on the green.

If the Italian had had the courage to observe, rather than seek a nicotine infusion, he would have seen the volcanic eruption of bunker sand. Then as the sand fell back, the golf ball continued, soaring gracefully clear, on its own trajectory. Few present would have given him the slightest chance of getting out of the bunker and onto the green in a single shot. Even Jaycee, watching from the clubhouse steps, believed that it was over and done with. But he had been in the game too long to dismiss miracles. Anything was possible in this game and more especially so when the golf ball lay at the feet of Cameron Cameron. The Scot never accepted defeat. And Jaycee was the first to applaud when the ball hit the apron rolled down the slight slope and came to rest on the edge of the green. Cameron had hit the sand with such skill that the ball had climbed almost vertically to escape from the bunker. As it came down it caught the green's contours that funnelled it down towards the hole.

There was no hiding now. All eyes were on Bonetti. He had been left with a putt of some twenty feet. It was a putt to win! In any circumstances it was a tricky situation with the hole positioned on the crest of a rise. If the putt was too weak, then the ball would never arrive. Too strong and it would carry past the hole and downhill towards the water. All this was of course, hypothetical, because Bonetti didn't have to worry about the water, nor being short. The only shot that mattered was one that put the ball in the hole. There were no half measures. Cameron's brilliance had given him the chance, so the one conclusive thing about Bonetti's effort was that it had to be positive. His caddy had offered only one, needless piece of advice. 'Don't be short!'

'Thanks for that.' Bonetti had retorted sharply. 'That ees the easy bit. How about the rest of it?'

Normally, he would have briefly stooped to look at the line, before hitting the ball in a direction as close as he could to the determined path. On this occasion however, the gravity of the situation made its mark. He had considered taking the easy way out and just walk up to the ball and push it in the general direction and hoping to God and Mamma that they would see it home. If he had been just playing for himself, then he might have seriously considered it. But his partner, Cameron, had been playing out of his skin and now especially when the Scot had conjured up this glorious chance, further deliberation was justified more than ever before. He observed from every angle. It even occurred to him to consider the direction in which the grass was cut, the incline of the transverse slope as well as that of the downhill contours. If the truth were known, Bonetti couldn't see much of this detail. He was simply going through a routine which gave him a few moments to build up the strength and courage to hit the ball. It was as if his very life depended upon this moment – and it did!

Bonetti's eyes glazed over. For the moment he felt transported – back to his beloved green hills of Toscana. Olive trees bent in the breeze. His Mamma *was* there by his side as he finally took his stance. Her presence, albeit an illusion, was enough to steady his eye, and to the bewilderment of those who stood close enough, he could be heard to be humming softly. The gentle tones were of something that any Italian would readily recognise as a passage from the Adagio da Albinoni. Bonetti was totally immersed in it. He relaxed, and let the melody take control. His massive hands became as sensitive as the musician's now playing for him. He drew back the putter and slowly brought the club-head back to the ball. Adagio was the music and it was with *adagio* that Bonetti set the ball on its way.

He knew it, and so did those watching the line. So sure was he that Bonetti was able to turn away from the putt without needing to wait for the ball to meander along its course, destined eventually to sink into the hole.

'Era mio destino!'

CHAPTER 23

Party Time

The Burj Al Arab Hotel was built with a view to attracting special people, notably people with a special bank balance. The Sky View Bar was located as a spar across the top of the billowing sail, some two thirds of the height of the hotel. Despite the mass constructions around the city centre which had become the home of the tallest building in the world, *The Burj Al Arab*, with its distinctive futuristic shape, dominated Jumeirah and the Dubai coastline. If it was a dramatic scene during daylight hours, then at night it offered an even more unforgettable sight, being surrounded by choreographed colour sculptures of water and fire. This all-suite hotel reflected the finest that the world had to offer and at $2000 per junior suite, per night, it also reflected in the finest room rates.

Premier Blair looked out over the southern reaches of the Persian Gulf, marvelling at the magnificent view from the Sky View Bar. The Rolls' reception had been a good natured, non-extravagant, laid-back affair, and the elation of the company's management team had been genuine. Their success at DUBEX had been the culmination of many years of high tech research, planning and finally marketing. The Prime Minister was more than happy to climb on the celebration bus, wishing that a few more British corporations would exhibit the same entrepreneurial skills as Rolls Royce in the face of extreme competition. In the course of his duties, he had spent the night in castles, palaces and presidential homes, but having been given a quick tour of some of the hotel's grandest rooms, he regretted the missed opportunity to spend the night in what were the most luxurious rooms that he had ever seen. As it was, there would be no lounging in a Jacuzzi on this occasion. Anyone following his line of vision out over the shimmering sea, would see where he would be laying his head that night. It was out there – in the distance – some two kilometres off-shore, in the cramped quarters of the Executive Officer who'd been gallant enough to vacate his den in favour of the country's leader. It wouldn't be the first time that he'd had to spend the night on a British warship. In any case it was good for his image. To be seen *supporting* the navy went down very well with the media and armed forces, and he did genuinely like the opportunity to mix with its officers and men. It also silenced his critics who were always eager to sing high their outrage when tax payers' money was seen to be funding his excesses. So apart from taking the advice from MI6, albeit founded on speculation of an uncorroborated threat of a terrorist attack in the region, there *was* something to be gained by sleeping with the navy.

Blair waited for his helicopter pick-up with some disquiet, as the party dispersed with surprising speed around him, leaving a few die-hards who were determined to disperse only when every bottle was drained. He found it unusual – not to be the first to leave, and the delay left him tired and ill prepared for the enforced fill-in of casual chit chat.

***

Sheikh Zayed Highway, six lanes in each direction, was stationary. The weekend rush had started early as local businesses disgorged their staff onto Dubai's creaking transport infrastructure. All were intent on making the dash to their own Emirate for the holiday. No matter how many millions the ruling party threw into the relief of congestion, for every new metre of tarmac that was added to the city's network, there seemed to be a hundred Mercedes or a thousand Toyotas waiting to fill it. From the elevation of the hotel's helicopter pad, Cameron and Jaycee could see that Bonetti was going to be late.

The American, like many of his fellow countrymen was actually residing at The Burj Al Arab, but impressive as it undoubtedly was, Cameron and BBC always tried to escape to some oasis of tranquillity. Cameron naturally, enjoyed his time on the golf course and nobody enjoyed a post game drink or two after the last putt had been sunk more than he – no matter where in the world that might be. Brigitte Blondaux-Cameron, having a parallel philosophy about fashion and shopping, similarly sought evening refuge from the mall crowds, in the company of her husband. They were in total agreement that even the best hotels in the world struggled to provide the same freedom and comfortable seclusion that they were able to enjoy in the privacy of a rented villa. Experience had led Cameron to seek a temporary home that was within striking distance of the Emirates Golf Club, yet not too remote from the city's shopping centres. Jumeirah was terribly busy but its convenience made it the natural selection. By coincidence Bonetti's home was not a million miles away.

After the golfing euphoria of the previous evening, Bonetti had other things to attend to. His role as head of communications security and consultant to the Lighthouse director demanded that his presence was required on the final day of the exhibition. Having been absent for two days due to his success on the golf course, Bonetti felt compelled to make his peace with his local sponsor. More contracts were bound to come his way after a trouble-free exhibition project and although the *Ping invitation* was an opportunity far too exciting to miss, dollars were dollars. – Especially if they were big dollars. As it happened, the Ping marketing team were equally loath to miss a good opportunity. Seeing that Bonetti's star was in the ascendancy, and that he presented an exploitable and unique figure who had been in the right place at the right time, they had compromised. They would wait for Bonetti!

***

There was an uneasy silence in the penthouse. As ever Stefan Larchey was totally engrossed in the statistical analysis of the algorithms. All three computers had been running at high speed for every minute of every day since the mathematician had first configured his private LAN. Now only two screens were streaming endless lines of data. The first had originally been working on the plain message but had now been re-tasked. Larchey, whether it had been intended to be simply informative for his partner or as Ashley thought more likely, a petulant statement of superiority, had stuck a hastily marked label on each screen. The second, identified by the SAM/BON Crypto label, was attacking the Bonetti-Samir ciphered fax message, whilst the third was engaged in a race-against-time brute force attack on the NAMES algorithm.

Ashley felt almost superfluous in the proceedings. He yearned to be wholly engaged in events, but it had to be admitted that the mass of figures displayed on every conceivable surface and paper in the room, were largely meaningless to him. The NAMES monitor simply showed two horizontal lines of binary digits, one red and one blue, that raced across, from left to right to fill the screen scan. When each line was completed, the screen would step down and so another line would begin, and then another, and another. The binary 1's and 0's flashed across the monitor with such mesmerizing speed that it was almost impossible to distinguish between the two logic states. It was only after a horizontal line had been completed that they became stationary and readable to Ashley. His colleague only occasionally viewed the NAMES attack and when he did so, it was with apparent indifference. Instead the analyst stared unblinking at the second monitor, from which he periodically extracted information, scratching it down on a paper pad, and then transferring a series of results onto one of the white boards.

The pale-faced mathematician never looked organized, in the personal sense. The loose, polo necked jumper, faded jeans and sandals were exactly the same as when he had first set foot into the Sheraton's suite. Add the tousled, unkempt hair that was now emphasised by several days of five-o'clock shadow and he could well have been mistaken for a stateless hobo. Ashley had not seen him eat. Since then the only sustenance that he'd seen the man take, were the copious cups of coffee and occasional glasses of water from the chiller. It seemed that his colleague simply fed on the digital output emitted by his beloved computers.

Ashley was not completely in the dark however. The first screen had taken his attention now that he knew what to look for. This computer had been re-tasked with a function that was of great interest to him. It was linked through the internet to the MOI computers in Dubai and also to GCHQ in Cheltenham. Both links were ciphered and their data streams were displayed on the split screen. The upper half was to represent whatever was monitored by the MOI and the lower half that monitored by GCHQ, and although nobody would confirm the original data source, Ashley took it to be an output from Echelon. The only thing about this link that Ashley was absolutely sure of, was that at the other end would be a familiar figure, in some ways not unlike Larchey. He could almost visualise through the screen, the sight of Zup with the waving arms of a ballet dancer, coupled with the perpetual attention to his schoolboy spectacles as they slid down the bridge of his nose.

It gave him confidence to know that resources were aligned behind him, even if his own contribution was minimal at this stage. The old adage that spying was waiting and listening, was never more true than at this moment. The only role that Ashley had to play was as observer – to keep an eye on screen one. Stefan's label simply said SAMIR COMMS.

Ashley, despite Larchey's initial reluctance, with the assistance of the MOI and their connections, had published the fact that Blair was enjoying the company of the Royal Navy. Much was made of the fact that the PM preferred to mix with the boys and escape the stuffy environment of consulate life. It went unsaid, at Blair's insistence that the PM didn't want to invoke media hostility by staying at the world's most expensive hotel.

Having given Samir and Faisal a stiff dig-in-the-ribs wake up call, Ashley was both hopeful – and confident that the farming would produce something to harvest. – Something that would give a clear indication of what Samir and his *Brothers* were up to. For the moment, the dual resource of MOI taps on the Lighthouse building and Faisal's fax number, plus Echelon's international watch, had revealed precisely one fact – no communication had taken place, none whatsoever!

***

Bonetti was stressed. The euphoria of winning the competition had been suppressed by the need to deal with business at the closure of the exhibition and then make the dash to The Burj Al Arab in time for the *Ping* photo-shoot. The business was essential and could be neither missed nor hurried, but the photo-shoot was the pinnacle of his aspirations to fame. The prospect of appearing in golfing magazines and posters advertising *Ping's* golf products around the world was beyond his wildest dreams. In business and society he'd worked so hard to climb the ladder, but had never thought of being a success within the golfing world. To be seen in the same company as the elite was one thing, but to be seen there amongst them as a winner was pure fantasy. *He* had been the right man, in the right place, at the right time. The circumstances of that final round and especially the manner in which he had sunk the winning put, had hit a chord with the equipment sponsor of both Cameron and Jaycee. It was the latter, as the *Ping* star, who had suggested that Bonetti be brought on board and they, seeing something of Hollywood in the Bonetti make-up, had jumped at the chance to introduce a new personality into their marketing world. Bonetti was no fool; he knew that it wouldn't last. He knew that it had been a divine intervention that had guided his putt home. When he recalled those final moments, he swore that he had no control over the event whatsoever. He was convinced that if he had hit the ball with the back of the putter, it would still have found its way.

Only one problem troubled him now, and it was the same problem that troubled the thousands of commuters fighting their way home – gridlock!

***

359

Gul was furious. He'd been promised the task of delivering the first of the new Pumas from DUBEXAIR to its home base. But as the senior military brass had gathered round the latest addition to the UAE's helicopter forces, it had been whispered into his ear that his co-pilot – Lt. Faraj, still his junior in rank, should take command. The Arabs didn't care about the years of devotion that he had given the service, and the promise of a final departing honour was so easily forgotten when some Colonel had wished to impress the attending royalty by letting them believe that a local UAE pilot was in command. Faraj, himself was shocked at the last minute decision. He had known that some time or other he would be expected to take over the command seat when Gul had gone, but he had expected that to happen back at the base, when there was only his ground staff around. Here, with the whole General HQ staff and members of the royal family in attendance, what had been an every day event which he could have carried out with his eyes closed, had suddenly become a task full of trepidation.

Despite his ire, Gul kept it under control. It just reinforced his conviction. The final outcome would be the same, Faraj was always going to be there and it didn't really matter which seat he sat in. Gul thought that it was his co-pilot's fate that his first flight as commander, would be his last.

What the Pakistani had not anticipated was that they would have a passenger.

***

Blair was the second man to be offended that afternoon. His aides had *still* not been able to come up with firm expected time of departure. Damned frustrating that he could see his destination, but could not get to it. So he decided to investigate for himself why his helicopter hop was being constantly delayed. In doing so, he came to find out why the Rolls reception had dispersed so quickly.

The helicopter pad of the Burj Al Arab was just one floor above the Sky-View bar, but whereas the bar faced the open ocean, the helicopter pad hung over the billowing sail like structure, facing the shore. His unanticipated arrival on the walkway to the pad caused a stir amongst the Rolls Royce crowd who'd congregated at the doors. Blair was quite amazed at the sight before him as he stepped through onto the walkway. There was the platform of the helicopter pad, its surface dressed in a short, close cut Astro Turf with the regulation H identifying the centre of the landing area. The great attraction for the gathering was the flags and buntings that decorated the periphery of the pad and the host of camera crews taking both still and video shots. The lenses were focussed on the two figures who were taking turns in hitting golf balls, high into the air and out of view into the blue beyond of the Persian Gulf.

Blair took a step forward beyond the crowd and immediately regretted his increased curiosity. As he traced the flight of the latest ball to be struck, his eyes lifted as the ball rose and then followed it as it fell and leant forward to watch it fall into the abyss below. He lost all sense of perspective as the white speck disappeared into the hazy background and felt his body sway, although in which direction, he was not sure. He'd been unprepared for the fact that, as he stepped out into the open, he was standing over six hundred feet above the ocean. As vertigo took a grip, a helping hand grasped his arm. Only pride prevented him from succumbing to a fear that left him wanting to crawl off the pad despite the keen interest in the golfing stars performing on the elevated stage. It was a timely departure as he was escorted to the beach where a Royal Marines' rigid inflatable was waiting to whisk him off to HMS Glamorgan.

Back on the helipad Cameron and Jaycee were coming to the end of their contribution to the photo shoot. The cameras swung round to prepare for Bonetti's role. Positioned behind the mock tees just vacated by the two professionals were two flags mounted into two artificial holes. Some ten metres or so from each was a line of new, sparkling white Ping golf balls, all arranged for Bonetti to come and replicate his feat of the previous day, putting them hopefully with the ease and style in which he had clinched the cut-glass trophy.

***

Ashley was close to despair. It was twenty four hours since they had released the news of Blair's change of plan, and still the cursors blinked at the ready on the blank screen of the first terminal. Samir and Faisal were still silent. Not a whisper. Ashley could not now believe that an attack was planned against the Prime Minister. Despite the fact that there was no hard evidence to support a threat, the decision had been taken to get Blair back onto British territory as soon as possible, even if it was afloat. It was Minder who called in to say that he had been picked up off the beach and that a few moments later; the group of windsurfers were packing their boards into four heavily laden Land Cruisers and returning from whence they had come. The SAS were going home. The tension had been building all day and both Ashley and Stefan breathed a sigh of relief when Minder broke the news. Ashley had had a personal invitation from Cameron to join in the Ping shoot. Much as he would have loved to have been there with his old friend, the pressure of Symphony was at its peak and confining him to Larchey's penthouse workshop. Cameron had promised him lunch after the Ping affair along with his new partner Bonetti and Jaycee - *El Presidente* as Cameron had mischievously referred to the American Open Champion.

'... Could it be?' Ashley lingered on the notion that now dawned on him. 'No it couldn't be him. Surely not?'

He must have spoken his thoughts out loud for Larchey interjected, 'Who couldn't it be?'

'It just occurred to me that there is another president in town!'

Larchey stopped what he was doing, his attention grabbed by Ashley's revelation. 'Like who? – which president?' he demanded.

'Like the American golfer, Jaycee. – How could I miss that? It was right there under my nose.

'American golfer?' Larchey almost spat it out in disgust. 'I thought you said another president?' and turned back to his computers in an air of disdain.

Ashley was too deep in his own thoughts to notice the mathematician's dismissive impatience. 'But you don't see it! The man is a national hero – twofold! The Americans love him because he is a champion – the best in the world. And secondly, he is a hero to all the Native Americans because he is one of them. So much so that in the US they call him *El Presidente* – he represents his ancestry, his race. My God! He would be a worthwhile target for... They could really strike deep into the American heart.' Ashley grabbed for his phone. Where was Minder?

∗∗∗

Bonetti had begun to despair of making the date with *Ping's* people but Sheikh Hamid had stepped in. One word to his brother, who just happened to be the Minister of Defence, opened up the opportunity, and the Italian had been driven to a remote part of the airport to await his VIP lift. It had been the plan that the Italian would take his limousine to the Burj and call in briefly at home to pick up Molly. Bonetti had had difficulty in persuading the reluctant partner to join him for the shoot. She had claimed that she was afraid of heights and as he already knew, she was happier when she was out of the spotlight. Yet, so enthused by her lover's success, she had reluctantly agreed to go. Now however, Bonetti had no choice but to text her to say that, after all, he would have to go alone. Relieved of this duty, Molly had slipped off her robe and slid into the pool to float lazily in the luxury of its refreshing water.

He heard it before he saw it. The Puma flew slowly across the airfield at a little over head height and eventually he picked up its low approach as it moved somewhat crab like towards him. Bonetti watched it settle ponderously, and when urged by the ground crew, grabbed his bag and in a crouching shuffle followed his guide to the aircraft door. The noise from the power units drowned his efforts to thank his escort and the downward draft of hot dust forced him to clench his eyes to mere slits as he was bundled on board. The Puma had different configurations and this aircraft had two up in the cockpit with a larger cabin for passengers, radar and the electronics package. Bonetti was alarmed at the confined space and the canvas fold down seat into which he had to fit. The helmeted figure in the

363

right hand seat turned and motioned to Bonetti in the rear cabin that he should belt up.

It was only with the help of the sergeant that he eventually found both ends of the seat belt, tugged them round his bulky torso, slotted them together and then cringed as the door was finally slammed shut. It was dark, with only a small window opposite to peer through. Apart from the deafening noise that still assaulted his ears, the vibration, the smell of fuel and dust brought on his distinct fear of claustrophobia. How could anybody do this for a living? It was only then that he realised the purpose of the co-pilot's frantic gestures and looking above and behind him, located and retrieved a head-set to clamp over his ears.

Bonetti was quickly overcome by the absolute immersion into the entirely alien environment. The initial schoolboy excitement of a chance to fly in a helicopter, coupled with the VIP treatment being laid on for him, had not prepared him at all for the reality of the situation. The Italian felt a wave of panic wash over him and decided that he should bale out quickly, before he lost all control. But it was too late and nobody could hear his explicative stream of protest. A thumbs up from the sergeant dispatcher, now retired to a safe distance, cleared the pilot to increase the power to the engines that were already screaming to a new threshold. Like it or not, Bonetti was on his way.

The Puma lifted off and swung away from the tarmac. The tilt and sideways motion incited Bonetti to search for the usual airline sick bag. But the Lear Jet was a million miles away, and this was not an airline – and sick bags were not a priority for clients with a fragile constitution. Bonetti closed his eyes and called for Mamma to get him out. The helicopter shook and strained as the nose dipped and it sped off over the airport perimeter. When eventually a crumb of courage had returned to him, the Italian opened his eyes to find that the aircraft had settled into a level flight and was slowly cruising across the city towards the coast.

From maybe one or two thousand feet, the reluctant passenger could only guess at which he had a splendid view of Dubai as he strained to look below. There in fact was sufficient reason for him to make such an uncomfortable trip. Confidence overcame fear as he became distracted by the panorama laid out beneath. As he had expected, the main highways out of Dubai were choked with traffic and it was immediately clear to see that the helicopter was the *only* means to meet the *Ping* deadline. Slowly as he settled down Bonetti began to take in the excitement of what was in front of him. The unique event at The Burj Al Arab would bring worldwide publicity, plus the kudos of arriving at the scene in a military helicopter, all conspired to elevate Bonetti to a new plane of contentment. He smiled to himself. He could cope with success and fame – he was born to it.

***

The throbbing beat of helicopter blades overhead alerted Molly to the fact that her Italian was on his way. She was relieved that she didn't have to make an appearance after all. She could wear all the fine clothes that Bonetti had bought for the occasion, at another time. Being Bonetti's Moll had its drawbacks, but as she had paraded in front of the bedroom mirror, adorned in the finest silks that money could by, she momentarily found a soft spot for him. Business is business she had hastily reminded herself and once more assumed her assigned role. However the chance to take a view from the helicopter pad of the hotel had been tempting. On the other hand she felt more comfortable being out of the picture and watching events from afar and from ground level. The water had amplified the sound of the Puma. She swam lazily under the water as the aircraft's signature beat throbbed in her ears but it was a few seconds after she had slipped out of the pool before she spotted the speck in the sky. The sudden awareness of her nudity, made her reach for her bathrobe. She pulled the silk wrap around her and settled on the lounger to watch the noisy bird make its final approach into the Burj.

Not far away, Brigitte Cameron took a first sip of her Gin and Tonic, and also sat so that she could look in the direction of the hotel. From this distance she could see nothing of the events taking place on the pad. But she knew that her husband Cameron and Jaycee, were having fun whilst engaged on the slightly serious task of promoting *Ping's* golf attire and products. She was happy that Cameron had found a renewed satisfaction in his career and they were both grateful for Jaycee's support and friendly rivalry. What she didn't know was that the pair was at that very moment signing autographs for the Rolls Royce drifters who had accumulated on the bridge to watch. Jaycee, ever alert to a commercial opportunity had hit upon the idea of making extra cash for the previous day's competition and hence the pair of them was signing Burj Al Arab bar menus for a impromptu charity donation of $50 a time. Cameron enjoyed the relaxed off-beat party atmosphere and was himself looking forward to a cool beer once Bonetti had arrived and done his thing with the putter.

***

Now Bonetti could see the silhouette of the hotel, against the setting sun. Not long now before they put him down on the ground floor landing pad. He took a glance through to the cockpit as they were running down the coast line. The pilot was pointing across to the right, across the man in the right seat and he could see that they were talking over the intercom. Bonetti strained but at first could not see the source of interest. The Puma changed direction and swung out to sea. As it did so, Bonetti's view through his tiny window also changed. The aircraft wheeled round, and he caught a brief glimpse of a ship, a very big ship! No wonder the pilots were so interested – then *he* could see it clearly and gasped at its size. He'd seen pictures of an American aircraft carrier before, and watched several television documentaries, but never really appreciated how one would look like at close quarters. Now he knew and called his mamma to see it with him. 'Dio Mio!' It was massive.

Bonetti sat back stunned by what he had seen through the

opposing window, but he was more than stunned when he sought to share the experience with the pilots. Not knowing how to operate the head set, he couldn't speak with them but still felt the need to communicate by some means such was this revelation about the carrier. He turned to look down into the cockpit expecting to exchange an excited gesture, give a thumbs-up. But what he saw froze him solid.

The co-pilot was holding a pistol, it must be in jest – it had to be! The pilot was looking at his companion – motionless. Bonetti was horrified. He stared unblinking down the cabin into the cockpit and was horrified to see the gun jerk in silent recoil. He could hear nothing through the earphones apart from the thundering engines just above his head. Was he mistaken? He looked again in disbelief – but he definitely saw the gun jerk – and then again!

The pilot's arm flew up, his harness fixing him captive to his seat, but the arm extended as if to parry the bullets that had thudded into his body. Bonetti retched and crumpled forwards. He was not able to make any sense of what he was a witness to. Had he been able to look up again, he would have seen another round of recoils. He wanted to believe that it was some strange game being enacted out. Perhaps some entertainment for their passenger – that the pistol merely held blanks. The jets of blood that hit the inside of the windscreen removed all doubt about what was fact and what was illusion.

Bonetti did look up when he realised that he had been a witness – the only witness to a savage and unprovoked murder. The pilot had slumped down over his harness. His blood had formed a bright red curtain that closed down over the windscreen, as if bringing his life to a close on some staged drama. The Italian turned away when the whole horrible inevitability became clear. He stared ahead, at the padded bulkhead facing him, squeezing back his enormous girth, seeking protection from the cockpit partition at his left shoulder. Try as he might, he could not conceal himself from the co-pilot's line of sight. Bonetti was seated on the opposite side to the co-pilot. Had he been sitting on the other side, then he would have been out of sight – if that really mattered at all. As it was, he was at the mercy of the anonymous helmeted figure that was now wrestling with the helicopter controls. The aircraft was going into a dive and starting to rotate, still under the grip of the dead pilot.

Bonetti chanced a look round the bulkhead. The co-pilot was trying to push his victim back, away from the controls with one hand, whilst at the same time pull the stick back with the other. Bonetti found himself urging, no – *praying* to Mamma that he succeeded. The Puma's engines were screaming louder than ever and all he could see out of the window was the grey-blue sea spinning below.

The seconds stretched into minutes as the aircraft bucked and weaved. Bonetti held his breath and braced his body against the restraints, but his heart was beating so powerfully that he expected blood vessels to burst at any moment. Surely his body would collapse from the stress of the G forces, before any impact from outside finally crushed the life out of him.

At last he felt the gyrations become less violent and eventually the new pilot brought the Puma back onto an even keel. The scream of tormented engines subsided as the throttles were eased back. Things were back to normal, if ever they could be – and with that realisation Bonetti prepared to face the next threat to his life.

From the ground, although still some distance away, the helicopter seemed to be dancing, with its tail swinging from side to side. A *snake walking* was how she remembered it. One minute it had been flying slowly towards the hotel and the next it was weaving and dancing all over the place. Molly knew nothing about helicopters, but even her ignorance could not hide the fact that there was something wrong with Bonetti's aircraft. And then, just as she stood in alarm, the noisy beast righted itself and continued on its path. She let out a sigh of relief and her pulse eased a little as she thought the crisis over. But it had only just begun.

Brigitte Cameron too had stood to watch, her glass held anxiously to her lips, unable to take a sip. Since their arrival in Dubai, it was part of the daily routine for helicopter flights to pass overhead. Some were tourist viewings, some were VIP's being dropped onto the Burj pad above, whilst others that just flew up and down the coast were on military exercises or patrol. Anyway, whatever had been the problem it appeared to have been resolved as the Puma was lining up to make a normal approach, just as others had before.

Bonetti waited, alternately peering fearfully round the partition and then pushing himself back into his seat. He tried to be invisible, all the while muttering a prayer to his Mother of God. Now that the Puma was back under control, the Italian feared the worst, and as he looked down towards the cockpit, he was horrified to see the co-pilot turning back to look at him. Bonetti yelped and once more sat back pressing against the aircraft's internal padding, sweat now pouring from under the headset. A punch, or was it a kick hit him in the knee. Bonetti screamed in pain. The shot had been silent in the engine noise, but the pain was excruciating and blood was flowing freely from his shattered leg. Just to make sure that he had been totally incapacitated, another bullet slammed into the soft flesh of his right thigh. Bonetti screamed again. The first bullet had smashed the left knee joint into fragments of bone and cartilage. Excruciatingly painful as it was, it was not, on its own, life threatening. But the second shot certainly was. It had severed his femoral artery leaving Bonetti only minutes to live if he didn't get immediate attention. He gripped the wound and stared in disbelief as he felt bright red blood pulse through the torn trousers, already feeling weak, whether it was from shock or blood loss, it mattered not.

It was anger, sheer animal anger that drove him to his next and final act. Through all the pain and bloody mess, Bonetti fumbled with his straps and unbuckled the harness, sobbing all the time. He slumped to the floor and was shocked at the red pools already collecting there. The pilot had returned to the process of flying, confident that both Faraj and their passenger were either dead or very close to it.

Bonetti dragged himself forward. The helicopter was still now, hovering to the seaward side of The Burj Al Arab, level with the Sky View bar and restaurant two hundred metres above the beach. If only I had live missiles on board, thought Gul, then I could really take the place apart. But the Sidewinders fixed on the weapons racks were only mock ups with neither fuel nor warhead. Just there for the show and the satisfaction of the DUBEX audience.

The *Ping* shoot was about to wrap up. Both of their stars, Jaycee and Cameron had put on a show with the photographers and camera crews getting every shot they could wish for. Protests from the hotel management were beginning to become more agitated as the golf circus had overstayed its rental session. Bonetti had failed to turn up, obviously due to the traffic congestion, but they couldn't wait any longer.

Cameron was searching out all those Rolls Royce guys who had not yet made their contribution when he heard a helicopter approaching. In fact it was getting very close although neither Cameron nor the crew retrieving the scene props, could see anything. It must be below – making a landing at ground level, was the consensus of opinion.

Bonetti was bleeding profusely and his strength was fading fast as life drained from his body. Sheer anger and determination drove him on to tear this murderous pilot apart.

Gul was quiet and focussed now. He let the Puma hover about fifty metres away from the Sky View bar. As he faced the darkened windows of the hotel's topmost floors, he could see the reflection of the helicopter in the mirror-like glass. He could imagine the diners and drinkers inside. Some would be fascinated by the close up view of the aircraft and others would be fearful that a tragic drama was unfolding. Gul could imagine their fascination change to panic as he brought the helicopter forward and in his own mind a sense of achievement was growing as the final act of his life, his last service to the UAE armed forces took its path. He reached for the throttles – the time had come.

Bonetti's eyes had lost all peripheral vision and what remained of his sight was contracting rapidly to a narrow beam of tunnel vision. Through the windscreen the hotel frontage seemed within touching distance. The pilot's intentions were clear to Bonetti. He made one final lunge to grab Gul around the neck and pulled the head back with all that remained of his failing strength.

Gul was taken by surprise, he had been convinced that the Italian had been incapacitated and had concentrated solely on smashing the Puma into Dubai's tower of Babel. Bonetti pulled again on the helmeted head in one last effort so that Gul was forced to release the controls. Once more the helicopter bucked and weaved like a rodeo bull throwing Bonetti up against the roof of the cockpit and then down over Gul.

It was the last thing that Bonetti was aware of before he lost consciousness. His huge frame was wedged over the cyclic control and ramming the collective forward. The Puma's engines roared as it leapt forward and upward in a steep climb. If it had been Bonetti's desperate intention, to steer the helicopter wide of the hotel, then he had succeeded. Gul, try as he may, could not keep the aircraft from pulling to the left and missing his target.

By now the roar of engines and the heavy beat of the helicopter blades could be felt by all who remained on the pad. But still they couldn't see it. Then like a wounded bull, it shot into view and roared up and over the edge of the pad. What items remained of the *Ping* shoot, flags, banners and cameras and their crews, were swept from the pad, over and beyond the peripheral safety net and down to the sea far below.

Cameron, Jaycee and the autograph hunters dashed for the bridge and the relative safety of the main building, but for most it was a dash too late. The big helicopter almost cleared the pad, but when the tail rotor caught the concrete rim, it was destined for destruction. The aircraft staggered, rose again and hovered for a second with its blades clawing desperately at the air. Then, having lost its rotor, the tail swung round as it fell into a helicopter's characteristic death throe spin. It swung into the bridge sweeping all those still on it, into the chasm below, and crashed into the glass fronted lobby. A million deadly shards of glass plate tore through the bodies of all those who had made it to the refuge. The body of the Puma crashed down on its side, onto the pad with its main rotor still beating. Flames erupted from the fractured fuel lines and the shattered carbon fibre blades ripped through the air in all directions, ripping through anything that happened to be in the path. What remained of the rotor acted like a paddle and propelled the Puma's body to the edge of the pad. There it hung, as if undecided whether to jump in a final suicidal dive, or come to rest on the pad. Fortunately for those who had survived the first destruction, and made it into the hotel, the momentum carried it slowly over the precipice as gravity took control. Seconds after, the flames reached the helicopter's fuel tanks and it erupted into a fearsome fireball.

The flash fire seared everything that remained above. Those who lay injured were quickly put out of their misery as they were incinerated by burning aviation spirit.

Less than two miles away, Brigitte Cameron stood and watched in despair as the high drama was played out above. She hoped and prayed that the photo shoot had gone to plan, and that her husband and Jaycee had retired to the bar for lunch together as they had intended. If, from what she had seen, they were still on the pad when the helicopter crashed, then she could not see how they could possibly have escaped. She dashed inside and returned with her mobile phone and dialled Cameron's number. First in Arabic and then in an American accent, the operator informed that the mobile number she was dialling was either switched off, or out of coverage – it would never ring again!

Molly had known instantly that Bonetti had perished. She knew for a fact that he was on board the helicopter and had watched with growing apprehension the antics it performed during those final dramatic minutes of its flight. From her location it had seemed that at the last minute, there had been a chance of the helicopter coming to rest safely on the pad. But then the agonising wait whilst it teetered on the edge, brought her hands to her face, whether in prayer or horror, she was not sure. The explosion had ended any hope. She was never to know that Bonetti had already died even before the Puma hit the hotel. Once the initial shock allowed, she too reached for her telephone. It wasn't Bonetti's number that she called.

CHAPTER 24

Little Boys Blue

Samir had been sitting in the Toyota, right in the middle of the evening's urban crawl, when he noticed the fireball surrounding the top of The Burj. There were always helicopters landing and taking off from the hotel sky pad, it was an everyday event. So it was hardly surprising that from time to time accidents would occur. Samir simply expected it to be the flight of some filthy-rich mogul eager to spend his ill-gotten fortune, and getting his just deserves a little earlier than expected. Not for a minute did he suspect that the aircraft had been carrying his boss. Bonetti had been busy, out of office for most of the week, and so Samir had lost track of his movements. He would find out later that it was the Italian, and feel no remorse whatsoever. Insha'allaah. It was God's will that he be taken from this life, and would be no loss to *this* world.

✳✳✳

Ashley took the news in stunned silence. Minder's call came to the penthouse, direct from the beach at Jumeira. He had lingered after the British Navy had evacuated the Prime Minister from the hotel and had witnessed the whole incident from the shoreline. Ashley's emotions were torn between his immediate concern for Cameron and Jaycee and the fact that he and Larchey had identified Samir's target when it had been too late to instigate any action. In the event, all their attention and resources devoted to the electronic eavesdropping had diverted their focus from the power of basic human reasoning. If, as now seemed certain, both of the golfers had died in the attack, then Ashley felt that he was to be condemned for the rest of his life by the awful guilt of failing his best friend. Ashley nervously paced the room, waiting for Minder to call again with a more detailed report and the inevitable confirmation of his greatest fear. Larchey said nothing but just continued to stare at his machines as if any answer they flashed up might offer explanations. For once he too thought that he had failed. It was a difficult concept for him to accept.

***

No, there was not much point in coming down – too much traffic – too many firemen, ambulances, and police. Don't worry – the MOI could handle this. When Minder had finished, Ashley stayed on the line, deliberated about his next course of action and eventually spoke to ask about the casualties. He had expected many deaths, perhaps even the whole hotel to be destroyed taking all within it. So he was both relieved and at the same time puzzled when the answer came back to identify 22 dead with about 10 injured – mostly burns, including some critical casualties. Most of the fatalities were made up of hotel staff and the *Ping* media crew, but two famous golfers had also perished, although Minder didn't, at that moment, know their identities. Ashley's feared that *he* did. They both agreed that as it was now dark, Ashley wouldn't even be able to get to the site and it would be wiser to wait to survey the scene in daylight hours.

A delicate call to Brigitte confirmed what he already feared. Cameron was not answering his phone and that yes, he would have been at the Burj Hotel at the time. Brigitte was alone in her grief. Ashley was immediately taken back to that fateful evening in Jakarta. He found his hands were shaking uncontrollably as he closed the call and now experienced, at first hand, how dreadful Cameron must have felt on that stormy night in Indonesia, when his friend had told him of Fitri's death. What more could they have shared in any life? Ashley felt tears on his cheeks, Brigitte needed him desperately but everyone was making demands for his time. Despite the evidence that the attack that they had anticipated had been carried despite, Ashley's intuition told him that it wasn't all over yet. If that was the case, then their investigations had been well wide of the mark. JC, El Presidente had been assassinated and the USA would mourn the loss of a sporting hero. Whatever the outcome, he knew that he would not let Cameron down, never mind what onerous tasks that it might incur.

✳✳✳

'So you were right then,' said Larchey after Ashley had haltingly relayed the message.

'Yes – I suppose I was,' Ashley murmured without conviction.

'Why so reticent? After all we did get Blair out in time – and *that* was *your* main purpose for being here. And you were right about the Rolls' guys. You found the connection with RR. So London should be pretty pleased with the way things panned out.' Larchey spoke lamely. He had been largely oblivious to Ashley's personal pain, he still being almost totally engrossed in his computers, one of which Ashley noticed, had suddenly come to a halt.

Ashley however needed a moment to himself and walked out once more to view the city from the balcony. In the dark he could not see as far as Jumeira. The scars of the Burj were hidden in the humid air. Etched in his memory, for ever after, would be the impression of the electric drummer still beating his nightly tattoo on the Lighthouse Tower, oblivious to the evening's drama. Whatever its connection was with the function of the Lighthouse Company, he would probably never know. The figure dominated the skyline of night-time Dubai but despite its prominence, he suspected that the local populace probably didn't even notice it anymore.

Perhaps Larchey was right; perhaps he *had* done a good job as far as London was concerned. True, they *had* pulled the PM out – and just in time. But as far as the Emeratis were concerned, the mission was not such a success. The immediate official response was quick

376

to label the whole affair as an unfortunate accident – a pilot error due to the crew's lack of experience with the new aircraft. The fact that there were no claims of responsibility from any terrorist body conveniently supported that theory. However, suspicions would persist and the incident would undoubtedly raise concerns about the nation's security. Ashley dismissed the official accident claim and was certain that the whole event would be seen for what it was, a failed attack on the British Prime Minister. The stance of the citizens of Dubai was inevitable. A terrorist attack on Dubai would have disastrous repercussions for the nation and there was much hope that as an accident, it would be largely forgotten within a few weeks. And there was the irony. It would no doubt hit the world's newspaper headlines and perhaps *the accident*, so close to the Premier, would even warrant a few seconds of CNN's screen time. In fact, the more Ashley thought about it, as far as terrorist attacks were concerned, the 'Burj event' hardly registered on the Richter scale. If the attempt on either Blair's or JC's life was the objective of Samir and his cronies, then it had been a pretty mediocre effort. Was it such a poorly worked scheme? – Just the half hearted, no! half-witted endeavour of a group of amateurs seeking fame or martyrdom by carrying out a copycat-like 9/11attack? Ashley felt a sense of anti-climax, even disappointment swell within him. Nowhere could he find the slightest inclination of success or satisfaction that some heinous act had been averted. He wanted to believe that it was simply the death of Cameron that left him devoid of emotion. Throughout his life, he had always given great credence to his gut feelings. Undoubtedly, over the years, his basic instincts *had* sometimes been wrong. But these were very rare occasions and this was not one of them. This confidence, along his study and analysis of Samir's mind-set, left him with the distinct feeling that the Jordanian's knowledge of security and his logical approaches should have produced something more. – Something greater than this bungled attempt on Blair's life.

Putting himself in Samir's shoes, Ashley believed that the Jordanian must be feeling totally disillusioned if the destruction of one helicopter and some superficial damage to the hotel's landing pad was the pay/off for what had to be a totally disproportionate effort. He couldn't for the life of him imagine that this was their ultimate objective. It didn't even rank as a near miss. To date, all that had been achieved was to put the local security services on high alert thereby placing any subsequent action in jeopardy. This just didn't have the main-stream Al Qaeda stamp of quality on it.

His meditative reflections were disturbed by a movement from behind. A distant door bell rang. 'It's your friend Bonetti,' Larchey spoke from the doorway. Ashley, still thinking of Cameron, wondered if the Scot could have survived after all, moved to pass by in order to take the call. Strange that he had not heard the phone ring. But Larchey blocked the doorway not moving aside to let Ashley through. He was about to protest but Larchey held his ground – 'Bonetti was in the helicopter!'

***

Even Minder, usually the one to suppress any show of speculation or emotion, was noticeably relieved that it was all over. He was positively buoyant when he picked up Ashley the next morning and his relaxed deportment was evidently reflected in the MOI surmise that it was now just a wrap-up. Ashley was astounded at their naivety, just as was Stefan Larchey – when he had finally managed to drag the man away from his own mission. Larchey's idea of debate was minimalist. Simply a few single-line sentences that merely left Ashley the impression that he was on his own and that the crypto man had other things on his mind precluding any constructive consideration. Ashley began to wonder if he alone was sceptical that Symphony had come to a conclusion.

***

For the *boys in blue*, the afternoon shift was always the worst. Even though winter was around the corner, working outside in the 40-degree heat with the fifty percent humidity to follow in the evening, was a gruelling day's labour. For the ten hours' work, keeping the Jebel Ali naval base clean and free of trash, they were paid a mere pittance. There was little respite even when they were eventually bussed back to their accommodation compound for a simple meal and then sleep. It was a soulless routine, with the only grace being that they were actually in employment and earning just enough to survive and send a few dollars back to Dhaka or Colombo to support their families. The families they would not see between the biannual ends-of-contract flights home were just a little better off than if their men had stayed home in Bangladesh or Sri Lanka. In their own countries these labourers had the dubious status of being the lowest of the low. Mere street urchins, begging for subsistence and scratching around rubbish dumps to survive. Here too in Dubai, they were the lowest of the low. The difference being that in the Gulf state, the disparity between those who had, and those who had not, was indeed a gulf in itself. Not for them, the Mercedes nor the BMWs. Not even a Toyota amongst them, and if ever they had the time, or the fare to make it to one of the great shopping malls, then they would have been ushered out the moment they stepped inside by security staff who knew full well that they were not there to spend. The *CleanOps* boys' monthly highlight would be when they were able to scratch enough Dirhams together to afford a call home, at some back-street store that ran an illegal internet telephone. And their few precious moments with their kin would take place in front of a stinking, clamouring crowd of fellow expatriates, all waiting to grab the phone when their compatriot had had his moment.

So it was with an air of despair and submission that the hapless bunch squatted in the dust of the roadside, dressed in their CleanOps, standard issue, light blue boiler suits, waiting for their bus to pick them up and deliver them to the base. Six days a week, for the foreseeable future, it would be the same schedule with no option but to keep pace on the dreary, mind numbing treadmill.

In the distance, they could see the bus threading its way through the traffic. It had seen many years of service as an American school bus. Its long, rectangular box form being a familiar sight on the school run in any North American community. What was once bright yellow was now faded by the sun and the grimy brown dust that encrusted every surface. The unwashed windows took on the same hue and texture as the coachwork. To a newcomer, the interior was equally repugnant. The A.C. had not worked within living memory, so windows were permanently forced open. Some were adorned with tatters of curtain that at some time had given protection against the searing summer sun. A nauseating stench pervaded the interior, which even the generous rush of air that flowed through it could not disperse. When, in the height of summer, the bus was stationary, the heat was intolerable. Yet none complained as submissive apathy left the boys in blue impervious to all but the most excruciating of discomforts. The barred windows seemed to reinforce the human conditioning by imposing a sense of imprisonment on its passengers. They sat on filthy, torn seats stained with the sweat of workers long gone. The present crew now reluctantly stretched themselves to their feet in anticipation that their long day in the sun was about to begin. Relief would come soon. It was, after all, their final day of labour.

***

The bus approached as though it would make its habitual stop to pick up the group – but then, to the amazement of the afternoon shift, it sped by with no hint of stopping. Some, at first, thought that it was the wrong bus but others argued that they had seen the blue CleanOps logo on the rear windows. There was no mistake. It was *their* bus. What was perhaps most alarming about it, was the fact that it was not empty. It had been full of workers, all attired in the very same company blue overalls as worn by those now left stranded by the side of the highway. Their disbelief was gradually replaced by frustration and anger as the notion grew that they yet again, would be deducted one day's salary for not arriving at the base on time, even though it was no fault of their own.

Had the driver cared to look in his mirror, he would have seen the shaking of angry fists, and had not the roar of the wind blasting through the open windows drowned out the barrage of curses, he would have been most apologetic. But the pressure of the pistol muzzle pressing though the thin backing of his seat and into the base of his spine left him in no doubt that his attentions should be focussed on what lay ahead. The bus thundered on, with its new work crew sitting silently, staring out at the Jumeira skyline.

No more than a few minutes had elapsed before a bus did finally stop at the rendezvous point. A number of the boys had started the long drag back to their compound but most of these had turned back when calls from their companions announced the arrival of the substitute transport. One or two were either out of earshot or chose to ignore the calls, and in any case were set to continue their way back to the camp. In the aftermath, they would be the ones to count themselves the lucky ones.

For the rest, a new foreman and his assistant welcomed the irate labourers with news that they were destined for a new site and that rather than losing a day's wage, they would in fact be compensated for the misunderstanding with each one receiving a generous bonus. Placated and satisfied, they boarded like sheep, happy to embark on a new routine and already planning on how to spend the extra income.

**

Samir had gone ahead to check the gate situation. He was apprehensive and with good reason. His own little private entry through the building site was closed, whether by an intentional increase in security, or because of some change in the building site perimeter, he didn't know. Whatever the reason, there was no option but to brave it out and stand in line with the other vehicles waiting in turn to be searched at the navy gate.

The searches, as his experiences had borne out, were usually cursory, especially if a familiar face was behind the windscreen. This afternoon however, was different. Normally at this time of day, there were few trying to gain entry. Most of the traffic was in the opposite direction as early skivers were sneaking out to beat the rush-hour congestion. But on this day, of all days, there was a delay. From his position on the bend in the road, Samir did not yet have a clear view of the gate itself, but expected that somebody didn't have the right stamp on his paper. He was confident of his own credentials but the thought of what lay ahead cast a dark shadow of apprehension over him. So much was at stake and so much could go wrong and already the signs were that it was not going to be as straightforward as they had planned. Maybe there was a security alert as a result of the previous day's Burj Hotel incident?

At last the queue edged forward. He advanced just a car's length, but it was sufficient for him to make out the reason for the hold up. His heart stopped when he saw *who* was on guard duty. There were two checks at the gate. At the first were the usual local guards checking the paper work, but a few metres beyond that, concrete blocks had been laid to narrow the entrance to single lane traffic and at the side was a Humvee with a manned machine gun mounted on its roof. On the opposite side was a squad of troops swarming over a four-wheeled drive vehicle. The doors were wide open, the hood and bonnet aloft and, simultaneously, the underside was being searched by two troopers with mirrors.

His familiarity along with the usual off-hand fraternisation with the guards would be of little avail today. The Americans didn't know him. They didn't know that he was Samir, *the* Samir, the lifelong supporter of the UAE naval forces. The man who knew every ship, every officer, and their orders and a clandestine party to their most sensitive secrets, whether they be martial or marital. Samir fought the panic that was welling up inside. But as the four-wheeler was cleared and the queue edged forward, it was too late to abort. Pulling out of the queue would just attract further unwanted attention and the brothers needed his directions once they got inside the base.

Shit – the Americans! He should have thought of that. Of course they'd never trust their major naval assets to local security. The queue shifted again, so that he was next in line – he had to take it easy – say nothing – do as he was told – and rely on his papers. They were genuine at least, and on this, his final visit, the plastic tubes in the back of the Toyota were empty. Maffi Mushkula!

***

The helicopter had broken apart on impact. The tail was some distance away and though Ashley was no accident inspector, it was clear to see that it had been ripped off before the aircraft had hit the beach. The engines were still missing, lying in the shallow water directly in the shadow of the helicopter pad, three hundred feet above. The cockpit, or what remained of it, was just a crumpled mess and only distinguishable as the cockpit by the mass of instrumentation within it. What immediately struck Ashley was the fact that although there were only two seats at the front, there were three bodies. The two still strapped into their seats were obviously the captain and his first officer. Some burning from the flash fire had taken place before the helicopter hit the water, but the bodies were not entirely incinerated. The pilots were unidentifiable in their flight helmets, but the third body was just as easily recognisable. The immediate question in Ashley's mind was what the hell was Bonetti doing wedged between the crew and the control panel? Even the extreme forces that had destroyed the aircraft could not explain how Bonetti, who would should have been strapped in the rear cabin for the flight, came to be where he now was, right up front. The circumstances spoke of a struggle and briefly Ashley wondered if Bonetti had been trying to take over the helicopter. But he quickly dismissed the idea. Bonetti was no suicide pilot and he couldn't picture him as hero either. The Italian had far too many long term ambitions and enjoyed life too much to bring it to a premature end. Besides, Bonetti had no allegiance to anyone other than himself. Ashley, once again, thought back to the Franklin quote, 'Three men can only keep a secret – if two of them are dead,' – and now two of them *were* dead.

***

The *CleanOps* boys were beginning to fret. They'd been travelling into the desert for nearly an hour and there was no sign of *the* new project. And the sinister Jeep with blacked out windows that followed in the dusty wake of the bus, even when there was ample opportunity to overtake, created a further sense of unease in those who had noticed it.

***

There had been no positive identification of either Cameron's or Jaycee's bodies. Ashley was utterly depressed at the sight of the flotilla of inflatables coursing around the hotel, searching for whatever remains that had surfaced. He had long since given up any hope that his friend had survived and feared that he, having been in the midst of the fireball, would be one of the many charred corpses recovered at the break of dawn. If that was really the case, then the fact that he had volunteered to be the one to identify Cameron's body to save Brigitte the pain of the horrendous procedure, would be taken out of his hands. It would require genetics or dental inspection to determine who was who. Ashley felt totally helpless and the guilt that he had experienced when first getting Minder's dire message persisted at the back of his mind.

The Americans had responded quickly and Ashley was taken aback by the number of security personnel that had descended on the scene. But where were they all *before* the attack? Surely they had resources devoted to Jaycee's protection. He was, after all a national figure. More popular than any elected President and the hero of every American sports fan. The fact that the British had overlooked this *president*, the people's president, was one thing but that fact that the American security forces had apparently not considered him worth protecting was quite amazing. It looked as though once Bush had declined the invitation to attend DUBEX, the CIA had totally opted out. Even at this early stage, the newspaper headlines that would greet the breakfast readers in New York would be scathing of the American authorities.

***

'Little boys blue come blow your horn.'

'What?'

'The message was – "little boys blue come blow your horn,"' came the testy response down the telephone.

'When?' demanded Ashley.

'We transcribed it just twenty minutes ago! From Samir to Faisal, and to one other – an overseas number – Pakistani,' replied Stefan. 'And we cannot be sure at this point in time where the third party is in residence.'

'You mean, you don't know if it was received in Pakistan, or …?'

'… or here!' Stefan answered, reading Ashley's thoughts. – 'But I *can* tell you where *Samir* was when he sent the message.'

'So?' Ashley felt that his colleague was playing with him, testing him. He quelled the frustration, bit his tongue, and waited for Stefan to continue.

'Jebel Ali. – The call originated from a GSM cell close to the port.'

'Ok, thanks. We are still at The Burj site, but the Jebel Ali port is pretty close. We'll take a look, just in case.' Samir had broken silence. Why, after all this time? And what of the message content? – Yet another riddle from the Jordanian.

Ashley collected Minder from a conversation with a group of police officials, and swept him into the driving seat of the car, 'Jebel Ali – and fast!'

'Sidi, if you want to enter the port, it's quite a detour. But if you just want to see the port, we can get to the headland – opposite, in less than five minutes?' – The need for urgency was tangible.

'Go for the headland!'

✱✱✱

Samir had been as passive as he could be. How he suppressed the urge to run, he did not know. He had passed through the formalities of the first inspection, trying his best to sound his customary, casual self with the local guards. But they knew him, and merely glanced at his gate pass before waving him through to the Americans.

One guard held him short of the inspection area until the others had dispatched the vehicle in front. The heavy boom was lowered and the guards moved behind the concrete barriers, before waving him forward.

The instructions were firm, yet polite, even respectful, 'Stop the car sir; please open the front – and the rear. Now please step outside the vehicle. – Thank you sir.'

The Sergeant once more checked his pass. Samir was not sure if he could read Arabic, and with a name tag that identified the guard as Rodriguez, he thought it unlikely, but the photograph was sufficient to satisfy the soldier.

The examination was as thorough as it ever could be under the circumstances. All the cavities within the Toyota were explored, internal, and external, the engine compartment, glove box and door panels. Samir was forced to smile as the cargo of plastic tubes was checked – if they only knew. Two days too late he thought, and yet he could see that without the presence of a sniffer dog, if one wanted to hide an explosive device, then there were still possibilities. Embedding it within a tyre, a false gas tank, or in the upholstery would be ideal places. It was a good job that he had brought all the hardware in on previous trips, so that he was clean on this final visit.

'Thank you sir.' – He was through. He drove slowly and purposefully through the gate and into the base, turned right and parked, as he had done a thousand times before, outside the communications centre. Time for tchai, he decided, but first he had to attend to his penultimate task – and took out his mobile to finger in a message. Samir smiled, he was delighted with himself. His job was almost done and he felt almost jubilant, so relieved at having successfully got to this stage without mishap.

The moment got the better of him, inspiring his newest cryptic message. A classy touch, he beamed to himself. The Little Boys Blue were on their way.

✳✳✳

Minder knew the place well, and true to his word, they pulled up at the root of the headland that projected out from the shore to the east of the port. As they drew to a halt on the causeway, Ashley gasped at the immensity of the ship opposite them. It completely filled the windscreen.

He knew immediately that it was the MSC Rachelle, recognising her as the very same container ship that he'd seen some days ago on the local newscast. She looked impressive on television, but as he got out of the Land-cruiser, the vessel took on a whole new dimension as perspective came into play. She was over three hundred metres long, forty metres wide and the height above sea level came to? … He counted the stacks of containers that had just been loaded …… …… seven! – So in total she must be carrying some seven thousand containers. By the look of her, and the movement about the dockside, she was almost ready to sail. Probably waiting for the next tide so that she would be safe heading out to sea? thought Ashley. He took the glasses that Minder had been using back at the Burj and slowly panned along the row of buoys marking channel to deep water. A second transport, a freighter was out past the outermost buoys and looked as if she was hove to, waiting to enter the port when the time was right. But when he turned again to the Rachelle, it completely filled his field of vision. He could not fail to be impressed by the sheer bulk, and for a moment completely forgot their reason for being there.

Then he was back on the task. Here, *surely*, was a target worthy of a terrorist attack, or perhaps hijacking? That would be a new one for Al Qaeda. Commandeer the biggest commercial ship in the world, right under the noses of the western forces, and either sue the insurers for a million or two, or scuttle her – perhaps in the middle of the Straits of Hormuz. And, thought Ashley, there would be fewer more attractive sites for that than at the narrow entrance to the Persian Gulf. Perhaps even block the flow of the major ships into the most sensitive waters of the world. He knew the straits were not so deep, so perhaps it was not just idle speculation. It became even more of a reality when he considered that the would-be pirates might even be on board at that very moment! Blocking the Straits of Hormuz would prevent any new American ships entering the gulf and at the same time trap those that were already in it.

Ashley quickly raised the glasses to his eyes and slowly, this time, inspected the dockside, picking out individuals and vehicles, searching particularly for somebody resembling Samir, or his Toyota. Of the twenty or so figures working in the vicinity of the Rachelle, none looked the slightest like the Jordanian. There were only a few vehicles around on this particular dock: a delivery van that looked as though it was unloading provisions for the crew, one or two private cars, a minibus probably for the dockers' transport, and then – half hidden in the shadows, Ashley picked out the nose of what looked like a jeep, no, it was a Landrover. Holding steady for a moment, Ashley saw two men sitting in the front of the open-topped vehicle, inevitable puffs of smoke could be seen, and then it was clear. They were security men, dressed in camouflage jackets, ostensibly there to monitor the comings and goings of the crew and dock labourers. Ashley felt some relief. At least there was some security around, and judging from their casual demeanour, they had seen nothing to worry them. All seemed peaceful enough.

It was when he switched his attention to the Rachelle's bridge that something seemed out of place. Not on the bridge, but in front of it, protruding above the stacked containers.

There was a mast, where he had not expected to see one. Not only that, but it seemed quite out of place with the Rachelle – Different in colour and structure to the towers of the container ship. Ashley had some trouble focussing on it as if the perspective was wrong. He played with the focus of the binoculars and as the containers became blurred, the mystery tower came clear. It flew a flag – the Stars and Stripes!

'My God, it's not the same ship! – Minder, there's another ship behind!'

Seeking a clear view of the hidden vessel, Ashley jogged along the headland path with the Arab hobbling on behind. Then with renewed urgency Ashley broke into a sprint to clear the stern of the Rachelle. With each stride, a little more of the grey ship came into view and it was soon obvious that it was military and an aircraft carrier. – And American. The flag caught in the stiff, offshore breeze, as if to signal that there could be no doubt whom she belonged to. The flight deck was crowded with aircraft and more could be seen through the apertures of the hanger deck.

The container ship was impressive but this was a fighting ship and Ashley was wowed back into his school boy days. Although comparable in size with the Rachelle, the three hundred and fifty metres of aircraft carrier immediately gave the impression of sheer power. She wasn't the first carrier that he'd seen by any means. There had been several opportunities whilst on courses in Portsmouth, to catch sight of the Royal Navy carriers. But they were mere toys carrying a squadron of light jets and a handful of helicopters, compared with this monster. The Nimitz class of super-carriers supported about eighty aircraft with a crew of over five thousand. One single ship had the fighting force of that of a small, even a moderately sized nation, and Ashley guessed that the Americans must have ten or more such vessels, each accompanied by their supporting task force. He remembered reading about the steady influx of American naval resources, on the flight out of London. This one had obviously been either patrolling the northern Gulf, around the Iraq/Kuwait waters and was heading back home to Norfolk, Virginia or San Diego after completing a tour of duty, or she had just arrived as the US response to Iran's nuclear sabre rattling.

Ashley took up the binoculars and swept down the length of the carrier taking in the ominous brood of steel birds of war with their folded wings – sleeping like hooded crows on the deck. Once on the open sea they would take to the wing again, to patrol the troubled skies over the northern Gulf and its eastern perimeter. She looked invincible. The island must have been twenty stories high with not a single space for the niceties of naval life. This was a pure fighting machine and built for one purpose – destruction! Nevertheless the sight of this amazing vessel would be enough to deter most aggressors – so maybe Bush's toy did have justification.

Minder asked the name, so Ashley looked to the stern, expecting to find it there, but if it was there, he couldn't see it. He swivelled to take in the whole length of the hull checking each marking as he went and then moved to the island. The designation CVN 76 could be clearly seen and would have identified the ship to any American navy man, but neither Ashley nor Minder knew what it meant in layman's terms. Astern of the bridge Ashley found a wooden plaque and adjusted the focus in and out, and held steady. What he read froze him to the spot. He stared in disbelief – and then the crossword clues started to fall rapidly into place.

Still with the glasses pointing ship wards, he turned to Minder: 'It's the Ronald Reagan! – the bloody U-S-S *Ronald Reagan*!' He turned back to the ship and recalled the message that Samir had transmitted, 'All the president's men will never put RR together again. – So! My friend, we have found *the* president.'

Minder was already on his telephone. He'd immediately put one and one together, if Samir was in Jebel Ali, as was the *Ronald Reagan*, then it was time to blow the whistle.

For Ashley and Minder, now that RR had at last been identified, their next objective was to find Samir. They were close to the seaward entrance of the port, which split into two parts. To the east where the Rachelle was moored, were the freight terminals – with the naval port on the western side. The two men were separated from the naval port by a stretch of several hundred metres of water. Immediately opposite was the Ronald Reagan, tied up close to the entrance. Beyond the carrier, in the background were moored the two frigates of the UAE Navy. Ashley could not get to the naval side unless they drove back to the Sheikh Zayed highway and then looped south round the whole of the port. It would take too long, but at least Minder had found a spot from which they could observe and report.

***

About five hundred metres away, Samir was also observing. It had been his intention to spend the time socialising with one or other of the engineers with whom he often shared a glass of tea or coffee, but the stress was too great. Instead he remained seated in the Toyota cab with one nervous eye on the gate and the other on the derelict landing craft containing the arms cache. In this condition he could not relax and feared that he would not be able to hide his anxiety from anyone he met face to face. Better to stay out of the way. With few distractions the time was passing so slowly that he had to double check his watch to make sure that it was still running.

His breathing had become shallow, more like a rapid pant, and the growing fear was beginning to take control of his body functions. Even the occasional sip from the water bottle was enough to trigger nausea that he had to fight to suppress. The urge to be out of this, was building by the minute. The inactivity was killing him and he began to wonder what it was that held him there. He felt alone and frozen to the spot, like a hare in the headlights of a car bearing down on it. He checked his watch once more – they must be here soon. Where were his boys?

The tap on the window nearly stopped his heart. – It was one of his tea-drinking associates from the signals office. Samir reluctantly wound the window down to respond and fearing that his pallid face would attract unwanted concern, swept up his phone to his ear to embark on a phantom phone conversation. The uniformed figure leant in through the passenger's side window, but on seeing Samir engaged in conversation, mouthed the word *tchai* and indicated with his hand that he should pass by the office for the usual drink and chat. Samir nodded his intention to accept and continued to converse with himself until the man disappeared from view. With great relief, he breathed deeply and looked out across to where the American carrier lay tied up. It had only been there an hour or two, but already a whole convoy of support vehicles had arrived at the dock to deliver enough provisions to feed the Reagan's population. He could see that a number of marines had taken up guard positions by the gangways and others were manning a check point that effectively sealed off that part of the jetty from all but those with passes. – A glance, once more at the port gate caused his pulse rate to surge. The *CleanOps* bus had arrived and was already through the local check of paper work and permits. Samir started the Toyota, ready to roll.

As he had done for the last two years, Shoab Malik had collected the work permits from the cleaner squad, to present them at the guardhouse for the inspection ritual. The local guards, familiar with the foreman simply waved them through. To them, the scruffy bunch of blue boys were the same ones who passed by yesterday and would do so on the morrow.

The bus had crawled forward to the American checkpoint and a burly sergeant, made to look even more bulky by his body armour, mounted the steps to look down the length of the interior. The hot, stale, pervading smell of sweat and dust deterred him from entering further, but his instruction for the labourers to dismount was clear to all. No need to translate into Urdu or any of the other sub continent languages, the motion of the soldier's sub machine gun was clear. As the last man alighted, the marine sergeant waved two of his charges into the bus, to clear it for entry. Disgust was written on their faces as they moved to the back searching seat to seat, checking the contents and belongings of its passengers. Two other guards checked the work permits, trying to detect likenesses amongst the crowd of blue suits. Many wore a turban type headdress of chequered material; others wore just a dirty cloth that was casually wrapped around the head whilst the rest had baseball caps that had seen better days. To the newly arrived Americans the dog-eared photographs on the permits all looked much the same, though if the truth were known, none of them belonged to those paraded in front of the bus. They would have identified however, the original boys in blue whose bullet-ridden bodies lay in the second bus, hidden in a distant desert wadi.

In the end, the local military had granted them access readily – a head count was seen as sufficient. The inspection of the bus had revealed nothing untoward, so the decision to let the poor bastards through was just a matter of course.

Samir was relieved to see that the bus had made it and was now pulling clear for the gate. This was his moment and as he changed into gear. Samir was happy to be on the move, at last. He moved slowly into the path of the bus and keeping a safe distance in front, led it out towards the area where the carcases of dead ships lay. Amongst them was the derelict landing craft that had concealed the guns, missiles, mines and mortars for almost a week awaiting this moment. He pulled up to a halt and watched the bus do likewise. Without a hint of urgency, the CleanOps team alighted and moved casually to retrieve the weapons that Samir had deposited.

To any casual observer, it just looked as though – at last, somebody was clearing the place up. But under their guise of simple cleaners, a metamorphism was taking place. No longer were these the detritus off the streets of Karachi or Chittagong, they were being transformed into the dedicated warriors of Islam. – A fighting unit that had been preparing for this day in the hills of Peshawar.

Hidden by the bus from the buildings and offices of the headquarters, The Brothers prepared for the demise of the President Reagan. Those who were not involved in setting up the mortars collected pistols, grenades, and assault rifles and crammed into the Toyota.

***

The subversive activities that were gaining momentum in the naval port might not have been observable from within the port itself, but across the water, the powerful binoculars of Mike Ashley had been following events. The one remaining riddle from Samir had been at the back of his mind ever since the call came after Stefan's interception. So when he panned across the vista in front of him in his search for Samir, the collection of blue figures milling around the port entrance had stirred his suspicions. It was too much of a coincidence. As Ashley watched events unfurl, he found himself willing the guards to discover some clue as to what was happening and who the boys in blue overalls really were. Surely they would turn up the weapons hidden on the bus. Surely they would be able to identify the troupe as impostors. Minder was on his phone giving a running commentary to the MOI, coordinating events, but to Ashley's dismay the blue team had boarded the bus and were being waved through. He shouted abuse, a warning, but it was lost on the air.

It was when he saw the Toyota pull out in front of the bus that his worst fears were confirmed. Samir and his little boys blue were into the final stages of their treachery, though how they were to achieve the objective against the mighty warship it was not immediately clear. Minder was still shouting down the phone when Ashley saw them split up. One group, maybe twelve, maybe fifteen men all told, were working on the flat bottom of a landing craft and the remainder, he could not guess how many, had jumped in with Samir. He was left with a little confusion as the Toyota was not heading down the dock side, in the direction of the Reagan, but had instead turned away to the far eastern dock where the two UAE frigates were berthed. From the increased distance, all Ashley could discern was that the Toyota had come to a halt at the gangway to one of the ships. Then, if there has been any doubt at all about their intentions, it was immediately dispelled by the flashes of gunfire that he saw in the gathering gloom.

∗∗∗

Samir had never thought about events beyond this point. And he hadn't for some strange reason, given his role in the build-up ever expected shots to be fired. So when The Brothers piled out of his cab and off the back of his vehicle, and then surged up the gangplank, the first crack of gunfire from the assault rifles came as a big shock. He'd never heard a firearm discharged at close range, not even an air pistol. It was all just a bad dream. Shots were fired and bodies fell, but it was surreal. Samir was confused. He fully expected the slain men to rise and dust themselves off, but the spreading pools of blood were no illusion. Death was real.

Four of The Brothers took up the posts vacated by the dead UAE navy guards, whilst the other ten raced onto the ship, shooting down anybody in their way. Within seconds, the invaders had disappeared into the bowels of the frigate. It was at that moment that Samir looked around him, woke from his trance and for the second time that afternoon felt incredibly lonely. His life suddenly seemed devoid of purpose. As far back as he could remember there had always been his family around him, friends at the mosque, even his colleagues at the Lighthouse and beyond, the warm tenderness of his father during those halcyon days to the north of Amman.

The Toyota was still ticking over, waiting for its driver to make a decision. But Samir was past making decisions. He never heard the dull thud of the sniper's bullet as it shattered the windscreen, nor did he feel the impact as it smashed into his forehead. He sat back with nowhere to go.

***

At last Ashley could see further action taking place. Special Forces had just made their entrance onto the scene and their Humvees could be seen hurtling through the gate. Guards were dashing everywhere and the wail of a siren added to the commotion.

It was too late, the first crump of mortar fire tumbled across the water and Ashley quickly turned to see what was happening on the Ronald Reagan. Here too action was gaining pace and he could hear alarms ringing as marines rushed to their posts. Two splashes on the water signified that the mortars were short of range, but it wouldn't take the gunners long to hit their target. Ashley was struck by the sudden awareness that the great behemoth was actually vulnerable to the simplest of attacks. Impregnable at sea – but in port it massive firepower was useless in defending itself. But she was not going to be sunk by mortars alone.

Another mortar round flew across the port. Ashley could see the smoke from the launch site. The deck of the landing craft was below the level of the dockside and was difficult to spot if you didn't know where to look. He turned to sight the carrier – and this time there was a hit. It just caught the edge of the flight deck, towards the bow – doing little damage. But it was followed immediately by another explosion – and this was a big one, followed by a secondary eruption as an aircraft fuel tank ruptured. Ashley instinctively ducked as the shockwave hit him. More mortar bombs were soaring into the sky destined to wreak destruction on the Ronald Reagan's flight deck. The terrorist team had their target in their sights.

Smoke and flames shot skyward as one of the parked fighters took a direct hit. Ashley swung the glasses around to the fire. Crew were dashing all over the place, some to escape and others to tackle the spreading blaze. Black oily smoke billowed across the water enveloping Ashley and stinging his eyes. The sleeping giant was awake.

***

On the Frigate Fujairah, Weapons Officer Hassan Iqbal could feel the throb of the frigate's propulsion units as his allies on the bridge took command. She'd be soon under way heading to ram the carrier amidships. The charges now being laid in the bow would explode on impact with the American hull. Hassan was getting the missile systems powered up. It was all familiar stuff to him and with his comrades he had prepared everything over the last week and ensured that the Harpoons were pre-armed and ready to be fired. Hassan punched numbers into the Command Launch System, which then initialised the first missile's digital computer. In normal flight data on speed, altitude, location, and the target would be constantly updated to guide the high explosive warhead home. Basically, Hassan knew that it was an old missile that first came into use with the American Navy in the early eighties, but constant updates and new technologies meant that the AGM-84 Harpoon remained one of the world's most destructive anti-ship weapons.

One hit from a 5 metre long Harpoon, usually meant a dramatically volatile end to any vessel that happened to be in the wrong place at the wrong time.

The Ronald Reagan was certainly in the wrong place. It was too close – almost point blank range. At a distance of about one kilometre, the Harpoon would normally only just have time to automatically arm itself after launch. Hassan had been promised that the first two missiles that he would launch *would* be pre-armed. The second fear he had was that they might not get low enough in time to strike the hull of the American ship, even a sea skimming Exocet would be hard tested to get down to its cruise level in the limited distance available. But these were the tools he had to work with and the strike capability of the Harpoon was second to none. In the past he had hit the target on every occasion he had launched, even if they were all beyond the horizon. Hassan thought that at half a million dollars per missile, he should be getting value for money. He looked at his watch. He was ready, just waiting confirmation from above that the mortar attack was under way. – It was!

On the deck of the Ronald Reagan, the rain of mortars was taking its toll on the aircraft parked on the flight deck. He'd counted six strikes but it was impossible for Ashley to see what level of destruction had been inflicted because of the dense pall of black smoke covering the ship.

Back across the port, the navy guards had swarmed in and made contact with the mortar team. Ashley could hear the exchange of small arms gunfire as the Special Forces bore down on the derelict landing craft. The flow of mortars dwindled and then abruptly ceased as the Brothers were overcome. It was a suicidal situation and once they had been discovered it was obvious that there was no possibility of escape. But they'd done their job. From Ashley's point of view, he wondered why fanatics gave away their lives so cheaply. Certainly, looking over to the Ronald Reagan, there was much destruction, maybe a dozen aircraft lost or damaged and without doubt there was loss of life on the carrier from which smoke was still billowing. But a mortar attack was never going to sink the American warship. Even as he watched, the fire teams were battling to get things under control and jets of foam were beginning to smother the burning aircraft. Undoubtedly rescue teams were also at work tending the injured and with the resources below decks, he had no doubt that those unfortunate to have been caught in the assault, would be receiving the best treatment available, with little delay. The American was injured and had taken a bloody nose, but, like the helicopter incident, it seemed a half-hearted affair that had not seriously threatened the Reagan. Perhaps that was the point. Perhaps it was the fact that they could threaten the Americans, in any theatre, at will, with minimal cost, slowly dragging the 'satanic nation' to its knees – that was the objective? They were like a pack of hunting dogs nipping and biting at the heels of a cape buffalo until the great beast tired and succumbed to their persistence.

'She's moving!' yelled Minder. He'd seen the Frigate cast off and the storm of propeller action was driving the ship from its moorings. 'She's going to ram!'

Ashley's thoughts went back to a similar attack in the Yemeni port of Sanaa, where the US Cole was blasted and lucky to survive. In military terms, the US navy was barely scarred, but the up-welling of public discontent and loss of faith was more damaging to the Washington Presidency. So it was with the guerrilla attacks in Iraq and Afghanistan. With the continuous loss of American boys, one by one, the resolve of the American people was slowly draining away. *Nine-eleven* was not forgotten, but the knee jerk swell of patriotism had ebbed away to be replaced by a growing concern about the continual arrival of Stars and Stripes draped coffins in the towns and cities of Wyoming and Kansas. The memory of the Cole jolted Ashley back into the present. The mortars had stopped, but he was on the lookout for anything else that might be thrown at the Reagan. Once more the binoculars were brought up to view the water around the American ship. It was just possible that another bombing was planned and he searched through the intense smoke, across the water for any vessel that looked as if it might be a menace. But the only movement on the water was from several inflatables that buzzed around carrying American Marines as a deterrent to any surface attack.

'Allah Akbar!, Allah Akbar!' – God is great, shouted Hassan, as he lifted the plastic safety cover and punched the launch button. The frigate rocked as the Harpoon's launch system burst into life and in the quiet of the control centre, the thunderous roar of the missile's engine could be heard above the background hum of the A.C. and buzz of electronics.

Ashley had seen the Security Forces approaching the Toyota at the gangway to the Frigate. He had to assume that Samir was a casualty of their response. As he looked once more through the glasses, he was troubled by the possibility that Samir had taken Goodwin's secret to the grave. Now all three were dead and it seemed more than likely that Goodwin's secret would remain just that.

The frigate was under way, swinging round and accelerating all the time.

Minder saw it first and immediately his shouted alert was drowned in the roar of the solid fuelled rocket. In the first instant, the launch tube was surrounded by smoke from the white hot flames of ignition, but then to their horror, the missile emerged from the tube as the booster accelerated the 1500 pounds projectile towards Mach 1. From the freighter port, the slender shape of the Harpoon belied its hidden peril – 500 pounds of Destex high explosive and it was hurtling towards the Reagan.

'Oh my God!' Ashley and Minder stood in awe, watching helpless as the missile first soared into the air and then slowly descended towards its cruising altitude as the turbojet kicked in. Time seemed almost frozen as the Reagan uttered a new alarm and the Harpoon slowly dived towards sea level.

'It's too high!' shouted Ashley. The missile *was* falling, but not fast enough – but it was headed at him! For a second it seemed to Ashley that they were directly in line, but the missile course was corrected and it accelerated towards The Regan. Minder dived to the ground as the missile roared hurtled across the water and just managed to glimpse the Harpoon zipping over the carrier, clearing the flight deck by no more than two metres. Those on the carrier who saw it coming ducked for cover. The relief was short lived. It cleared the Reagan but continued its course beyond.

The Rachelle had just cast off from her moorings when the missile plunged into the lower level of containers stacked on her deck. The armour-piercing warhead tore through half the width of the Rachelle's deck load before exploding. The blast flung Ashley to the concrete as shards of destroyed containers and their contents ripped through the air piercing his clothing and cutting exposed skin. He was too stunned to react quickly and remained prostrate after the initial shock. Salim was up and rushed to Ashley to drag him clear of the rain of debris.

In the depths of the Frigate Fujairah, the muffled explosion brought joy to Hassan and his team. They had hit! – Now for the killer blow! Even as the first Harpoon was leaving its launcher, Hassan was well into the routine of dispatching the second. Efficient as he was, he was not quick enough to beat the explosive entry into the control centre. The Special Forces team had had no option but to blow open the sealed control chamber using plastic explosives. The steep, narrow stepladders and cramped entrance way precluded the use of anything more sophisticated than a semtex charge. With expertise that came from the years of training and practice, the UAE's special forces had raced on board, laid their charges, retired, and finally detonated them. The blast ripped through the Brothers killing some directly, whilst stunning and disabling the rest. Those who were still alive after the blast were quickly dispatched by machine gunfire. The second Harpoon was ready and waiting – but there was no hand left to dispatch it on its deadly mission.

The Special Forces were at the key side. One after the other they fired rocket propelled grenades into the bridge. The command deck burst open like an exploding can of beans. No one survived to steer the ship into the ribs of the Reagan. All guidance and power destroyed, the frigate died in the water.

CHAPTER 25

For a Fool to See

The drama of events that had unfolded in front of him left Ashley sore and drained. It was after dawn when he eventually got back to the suite, showered, and collapsed into an uneasy slumber. The blast impact had picked him up and then flung him down on the concrete dock leaving him dazed and tattered with heavily bruised ribs and joints. The physical wounds though momentarily painful, were largely superficial. The mental scars would be more of a problem.

Mercifully Stefan had retired to his own room. It was the first time that Ashley had not seen him engaged with his beloved statistics. Throughout the fleeting hours of sleep he could still hear the percussion of mortar bombs, see the fires on the Reagan's deck and feel the explosive blast tug at his clothes as the Rachelle's cargo blew up. Ashley and Minder were first deafened by the explosion and then seconds later showered by burning embers that set light to Ashley's hair and clothes. The thick acrid smoke from both ships was swept landward across the dockside by the breeze, burning their eyes and lungs. They coughed and retched uncontrollably as they sought refuge through weeping eyes. The whole of the freighter terminal was covered in the smoking remnants of containers and their fragmented contents.

It had been like a wide screen movie – all the action taking place in front of his ringside seat and being so close it had been a fearful and exhausting event. Despite the dramatic pyrotechnics, and even though considerable damage had been done, neither the Reagan nor the Rachelle were fatally damaged. 'Insha'allaah,' Minder had deemed it simply as God's will, and Ashley's had to agree that it was not a long way short of a miracle that both ships had survived.

It had been difficult to assess what carnage had taken place on the carrier deck and there was still no word about casualties aboard the carrier. Nor was there any comment about how many aircraft and other resources the Reagan had lost.

Conversely, the damage to the container ship was clear to all. Her cargo had gone – blasted out over the sea and desert. But the fragile nature of the container construction had meant that the worst of the Harpoon strike had been fortuitously dissipated, saving the rest of the ship from serious, structural damage. Disaster, in the sense of complete physical destruction had, by a narrow margin been averted. Ashley wondered how on earth the local media managers would explain away *this* accident! They couldn't of course and it would just remain to be seen how much damage had been inflicted upon the confidence of the investors who had been pouring their money into Dubai as the new Mecca of the financial and property world.

***

The Cryptanalyst was back! Ashley woke painfully but did not to find him, as expected, punching keyboards, but relaxing, eyes closed with a cigarette in hand, laid out on a recliner on the balcony.

'So all the fun over and done with?' He spoke without opening his eyes, or even acknowledging Ashley's arrival.

'You could say that,' responded Ashley.

'The fireworks were most impressive – even from here.' Stefan at last opened his eyes but remained looking out over the balcony onto The Creek below. He lifted both arms to lock his hands together behind his head and sank lower into the recliner. 'Had my own fireworks, too,' he added.

'You sure did. – Have to say that your *Blue Boy* message was just in the nick of time. – Any later and the President's men *would* have been picking up the pieces.'

'I guess that your Jordanian friend is not in a position to relate what he knows, pardon – I should say *knew* – about the Goodwin thing?'

'Unless your satellites can eavesdrop on Saint Peter's gate, then that seems to be the case.'

Ashley detected a grin struggling to crease the younger man's face.

There was a long heavy pause. Ashley anticipated a sarcastic comment but it was such a long time coming that he had turned to the kitchen in search of the source of the coffee aroma.

'Mercury has ears everywhere. You'd be surprised to know. But don't quote me! – of course!' Came the shout from the balcony.

'If you shout any louder, I won't need to quote you – the whole bloody world just heard it first hand.' Ashley chuckled when he realised that he had forgotten for the moment that the suite might just be bugged.

The coffee was still hot as he walked to join Stefan outside. Picking up the local newspaper as he went, Ashley inadvertently disturbed the mouse of the second computer. The computer woke up and its screen sprung to life. *Little Boys Blue come blow your horn.* So that was how Stefan had received the message! He couldn't believe that it was only twelve hours ago that he had called Ashley with the news of the intercept. So much seemed to have happened since that trigger had been initiated. Samir's misplaced confidence had been his downfall. One unguarded comment had pulled the plug on The Brothers' well-hatched plan. Ashley confirmed to himself again what he always knew to be the case: *that spying was waiting and watching.* They had done exactly that and their diligence and resources had come up with the final clue right at the eleventh hour. Symphony had been at least a political success. History had not been changed and the collateral residue would in time slowly be forgotten.

Ashley moved outside and drew up the other recliner to sit close to the unkempt figure taking in the sun. He sipped the hot coffee, eager for the caffeine infusion to course through his veins, bringing vitality to the tired mind and body. 'I suppose you'll turn your attentions to the Goodwin problem when you get back home?'

'No need!' came the abrupt reply.

Ashley was aghast. 'No! – You mean to say that you've given up?' A mixture of anger and surprise creased his brow.

'Nope!'

'So what's the score?'

'Well, my friend, it turns out that Boy Blue was not the only message I got last night!' Stefan hesitated for effect, teasing Ashley to the last. He sat up, turned to face Ashley, and looked him directly in the eye and whispered, 'Peter Goodwin also sent me a message!'

Ashley was stunned by the statement and by the intensity of his colleague's delivery. Despite the eyeball to eyeball stare and that the advice was related with deep gravity, Ashley wondered if it had indeed been overheard at Saint Peter's gate, or discerned from some mysterious tapping in Morse code, emanating from Goodwin's grave? But such was Stefan's demeanour that he could see this was not a moment for sarcasm or jollity.

'As far as we can tell – and there have been many attempts by almost every mathematics faculty in the universe, to prove otherwise – NAMES remains intact.'

'But we know …!'

Stefan held up his hand, to interrupt Ashley's interjection. '…… Intact that is, until, as the whole world now seems to suspect, Peter appears to have found a way into the new algorithm. – Well he did – and now I know how he did it.'

Ashley's eyes widened, amazed at the news. But then scepticism took over. He sipped the coffee, pausing to demand, 'Show me!'

Now the cryptanalyst was in his element. 'Peter discovered a problem with the interface between the basic NAMES algorithm and the part that gives it backwards compatibility with BASE.'

'So this is why Samir was alarmed.'

'Well perhaps not alarmed. I should think more delighted than alarmed.'

This puzzled Ashley, but he let it ride for the moment, eager to get to the meat of what Stefan was about to divulge.

'You can think of it as two pieces of a jigsaw puzzle. One part is NAMES and the other piece, the backwards compatibility. How they fit together is the problem. There is a mechanism within this region that runs a check to make sure that the output, the data that is actually transmitted, is really ciphered. In order to do this it compares the plain input with the ciphered output to make sure that they are not the same.'

'But that seems like a standard procedure to me. – A built-in safety feature. What would happen if the two streams were the same?' 'An alarm would be given and the device would instantly stop transmitting. Yes, you are absolutely right, that's just about always the case. – *But* what Peter found out – and boy, is this serious stuff?' it was still a muted whisper, but as deafening as if the man was using a megaphone, 'is that the check mechanism can be switched off – disabled!

'Oh shit! …… But wait a minute, wouldn't the receiving machine detect that it was receiving plain information rather than ciphered stuff?'

Stefan was surprised that Ashley was still with him. 'Yes, right again!' he was impressed. 'But the NAMES algorithm still pretends that it is transmitting ciphered data. Can't you see it?'

Ashley thought for a moment. He could lie and perhaps preserve some pride, or he could plead ignorance and be enlightened. Having come so far with Symphony, he knew that later he would feel cheated if he never could get to grips with the final solution. Just as he'd felt, when he had given up on the trickiest of crossword puzzles. 'I'm all ears.'

'For ciphered communications to take place between two stations, phones, fax, radio, it doesn't matter which, both machines must have the same secret key and be able to synchronise the cipher/decipher operation. So the transmitter acts as the master and sends the message with bits of extra data that are used to set up the synchronisation. In a plain message the synch bits are missing!'

'So NAMES still injects the synch bits in order to fool the receiver?'

'Voila!' Stefan sat back on the recliner with a grandiose sweep of the arms as if he had just given the world to his pupil.

Ashley finished the tepid coffee. It had been in his hand the whole of the time, but with the intensity of the conversation, he had been unaware that he still had it. He stood and turned towards the city, digesting what Stefan had just said. Stefan laid back in his original pose, with hands locked behind his head. He appeared to be relaxing in the sun, but in truth he was waiting for the next question. And it wasn't a long time coming.........

'How is it switched off?'

'Bravo – *that* is indeed *the* question.' Schoolmaster Stefan Larchey assumed both his role and stood at the balcony rail alongside his student. 'Only three people knew this ...'

' And they are all dead,' said Ashley thinking again of Franklin's definition of a secret, and momentarily wondering if he, seeing what had happened to the others in-the-know, also wanted to join the club. But fearing the lifetime of frustration in knowing that there is a secret, without knowing what the secret was, he acceded to the lesser of two evils. And waited ...

Sensing Ashley's anticipation, Stefan continued, 'Goodwin discovered that there is a trigger to initiate the switch-off of the cipher check.'

'You mean that it can be switched off and on – as required?' Ashley was incredulous.

'Ha Ha! Gets *very* interesting, doesn't it?' Stefan turned to face the window, resting his back on the balustrade, 'And we *all* know *who* would be interested in having their dirty little fingers on the switch, don't we?'

'On everyone's switch!' added Ashley. It was all so clear now. No wonder Goodwin was irate about NAMES being accepted as the new standard for encryption. No wonder he wanted to lay everything bare in Toronto – and no wonder he had been prevented from doing so. 'But you have still not told me *how* it can be switched.'

'It will cost you a considerable number of beers and dinner tonight, ok?' chortled the analyst.

Ashley had never seen the man smile before, let alone laugh. Capricious lot these cryptologists he thought, not for the first time, and not for the last. 'The night is on me,' he declared, giving the mathematician a generous bash on the back. 'Show me you bastard!'

✳✳✳

The third computer screen had been full of data before Stefan cleared it. 'This computer has been running through the NAMES algorithm ever since I arrived here. The other two were running to catch any messages that Samir either sent or received, plain or ciphered, as you know. – But this little beauty has been tracking through the NAMES algorithm, searching for the back door that we think Goodwin discovered. It's an awesome task and it was launched more in hope than logic. On paper, the likelihood of finding it was, let me say – negligible, in my life time. But we linked up with some considerable computing power in London and – got lucky. Very lucky'

'Why didn't Goodwin make it more obvious?'

'Well, of course he was about to blow it wide open in Toronto, before somebody got at him. But Peter must have known that he was under threat, and so he left this legacy, just in case.'

'And didn't want to make it so obvious that the wrong people found it before the bad boys had the chance to disguise it, somehow.' Ashley began to see the real brilliance of Goodwin emerge.

'Correct – if it was more deeply hidden, it would have been almost impossible to find – if ever! So he left a flag in the algorithm that not only identified the flaw, but also the instigating party,' Stefan moved to sit at the computer and dragged the keyboard within easy reach. 'Watch this!'

The computer screen woke slowly from its sleep mode to show three boxes on a blue background. One was labelled *Key*, the second *Plain Transmit Message* and the third, *Ciphered Received Message*.

The cryptanalyst typed in the thirty two digits of the sample secret key, all ones – and then typed into the Plain Transmit Message box, *petergoodwin*. A fourth box appeared on the bottom line of the screen with a button marked *GO* at the side of it. Stefan moved the mouse over the button and clicked on it. After a few seconds, the lowest box filled with alphabetic data.

'You see that?'

Ashley peered at the text – but was disappointed to see no message or patterns that he could recognise. 'No,' he replied disappointedly.

Stefan nodded, apparently in agreement and went back to the keyboard. Ashley could see a new line appearing in the *Plain* box – *petergoodwinpetergoodwin* – as Larchey typed it in and then clicked on the *GO* button.

Once again characters began to file into the *Ciphered* box. –

ALLISPLAINTOSEEFORTHENSA

Ashley gasped. 'You mean to say that he is using part of the cipher process to send us this message?'

'Absolutely brilliant, outstanding – don't you think? – and the meaning of the message is really clear to see!'

'How the hell did you come up with that idea – typing Goodwin's name twice, I mean?'

'Ha! – well ……' Stefan sighed and seemed reluctant, almost embarrassed to divulge his next secret, but eventually continued: 'by accident, I have to admit. – You see, it was natural for me to try things, playing with his name and some of the weaker cipher keys. I got tired of typing *petergoodwin* for every different attempt – so I did a copy and paste, but on this occasion – by a typing error, I pasted twice!'

Ashley was absolutely amazed, how Stefan had found it and not least by his obvious mortification that it had come by means of his error. Stefan eventually turned and looked rather sheepishly into Ashley's eyes. He just had time to change the grin, pulling his mouth into a lopsided grimace that belied his humour of the event. He thought for a moment and then broke the silence. 'Ok, so this message tells us that the National Security Agency *can* read messages ciphered by NAMES – but it still doesn't tell me how! How can that output check be fiddled?'

Without a word, Stefan turned back to the computer and clicked paste again so that the Plain box held *petergoodwinpetergoodwinpetergoodwin* – then the GO button.

The *Ciphered* box output burst into life once again as characters were clocked into it from the left. –

Stefan spread his palms to intimate his revelation –

ALLISPLAINTOSEEFORTHENSA-AFOOLCANSEE

Ashley hardly dare ask. 'Another accident?'

Stefan nodded, but mitigated this with: 'but you see the plain input of *petergoodwin petergoodwinpetergoodwin* is thirty six characters – and so is the output. It just fits!'

Ashley exploded into laughter, slapping the computer man on the shoulder, 'and if you *paste* again?'

Stefan pasted again – but nothing changed. 'That's it.'

Ashley stifled his hoot, wiped a tear from his eye and let the moment pass. 'That's what?'

Now Stefan's moment had arrived, and for *that* moment he let Ashley roast on the spit a little longer. 'That's the trigger to change the check from its normal operation to it's – er – shall we say *compromising mode*. I asked myself, "when can a fool see?"'

'April the first!' Ashley shot back.

'Precisely – on the first of April! – So I used two of these computer stations to exchange messages. Everything worked normally. NAMES ciphered the message at the transmitter – and deciphered at the receiver – *AND* the message was ciphered all the way. – But!' and now the smile was on Stefan's face, a very smug smile indeed, 'when I changed the date of the transmitted message to April first ……'

'It was sent in plain!'

'And *all* the messages it sent subsequently were sent plain! – until, that is, you sent another message dated April first!'

410

'Then NAMES returned to its normal operation!'

'Bastards!' The pair broke out into loud laughter and punched each other in playful delight, and then amidst it all, a thought flashed across Ashley's jubilant mind – that if indeed, the room was bugged – then Goodwin's secret was no longer a secret!

***

Ashley had been quite surprised, but pleasantly so, when the MOI's Col. Ali Abdullah, presented himself as Ashley's departing escort. Ashley at first wondered if he had come to make sure that he was actually leaving the country, but his suspicions were dispelled by the warmth of the Arab's smile and the congratulations he expressed.

'Of course the UAE has not come out of this unscathed. Investment has fallen dramatically, as one would expect. But, on the positive side, we have shown – with your great help, of course, that we have the resources and intelligence, to deal with the problems that face the peaceful world. Insha'allaah, I think that from this knowledge, confidence will soon return to our country.'

As Ashley made to shake hands, the Arab, took it in both hands as a gesture of respect, even more than that – clasped Ashley by the shoulders, and then leant forward close to Ashley's face to touch nose to nose and forehead to forehead.

Admiration with affection. It spoke loudly in the face of the troubled world's opinion of the Arab race. *Muhabrah*!

***

Once through immigration, the Colonel had left him to his own devices. As previously arranged he met Cameron's wife Brigitte in the airline lounge. Ashley had to suppress the warm satisfaction of having brought Symphony to a successful conclusion and replace it with the warmth of affection for his friend's wife. Both of them had thought it best to travel together and Ashley could not help reflecting back to that dreadful night in Jakarta and Cameron's empathy

411